M.R. Macke
ter-driven cri
Glasgow, including an ongoing series of mysteries
featuring criminology lecturer Anna Scavolini.

The first book in the series, *In the Silence*, was shortlisted
for the Bloody Scotland Scottish Crime Debut of the
Year and longlisted for the McIlvanney Prize for Scottish Crime Book of the Year 2019.

The sixth, *The Secrets We Keep*, featured in the *Financial
Times*' Best Summer Books of 2025 (Crime and
Thrillers) and IngramSpark's 2025 Editorial Selection
(Mystery/Thriller).

Praise for M.R. Mackenzie

'One of the most consistently accomplished writers on
the current scene.' FINANCIAL TIMES

'Mackenzie has come up with something that defies
easy definition and is truly original.'
NB MAGAZINE

'Brings a fresh new voice to the field of Tartan Noir.'
JAMES OSWALD

'Writes with precision and passion.' CARO RAMSAY

'An immersive slow burn of a tale, peppered with
disquieting fire-crackers of revelation.'
MORGAN CRY

ALSO BY M.R. MACKENZIE

M.R. MACKENZIE

THE CRACKS BENEATH

AN **ANNA SCAVOLINI** MYSTERY

Cover design by
Tim Barber / Dissect Designs

Typeset in 10.5 pt Baskerville

First published in 2026 by Mad House

ISBN: 978-1-9160948-9-5

Text version 1.01 (9 April 2026)

mrmackenzieauthor.com
facebook.com/MRMackenzieAuthor
author.to/mrmackenzie

CAST OF CHARACTERS

Professor **Anna Scavolini** (40) – Professor of Criminology, Kelvingrove University

Zoe Callahan (40) – Anna's best friend

Jack Scavolini (6) – Anna's son

Pamela Macklin (28) – Anna's friend; solicitor

Sal Brinkley (31) – Zoe's girlfriend

DSU **Vanessa Tope** (43) – Detective Superintendent, Major Investigations Team

Dr **Farah Hadid** (29) – Lecturer in Criminology, Kelvingrove University

Dr **Marion Angus** (33) – Senior Lecturer in Criminology, Glasgow Caledonian University; Anna's former student

It is the little rift within the lute,
That by and by will make the music mute.

Alfred, Lord Tennyson, 'Vivien's Song'

PROLOGUE

Sunday 9 January 2022

There are thirty-six individual steps on the stairs leading down to the car park outside the former Springburn library and museum. A long way to fall, and even more so at 1 a.m. on a cold, damp night in early January.

At least, that's how it seemed to Fergus Michie as he stared down at the body lying flat on its front at the bottom. It was a bird – he could make out that much. Dressed in one of those long parkas with the fur trim his own missus had been on at him to get her for her Christmas. He'd eventually caved in. Bought her a knock-off at the Barras and crossed his fingers she'd not know the difference. So far, he seemed to have got away with it. He wondered if this one was the real thing. Hard to tell from this distance.

She wasn't moving. That didn't seem like a good sign.

'Aw, shite.'

He glanced back the way he'd come, towards Atlas Road, silent as a stealth fart at this ill-gotten hour. Like it or not, this was *his* problem.

'Aw, *shite*,' he repeated, this time with feeling.

Turning on his tail, he hurried back out to the road, looking both ways. All quiet on the western front, as his old man had been fond of saying – the meaning of which he'd never managed to work out. Then, he heard it. Quiet, far-off – a car approaching from the south, out Sighthill way.

A minute later, a police car came cruising into view. Blue lights dark, siren silent. In no particular hurry.

Acting more by instinct than conscious thought, Fergus stepped out into the path of the approaching vehicle, waving his arms like an air traffic controller and shouting, 'Oi! OI!!!'

The car slowed, coming to a halt a few feet in front of him. He watched, breathless from his exertions, as the doors opened and two officers – a man and a woman – got out. As they slowly approached the seemingly deranged man standing in the middle of the road, the older of the two, middle-aged and heavyset, raised a calming hand.

'Whoa, there, whoa!' called PC Gordon Waugh. 'Easy does it, sonny. Where's the fire?'

'It's no a fire!' Fergus shot back, practically spluttering in indignation at the cop's altogether too relaxed demeanour. 'It's a . . . it's a BOADY!'

'A body, is it? What sort of a body? Like a *dead* body?'

'Looked pretty deid fae where I wis staundin.'

'That right, sonny? Well, we shall have to consider this very—'

But Fergus was no longer listening. Concluding that the matter was unlikely to be resolved without drastic action, he turned, cutting Waugh off midstream, and set off at a decidedly ungainly canter, heading back towards the steps.

It worked. Whether by force of habit or because he genuinely believed the apparently unhinged man in front of him was trying to flee a potential crime scene, Waugh immediately gave chase, his younger colleague hot on his heels. They caught up with Fergus at the top of the steps and came to a halt, gazing down in unison at the bundle lying in the pool of the streetlamp at the bottom.

Waugh took in the sight for several seconds, then looked at Fergus, as if expecting a full and frank explanation as to how it had got there. For a moment, Fergus just stared back at him, eyes headlight-wide, before repeating the mantra uttered at least once in the life of every Glaswegian ne'er-do-well.

'It wasnae me.'

Waugh considered this for a moment. Then:

'Don't move,' he snapped.

He and his younger colleague made their way gingerly down the steps, Waugh's hand trailing the handrail lest he come a cropper himself. Fanning out, they approached the body cautiously in a pincer movement.

'Miss? You all right there?'

No response or sign of movement.

Taking his pencil torch from his duty belt, Waugh dropped to a crouch, tilting the beam this way and that as he examined the body. The woman's head was turned at a ninety-degree angle. The mousy brown hair at the back of her skull was matted with blood. A single, wide-open eye stared up unseeingly.

Tucking the torch behind his ear, Waugh dug out a pair of disposable gloves and snapped them on before pressing his fingers to the woman's neck, feeling for a pulse.

Nothing.

Slowly, Waugh got to his feet, dipping his chin as he murmured into the radio clipped to his stab vest.

'Control, this is Sierra Six-Four. We've got an adult female, unresponsive, query deceased, at the foot of the steps behind the old Springburn library off Atlas Road. Requesting immediate backup and ambulance, over.'

He turned to his colleague, who'd remained a few paces back, watching the entire performance attentively.

'Right, then, young PC Hardacre,' he declared. 'For the

avoidance of any doubt, it's vitally important that we preserve the locus and avoid interfering with the body until such time as the medical professionals get here. You may find it helpful to keep your hands in your pockets to avoid the temptation to touch anything.'

PC Kelly Hardacre – who, in her six and a half weeks as a probationer, had more than got the measure of her partner and would-be mentor – chose not to point out that all of this had already occurred to her.

'Aw, shite.'

The two officers turned to find Fergus standing just a couple of feet away, gawping wide-eyed at the body.

'I distinctly remember telling you to stay put, sonny,' said Waugh.

'But . . . but I know her.'

'You know her?'

'Aye. That's Leanne.'

'Leanne? Leanne who?'

'*I* dunno. Just Leanne. I see her about. Her and her man stay down on Millbrae Avenue. Two of 'em are aye at each other's throats. Their fights're the stuff o' legend round here.'

Waugh stared at Fergus, not sure what to make of this. Perhaps this big lumpen oaf wasn't the complete doughball he'd initially pegged him for after all. Mind you, it didn't do to inadvertently give the impression that a member of the public might know more about what was going on than you, especially in front of a junior officer. Time to take control of the situation.

'I'm going to have to ask you to step back, sir,' he declared, adopting his best 'dispersing crowds at Hampden Park' voice. 'You're contaminating a potential crime scene.'

'Crime scene?' Fergus's eyes lit up in excitement. 'Ye mean some'dy *pushed* her?'

'STEP. BACK. SIR!' barked Waugh.

4

Fergus did as he was told, reversing several steps. He stood and watched from a respectable distance, his expression verging on petulant.

Waugh circled the body, examining it carefully, stroking his chin. Hardacre continued to watch, thumbs tucked into her stab vest, her expression studiously neutral.

'Well, then, PC Hardacre,' said Waugh, turning to face her. 'This is quite a brain-tickler we have here, wouldn't you say?'

Hardacre, who knew by now that Waugh enjoyed few things more than the sound of his own voice, gave a mild 'mm' which she hoped conveyed the right combination of curiosity and unworldliness.

'Yes,' Waugh mused ponderously, 'once the forensic bods get here, I imagine they'll have plenty to say about the scene before us. They may note, for example, the positioning of the body: the lack of consistency with a fall. You'll see that her arms are down by her sides, whereas, if either you or I were to take a tumble down a flight of steps in the dark, we'd instinctively put out our hands to break the fall. With me so far?'

'So far,' agreed Hardacre, careful to play the part of someone whose own head was devoid of independent thought.

'They'll note, too, the lack of obvious injuries, besides that crack to the back of her noggin – almost *certain* to be determined as the cause of death at the postmortem. Again, hardly consistent with a fall down a flight of steps, is it?'

'If you say so, PC Waugh.'

Waugh wagged a shrewd finger at his colleague. 'I've been in this game for a wee while now, young Hardacre, and let me tell you, there's not much that slips past me. Of course, it's not our place to offer up our opinions on these matters. Best left to those of an appropriate pay grade. But we have minds, as well as eyes and ears, and we can deduce a lot, even *without* the benefit of a string of letters after our names.'

He clocked Fergus, listening every bit as attentively as

Hardacre – perhaps more so. He made a show of glancing down at the body again briefly, before once more addressing his audience of two.

'Make no mistake: someone *put* this young lassie here, with the express intent of her being found.'

PART I

FISSURES

'I'LL KILL YOU': BOYFRIEND IN COURT OVER STREET SLAYING

By Martin Glazer, Staff Reporter

A man accused of telling his girlfriend 'I'll kill you' during a blazing row has appeared in court charged with her murder.

Sean Kerevan, 29, is charged with killing 30-year-old Leanne McColm, whose body was found in the early hours of 9 January near Springburn railway station.

Kerevan made no plea during the hearing at Glasgow Sheriff Court. He was formally charged with murder and remanded in custody.

Prosecutors allege that Kerevan, an electrician, assaulted Miss McColm en route from Springburn station to their home on Millbrae Avenue, before staging the scene to resemble an accident. A witness reportedly told police she saw him dragging her 'roughly by the arm' along Trongate in the Merchant City just hours before her body was found.

Another member of the public is said to have come forward claiming they overheard Kerevan threaten to kill Miss McColm during an explosive argument in a city centre pub late last year.

Sheriff Moira Black denied Kerevan bail, citing the seriousness of the charge and concerns over public safety due to his previous convictions for aggravated assault. A full committal hearing has been provisionally set for next Friday.

Miss McColm's family have described her as 'bright, kind-hearted and full of life'. A spokesperson said they are 'devastated' by her death and are urging anyone with information to come forward.

Kerevan will remain behind bars until his next court appearance.

1

Friday 18 February

She was running late, which wasn't like her at all.

Anna hurried up the steps to the upper level of Edinburgh's Waverley Station, pushing through crowds of people in considerably less of a hurry than her while clutching the metre-high, plastic-wrapped devil's ivy she'd belatedly remembered to buy as a housewarming gift. 6:45 on a Friday evening – you'd think, after a long week at the coalface, this lot would want nothing more than to get home as quickly as possible.

She emerged into the late winter darkness of Princes Street and spent a few seconds getting her bearings. Despite its relatively close proximity to Glasgow – a mere forty-seven minutes on the express service – she'd never had much cause to visit Edinburgh, and the place always struck her as vaguely foreign in a way that even the various capitals of mainland Europe in which she'd spent considerably more time never had. Perhaps it was all the tourist trappings – the souvenir shops and crowds of holidaymakers fresh off the bus, constantly reminding you that you were an interloper.

At least she didn't have far to go. Her destination, a flat in the New Town, was a brisk fifteen-minute walk west of the station, along Princes Street and up towards Queen Street Gardens. Even so, she was a little breathless as she strode along Queen Street, past the rows of elegant Georgian townhouses until she came to the one at the end with the brightly coloured flower baskets hanging from the ground floor windows. She consulted the column of brass name plaques, each with its own buzzer, before ringing the one for Flat 0/2.

A moment later, the door opened, and bustling, birdlike Pamela Macklin was beaming out at her from the communal foyer.

'*There* she is! About time, slowpoke! We were beginning to think we'd have to send out the sniffer dogs. Come here, you!'

And then, before Anna had time to prepare herself, Pamela pulled her into an enthusiastic hug, which Anna tried to reciprocate while simultaneously avoiding crushing the plant she was carrying.

Pamela released her, giving her an appraising look.

'Well, look at *you*! Who'd have thought you'd scrub up so well? Is that some rouge on your cheeks or is it just because it's so blooming parky out there? Come in, come in. Shut out the night!'

Anna gratefully stepped over the threshold, fighting to manoeuvre both herself and the plant through the narrow doorway.

Pamela raised an eyebrow. 'Taken up a new career in forestry?'

'What? Oh, uh, no. Just a little housewarming present.' Anna gave a sheepish shrug. 'It looked smaller in the shop.'

'Well,' said Pamela amiably, as Anna followed her across the communal hallway towards a glossy black front door with a polished brass numberplate, 'you didn't have to, but thanks all the same . . . though I'm not sure where we're going to put it. Can you believe this place was once a single house? Now there's six of us, all living on top of each other like sardines in a can. Still, all in all, I'm moving up in the world, wouldn't you say?'

She ushered Anna into the flat. Anna took in the hallway's dark wood flooring; the high ceiling with its ornate cornicing. The smell of something rich and savoury hit her nostrils, accompanied by what she thought of as 'dinner party music' – agreeable, unintrusive and utterly, utterly forgettable.

'Ger!' called Pamela. 'She's here! Get yer bahookie out here!'

The door to what looked to be the kitchen opened and a man in his early thirties emerged, sporting red hair tied back in a bun. He was a large man in every sense of the word – both tall *and* wide, with an ample gut that strained against his T-shirt and the apron he wore over it.

'Anna, this is Gerry Kerevan,' said Pamela. 'My other half, as you might say. Ger, meet Anna Scavolini, the friend I've been talking your ear off about.'

Anna smiled and gave Gerry a polite but restrained nod. 'Gerry. Pleasure to meet you.'

'Likewise,' said Gerry jovially.

And then, before Anna knew what was happening, he stepped forward and folded her into a fulsome hug. For a moment, she was completely taken aback, her defensive instincts kicking in automatically – but then she found herself relaxing into it, feeling oddly safe and secure in this bear-like man's arms.

'Well,' she said, laughing awkwardly as they finally broke apart, 'hello.'

Gerry laughed too, somewhat sheepishly. 'Sorry. I'm guessing Paz didn't warn you I was a hugger.'

'She didn't . . . but it's OK. Though I'm afraid the plant might have had it.'

Together, they inspected the now rather crumpled devil's ivy.

'Oh dear,' said Pamela, appearing genuinely crestfallen as

she assumed custody of it from Anna, who now wished she'd had the presence of mind to hand it over as soon as she crossed the threshold.

'It's true,' Gerry agreed, rather soberly. 'I'm a big brute who doesnae know his own strength.'

'Gerry's a Weegie like you,' Pamela chimed in, as if this fully explained the overly familiar manner in which he'd greeted her.

Gerry grinned amiably. 'Aye – abandoned the motherland a couple of years back on account of a certain special someone.'

'Aww,' Pamela cooed, slipping an arm through his.

Looking at the pair of them, Anna doubted she'd ever seen a more mismatched couple: Gerry so big and scruffy; Pamela, in her crisp white blouse and pleated skirt, such a prim little slip of a girl – *woman*, she hastily corrected herself.

'So,' said Gerry, giving Anna an appraising look, 'the famous Anna Scavolini! I've gottae say, it's been a long time coming, putting a face tae that name. I've been hearing no end of chatter about you.'

'All of it good, hopefully,' said Anna, trotting out the one line she'd learned as a response to that comment and continued to deploy, despite knowing full well how utterly corny it was.

Gerry grinned. 'Ah, now, that would be telling.'

There was a lull of silence, during which Anna belatedly realised it was her turn to say something.

'Um . . . you have a lovely house . . . flat. Houseflat.'

Ugh. What was it with her and words tonight?

'Quite something, in't it?' Gerry agreed. 'Miles away from the sort of dives I'm used to, lemme tell you. Still keep thinking some *Jeeves and Wooster* type in a penguin suit's gonnae pop out of the wall panels and give me intae trouble for putting my feet on the upholstery or using the wrong soup spoon.' He shrugged fatalistically and nodded to Pamela. 'But

14

this one had her heart set on it, and I could hardly say no to these dimples.'

Pamela gave a little squeal of contentment and clutched Gerry's arm tighter. Anna smiled awkwardly.

For a few moments, the three of them just stood there in the hallway, smiling vacuously at one another. Then, mercifully, the spell was broken by the sound of a timer beeping in the kitchen.

'Um, I'd better get back in there,' said Gerry, jerking a thumb over his shoulder. 'The tajine's at a critical point.' He turned to go.

'Ger, lovely,' said Pamela, 'be a sweetie and take this off my hands, will you?'

She handed the devil's ivy to him. He accepted it gingerly, evidently concerned he might do further damage to it.

'Don't chuck it out just yet,' she called after him as he departed with the unfortunate plant. 'We'll take it out back later and give it a proper Christian burial.'

As the door to the kitchen swung shut again, she turned to Anna.

'Shall we . . . ?'

Together, they headed through to the living room – a rather sparsely furnished affair, with a sofa, an armchair and a coffee table but no ornaments or nicknacks on the mantelpiece and only a solitary print of an acrylic landscape hanging from the wall. The whole thing had the air of a work in progress.

Anna raised an eyebrow at Pamela. 'A man who cooks? You've hit the jackpot there.'

Pamela grinned. 'He cleans too. I've got him trained well.' She gestured to the sofa. 'Now, put your feet up, and you can tell me all your news and I'll tell you all of mine. It's been such a long time since we last saw each other. Shocking, truly shocking state of affairs.'

'We've spoken on the phone,' Anna pointed out, slightly defensively, as she took a seat at one end of the sofa.

Pamela settled into the other, giving her a look of mock consternation. 'Anna, you know it's not the same. I've missed seeing your bonny face. I can't believe it's been – actually, how long *has* it been?'

'Since before lockdown,' said Anna, knowing for sure that she was responsible for this shocking state of affairs and feeling suitably guilty about it.

'It was the New Year bash at your place,' recalled Pamela, 'right before you upped sticks for Italy. Back when we were all still labouring under the illusion that the whole world wasn't about to change beyond recognition. But listen to me, still wittering on like a mad loon! Tell me, what's new in Anna Scavolini Land? Is it true you've gone part-time? You jammy so-and-so! Me, I'm rushed off my feet as per. But I can't complain. It's good to keep busy. Never enough hours in the day, though, am I right?'

Anna smiled. 'No, there certainly aren't.'

She'd forgotten what a motormouth Pamela could be, capable of talking your ear off till the cows came home, barely giving you a chance to draw breath. Still, right now, Anna was more than happy to let her host dominate the flow of conversation. Indeed, the prospect of listening to Pamela rabbiting on about her various trials and tribulations sounded far preferable to confronting her own present worries, which she was determined to park for the duration of this evening.

'Why don't you tell me your news first?' she suggested. She gestured to their surroundings. 'All this, for a start. Last time I was through to see you, you were still renting that pokey bedsit in Newington.'

'It's true,' said Pamela happily. 'I've finally got my foot on the property ladder – which, in this economy, is no mean feat, let me tell you. A part of me thought it was never going to happen. And now, look at me.' She spread her palms wide, inviting Anna to behold her in her triumph. 'I'm a grown-up. I have ARRIVED.'

Anna smiled, amused by Pamela's obvious pride. 'I know. A designer flat, a joint mortgage – talk about your major commitments. All you need now is a Golden Retriever and you'll have the full domestic package.'

'Oh, I couldn't get a dog,' said Pamela earnestly. 'I'm allergic.'

And I'm the one who gets accused of being overly literal, thought Anna.

'Speaking of commitments,' said Pamela, with a playful little eyebrow-raise, 'notice anything?'

It took Anna a moment to cotton on to what Pamela was referring to. In fact, it wasn't until she'd inspected the younger woman from head to toe and Pamela had helpfully held up her hands, fingers spread out, that Anna finally noticed the small diamond ring on the third finger of her otherwise unadorned left hand.

'You *haven't.*'

Pamela nodded, giddy with excitement.

'But that's . . . Pamela, I'm so made up for you.'

Pamela grinned. 'Ger popped the question on our first night here. Got down on one knee and everything, even though the floor wasn't carpeted and he's got dodgy joints.'

'Well, that certainly demonstrates dedication to the cause.'

As someone who regarded the institution of marriage with a deep distrust she wasn't sure she could fully justify, Anna had always struggled to feign enthusiasm for what, at the end of the day, she saw as an administrative formality at best and an archaic act of subjugation at worst, so she hoped she'd managed to sound suitably pleased. At the end of the day, she was happy Pamela was happy, and she supposed she ought to leave it at that and not overthink things.

'Actually,' she smiled, 'I *did* wonder why you'd invited me over at such short notice. But it all makes perfect sense now. You know, if you'd given me advance warning, I'd have brought something more substantial than a plant.'

'It's true,' agreed Pamela, 'though, if it makes you feel any better, I had other reasons too. I suppose . . .'

She hesitated, an apprehensive frown replacing her previous expression of contentment.

'Well,' she began again, 'I suppose you could say I had something of an ulterior motive.'

'Oh?' said Anna, intrigued by this development and, if she was being honest with herself, finding it a bit ominous. 'Tell me more.'

Pamela hesitated for a moment, then leaned towards Anna with a furtive expression, beckoning her closer.

'The thing is, I was sort of hoping to talk business with you. That's if—'

But at that moment, the door swung open and Gerry came lumbering in. Pamela's lips snapped shut like a Venus flytrap.

'Well, then,' said Gerry, a note of amusement in his voice, 'what are you two girlies conspiring about behind my back?'

Red-cheeked and flustered, Pamela said nothing. Anna realised she was going to have to salvage the situation herself.

'Pamela was just telling me about your big news,' she said, smiling up at Gerry. 'I gather congratulations are in order.'

Gerry grinned. He headed over to the sofa and perched on the arm next to Pamela. Pamela glanced briefly in Anna's direction. To Anna's eyes, she looked decidedly uncomfortable – almost guilty.

'And I was saying to her,' Anna went on quickly, 'I still haven't heard the story of how the two of you got together.'

'You mean she hasn't told you? It's actually quite a funny story. We met at a *WoW* convention.'

'Wow?' Anna repeated uncomprehendingly.

'*World of Warcraft.*'

'Oh,' said Anna, not really any the wiser.

'It's an MMO,' put in Pamela, recovering some of her composure. 'You know, a massively multiplayer online game. You've *literally* never heard of it?'

'I've heard of it,' said Anna, somewhat defensively. She vaguely remembered Sal, Zoe's girlfriend, having mentioned it at some point. 'I just never figured you for a fan.'

Gerry she could readily picture. With his ample belly and scruffy T-shirt, he had 'gamer' written all over him. But prim, workaholic Pamela? She supposed it took all sorts.

Pamela grinned, though, to Anna's eyes, her good humour still seemed a bit forced.

'Guilty as charged. It was about two years ago at the SEC – the last one they put on before lockdown. I was there cosplaying as a Night Elf huntress. Ger was an Orc druid.'

Gerry winked at Anna. 'She rocks a chainmail bikini.'

Anna felt her eyes widening involuntarily.

Pamela's cheeks flushed once again – though it seemed to Anna with pride this time rather than embarrassment.

'I was behind him in the line at the concessions stand,' she explained, 'and I'm afraid I wasn't looking where I was going, so I sort of trod on his robe . . .'

'In the process, very nearly causing a serious wardrobe malfunction.'

'And he said to me . . .' She adopted a deep, pompous baritone. ' "Don't you ever look where you're putting your feet?" '

'And *she* said to *me* . . .' Gerry adopted a squeaky but equally haughty voice. ' "Well, I wouldn't *have* to if you didn't drag your robes on the ground!" '

'And we just sort of stood there looking at each other for a few seconds.'

'And then we both started laughing like a pair of right eejits.'

'And we just . . . hit it off.'

'It should never have worked,' declared Gerry philosophically. 'I'm Horde, she's Alliance . . .'

'Sworn adversaries,' said Pamela, deadly serious.

'But it was like it was fated to be. Two warriors from rival factions brought together by the irresistible pull of forbidden love. And now, she's my wee elven princess . . .'

'And he's my big cuddly teddy bear.'

As much as the cloying sweetness of the scene threatened to set off Anna's gag reflex, there was a part of her that couldn't help but feel ever so slightly envious of what they had – or, if not their specific set of circumstances, then at least the happiness it so clearly brought them.

She cleared her throat. 'It's nice – that you managed to find each other.'

'Tell me about it!' said Gerry. 'Still have to pinch myself that someone like her would so much as look twice at someone like me.' Detaching his arm from Pamela, he got to his feet. 'Anyway . . . I was just coming to tell you, food'll be on the table in five minutes.' He glanced at his watch. 'Make that one and a half.'

With that, he ducked out of the room.

Pamela turned to Anna brightly. 'Better shake a leg.' She got up to follow Gerry.

'You were saying you wanted to—' Anna began.

But Pamela just silenced her with a brief, firm headshake, before hurrying out of the room without meeting her eye.

Mystified – and, if she was being honest with herself, more than a little troubled by all this cloak-and-dagger business – Anna got to her feet and followed her.

2

A couple of hours had passed. Justice had been done to the tajine, the dinner plates had been cleared away, and, over wine and a variety of cheeses, Anna, Pamela and Gerry continued their conversation at the dining room table. Gerry, it turned out, was most interested to hear about the work Anna did and questioned her about it relentlessly. In the process, Anna found herself having to correct more than a few of the misconceptions people commonly held about the role of a criminologist. No, she didn't profile offenders for a living. No, she didn't visit crime scenes and determine, based on the length of the perpetrator's stride, that he was a thirty-six-year-old white male who lived in a three-storey tenement in Baillieston with his ailing grandmother.

Not officially, at any rate.

'And what is it *you* do, Gerry?' she asked – thinking, not for the first time, that our obsession with finding out what people we'd only just met did for a living must say something rather damning about humanity as a species . . . and about herself for contributing to keeping the convention alive.

'Oh, he's a *total* computer genius,' said Pamela, cutting in before Gerry could respond.

Gerry laughed self-consciously. ' "Genius" might be over-stating it just a *tad* . . .'

'He's just being modest,' Pamela said to Anna. 'Couple of years back, he developed this app that's the toast of the town. Made a proper mint off it, so he did. How else d'you think we were able to afford this place? Not on *my* poverty wages, that's for sure.'

Gerry took a sip of wine and shook his head. 'Oh, I'm nothing special. I just spotted a gap in the market and took advantage of it. My business partner, Richard – now *he's* the one with *real* nous. Got us into all the right meetings with the right people. You can have all the brainwaves in the world, but, when it comes down to it, it's all about knowing the right people.'

'It's the way of the world,' said Anna, once again feeling rather guilty. After all, did she not owe her current, highly desirable employment status to having the university principal's ear?

'It's true,' agreed Pamela, pushing a bit of cheese around on her plate in a way that seemed far too casual to actually *be* casual. 'Whether we like it or not, it's all about making use of the connections we have to get the outcomes we want. We shouldn't feel guilty about making the most of the cards we're dealt.'

She lifted her glass to her lips and drained it in a single gulp.

Here we go, thought Anna. This was it: the point they'd been leading up to, ever since Pamela's cryptic reference, several hours earlier, to wanting to 'talk business'.

'Anna,' said Pamela, studiously casual, 'what do you know about the Leanne McColm case?'

There was a loud clatter as Gerry dropped his knife. He looked at Pamela, askance.

'Not much,' said Anna carefully. She could tell Gerry was far from happy and had no desire to compound this by saying the wrong thing. 'Just what's been in the papers. She was found at the foot of some steps in Springburn near the start of the year with a fatal head injury. Her partner was charged with her murder a few weeks later.'

Pamela nodded. 'That's right. And he's currently languishing in HMP Barlinnie, in spite of his protestations of innocence.'

'Paz . . .' Gerry began.

'Hmm?' Pamela glanced at Gerry with a look of mild surprise, as if she had no idea what he could possibly be objecting to.

'Why are you doing this?' he hissed in a low, aggrieved voice.

'What do you mean?' she retorted, matching his volume, as if that was somehow going to stop Anna, sitting right next to them, from hearing. 'You *know* Anna's good at this sort of thing. She looks into cases just like this. Gets results.'

'That's just *it*,' Gerry snapped. 'I don't *want* her looking into this one.'

'I don't understand,' said Anna, feeling both awkward and vaguely irritated by the feeling that she was being set up in some way. 'Is the accused a client of yours?'

Pamela, seemingly remembering her manners, swivelled back round to face Anna.

'Unfortunately not. I wish I *could* represent him, but it's not possible because of the . . .' She glanced at Gerry. '. . . family connection.'

'Family?' repeated Anna, still mystified.

'Sean's my brother,' said Gerry sourly.

Of course. She remembered the accused's name now – Sean *Kerevan*. She even had a vague memory of his face, emblazoned on the television screen during the evening news on the day he was charged. Not much of a family resemblance, she thought. The face she remembered had been harsh and intimidating, with a Hitler Youth buzz cut and dark, unfriendly eyes

– about as far a cry from big, cuddly Gerry as you could imagine.

She remembered, too, the corresponding photo of the victim: a young woman with a slight build and a mousy brown fringe, captured in a pub on a night out, glancing over her shoulder at the camera with a rather guileless smile. 'Plain' was how an unkind person might have described her, but, even from the blurry photo, it was clear she had the sort of warm, inviting personality that made it impossible for folk not to like her.

Now Gerry and Pamela were hissing at each other again, arguing back and forth as if Anna wasn't there.

'We agreed we weren't going to involve anyone from outside,' said Gerry.

'Can't think why,' retorted Pamela, almost indignantly. 'Surely you want him to get the best possible chance?'

'Sean made his bed. If he really didn't do it, he can put his trust in the system, same as every other man in history who's been accused of murdering his girlfriend. In case you're forgetting, he's already *got* a solicitor.'

'An old clock-puncher who never saw a corner he didn't feel like cutting!' Pamela all but spluttered.

Gerry shot a brief glance at Anna before turning to Pamela again.

'This was supposed to be a private family matter!'

Pamela scoffed. 'Family! What family? When was the last time you even *saw* your brother? If you and him are so tight, why is it you've never so much as introduced me to him?'

'Excuse me,' said Anna.

Jarred by her unexpected interjection, the pair stopped arguing and turned to face her.

'I think you're both forgetting something,' she went on, keeping her tone firm but even-tempered. 'All of this is immaterial since neither of you has stopped to ask me whether this is something I have any intention of getting involved in.

'Which I don't, incidentally,' she went on as Pamela opened her mouth to speak. 'Quite apart from anything else, I'm not the virtuoso private eye you're making me out to be. I'm just an amateur who happened to get lucky a couple of times. Plus, in order to do something like this any sort of justice at all, I'd essentially have to put my life on hold; devote every spare hour I have to it. And it's not as if I have a surfeit of those to begin with.'

'You work part-time,' said Pamela quietly. 'You've got more time on your hands than anyone else I know.'

Anna ground her teeth. She'd walked right into *that* one.

'It's just not going to happen,' she said, with what she hoped was sufficient finality to put the matter to bed. 'I'm sorry.'

She hadn't mentioned the third and perhaps most compelling reason of all for not wanting to get involved: the element of personal risk. Supposing, just supposing, Sean *was* innocent after all, it meant the real killer was out there somewhere, lying low. And people who'd literally got away with murder tended not to take kindly to amateur sleuths trying to uncover their crimes. Pamela ought to know that better than anyone. Anna wondered whether she'd told Gerry how she'd got the scar on her abdomen, or why she didn't have a spleen.

Wordlessly, Gerry scraped back his chair and got to his feet. Anna and Pamela sat in silence as he lumbered around the table, noisily gathering up the empty plates before departing towards the kitchen with them, almost but not quite slamming the door behind him.

'I'm sorry,' said Pamela, once the dust had settled. 'He's not normally like this.'

'It's fine,' said Anna. 'He's obviously going through a tough time.'

Neither of them was able to meet the other's eye.

'You wouldn't think,' said Pamela pointedly, 'given how little he says about it.'

'No one likes airing their dirty laundry.'

Anna realised, as soon as she'd said it, that it had sounded like a rebuke. That hadn't been her intention, but it was now too late to take it back.

Pamela gave no response. She sat, staring morosely at the table. She must surely have known a bust-up like this was inevitable as soon as she broached the topic. That was why she'd been so insistent on waiting till dinner was out of the way, Anna realised: to avoid spoiling their meal. Though, in retrospect, she wondered if it had really made any difference. The tajine, which had seemed so rich and satisfying at the time, now sat like a lead weight in her stomach.

'Dinner was lovely,' she said, feeling obliged to say *something* to break the silence. 'I'll need to get the recipe from you.'

'Of course!' said Pamela immediately, eagerly latching onto this safe, uncontroversial topic. 'I'll forward it to you.'

'Got much on next week?'

'No rest for the wicked.'

'Heh, tell me about it.'

The silence returned, even heavier and more awkward than before. Both of them, it seemed, were determined to avoid acknowledging the elephant in the room.

At length, judging that she'd left it long enough, Anna stirred in her seat.

'Right, then – I'd probably best be making a move. It's a fair old trek back to Glasgow, and I've got the babysitter on the clock.'

She knew she was clutching for excuses.

Pamela looked up, her face crumpling in disappointment. 'Is this because I asked you to . . . ?' She trailed off. 'I hope you don't think the only reason I invited you here was—'

'No, it's not,' said Anna firmly. 'And I don't. The truth is, I'm feeling a bit wiped out. It's been a long week.'

And it was true. The 'wiped out' part, at any rate – though, now that she was only working three days a week, it felt somewhat churlish to complain, especially to someone who put in far more than the typical hours of a full-time job.

Pamela studied her intently. 'It's true – you *are* looking a bit peely-wally. Hope it's nothing contagious! Ger and me both had COVID over Christmas. Total nightmare!'

Anna felt suddenly self-conscious. *Was* she looking under the weather?

Pamela got to her feet. 'Well, if you're dead set on going, at least let me walk you back to the station.'

'You don't need to.'

'Honestly, I insist. We don't want you keeling over on your way down Princes Street and being left dependent on a good Samaritan stopping to help you!'

'I . . .' Anna began, then stopped. It occurred to her that Pamela's offer probably wasn't wholly born out of altruistic concern for her. Odds were, Pamela was simply looking for an excuse – *any* excuse – to get out of the house, delaying the inevitable clash with Gerry. Anna met her eyes, caught the faint glint of desperation in them and knew she had no option but to play along.

'All right,' she said. 'You can make sure I don't come a cropper.'

Pamela grinned. 'That's more like it. You sit tight. I'll get our coats.'

3

They set off at a leisurely pace, walking side by side through the darkened city. As they made their way along Queen Street, Pamela slipped her arm through Anna's. It took a considerable effort on Anna's part not to pull away. Physical contact like this had always made her feel vaguely uncomfortable, particularly when the other party didn't ask before initiating it. She worried that people might assume they were a couple, then worried about what it said about her that she considered that something to worry about.

As they walked, they talked about this and that, mostly catching one another up on various bits of news about mutual acquaintances. Anna once again found herself wracked by guilt over how long it had been since they'd last seen each other. It really shouldn't have taken something as quasi-official as an invitation to a housewarming to haul her through to Edinburgh.

As they turned down Frederick Street, she realised that, without having been conscious of it, they'd begun to speak about the two Kerevan brothers. She wasn't sure which of them had initiated it, though she suspected Pamela was the one who'd steered their conversation towards the subject. After all, she was the one who had something to gain by bringing it up.

'Gerry's the older of the pair,' she said. 'By about three years, I think. They grew up in Easterhouse – a proper "school of hard knocks" upbringing, from what I can gather. Their parents both died young, and they didn't have any other family they were close to – so as you can imagine, they both had to make their own way in the world.

'Gerry's the one who left it all behind him; you know, made something of himself. Sean never really managed to break free of his roots, and I think there's always been a wee bit of resentment there. On *both* sides, I hasten to add. At least, Sean resents Gerry, and Gerry resents that Sean resents him . . . if that makes sense.' She paused. 'There's also the Leanne of it all.'

'What d'you mean?' said Anna.

'She and Gerry used to go out before she got with Sean.'

Anna's eyes widened in surprise.

'They weren't together long,' Pamela clarified, as they turned onto George Street. 'At least, as far as I can tell. From what I understand, Leanne ended it with Gerry more than three years ago, and she got together with Sean shortly after. That was a good year before Gerry and I met. Not that Ger likes to talk about that period in his life. And I mean, it's understandable. Would *you* tell your current squeeze every last detail of your last relationship?'

'I haven't got a current squeeze.'

Pamela rolled her eyes and smiled indulgently. 'My point still stands. I'm willing to bet it still smarts – you know, this sense that, after things didn't work out between them, Sean sort of muscled in on his turf.'

'That's one way of looking at it, I suppose,' said Anna.

It said a lot, she thought, about men – about their territorial nature and their undying belief that they 'owned' the women in their lives; an ownership that still persisted long after they and the woman in question went their separate ways. The thought that even one as seemingly wholesome and gentle as Gerry might not be immune to such attitudes was, for some reason, deeply disappointing to her.

'The point is,' Pamela went on, 'I'm not trying to make out Ger's a saint in all of this. But it does explain why he's got the blinders on a bit when it comes to Sean. It's hard for him to think anything but the worst of him.'

'Have you ever met him?' Anna asked.

Pamela shook his head. 'Not in person, though I did talk to him on the blower once when he rang looking for Ger, not long after we got together.'

'And what did you make of him?'

Pamela hesitated – reluctant, it seemed, to share her true feelings.

'Truth be told, I didn't like him much. I thought he was . . . loutish, if that's not too prejudiced a term. He just seemed . . . sort of closed off, you know? Like he wasn't interested in us becoming friends, so he saw no point in being civil to me.'

Anna didn't say as much, but this description chimed a lot with her own assumptions about the man based on his mug shot. She supposed that said more about her than it did about him, but she couldn't help wondering why Pamela felt so compelled to go out of her way to help someone with whom, by her own admission, she hadn't exactly hit it off.

'I'm pretty sure that was the last time Ger spoke to him too,' Pamela said. 'I'm not saying he cut Sean out of his life on *my* account – like I say, there were other factors at play. But I suppose there's a teensy wee part of me that clings to the thought that he chose me over him.'

They crossed Hanover Street and continued towards St Andrew Square, the Melville Monument looming tall and dark against the night sky ahead of them.

'The case against Sean,' said Anna. 'What does it hinge on?'

There was a certain weary inevitability to the question – as if, deep down, and for all her protestations back at the flat, she'd known all along that it was only a matter of time before her resolve crumbled.

If Pamela was in any way elated by Anna's expression of interest, she did an impressive job of hiding it.

'From what I can gather, it's mostly circumstantial. The body was found within walking distance of their house in Springburn, but the theory is she never made it home that night. An eyewitness saw the two of them in the city centre a couple of hours earlier, heading up Trongate. She – the witness – gave an interview to one of the tabloid rags. Said Sean was dragging Leanne by the arm and yelling at her.

'Then, not long after, the two of them were caught on CCTV together at High Street Station, and again getting off a train at Springburn. At least, the police *say* it's him. He's got his hood up, and the quality's about what you'd expect. But the guy in the footage has Sean's build, and the hoodie he's wearing matches one Sean owned. The news programmes broadcast it as part of an appeal, not long before they charged him.'

'I know,' said Anna. 'I remember it.'

It wasn't exactly the sort of thing you forgot in a hurry: a fuzzy, high-angle, black-and-white video of two figures passing through the doors at High Street Station, Leanne in front and the man alleged to be Sean close behind, practically frog-marching her. For some reason, footage like that always seemed to accentuate the existing characteristics of the people it captured – in this case, making Leanne seem even smaller and more vulnerable, and Sean even more ogre-like than he'd appeared in his mug shot.

'No evidence to suggest she was killed at home, then?'

Anna asked. 'I mean, if they reckon she never made it back . . .'

'Right,' said Pamela. 'No evidence of a struggle, no blood, no anything. But – and here's the interesting part – wherever she was killed, it wasn't where the body was found.'

'No?'

'The SOCOs performed a thorough examination of the crime scene and surrounding area. There was none of the blood splatter or other forensic evidence you'd expected to find, and the body bore all the hallmarks of having been badly staged. Like, whoever put her there wanted it to look like she'd fallen down the steps – only the positioning of the body bore no resemblance to a fall. And the only injury was a single blow to the back of the head – again, inconsistent with a fall.'

'What would someone have had to gain from moving her?'

'Beats me, but whatever happened to her, it didn't happen where she was found.'

They passed the old Capital Building, now an Italian restaurant, and headed south along St David Street towards the imposing landmark of the Scott Monument.

'And what does Sean say to all of this?' asked Anna.

'He says he didn't do it, obviously. And that the eyewitness sighting and the CCTV footage aren't him.'

'Does he have anything approaching an alibi?'

Pamela winced. 'That's where things get a little tricky.'

'How so?'

'Well, at first, he claimed he'd been out visiting a friend at the time. Then, when he was asked to identify the friend, he changed his story. Said he'd got mixed up and he'd actually been out for a run.'

'What about tracking data?' said Anna. 'His phone or a FitBit or whatever.'

She thought of her own morning runs, which she still tried to fit in at least three times a week, whenever work or ferrying Jack to school didn't get in the way. Her every movement tracked on her watch, all in the name of refining her route and trying to better her time. Best not to think too much about who was collecting all that data, and for what purpose.

'He says he forgot to take them with him,' replied Pamela. 'The tracking data bears that out.' She looked at Anna and winced again. 'I know. Not the best look given what he's accused of.'

'It's really not. Also, who mixes up visiting a friend and going out running? Especially on the same night someone supposedly murdered your girlfriend.'

The road began to slope downward as they neared Princes Street. The monument loomed ever larger, ever blacker against the night sky.

'It's true,' Pamela agreed. 'He's definitely not telling the whole story there. But it just doesn't seem right, condemning the man off the back of a memory lapse, however much of a stretch it might seem.'

'Plenty of men have been convicted for less,' said Anna.

'You're not wrong there,' said Pamela quietly.

They continued on in silence, crossing at the traffic lights and cutting through the eastern edge of Princes Street Gardens towards the station's Waverley Bridge entrance.

As they made their way down the steps and into the station, Pamela piped up again.

'There's something else I should probably mention. Leanne was pregnant.'

For a moment, Anna didn't respond. She wasn't sure whether it was some ingrained biological response born out of being a mother herself, but this news had left her feeling profoundly queasy.

'Did Sean know?' she asked eventually.

'Not till the police ambushed him with the news following the postmortem. At least, that's the impression he gave, according to what I've been able to piece together through the legal grapevine.'

'But you suspect otherwise?'

'I don't know. I'm just thinking, if he *did* know . . . well, it makes it that much harder to picture him killing Leanne, doesn't it – knowing full well he was killing his unborn child too?'

Anna wasn't so sure. Untold numbers of pregnant women, battered or killed by their partners, suggested otherwise. As experienced a solicitor as Pamela was, having no doubt seen more than her fair share of the damage humans were capable of inflicting on each other, she could be profoundly naïve about certain things. Anna knew she was predisposed to see the best in people, and had long suspected that this was especially true when it came to those accused of the worst offences – as counterintuitive as that might seem.

They continued through the station, heading down the escalator to the lower level.

'You mentioned something about Sean's solicitor,' said Anna. 'Something about him being a clock-puncher?'

Pamela made a disgusted face. 'Maurice Hanley. He's a horror. Spends all his time on social media ranting about asylum seekers and trans people. I wouldn't trust that man to represent my budgerigar, let alone my own flesh and blood.'

Was that a dig against Gerry, Anna wondered? With the fortune he'd supposedly amassed from the app he'd developed, he could presumably have afforded to secure his brother the best legal representation money could buy, had he felt so inclined.

'Word is he's already written Sean off as guilty and is doing the bare minimum he can get away with,' Pamela added.

Anna gave her a look, trying to gauge whether Pamela had credible grounds for believing this or was simply letting her own pre-existing views on the man feed her imagination.

Pamela shrugged defensively, as if she'd guessed Anna's

thoughts. 'It's a high-profile case. People talk.' She hesitated, then added, 'The fact Sean has past convictions for aggravated assault probably doesn't help matters.'

'Probably not, no,' said Anna, wondering if this man, of whom she already felt she well and truly had the measure, had *any* redeeming qualities.

'I also seem to recall something in the press about him having been overheard threatening to kill Leanne,' she said.

Pamela's expression became increasingly strained. 'Ah, yes, that,' she said, as if she'd been hoping Anna wouldn't bring up that particular detail. 'I'll admit, that doesn't exactly do him any favours. Still, there might be another explanation . . .'

Anna gave her an incredulous look, and Pamela visibly wilted under her gaze.

'. . . though, if there *is* one, I can't think of it right now,' she admitted.

They came to a stop not far from the ticket barriers. Anna turned to face Pamela.

'I'm going to regret it if I don't ask this, so I'm just going to come out and say it. Given everything we already know about this man, what is it that makes you so keen to help him?'

Pamela raised her arms helplessly and let them fall to her sides with a slap. 'It's like I said to you once before. It's not up to me to determine someone's guilt or innocence. That's for a jury to decide. But I do believe, deep down in my core, that everyone, whoever they are, has a right to fair trial.'

'And your feeling is that Sean won't get that.'

For a moment, Pamela was silent, chewing her bottom lip and avoiding Anna's eye as she mulled over whether to continue. Eventually, she seemed to come to a decision.

'A few years back,' she said, 'when I was still a baby solicitor, I had a run-in with Hanley. We didn't work for the same firm, but, due to a bunch of circumstances too complicated to go into here, he inherited one of my clients from me. At the time, I passed him everything I had on the case, including crucial evidence that would've holed the prosecution below the waterline.

'He didn't use it. Either he deliberately sat on it or else he simply forgot about it. But, whether due to outright malice or just workaday incompetence, my client went to prison for something we could have *proved* he didn't do.' She paused. 'And now that man's representing my future brother-in-law.' She looked at Anna, her eyes wide and plaintive. 'You can see my dilemma here, surely.'

'Yes,' Anna admitted – though she still felt, if she was in Pamela's shoes, that she'd be leaving Sean to sink or swim on his own steam. She supposed that was simply further proof, if any was needed, that she lacked her younger friend's far greater capacity for human compassion.

'Come and see him with me,' said Pamela suddenly, her voice urgent and insistent. 'I can get us a meeting with him – I know I can.' And then, before Anna had time to process this, let alone respond, 'Just a meeting. That's all I'm asking. No strings attached.'

'I—'

'Please. The case is still a way off going to trial. Right now, they're in the middle of precognition – statements, expert opinions, all of that. There's still time for us to make a difference. But the clock's ticking.'

Anna's eyes strayed to the departure board. She had less than three minutes before her train was due to leave, and then it would be a twenty-five-minute wait for the slow train – the one that stopped at every station between Edinburgh and Glasgow and took twice as long. The clock was ticking in more ways than one.

Her eyes met Pamela's again, and she realised there was no way she could both let Pamela down gently *and* make her train. It was one or the other . . .

Or say yes.

'Just a meeting,' she said.

'Just a meeting,' said Pamela.

'I form my own opinion of the man. If I don't like what I see, I get to walk away without being made to feel like I've broken a promise.'

Pamela nodded emphatically, lips pressed together in a desperate smile.

Anna sighed inwardly, her fate sealed.

'Fine.'

Pamela bunched her fists and let out a little squeal of triumph. Sensing that she was about to either jump for joy or threw her arms around Anna, Anna decided she was going to have to defuse the situation – and fast.

'Uh-uh. Any public histrionics and the deal's off.'

With a considerable effort, Pamela managed to contain herself, clasping her hands together in a bid to prevent them from doing anything inappropriate.

'I'll get back to you with a date and time ASAP,' she promised.

'You do that.' Anna glanced at the departure board again. 'And now I really do need to go.'

'Of course. Go-go gadget! Catch your train. Love to Jack.'

Anna, already hurrying towards the turnstile, nodded distractedly. She fished her phone out of her shoulder bag as she went, scrambling to open the ScotRail app and select the return ticket, before buzzing herself through. She boarded the train and collapsed into a seat just before the doors slammed shut.

As the train thundered westwards towards Glasgow, the carriage bucking and swaying with every join in the track, Anna took out the reading glasses she still couldn't get used to, despite having worn them for the last several weeks. If it wasn't the frames interfering with her field of vision and distracting her from what she was trying to read, it was the fact they picked up every speck of dust going, as well as umpteen finger-prints she swore she hadn't put there, resulting in her constantly having to clean them . . .

Doing her best to ignore the growing pain behind her right eye – a dull ache that had started to come on over dinner, and, going by past experience, would only get worse as the night wore on – she tapped 'Leanne McColm murder' into Google, opened the first article, and began to read.

4

Monday 21 February

'Thanks for your attention today,' Anna called as the lecture theatre began to empty. 'Don't forget, read Hagan pages 172 to 196 for next week.'

She unplugged her laptop and gathered up her things, heading for the door behind the last of the stragglers. As she emerged from the lecture theatre, she clocked the familiar bespectacled, curly-haired figure of Farah Hadid waiting for her in the corridor.

'Hey, you!' Anna grinned, heading towards her. 'What brings you out to the back of beyond?'

With rooms in the Hutcheson Building – the School of Social and Political Sciences' base of operations – at a premium, classes tended to be booked wherever they could be accommodated, meaning that multiple treks from one end of the sprawling campus to the other were not unheard of during any given day. This afternoon, Anna was in the Ingram Building, down on the southern edge of the campus, almost half a mile from her office.

Farah shrugged amiably. 'I thought to stretch my legs . . . and I wanted to catch you; see if you fancied a late lunch.'

Anna checked her watch and winced. 'Love to – but I can't. I'm heading back to the office to answer some emails before I have to hoof it over to the Rutherford Building to give the fourth-years their lecture on crime and intersectionality at three.'

'*Bof!* In that case, we'll walk together?'

They fell into step, weaving their way through the throng of students as they made for the exit.

'Later this week, then, perhaps?' said Farah as they walked. There was a faint whiff of desperation in her voice. 'It's hard pinning you down. You're hardly ever here, it seems.'

'A *slight* exaggeration,' said Anna.

But she knew what Farah meant. Though, nominally, her contract stated that she worked three days a week, in reality it worked out as two full days and two half-days, meaning that their regular lunch dates had largely become a thing of the past. If anything, her reduced hours on campus left Anna feeling run even more ragged than before – though, just like with Pamela, she felt it would be in poor taste to complain about her situation to Farah, who did the full five days . . . and then some.

They began to make their way up through the campus towards the Hutcheson Building. As they climbed the steps behind the student union, Anna's phone pinged an alert. Instinctively, she slowed to dig it out of her shoulder bag. She hoped it wasn't Jack's school again. It had been nearly three weeks since they'd last summoned her because he'd had a meltdown in class – the longest incident-free stretch yet. *Please, don't ruin this good streak.*

But it wasn't the school. The message was from NHS Greater Glasgow and Clyde:

Anna Scavolini, please remember your appointment on 01/03/2022 at 17:45 . . .

'It's bad news?'

Anna stirred at the sound of Farah's voice. She quickly rearranged her face, which she realised must have given away her mood.

'What? Oh, no. Nothing important.'

She pocketed her phone.

Farah gave her a brief, probing look, evidently unsatisfied with this response, but she didn't push the matter.

They continued into the Hutcheson Building. As they headed up the stairs towards Anna's office, Farah broke the silence into which they'd lapsed.

'So it seems Simon is definitely leaving the course director position at the end of the teaching year.'

'Well,' said Anna, not surprised, 'we always knew he didn't want it long-term.'

'You won't consider taking it up again?' said Farah, a slight note of disappointment in her voice.

'Me?' Anna laughed. 'No chance. I'd never be able to do it justice on my reduced hours. Besides,' she went on as they alighted on the third floor, 'I can't say I'm in any great hurry to don my administrator's hat again.' She glanced at Farah. 'There are others who are eminently qualified.'

'It's true,' said Farah, failing to take the hint. 'Agnieszka would be very good, if she fancies to take on the workload. So would Robert.'

Anna bit her tongue and said nothing. She desperately wished Farah could see that she'd be ideal for the role herself, but she didn't want to put her on the spot. That would only embarrass her and, in all likelihood, scare her off altogether. It wasn't as if Farah lacked the experience: during Anna's last couple of years as course director, the two of them had effectively run the undergraduate programme together, even if Farah would never have admitted it. The challenge was going to be finding a way to persuade her younger colleague – who always believed there were other people out there more qualified, more deserving, than her – to put herself forward.

At least, Anna told herself, Farah was finally on the lecturer scale, with job security and a wage commensurate to her ability and workload – both of which she'd been denied for far too long. As far as Anna was aware, Farah had no inkling of the role she herself had played in getting her the post, and she had no intention of enlightening her. Far better to let Farah believe that the university's management, which had long treated her as a source of cheap, uncomplaining labour, had finally recognised her considerable talents and decided to reward her with the title and the wage that should both, by rights, have been hers years ago. Once Anna's student, then her teaching assistant, now her peer, seeing Farah finally getting her due was a source of no small amount of gratification to Anna – and, if she was being honest with herself, more than a hint of pride.

They reached Anna's office. As Anna headed over to her desk to hook her laptop up to her monitor, her phone began to ring again. She fished it out of her bag, checked the caller ID and immediately took the call.

'Martin, hi. It's Anna Scavolini. Thanks for calling me back.'

She glanced across at the doorway, where Farah mouthed some variation of *We'll catch up later* and began to back out. Anna smiled and nodded cheerio as she continued to listen to the voice at the other end of the line.

'That's right,' she said, settling into her chair. 'I'm doing a bit of . . . well, I suppose you could say "research" into the Sean Kerevan case. I saw on the *Chronicle* website you also covered his aggravated assault trial in 2018. I was wondering if you'd mind filling me in on some of the details. Perhaps something that didn't make it into the papers . . .'

5

The sun was setting as Anna approached the multi-storey block of flats on Dundasvale Road – a long slab of grey concrete softened only slightly by the lines of trees out in front. Glass-fronted stairwells jutted from its façade, breaking up the otherwise monotonous run of balconies and roughcast walls. The place had the air of something designed for efficiency rather than style – one of those postwar estates built to rehouse the city's poor from the tenements, overlooking the roar of the three-way overpass at Cowcaddens. She took the stairs up to the fourth floor and made her way along the outdoor walkway before ringing the bell to flat 11.

Immediately, an almighty yapping noise started up beyond the door. Anna instinctively took a step back, surprised and just a little bit alarmed.

'Och, wee *soul*!' crowed a voice. 'What's the matter? Who is it? Who's at the door?'

The first thing Anna registered when the door opened wasn't Zoe, dressed in leggings and a comfy, oversized pullover, but rather the corpulent pug at her feet. White apart from its jowls and ears, which were both black, it stood with splayed legs, staring up at Anna with a deranged look in its large, bug-like eyes and bellowing at her with all the ferocity it could muster.

'Oh *hey*, doll!' gushed Zoe, delighted. 'Fancy seeing *you* in these parts. What brings—'

'What?' Anna shouted, struggling to compete with the pug's incessant barking.

'I said . . .' began Zoe, raising her voice, before giving up. 'Haud on.'

Bending down, she scooped the pug up and cradled it against her chest like a huge, misshapen baby. Instantly, the creature fell silent and nestled in Zoe's arms, tongue lolling in time to the sound of its rasping breath.

'There,' said Zoe, 'that's better. I was saying, what brings ye out thisaway?'

'I . . .' Anna began. 'Can we . . . ?'

A look of recognition dawned on Zoe's features as she remembered her manners.

''Course ye can! Step right this way.'

She ushered Anna inside.

'Urm . . . gonnae do me a favour and take yer shoes off?' she said, as Anna stepped over the threshold. 'I don't wannae come off like some sorta hypochondriac – only I've just hoovered and—'

'It's fine,' said Anna quickly, and dutifully stepped out of her shoes, wondering what had brought this on. The two of them had never done the whole 'shoes off at the front door' ritual – not in either of their respective homes.

''Preciate it, doll. These light carpets are a pure pest. Show up every speck of dirt.'

'Doing a spot of dog-sitting?' Anna nodded at the pug, continuing to luxuriate in Zoe's arms.

'Huh? Oh no, he's mine. My own flesh and blood. Well, no in the strictly literal sense, but they say family's what ye make it, right?'

Anna gave her a perplexed look.

'I've adopted him.'

'You've . . .'

'Adopted him,' Zoe repeated. 'Me 'n' Sal were at the dog shelter this weekend past,' she explained, as Anna continued to stare uncomprehendingly at her. 'Y'know, just going for a wee look-see. And he was sitting there all on his lonesome in this big auld cage, no pals, no creature comforts, no even a squeaky chew toy. And he's only two – which means he's still just a baby, really. And I just thought, I cannae leave him there. I'm no having that on my conscience. 'Sides . . .' She lifted the dog up so its head was level with hers. '. . . who could say no tae a face like that?'

Anna met the animal's vacant gaze and concluded that it would be best not to offer an opinion on the matter.

'Has he got a name?' she said instead.

'Aye.' Zoe nodded proudly. 'Pugwash. Captain Horatio Pugwash.'

'I suppose I asked a stupid question.'

'No such thing.'

They made their way through to the living room, Zoe leading the way. The flat was small, but Zoe and Sal had made the most of the space available to them, and the place had a homely, intimate feel that always made Anna feel a sense of warmth and security whenever she dropped by.

Spotting a pair of purple knickers lying on the floor, Zoe bustled over and, tucking the dog under one arm, bent down to scoop them up.

'Sal!' she sighed. 'If I've told that clatty besom once, I've told her a hunner times.'

'She not in?'

Zoe straightened up. 'Late shift at Costa. So of course I'm left minding the fort . . . and clearing up after her slovenly ways.'

She said it without any ill-feeling – as if it was all par for the course and she was perfectly content with this state of affairs. Still, not for the first time, Anna couldn't help noting how uncharacteristically house-proud Zoe seemed to have become since she and Sal had finally got their own place a couple of years ago. Zoe, who used to leave her own used undies hanging from door handles, but now instructed guests to remove their shoes at the door.

Zoe settled on the sofa with the pug still in her arms. Anna chose the armchair facing her. The dog stared across at her, mouth lolling open, making a rasping sound not unlike loud snoring.

'Is he supposed to make that noise?' Anna asked.

'Huh?' said Zoe, as if she was completely unaware of it. 'Och, that's just him breathing. He's fine.'

'Oh.'

'So, back tae my original question. What's the dealio? I mean, don't get me wrong – it's aye a pleasure, day or night, but it seems we don't see a whole lot of you these days . . . not unless ye're swinging by tae pick Jack up.'

The routine had been the same since Jack started school in January. On Tuesdays and Thursdays – the two days Anna put in a full shift at the university – either Zoe or Sal picked him up from school and brought him back to the flat till Anna finished work, while, on Mondays, when Anna was on campus in the afternoon, a neighbour with a child in Jack's year, Theo, took him to theirs. He'd be there right now, no doubt tucking into burgers or chicken nuggets or one of the other ultra-processed meals Anna wasn't sure she entirely approved of.

'Actually,' she said, already experiencing a pang of guilt at the imposition she was about to place on Zoe, 'that's sort of why I'm here.'

Zoe looked at her quizzically.

'I wanted to ask, would you mind keeping him for a bit longer next Tuesday? It's just, I've got this appointment at six, so I'm going to be a bit later getting here, and I just wanted to give you plenty of notice, in case you had plans . . .'

'What kind of appointment?' asked Zoe.

'Just a routine medical thing,' said Anna, too quickly. 'Nothing serious.'

Zoe shot her a curious look, not unlike the one Farah had given her earlier on the steps behind the student union. For a brief moment, it felt to Anna as if Zoe could see right through her. She quickly lowered her eyes, reluctant to meet Zoe's gaze.

'Aye, nae bother,' said Zoe, after a moment. 'Ye know we always love having him . . . and hey, it'll give him time tae get acquainted with Captain Pugwash – won't it, schnookums?'

She bounced the dog on her knee. It responded with a loud belch. Zoe stared at Anna, eyes and mouth wide with the same sort of excitement and wonder as if her firstborn child had just uttered its first word.

'Is that no the cutest thing you ever heard?' she whispered in hushed awe.

To keep the peace, Anna agreed that it was.

'Ye have tae be careful wae pugs,' Zoe went on sagely. ''S dead easy for them tae get overweight. Then they get all sorts of health problems 'n' whatnot. His old owners never gave him the proper amount of exercise. That's how come he's such a porker.' She turned to address the dog directly. 'Gonnae have tae put you on a diet, aren't we, wee man?' She rubbed its protuberant stomach. 'Who ate all the pies? *You* did! Yes you *diiiid!*'

Anna felt vaguely nauseous. Observing Zoe's manner towards the creature, and also her increasingly fastidious attitude towards the flat, Anna couldn't help but think she increasingly resembled a mother hen. And then it hit her. Was Zoe becoming broody?

Surely not. Not Zoe, who'd once told her she had no desire to have children, even talking about getting her tubes tied. But then, that had been during a much darker period in her life. Perhaps, now that she had a full-time job, a long-term partner and her own wee flat, her biological clock had belatedly started ticking . . .

'Listen,' said Zoe, 'whilst we're on the subject of doing favours, I was wondering if mibby I could talk you intae doing one for *me*.'

'Why not?' said Anna, her mind already turning to apprehension at the thought of what this favour might involve. 'Fair's fair.'

'It's nothing big,' said Zoe, as if guessing her thoughts. 'Just . . . well, it's sort of about Sal.'

'What about her?' Anna experienced a sudden pang of concern. 'The two of you aren't breaking up, are you?'

'What?' Zoe sounded rather alarmed herself. 'No, no, nothing like that. Only . . .'

Again, she hesitated, absentmindedly stroking Captain Pugwash's ear as she chewed her bottom lip. When she next spoke, it came out in a somewhat breathless rush.

'See, thing is, I was sorta hoping mibby she'd've got her act together by now. I mean, I'm no saying we all need tae settle for a nine tae five office job, slaving away for the Man. But, like, she'll be thirty-two before much longer, and she still hasnae got any sense of direction in her life. 'Less ye count part-time shifts at Costa and that gaming channel on Twitch wae three hunner followers as a direction.'

She looked at Anna, inviting her to disagree. Anna nodded soberly, wondering where all this had suddenly come from – and what role she was expected to play.

'I don't want ye tae think I'm on her case the whole time like some auld nag,' Zoe put in quickly. 'Truth is, I've no said anything tae her . . . which is why I was kinda sorta wondering if ye'd, y'know . . .'

She gave Anna a pointed look, as if the meaning was implicit. Anna met her gaze blankly.

'I was hoping ye'd say something tae her.'

It came out in a rush, as if getting through it as quickly as possible would lessen the obvious discomfort Zoe felt at making the request.

Anna blinked at her in surprise. 'Why me?'

'Well, you're . . .'

'I'm what?'

'You know.' Zoe gestured to Anna as if it was self-evident from just looking at her.

'An old nag?' suggested Anna.

'Got-together. Sensible. *Responsible.* You don't sit on yer arse playing video games every night when ye get in fae yer minimum wage sixteen-hour-a-week gig at the coffee shop. Ye've got goals. A career. A whole mission statement. Point is, ye're a positive role model. Something tae aspire to.'

'And you think if I have a chat with Sal – what, some of that's going to rub off on her?'

She knew she both looked and sounded incredulous, but she saw no point in trying to hide it. Truth be told, she was far from convinced Zoe had thought this plan through.

'I'm just saying,' said Zoe, 'she might be more inclined tae take it seriously coming fae you than fae me.'

She deposited Captain Pugwash on the seat next to her. The dog looked around, disoriented and disgruntled, as if he had no idea how he'd got there.

Zoe leant forward, staring at Anna imploringly. 'Look – I just don't wannae see her make the same mistakes as me. I pissed away my twenties and most of my thirties. Took me pure *ages* tae get my shit together. And I was lucky. I found something I was good at *and* managed tae blag my way intae a nursery job pretty much straight out the gate. But there's no many options out there for thirtysomething slackers wae no college degree.'

As she spoke, it dawned on Anna why Zoe wanted her to be the one to do this. She was worried that taking Sal to task herself would drive a wedge between them. She needed someone else to be the sacrificial lamb. Which left Anna feeling an awful lot like she was being set up to take the rap for something that had nothing to do with her.

Still, when it came down to her, she didn't see how she could possibly say no. Not when she'd explicitly come here to get Zoe to do something for her – on top of everything else she was already doing for her regarding Jack.

'All right,' she said, with a heavy heart. 'I'll do it.'

'Ye'll talk to her?' Zoe's face brimmed with hope.

'Provided the opportunity presents itself.'

And then, before Anna could prepare herself, Zoe was on her feet and coming towards her, arms outstretched. Anna stood up and allowed herself to be smothered in Zoe's embrace. Captain Pugwash, clearly thinking this was a most magnificent game, jumped down from the sofa and circled around them, barking joyously.

'Ach, ye're one in a million, you are,' said Zoe, still clinging to her. '*Knew* I was daein' the right thing, coming tae you.'

Anna patted Zoe's shoulder awkwardly. 'Don't mention it.'

Zoe released Anna from her embrace but continued to grip her upper arms.

'I'm serious. Total diamond is what you are.' She grinned. 'Here – I'm liking this whole "you scratch my back" arrangement. Ye've no idea what a weight off my mind this is.'

'Happy to help,' said Anna, cheeks aching from the rictus grin she was forcing.

Anna stayed a little longer, chatting with Zoe, before diplomatically drawing things to a close, using the excuse that Jack was waiting for her at Theo's. In reality, the main motivation was that Captain Pugwash, having tired himself out after all the excitement, had taken to lying on the sofa with his stubby legs in the air, breaking wind at regular intervals, the results of which were both noisy *and* pungent.

As she made her way down the stairs, she reflected on what

she'd said to Zoe. *Provided the opportunity presents itself.* In reality, she'd been somewhat underhanded with her choice of words. Given how rare her interactions with Sal actually were, a part of her, she supposed, was hoping the opportunity might *never* materialise. Because she really had no idea where she was going to begin . . .

As she reached her car, her phone pinged an alert. She fished it out of her bag, half-expecting it to be another text from the hospital, telling her the date of her appointment had changed. It wouldn't be the first time.

But it wasn't. It was from Pamela.

Game on. Monday 28 Feb at the Bar-L. x

6

Monday 28 February

Anna got out of her Skoda and gazed up at the visitor's entrance to HMP Barlinnie – an incongruous-looking glass hexagon jutting out of the imposing brick façade. Of course, this was only the public face of the prison. The five blocks that housed the roughly 1,400 inmates (400 more than its official capacity), built in the nineteenth century and kept firmly out of the view of the public, constituted a far grimmer sight.

She checked her phone for the umpteenth time. It was five minutes to ten and there was still no sign of Pamela. Not even a text to say she was on her way. If she wasn't here in the next couple of minutes, Anna was either going to have to go in without her . . .

Or get back in her car and forget the whole thing.

On multiple occasions during the last week, she'd thought about backing out. She could ring up Pamela; tell her she'd changed her mind and couldn't get involved. As recently as last night, she'd considered simply not turning up at the prison. But she'd found she couldn't do it. She hadn't exactly sworn a blood oath to Pamela, but she'd agreed to talk to Sean, and she wasn't someone who backed out of her commitments. Besides, the cursory steps she'd taken so far – reading what she could find online about the case and contacting the *Chronicle* journalist who'd covered Sean's court hearing, among other measures – had left her with questions. Questions she knew she wouldn't be able to set aside till she had answers.

She turned at the sound of an approaching vehicle. A Mini Cooper trundled into the car park. Anna spotted Pamela, a nervous driver at the best of times, hunched behind the wheel, glancing furtively this way and that as she tried to identify a place to park. Anna raised a hand in greeting and gestured to an empty space at the end of the row. Pamela waved her thanks and pulled in.

'I know, I know,' she said as she got out, 'no excuses. Traffic was a total 'mare, though. Glasgow's always so much further from Edinburgh than you think, don't you find?'

Anna allowed herself a small, private smile. At this point, expecting Pamela to change was an exercise in futility.

Pamela shrugged expectantly. 'Shall we shake a leg?'

'You never told me what you said to Sean to get him to agree to this,' said Anna, as they crossed the car park towards the entrance.

'Oh, not much,' Pamela responded airily. 'Just that you were an internationally renowned professor of criminology who'd taken a keen interest in the case.'

Anna gave her a look.

'What? I had to tell him *something* to get him on side. Besides,' she went on, as they headed through the revolving door and into the foyer, 'I never said you were a shoo-in to help him. Just that you were interested. And you wouldn't be here if you weren't just a *bit* curious, would you?'

Anna, who couldn't think of anything she could say to refute this point, chose to say nothing.

They passed through security in the usual orderly fashion. Both of them had done this dance many times before, so they were familiar with the process: handing over their identification at the booking desk and being allocated a table number; stowing their coats and belongings in the blue lockers in the foyer; then progressing through to the waiting area, followed by a protracted wait on the uncomfortable plastic seats along with a myriad of other visitors before a prison officer came through and began to summon them by table number. Anna and Pamela were part of the first batch to be called, and they followed the officer and other visitors through the security doors for a pat-down search – the final hurdle before they were allowed to proceed to the visitation room.

The room itself was a low, windowless affair with tables and marginally more comfortable chairs, plus a children's play area and an array of vending machines. The prisoners themselves were already seated – a mixture of ages and body types, some in prison-issue blue sweatshirts and grey jogging bottoms, others – those still on remand – wearing their own clothes.

Anna looked around, trying and failing to spot Sean, before realising Pamela was doing the same.

'Which one were we, again?'

'Eleven,' said Pamela, a note of confusion in her voice as she stared at the empty table.

Before either of them had a chance to speculate as to what was going on, a large, affable-looking officer made his way over to them.

'Are yous here for Sean Kerevan?' he asked.

'That's right,' said Anna, sensing that things were likely to progress more smoothly if she assumed command of the situation. 'Where is he?'

'He's been a wee bit held up,' said the officer. 'It's nothing tae worry about,' he added quickly, as Anna saw Pamela's features crumpling in alarm. 'He'll be along in a minute or two. Why don't you ladies take a seat in the meantime and we'll bring him through when he's ready?'

Mystified and, if Anna was being honest with herself, a little unsettled, she and Pamela took their seats at the empty table and sat in uneasy silence while, all around them, prisoners and their visitors greeted one another with varying degrees of enthusiasm.

'Maybe we should get him something from the machines,' Anna suggested.

She figured having something to do while they waited would keep Pamela from fretting. It might also make Sean more amenable once he finally arrived.

'That's a lovely idea!' said Pamela, lighting up. Then her face fell. 'Oh, bosoms! We've no idea what he likes.'

'We'll get chocolate, then,' said Anna firmly. 'Everybody likes chocolate.'

They ended up buying half a dozen different varieties, spreading them out on the table like a serving suggestion. As they continued to wait, Pamela unwrapped a Dairy Milk and gnawed on the end of it pensively. Anna wasn't sure what was making her so nervous. She'd assumed, at first, that it was the prospect of coming face to face with Sean that was putting her on edge. But the longer she watched her, the more it struck her that Pamela's nerves had less to do with Sean and more with how Anna herself would respond to him – whether she'd judge Sean to be someone worth fighting for, or simply walk away, leaving him to his fate.

They'd been waiting for just over five minutes when the blue door at the back of the room opened and two figures emerged, one wearing the white shirt and black trousers of a prison officer, the other a T-shirt and joggers. Despite his hunched shoulders and bowed head, Sean Kerevan towered over his escort, well-defined muscles straining against the fabric of his top.

It wasn't until he sat down facing her and Pamela that

Anna noticed he was sporting a recent injury: a cut just above his left eyebrow, sealed with steri-strips.

'Oh!' squeaked Pamela, audibly alarmed. 'What happened? Is everything all right?'

Sean gave a thin smile. 'Should see the other guy.'

Anna's eyes strayed to his hands, folded in front of him on the tabletop. In addition to the words 'PAIN' and 'GAIN' inked on the bases of his right and left fingers respectively, his knuckles bore evidence of old scarring, consistent with having hit something – or some*one* – hard and repeatedly.

Pamela gestured to the snacks. 'We thought you might like something to eat.'

Sean barely glanced at the selection before shaking his head disinterestedly.

'I'm not hungry.'

Pamela looked momentarily crestfallen, then pasted on a bright, encouraging smile.

'So, how have you been getting on?'

Sean sucked his teeth noisily, his contemptuous eyes briefly meeting Anna's. She felt herself beginning to mirror his expression and quickly stopped herself.

Pamela lowered her eyes, chastened. 'All right,' she murmured. 'Daft question, I know.'

Then, switching into what Anna recognised as her 'business voice' – brisk, clear and just a little too pompous, she continued:

'Well, first of all, I'd like to thank you for agreeing to see us. You already know who I am, obviously, so I won't waste time reaming off *my* curriculum vitae.'

In a movement that felt decidedly rehearsed, she turned to Anna, gesturing to her like a salesperson showing off a prize exhibit.

'But I *would* like to introduce Anna Scavolini, Professor of Criminology at Kelvingrove University *and* a published author.

As I mentioned in my email, Anna's taken a strong personal interest in your case.'

'Well,' Anna began, 'I wouldn't go as far as—'

'S'pose I'm meant to be flattered,' growled Sean.

There was a cruel, mocking note in his voice that Anna found profoundly unpleasant – which, she supposed, tallied with just about everything else she already knew about the man.

'You should be,' Pamela told him, chastising him like an errant child. 'Anna's taken time out of her busy schedule to come here to see you today.'

Sean continued to look unimpressed.

'Anna's been responsible for solving a *string* of cases,' Pamela went on, 'including several miscarriages of justice. You're extremely fortunate she's taking the time to speak to you, let *alone* considering helping you.'

For Anna, this was the limit. There was putting your best foot forward and then there was gilding the lily with abandon. She saw now that she was going to have to put her foot down, and sharpish.

'Now hold *on*,' she said. 'I haven't solved a *string* of cases. I've looked into a handful, purely as a layperson, and in most instances, my role in solving them was tangential at best. And,' she concluded, shooting a pointed look in Sean's direction, 'I never said I was considering helping him.'

'Good,' Sean snapped, before Pamela could respond, 'cos I don't need your help.'

Anna heard Pamela's shocked intake of breath – practically a squeak of horror.

'That's enough, you!' She turned to Anna. 'Don't you listen to him. He's just upset. He doesn't know what he's saying.'

'I'm bloody *not* upset!' said Sean, his voice rising angrily.

But Anna's back was well and truly up now. She knew she shouldn't rise to the bait, but something about Sean's reaction – perhaps his general arrogance, perhaps his blunt dismissal of

Pamela's admittedly overblown cataloguing of her star-studded credentials – had struck a nerve. She wasn't going to sit here and be condescended to. Not by this man. Not with what she knew about him.

'No,' she said, addressing Pamela but staring belligerently at Sean. 'Let's hear why he's so convinced he doesn't need any help. Given the evidence stacked against him, I can only assume he must have some sort of rabbit he's going to pull out of his hat. Otherwise I can't *begin* to imagine what could possibly make him so confident.'

She sensed Pamela squirming in the seat next to her, but she continued to stare at Sean, who held her gaze, saying nothing. There was a look of surprise in his eyes, accompanied by something else. Something almost like . . . respect.

'If you don't need our help,' said Anna, 'then why *did* you agree to see us?'

A moment passed, then Sean gave an ill-tempered shrug, reverting back to his earlier sullen truculence.

'What else'm I gonna do with myself?'

'Oh,' said Pamela. Then, as if it had all suddenly become perfectly clear to her, *'Oh.'*

Anna and Sean both looked at her questioningly.

'We're the first visitors you've had, aren't we?' said Pamela softly.

'Yeah, well,' Sean muttered to himself, 'find out who your *real* friends are when you're slapped with a murder charge, don't you?'

Pamela didn't appear to know what to say.

'I thought Gerry might show his face,' Sean continued, still seemingly addressing himself. 'But he's never even written. Not even once.'

For a moment, an unfamiliar note came into his voice – one almost akin to vulnerability. To hurt. Then he caught himself, and his expression hardened.

'Fucking wanker. Thinks he's too good for this place. Can't

have his poncy new mates knowing he's got a brother who's a common crim.'

Anna studied Sean carefully, intrigued by this momentary lapse. There was, she thought, something more than a little forced about the part he was playing – almost like he was over-compensating, acting the tough guy because it was what was expected of him. Like Pamela's overblown trumpeting of Anna's problem-solving credentials, it was all being laid on just a little too thickly. Anna wondered what really lay behind the façade. One thing was for sure – they were never going to find out if they continued to treat him with kid gloves.

'And how's your case progressing?' said Pamela, keen to end the standoff. 'Is Mr Hanley treating you well?'

Sean snorted. 'There's someone else who never visits. Or *hardly* never. Keeps calling to reschedule at the last minute. Something always seems to come up.'

'But you *have* had a chance to discuss things with him?' Pamela sounded faintly desperate. 'He knows how you want to plead?'

Sean smiled humourlessly. 'Well, let's just say how *I* want to plead and how *he* wants me to plead ain't exactly the same thing.'

'He wants you to plead guilty.'

It was a statement of fact rather than a question. Pamela sounded genuinely crushed.

'He keeps saying how bad it looks,' Sean went on. 'How, in his "considered opinion", I should fess up and admit I did what they all say I did.'

'Now *there's* an idea,' said Anna glibly.

Pamela gave Anna a sharp look, disapproval writ large in her expression.

Anna ignored her. She knew what she was doing. She sat, arms folded, staring at Sean, silently challenging him to respond.

Pamela leaned across the table towards him, trying in vain

to get him to meet her gaze rather than Anna's. 'It's *vital* that your solicitor follows your wishes,' she implored. 'He can advise you, but at the end of the day, it's you who's on trial. He has to submit the plea you tell him to.'

Sean shrugged indifferently, as if it was neither here nor there to him. He sat, arms folded, glowering at the tabletop.

'What about your alibi?' Pamela persevered. 'Are you any clearer in your head about where you were that night?'

'I already said I was out for a run.'

'But that's not what you said at first,' said Anna. 'You told the police you were visiting a friend. What made you change your story?'

'I just . . . got confused, is all.'

Anna stared at him incredulously. 'That's your answer? You got *confused*? You mean you can't tell the difference between going for a run and visiting a friend?'

Pamela gave Anna another warning look, which she pointedly ignored.

'I just forgot, OK?' Sean snapped.

'Out of curiosity,' said Anna, 'where were you when you heard the planes had flown into the Twin Towers?'

'School,' said Sean, without giving it any thought.

'Uh-huh? Which year?'

'P4,' said Sean, again coming up with the answer immediately.

'Hmm,' said Anna. 'Funny.'

'What is?'

'Well, it's just that you remember, with crystal clarity, where you were when you heard about an event twenty years ago that didn't even involve you . . . and yet you appear to have infinitely more difficulty remembering where you were on the night your girlfriend and her unborn child were killed.'

This time, Pamela stared at Anna open-mouthed, not even *trying* to hide her disbelief. Anna continued to watch Sean, who stared her down insolently, nostrils flaring as he breathed heavily through his nose. Perhaps it was simply her imagination, but it seemed to her that he was expending a considerable amount of effort to maintain that expression.

Eventually, he gave a thin smile and a dry, sneering laugh.

'What can I say? I'm forgetful.'

'Well, that's one word for it, I suppose,' said Anna quietly.

Pamela prodded Anna's leg under the table with her foot – not a full-blown kick but considerably more than a mere nudge.

'And just so we're clear,' Anna went on, ignoring her, 'your assertion is that the eyewitness sighting of a man dragging Leanne along Trongate shortly before her death – a man matching your physical description, wearing an item of clothing identical to one you own – wasn't you?'

'It's not my "assertion". It's the truth.'

'And the figure captured on CCTV with Leanne at High Street and Springburn railway stations – not you either?'

'No.' Sean's voice was a low growl.

'You weren't on Trongate or at either station?'

'No.'

'And there's no possibility you simply forgot you were there, just like you initially "forgot" about your run?'

'NO.'

He drew the word out, his lips moving slowly and emphatically, eyes all the while fixed on Anna.

'Has Mr Hanley spoken to you at all about character witnesses?' Pamela blurted, a ring of desperation in her raised voice. 'It's worth having a think,' she went on, seeing that she had Sean's attention, for however brief a time; 'seeing if there's anyone who could speak up on your behalf. A long-term friend, or, failing that, a past employer . . .'

'That'll be right, aye,' said Sean. 'All these great friends of mine who couldnae even wait till I was charged to shaft me. Some of 'em even went to the press – told 'em they always knew I was a wrong 'un. Apparently I'm violent and "prone to outbursts of aggression".'

'Yes,' said Anna blandly, 'I imagine the previous convictions for aggravated assault might go some way towards explaining that characterisation.'

An angry look flared in Sean's eyes. 'That was . . .' he began, then stopped, seemingly changing his mind about whatever he'd been going to say. 'The other bloke started it,' he said sullenly.

'Somehow I had a feeling you were going to say that.'

This time, there was no uncertainty about it: the contact Pamela's foot made with Anna's leg constituted a full-blown – and rather vicious – kick.

Ignoring it, and the stinging pain in her calf, Anna selected a KitKat from the table and slowly, deliberately, began to unwrap it.

'If you don't believe me, fine,' snapped Sean, 'but it's true. It was self-defence.'

'Self-defence which, I'm reliably informed, involved a glass bottle.'

Sean said nothing, but he didn't look happy. Nor, for that matter, did Pamela, who, for now, seemed to have abandoned any thought of getting Anna to stop through the force of her feet and was sitting, arms clutched about herself, staring morosely at the tabletop.

'All right,' said Anna, 'let's park the grievous bodily harm for now and move on to the threat you made against Leanne's life at The Raven on Renfield Street on the nineteenth of December last year. Or are you going to tell me that was self-defence too?'

At this, Sean practically laughed – an angry, frustrated laugh, but a laugh nonetheless.

'This again? Christ, how many times do I have to explain it to you people? It was a figure of speech! Some wee clype went running to the polis on account of a bloody FIGURE OF SPEECH.'

Anna gave him a nonplussed look. He sighed, clearly resenting having to explain himself.

'You mind that song "Baby Shark"? Some woman had been playing it for her wean on the bus earlier, and I'd said to Leanne, "Is that no the most annoying thing you ever heard?" 'Course, after I said that, she knew exactly how to push my buttons for the rest of the day. Kept singing it, trying to get me to blow my top. She started up again with it in the pub that night. And I'd had enough. I said something to her like, "See you, if you don't stop, I'm gonnae kill you." ' He jerked his shoulders in an angry shrug. 'That's all I said. Doesnae mean I was literally planning on *murdering* her.'

'Still,' said Anna coolly, 'not a great look – especially when you factor in the domestic disturbances.'

She felt Pamela shift in the seat next to her. *That's right, Pamela – I know all about those.*

'Three calls to the police in the last six months from your next-door neighbours,' she went on. 'Raised voices, sounds of breaking glass, a woman screaming over and over. Let me guess – all that was just her trying to get you to blow your top too.'

'All right – so we fought. Couples do. It doesnae mean anything. And it's not like she didnae give as good as she got.'

'Is that right?' Anna's voice was a complete monotone.

'Aye.' Sean glowered at her from beneath hooded brows. 'That auld witch next door – she's never liked me. Her *and* her gimpy son. Had it in for me since the year dot, they have. They'd swear up was down and black was white if it meant getting me put away. 'Sides, she's got some fucking nerve complaining about noise, the volume she leaves the telly running at all day.'

Anna said nothing, but made no effort to hide either her incredulity or her disdain.

'I know what you're trying to make out,' growled Sean.

'Care to enlighten me?'

'Same thing the cops made out. That I'm some sort of monster with violent urges I can't control. That I lost the plot and bashed my own girlfriend's head in. Well, it's not true. I'd never hit her – her or *any* lassie. That's not who I am.'

'Really,' said Anna.

'Aye,' said Sean. Then, mimicking her accent, far more cut-glass than his own, *'Reeeeeally.'*

For Anna, this sort of mockery was water off a duck's back – especially when it came from someone like him who was in no position whatsoever to take the moral high ground. Without missing a beat, she moved on.

'I'd like to circle back to the aggravated assault convictions from 2018. Note that I said "convictions" plural. Because the other bloke who quote-unquote "started it" wasn't the only victim, was he?'

Sean's face tightened. Anyone could see he knew precisely what was coming.

Anna locked eyes with him. 'You assaulted two people that night. The second victim was a woman.'

Beside her, she heard Pamela's shocked intake of breath. Clearly, this was news to her.

'That's not what happened,' said Sean immediately. 'I never assaulted her.'

'She needed fifteen stitches in her cheek.'

'Only cos she never looked where she was going. How was I to know she was gonnae walk past me while I was . . .' He trailed off.

'Swinging a broken bottle?' Anna suggested.

Sean said nothing. At this point, he must surely have known it would be pointless.

'From where I'm sitting,' said Anna, moving into what, if she was giving a lecture, she'd have regarded as the summing-up phase, 'it sounds like you inhabit a world where you're this perennially misunderstood, maltreated victim of circumstance for whom the entire world has it in. Your entire defence is one long, plaintive cry of "it's not what it looks like". Well, I put it to you that it's *exactly* what it looks like. Would you like to know what I think happened to Leanne that night?'

Sean merely continued to stare daggers at her.

'I think you followed her into town and had it out with her. You hauled her back to Springburn and, on the way to your house, things escalated and you hit her on the back of the head. Whether you actually *intended* to kill her with that blow is for the courts to decide. Either way, it resulted in her death.'

Sean listened, his jaw set, breathing heavily through flaring nostrils.

Casually, Anna broke the end off the KitKat finger she'd unwrapped earlier and popped it into her mouth.

'You then attempted to move the body and stage it to look like an accident, only you didn't do nearly as good a job of it as you thought you had. As a result, the police saw straight through your attempt the moment they clapped eyes on it. Am I right?'

'No.'

'I think, in your arrogance, you never for a moment imagined they'd suspect you, and so, a few hours later, when you got back to the house to find them already searching it, you hadn't even thought to prepare a halfway plausible alibi. That's what happened, isn't it? You did it, and you banked on everyone else being too stupid to notice.'

'No.'

'You killed her, didn't you, Sean?'

'No.'

'You killed Leanne, and you killed her unborn baby.'

'NO!!!'

Sean's outburst was sudden and explosive. His voice filled the entire room, causing every other conversation to immediately cease. A couple of nearby prison officers advanced towards the table, braced for violence.

'It's OK,' said Pamela, waving them back. 'It's fine.'

Reluctantly, the officers came to a halt, though they remained a few paces away, ready to spring into action if things flared up again. Slowly, almost reluctantly, the other prisoners and their guests resumed their conversations.

Anna kept her eyes on Sean, stewing on the opposite side of the table, barely keeping a lid on his emotions.

'I bloody loved her, all right?' he said, his voice a low, insistent hiss. 'She was everything to me. And that baby . . . I'd never . . .'

He trailed off, swallowing down whatever sentiment had been on the verge of bubbling to the surface. A moment later, he continued in the same insistent whisper.

'Every man and his dug's already made up his mind about me. But if I was gonnae kill her and stage the body, why would I make such a bloody half-arsed job of it? You tell me that. How they found her, no one with half a brain would think she actually fell.'

He looked at Anna and Pamela in turn, on the verge of desperation. Neither of them spoke. They were each waiting to see what he said next.

'And,' he went on, marginally calmer now but no less insistent, 'why take the risk of moving her when someone could've easily caught me in the act? Why not just leave her wherever it happened and get the fuck outta there? Way I figure it, someone *wanted* that body found, and they *wanted* it to look staged so the cops'd be looking for the killer . . .'

He turned his gaze to Anna, his expression sour and contemptuous, convinced he had her number.

'Simplest answer's always the best one, right? And who's gonnae be suspect number one if not the boyfriend?'

Anna didn't respond.

Sean folded his arms, resting them on the tabletop and leaning towards the two of them, chin jutting out obstinately.

'So,' he concluded, clearly entering into a summing-up phase of his own, 'either I'm the dumbest fucking murderer in the whole of Glasgow . . .'

He paused for a beat, letting it hang.

'Or maybe . . .'

He looked Pamela dead in the eyes.

'Just maybe . . .'

Then Anna.

'I. DIDN'T. DO. IT.'

7

'What in the name of God Almighty was all *that* about?'
Pamela demanded as they stepped out into the fresh air.

She was moving fast, striding down the wheelchair access
ramp at the front of the building on her skinny, bird-like legs,
forcing Anna to hurry after her.

'Needling him like that, nearly getting him to blow his top
. . . Honestly, it's a miracle we weren't both turfed out of there
for starting a total brouhaha!'

'I know,' said Anna, doing her best to keep her own tone
calm and level. 'But I decided it was worth the risk. I needed
him to stop stonewalling us, and I figured the best way of
doing that was to chip away at the emotionless hard man act.
Get him to lose his cool.'

'And? Get what you wanted?' Pamela stopped at the
bottom of the ramp and swung round to face Anna.

Anna didn't respond. Truthfully, she wasn't sure what her
answer should be. In many respects, Sean remained an enigma
to her – a maddening, self-contradictory enigma.

After a lengthy moment had passed without Anna answering, Pamela spoke again.

'So, then – what did you make of him? What did you think?'

Anna opened her mouth to respond, then stopped. She remained silent for a moment as she got her thoughts in order, then began again, choosing her words carefully.

'I think Sean Kerevan has a hair-trigger temper and is trying his best to suppress a serious amount of pent-up aggression. I also think, if this case goes to trial and he takes the stand, any halfway competent prosecutor is going to make mincemeat of him.'

'Agreed. But . . . ?'

'I'm not sure there *is* a "but". I believe him when he says he loved Leanne. And I don't doubt that he's a whole lot more upset about her death and the baby's than this whole macho routine he's got going allows him to admit. But none of that proves he didn't kill her. They're known as crimes of passion for a reason.'

She looked at Pamela, standing there, sucking in her cheeks disapprovingly.

'You don't agree?'

'I don't know,' Pamela admitted. 'I just . . . I can't help thinking a guilty man would have tried harder to sell us on his innocence, not to mention his grief. But he wasn't having any of it until you bullied . . .' She caught Anna's look. '. . . I mean, coaxed it out of him. That's got to count for something, surely?'

Anna frowned. 'I find that sort of reverse psychology a bit overly reductive. "He looks guilty. That must mean he's actually innocent." '

Pamela opened her mouth to object, but Anna beat her to it.

'And I know that's not what you're saying, but my point still stands. Just because he wasn't going out of his way to convince us he didn't do it doesn't mean he *didn't*.'

69

Pamela said nothing. She lowered her eyes, obviously disappointed.

'Still,' said Anna, after a moment, 'I won't deny he had a point about moving the body, and the incompetently staged nature of the scene. Why take the trouble to move it in the first place, and cock it up so badly – unless you *wanted* people to think, "Someone staged this"? Sean's obviously not stupid. I can't see him making such a pig's ear of it – not unless the whole thing was one massive double bluff.'

'You mean, make it look so obviously staged the natural conclusion would have to be that someone was trying to frame him?'

Anna gave a sceptical grimace. It seemed even less likely now that Pamela had spelt it out.

They stood there in silence for a while, each consumed by their own thoughts. A prison officer emerged from the building behind them, phone clamped to his ear, deep in murmured conversation.

'How come you never told me before we went in that the second victim in the assault case was a woman?'

Pamela's question seemed to come out of nowhere. She sounded genuinely aggrieved.

'Would it have made a difference?' asked Anna.

'I'm not sure,' said Pamela, a sullen note lingering in her voice. 'Just . . . would've been nice to have known, that's all.'

Anna sighed, running a hand through her hair. 'I wanted to see how Sean would react when I sprung it on him, but not till I was sure I had all my ducks in a row. I couldn't risk you preempting it. Anyway,' she went on, remembering something, 'I could level much the same accusation against *you*.'

Pamela looked confused. 'Come again?'

'When you told me about the case against Sean, you never mentioned those domestic disturbance callouts. You left me to find out about them myself. I know you knew about them, so don't pretend.'

'It's true,' Pamela admitted, a note of genuine regret in her voice. 'I knew about them. I just . . .' She gave a small, wincing smile. 'I don't know. I suppose I was worried that, if I *did* tell you about them, it'd make you even *less* likely to give Sean the time of day.'

Anna looked at Pamela, standing there, looking so forlorn and contrite. She shook her head.

'This won't work, you know.'

'What?'

'You, keeping things from me. The only way it can work is if you're completely honest with me.'

Pamela's eyes lit up, immediately seizing on the subtext of Anna's statement.

'Does that mean . . . you'll help?'

'I have to know absolutely everything,' Anna went on, ignoring the question. 'Everything, down to the slightest detail, however trivial.'

'Agreed. No more secrets.' Deep breath. 'So are you going to help?'

For almost a full minute, Anna said nothing. She stood, hands jammed into the pockets of her overcoat, head tilted back as she gazed up at the overcast sky. Every synapse in her brain was telling her to walk away. To refuse to have anything to do with this. How many times now had she said she didn't do this anymore – whatever 'this' was?

It wasn't even as if she was remotely convinced Sean was innocent. At least, then, the whole thing would be considerably more cut and dried. On the contrary, she still believed the most likely explanation was that he killed Leanne and did a thoroughly awful job of trying to cover it up. And he certainly hadn't done anything to endear himself to her. Indeed, the Sean she'd met in there had been even more unlikeable than the picture she'd formed of him in her head over the last couple of weeks.

She would never have said so to Pamela, but, when Anna

had agreed to come here, a part of her had done so with what amounted to an intention to deliberately sabotage the entire meeting. She'd planned to confront Sean with what he'd done – rub his face in it, leave him with nowhere to hide. It was possible she'd even allowed herself to believe that, if she bludgeoned him hard enough with the weight of the evidence against him, he'd eventually crack and give her the confession that had so far eluded the professionals.

But that hadn't happened. Instead, he'd held firm – and she had to admit, that said something about him . . . or at least, she *thought* it did. She might have dismissed Pamela's assessment of his demeanour as nothing more than reverse cod psychology, but, privately, she found it a whole lot harder to ignore the voice at the back of her head telling her that, surely, a guilty man would have made more of an effort to try to get a potential ally onside – especially a pre-eminent criminologist who'd supposedly taken a personal interest in his plight.

There was no question about it: something about the case didn't add up – at least not to *her* satisfaction. She wasn't sure what it was, but it was there, niggling away at her like a bit of gristle stuck between her teeth. And, as much as she hated to admit it, the part of her that found it impossible to ever let any unfinished business go desperately wanted to know what that 'something' was.

No, not wanted to know. *Needed* to know.

She lowered her head, feeling oddly calm about it. Resigned, even.

'It's looking that way, isn't it?' she said.

PART II

TANGLED WEB

8

Tuesday 1 March

Anna lay still, trying to ignore the growing discomfort in her lower back and to tune out the hammering pulses that seemed to rattle deep inside her skull. The clanging was relentless – a metallic *dun-dun-dun-dun-dun*, followed by a whirring sound, then a burst of electronic clicking, then a momentary interlude of silence, just long enough to lull her into believing the ordeal could be over, only for it to start all over again.

She'd said no when they offered her the option of music, on the grounds that she might well end up spending the next forty-five minutes being subjected to song after song that she didn't like, but now she was beginning to regret it. On their own, the headphones they'd given her were a woefully inadequate source of noise cancellation.

It had started just under three and a half months ago: a series of headaches and visual disturbances, accompanied by a feeling of pressure behind her right eye. At first, she'd put it down to tiredness and overwork, even though, on a part-time contract, she really did have very little to complain about in that department. Then, she'd thought it might be stress driven by the problems Jack was having at school, even though the symptoms had begun back at the tail end of the previous year, when she was still home-schooling him – or rather trying to – after having been too late to get him enrolled at a local school following their return from Perugia.

It wasn't until nearly six weeks had elapsed that she finally took herself to her GP, who recommended she avail herself of the free eye test offered by every optician in the country. The exam revealed minor deterioration in her right eye, resulting in her, at the grand age of 40, receiving her first ever pair of prescription glasses. She'd been a dutiful patient, wearing them every time she read anything, even if she was just checking her phone for a few seconds. And, at first, she'd managed to convince herself they were working. The pain wasn't *quite* so bad, the blurred vision not *quite* so severe.

But eventually, she'd been forced to accept that the problem wasn't going away. On the contrary, it was getting worse, the headaches more frequent and of greater intensity. A second visit to the GP led to a referral to a consultant neurologist, Dr Elizabeth Maitland, who promptly arranged for her to undergo the brain scan she was now receiving.

'It's unlikely to be anything to worry about,' Maitland had said to her. 'There are umpteen possible explanations for the symptoms you're describing, many of them completely benign. Still,' she'd added, with a slightly patronising smile, 'best not to leave anything to chance, eh? Worst thing you can do with a problem is to sit on it. *Potential* problem,' she'd corrected herself, and smiled again. 'Try not to worry. There's no point fretting about something that hasn't even happened yet.'

Sage advice. And yet, lying inside the MRI scanner, listening to it beginning its *dun-dun-dun-dun-dun* routine for the umpteenth time, Anna felt anything but reassured.

. . .

She came to with the realisation that someone was shaking her shoulder and saying her name. She opened her eyes to find herself out of the scanner and gazing up at the radiographer who'd checked her in what must have been nearly an hour ago.

'There you are, back with us,' she smiled. 'Did you have a wee sleep?'

Anna blinked her eyes, trying to force herself to wake up properly.

'Must have. Sorry.'

She reached up and lowered the headphones from her ears.

'Don't apologise!' said the woman. 'Happens more often than you'd think. Believe it or not, some of the patients say the noise is actually quite soporific. Anyway,' she went on, as she helped Anna to sit up, 'that's us all done. You can go ahead and get dressed now.'

Gingerly, Anna lowered her feet to the ground and, once she was sure they weren't in any danger of giving way under her, stood up.

'It's normally a one to two-week wait for the results,' said the radiographer. 'The doctor'll be in touch with you in due course.'

Anna nodded her thanks distractedly and headed for the door, the foam soles of her hospital-issue disposable slippers clinging to the linoleum like suction cups.

Shortly afterwards, having exchanged the hated hospital gown – the kind that never seemed to fully close at the back – for her own clothes, Anna emerged into the post-sundown twilight.

She halted in the shadow of the multi-storey complex, waiting for the voices in her head to settle before she even *contemplated* getting behind the wheel. Once again, she implored herself not to worry. It was probably nothing – and besides, the headaches hadn't been nearly as bad over the last few days. Or so she told herself.

She sucked in a deep breath. Above all else, she was determined not to bring her worries home with her. The last thing she wanted was to pass them on to Jack, who she knew from long experience was particularly adept at picking up on her moods.

Once she'd gathered her thoughts and composed herself, she headed up to Cowcaddens to collect Jack from Zoe and Sal's. Jack was sullen and uncommunicative with her when she got there, standing in the hallway in his Thornwood Primary uniform with his fists clenched by his sides, refusing to make eye contact with her.

'He's been like this since I picked him up,' said Zoe in a quiet voice. 'Don't ask me why. I've no been able tae get anything out of him.'

At least Sal wasn't about – some last-minute get-together with friends from her college days, Zoe said. Anna silently thanked her lucky stars. She doubted she'd have had the headspace for a brain scan, a sulky child *and* delivering life lessons in responsibility to Zoe's girlfriend with the strangely coloured hair.

In the car, Anna tried to ignore the mutinous atmosphere emanating from the back seat, cheerfully chatting away to Jack, asking him about his day and what he'd had for his dinner. Jack responded in a surly tone, giving one or two-word answers, staring straight ahead with his brows clenched.

At length, Anna concluded she was going to have to tackle the bull by the horns.

'What's the matter, Jack? Did something happen at school?'

'No,' Jack growled.

'What's the matter, then? Auntie Zoe said you'd been like this all evening.'

'I hate it there. Why do I have to go?'

'You hate it at *Zoe's*?'

'No. School.'

'Well,' said Anna, wincing internally at the unimaginative platitude she was about to serve up, 'everyone has to go to school. How else are you going to learn things?'

'I already know more than everyone there. They're such babies. Some of them can't even *read*!' He screwed up his features in disgust.

'Jack,' said Anna sharply, 'that's not very nice. Everyone has different things they're good at, and everyone develops at a different pace. I bet the ones who can't read are able to do other things you're not able to do yet.'

'I still don't see why I have to go,' muttered Jack, ignoring what she'd just said. 'Why can't we go back to you teaching me?'

Anna bit back a sigh. She should have known that question was coming. It was, she supposed, a bit of a tall order to expect a six-year-old to understand that what had seemingly been a perfectly acceptable routine three months ago was no longer so. The whole home-schooling arrangement had only ever been intended as a temporary measure, born out of necessity. And it wasn't just personal prejudice against the practice – though she had to admit that that prejudice had been sharpened considerably by the various nutcase conspiracy movements that had sprung up since the pandemic. Unlike the various cranks whose posts she'd encountered online, insisting that they were the people best placed to educate their children by virtue of having birthed them, Anna had enough self-awareness to know that, while she was perfectly at home in a university lecture theatre, she wasn't remotely qualified to properly educate a pre-pubescent child. Her efforts to provide him with a structured learning environment had verged on an unmitigated disaster, with any attempt to sit Jack down at the kitchen table with the worksheets she'd downloaded invariably devolving into chaos, ending with her giving up and letting him do as he pleased, telling herself that building Lego or a trip to the swing-park still counted as learning. Given how manifestly she'd failed to enforce any sort of discipline, she supposed it was only fair to apportion at least some of the blame for Jack's failure to adapt to the strictures of a formal schooling environment to herself.

'That was only ever temporary,' she said, as levelly as possible. 'It just wouldn't be feasible long-term. You have to go to school during the week, just like I have to go to work. That's just the way it is.'

'That's not true,' said Jack. 'You stay at home on Monday morning and Friday afternoon and all day on Wednesday. Why can't I?'

Anna opened her mouth to respond, then stopped. She didn't have an answer to that – at least, not one that would make sense to a child – even an unusually bright one such as Jack.

Remember what you decided, she told herself. *Don't pass your stress on to him.*

'We can talk about this another time,' she said, aware that she'd just delivered the cop-out to end all cop-outs, and, far from resolving the matter, was merely kicking it into the long grass.

Jack kept up his mood all the way back to the rental property in Jordanhill that, for the past six months, had been their home – and would probably remain so for the foreseeable future as well.

In the end, she'd decided to bite the bullet and let Terry and his crew of quite possibly cowboy builders loose on her beloved house on Clarence Drive, effectively handing them a blank cheque to do whatever was necessary to rectify the subsidence issue she'd been assured was a ticking time bomb. The last time she'd passed by to see how progress was going, she'd seen no sign of any work being done, but there was plenty of scaffolding in place and a large banner advertising Terry's services to other prospective clients.

Their current abode, on Southbrae Drive, not far from the old Jordanhill College, constituted a significant downsizing in comparison – a traditional red sandstone villa converted into a four-in-a-block. Anna and Jack had the front ground floor flat, with two bedrooms, a living room, kitchen and bathroom – which, all told, gave the two of them a more or less adequate amount of space but not much more beyond that.

In a way, the move had been something of a blessing: turned out it was considerably less hassle keeping a small flat in order than a three-storey townhouse. Still, Anna couldn't help but feel a little unmoored. The temporary nature of their current accommodation made it impossible to put down roots; to feel like it was really home. Plus, due to the lack of available space, several of her belongings were still in storage, leaving her with the constant nagging feeling that, at some point, she was going to find herself without immediate access to something she desperately wanted. It hadn't happened yet, but, as with so many worries, the anticipation was almost worse than the actual event.

Once inside, Jack soon forgot his earlier bad mood and reverted to his usual whimsical self, chattering away to himself as he tackled his latest Lego creation: a sprawling edifice that incorporated both medieval turrets and space lasers. Anna managed to keep up appearances until he was safely tucked into bed, then retreated to the easy chair facing the living room window with a large glass of red wine and allowed her worries to unspool. The headache she'd managed to convince herself was gone had returned with a vengeance. Maybe it *is* stress-induced, she wondered.

Or maybe it's exactly what you've feared it was right from the beginning.

It wasn't until she'd downed most of the glass and had had plenty of time to imagine every grim scenario under the sun that, on a whim, she checked her phone and saw that, while she was undergoing the scan, she'd received a text from Pamela Macklin.

> Through in Glasgow tomorrow seeing client.
> Early afternoon case conference if you're free? x

9

Wednesday 2 March

Anna was waiting on Great Western Road, at the foot of the steps up to Hillhead Street, when the number six bus pulled up. Pamela was the first passenger to disembark, proudly clutching her paper ticket.

'I made it!' she exclaimed, a trifle breathless but grinning through it. 'No crises or calamities!'

'So I see,' said Anna. It had long ceased to be a source of surprise to her that Pamela always regarded successful journeys on public transport as genuine accomplishments, to be shared and celebrated with her friends. 'How did things go with your client?'

'Trade secrets. You *know* I can't discuss that.' Pamela tapped her nose and winked.

'Of course. Um . . . I booked us a room in the university library, so we won't be disturbed. Shall we . . . ?'

They headed up the steps together and began to make their way along Hillhead Street, past the sandstone tenements and overhanging trees, still bare and exposed as they waited patiently through the last vestiges of winter.

Anna wasn't supposed to have been at the university today. Wednesday was the one day of the week when she had no work commitments whatsoever, and she always tried to treat it as a genuine day off, denying herself even the occasional paranoia email check. Her original plan had been for them to meet in town once Pamela had finished with her client, but she'd ended up being unexpectedly summoned to track down her paperwork for a student appeal after someone managed to mislay the only other copy. When she'd called Pamela, explaining that she'd be running late, Pamela had offered to jump on the bus and meet her here instead.

And now, here they were.

'How's Gerry feeling now about the whole "us looking into his brother's murder charge" thing?' Anna asked as they continued to walk. 'He come round to it yet?'

Pamela gave a pained grimace. 'I, um, haven't brought the subject up with him again. Not since that night you were over. I fancy he knows, or at least has an inkling, but it's . . . not something we talk about.'

To Anna, this didn't sound like a particularly healthy way to conduct a relationship, but she refrained from pointing this out.

'Were Leanne and Gerry still in touch at all, do you know?' she said instead. 'In the run-up to her death, I mean.'

Pamela shook her head. 'Not since she and Sean got together. I get the sense the feelings of betrayal pretty much closed the door on any future contact. Anyway, it's not as if it's something Ger talks about. For obvious reasons.'

'And how's he coping with it all? I know they were only together for a short while – but still, I doubt that makes it any easier.'

Pamela gave a strained smile. 'Oh, he's a real stoic, my Ger. Big with the whole "stiff upper lip" routine. But I know him better than he thinks I do, and I know it's done more of a number on him than he lets on. Plus, he didn't exactly find out under the best of circumstances.'

'Oh?'

'Yeah. Read about it in the papers. Passed the newsagent's on his way into work and there was Leanne's face slap bang on the front page of the *Caledonian*. You'd think someone could've called to warn him. Like, oh, say, his own *brother*.'

'I'm guessing Sean probably had other things on his mind,' said Anna, thinking this a not unreasonable concession.

But Pamela just continued as if Anna hadn't spoken. 'I was away at the time, visiting my folks up in Stornoway. It was a sort of belated New Year get-together – I'd had to work through the holiday period. Ger couldn't come because he was attending this big tech conference in Dundee all weekend. When he found out what'd happened, he rang to tell me straight away, but I couldn't get back down till the Wednesday, and by then, he'd already perfected his macho "I'm not bothered" routine.'

Anna found herself at a loss as to how to respond. It was obvious Pamela felt guilty over not having been there to support her fiancé, but pointing out that she couldn't have planned for this seemed an overly glib response.

'Well, you're there now,' she said instead, 'and I'm sure he knows he's lucky to have you. I mean, you're not there *now*,' she clarified. 'Right now, you're here with me.'

Pamela laughed affectionately. 'I knew what you meant, Anna. Thank you.'

She squeezed Anna's arm, briefly resting her head on her shoulder. Anna felt herself stiffening reflexively and hated herself for it. Pamela couldn't help being the touchy-feely type, any more than Anna could help being the polar opposite.

It was a source of some relief to her when they arrived at the library entrance and she was able to use the excuse of needing to fish her card out of her bag to extricate herself from Pamela's grasp. Shortly afterwards, they were on their way up to the third floor, Pamela clutching her freshly minted visitor pass like a sacred trophy.

The study rooms on levels two and three had long been among Anna's favourite places to go when she needed to get some work done undisturbed. Often, when she found herself with a looming deadline, she'd book herself a room, switch off her phone, disconnect her laptop from the Wi-Fi and lose herself in whatever task was at hand. So far, none of her colleagues seemed to have sussed out where it was she disappeared to on these occasions – and she was determined for that to remain the case.

They headed into the small, windowless room Anna had booked for them, with a quartet of chairs surrounding a laminate-topped table. As Anna shut the door behind them, Pamela took a seat, laying her satchel at her feet. Anna preemptively fished out her reading glasses and put them on.

'Thanks again for agreeing to meet like this,' said Pamela, as Anna took a seat next to her. 'I don't know about you, but I always find it helps to talk things through with another sentient human. Plus, it'll give us a chance to fill in any gaps in each other's knowledge, should any arise.'

Anna nodded and passed no comment. She was acutely aware that, to date, her commitment to the case had been patchy at best – distracted as she'd been by other matters, coupled with a general lack of enthusiasm fuelled by her continued antipathy towards the idea that Sean could be innocent. Instead, she fished out the A4 notepad she'd been using to record her observations about the case and set it on the table in front of her, pen at the ready. Pamela did likewise, producing a considerably daintier pocket-sized notebook from her satchel.

'Where do you suggest we start?' asked Anna.

'I thought perhaps it would be beneficial to run through

what we know about the case, and any potential holes we've identified. There's still plenty of gaps, but we're a pair of smart cookies, aren't we? We'll muddle through.'

'We are indeed,' Anna confirmed. 'No luck getting your hands on a copy of the case file, then?'

Pamela shook her head. 'No, and I can't say I'm all too surprised. That would require the cooperation of the police – or, failing that, access through Sean's legal team, and I can't see Maurice Hanley being too keen to share his homework with the likes of us.'

'Don't suppose there's any point in asking Sean to instruct him?' said Anna, without much optimism.

They'd left the prison the other day without having secured anything approaching an explicit go-ahead from Sean to look into the case on his behalf. Following his heartfelt insistence that he was innocent, he'd retreated once more into sullen, arms-folded silence, and the visit had drawn to a close shortly thereafter.

Pamela grimaced. 'I fancy we'd be unwise to count on his active cooperation anytime soon. Still, between the media coverage, what your journalist contact told you, and what I've been able to pick up from the legal grapevine, I reckon we have a pretty clear picture of the state of play.'

Anna consulted her notes. 'From what I've been able to make out, the case against Sean essentially rests on six key pillars. Number one: the sighting of him and Leanne on Trongate around two hours before the body was found.'

Pamela scrambled to find the relevant page in her own notes. 'Right. A bar worker, Kasia Wiś . . .' She frowned as she struggled to read the unfamiliar word. 'Wiśniewska? She gave an interview to the *Daily Post* in the early days of the investigation.'

'I bet the police loved *that*,' said Anna. She checked her notes again. 'According to her, she was standing outside the Strangeways Bar, about halfway between Candleriggs and

Albion Street, at around 11:15 when Sean came charging past her, dragging Leanne behind him. They stopped a little further up the street and he turned and yelled at her, before dragging her on again. They were heading east, towards High Street.'

She turned to the next page. 'Which neatly brings us to pillar number two. Well, it's actually number four on my list, but it makes sense to consider the two of them together. Anyway, pillar number two: CCTV footage of the two of them entering High Street station just over ten minutes later, at twenty-eight minutes past eleven.' She fished some printouts from her shoulder bag and spread them out on the table. 'Here. I screenshotted these from the *Reporting Scotland* appeal on the nineteenth of January. It wasn't on iPlayer, but fortunately someone uploaded it to YouTube.'

Together, they examined the printouts. Blowing them up to A4 size had done the footage no favours. On the contrary, it merely served to accentuate the fuzziness of the two figures stepping into the foyer, one small and female, the other large and male.

'It's not a great picture,' said Pamela, stating the profoundly obvious. 'That's definitely Leanne, but the man with her – can we really be sure it's Sean? You can't see his face.'

Anna had suspected Pamela would latch onto this. 'You said it yourself earlier – his hoodie matches one known to belong to Sean.'

Pamela looked sceptical. 'It's just a light grey hoodie. Half the men in Glasgow probably have one of those in their wardrobes. Heck, *I've* got one of those in my wardrobe.'

'It's not just any grey hoodie, though,' said Anna, pointing. 'See – it's got darker sleeves and a Nike logo on the front. There are photos of him wearing it on his social media. I can show you if you don't believe me.'

'Fine, if you say so,' said Pamela, clearly unconvinced – or, perhaps more accurately, *unwilling* to be convinced.

'Don't forget about the bar worker,' said Anna. 'Kasia. She identified Sean too. Presumably, she'll have picked him out of a photo line-up or something like that.'

'For what *that's* worth,' said Pamela – still, it seemed, unwilling to concede even this basic point. 'She must have seen him for all of two seconds on a pitch-black night.'

'Fine.' Anna could see she wasn't going to win here. 'Let's move on to number three: Sean's shifting alibi. As we've already established, when he was initially questioned, he told the police he'd been visiting a friend, then changed his mind and said he'd been out running. Care to explain *that* one away?'

'I can't,' said Pamela, 'and I reckon you probably knew that.' She sounded more than a tad resentful.

Anna decided to at least *try* to be charitable. 'Well, I've given it some thought, and I reckon, if – and I want you to note the emphasis on "if" – *if* either alibi was true, it's more likely to have been the initial one.'

'Right,' nodded Pamela. 'People tend to tell the truth first, before they've had a chance to think things through; to polish it into something more convenient.'

'Exactly. Once someone starts revising their version of events, you have to ask yourself: what are they trying to fix? Let's assume this friend *did* exist and Sean *did* visit him that night – what motive would he have had to cover that up?'

Pamela thought about it. 'Up to something dodgy together?'

'That, or the friend was someone he didn't want the police to associate him with. Though, even if that *was* true, surely any such concerns would have become secondary the moment he was accused of murder.'

'Unless they were involved in something worse than murder,' said Pamela, then grimaced as the ramifications of what she'd just said hit her. 'Actually, let's not go down that route.'

'Yes, let's not,' said Anna heavily, turning to the next page in her notepad. 'Pillar number four, or whichever number we're up to now: his past convictions for aggravated assault – including that of a woman – in 2018.'

'It's unlikely those would be deemed admissible in court,' said Pamela. 'Not unless the defence attempts to make a claim of previous good character.'

'But they would have featured in the police's report to the Procurator Fiscal – correct?'

'Oh, definitely. In fact, I'd lay odds on them having been what ultimately convinced the police to charge him – especially since one of the victims was a woman. The moment they found out he had priors, they'll have stopped looking anywhere else – I'll bet my life on it. Classic tunnel vision.'

'Which leads us onto pillar five . . . or 4B, if you prefer to lump them together: the domestic disturbances. Between July and December 2021, Sean and Leanne's next-door neighbours made three separate calls to the police reporting arguments involving shouting and property being smashed, as well as lodging a complaint with the council. Yet again, we've got a pattern of violent or, at the very least, threatening behaviour on Sean's part.'

'Not necessarily,' said Pamela. 'The complaints seem to have focused exclusively on the noise disturbance rather than any particular concern for Leanne's safety. Maybe what Sean said is true? Maybe she really *did* "give as good as she got"?'

Anna shook her head. 'I don't buy that. Mutually abusive relationships aren't a thing – not really. More often than not, they're a trope pushed by misogynists who try to paint domestic violence as a two-way street in order to downplay the fact that the victims in these situations are overwhelmingly women. "She was no angel", "she led him on", et cetera. It's classic minimalisation.'

Pamela folded her arms. 'I'm not talking about abuse here. All we have is noise complaints. Raised voices. A few smashed plates. Couples argue, some more vociferously than others. We have no idea what Sean and Leanne's personal baseline looked like.'

'Right,' said Anna dubiously, 'but there's also the final pillar: the threat to kill. Or are you going to give Sean the benefit of the doubt again and assume it was a figure of speech?'

'*Someone* has to,' said Pamela unhappily. 'And let's be honest for a moment: if you were planning to kill someone, would you go ahead and announce your intent in the middle of a crowded pub?'

'I don't know,' said Anna. 'I've never planned to kill anyone.'

She caught Pamela's eye. Pamela smiled, weakly at first, then shook her head and laughed softly. Anna found herself laughing too, though she wasn't sure she entirely understood why.

Pamela continued to shake her head ruefully. 'What are we like? You and me, sitting here, playing "good cop, bad cop". Bet you were in the debating society at school, weren't you?'

Anna gave a rather strained smile. She didn't *like* always playing the part of bad cop, but Pamela had so comprehensively staked out the territory of good cop, with a seemingly endless ability to put the most charitable spin on things, that she felt she had no choice.

'I suppose it's fair to point out we weren't there,' Anna said, attempting to invest the proceedings with a little charitability of her own. 'We don't know *exactly* what was said. And, without access to the case file, we've no way of knowing who this mysterious eavesdropper was, so it's not as if we can go and ask them.'

'No,' Pamela agreed. She perked up suddenly, an idea coming to her. 'Tell you what, though – we *could* go and talk to those neighbours. You know, the ones who complained to the police and to the council. We could go over there, you and me, and knock on some doors. Find out, from the horse's mouth, as it were, just what these fights were really like.'

'Maybe,' said Anna, aware of the note of reluctance in her voice. She reminded herself she'd committed to making a proper fist of this, and that that meant following up every possible lead. At any rate, she told herself, if she *was* going to go door-knocking, she'd prefer to do it on her own rather than have Pamela tagging along, no doubt interjecting at the most inopportune moments.

She wondered again just how she'd allowed herself to be talked into getting involved. Playing the part of bad cop wasn't much of an acting stretch on her part when the person at the centre of it all was Sean Kerevan. She slid her fingers under her glasses and rubbed her eyes. The bright overhead lights were making them hurt.

'Oh – did you bring the map?'

Anna opened her eyes and turned to Pamela, blinking.

'Sorry?'

'The map of Glasgow I asked you to bring. I thought it might help to track Sean and Leanne's movements that night . . . at least, inasmuch as we can infer from the info we've got access to.'

'Right. Yes, of course.'

Feeling somewhat knocked off her stride, Anna reached for her shoulder bag and dug out the large-scale map of the city she'd picked up at the bookshop on Hyndland Road on her way here. As she stood up to lay it open on the table, she experienced a momentary flutter of dizziness and had to clutch the back of her chair to steady herself.

The moment passed. She glanced at Pamela, who didn't seem to have noticed.

'OK,' said Pamela, once she'd run her finger over the map and found the spot she was looking for, 'so Sean and Leanne's house is here, on Millbrae Avenue, just north of the Sighthill cemetery.'

She tapped the cluster of residential streets, then dragged her finger in a northeasterly direction, coming to a stop at the point where the curve of Atlas Road bisected the railway line running through Springburn.

'CCTV footage shows Leanne arriving alone at Springburn Station at quarter past nine that evening and boarding the 21:23 train to Balloch from Platform 3.'

Once more, she ran her finger along the map, following the tracks south through Dennistoun before looping around in a semicircle and travelling west in a more or less straight line until she came to a stop at High Street Station, at the edge of the Merchant City.

'Ten minutes later, CCTV again picks her up, disembarking alone at High Street. It's not clear what took her into town. I understand Sean wasn't able to shed any light when he was asked. There's a further CCTV sighting of her heading west along Ingram Street at 21:37. Again, this comes from the *Reporting Scotland* appeal. But, after that, the trail goes cold for over an hour and a half.'

'What about mobile tracking data?' asked Anna. 'Surely the police will have been able to use that to work out where she went?'

Pamela shook her head. 'One thing I *was* able to ascertain from my contacts is that there's no mobile data for either Sean *or* Leanne that night. Seems she left her phone at home when she went out.'

Anna frowned. 'Does that not strike you as suspicious?'

'In what sense?'

'In the sense of her not wanting her boyfriend, who has a history of violent and aggressive behaviour, knowing where she was going.' She held up her hands, forestalling Pamela's objections. 'I know, I know. Bad cop.'

Once more, Pamela looked uncertain. 'Perhaps. Or perhaps she just forgot it.'

Anna considered asking Pamela when was the last time *she*

forgot her mobile when she was going out, but decided there was little to be gained by stoking further disagreement.

'All right,' she said. 'The next confirmed sighting of Leanne is on Trongate.'

'Right,' said Pamela. 'Kasia whatserface saw her and maybe-Sean passing Strangeways at roughly 23:10.'

'There's no CCTV of Sean heading into town?'

Pamela shook her head.

'He could have travelled by bus,' said Anna, thinking aloud. 'Not all of them have cameras.'

'Hmm.' Pamela didn't sound convinced.

'All right,' said Anna again, keen not to dwell on what was evidently going to be an impassible disagreement for them. 'We then have Leanne and maybe-Sean entering High Street Station at 23:28 and hanging around the platform till they board the eastbound train at 23:37.' She checked her notes again. 'CCTV again shows them leaving Springburn Station ten minutes later at 23:47.'

'And then,' said Pamela, taking up the narrative, 'that's the last sighting of her till around 1 a.m., when a local man, Fergus Michie, finds her body at the foot of the steps behind the former library. He flags down a police car. The officers attending secure the scene and call for backup. Mr Michie recognises Leanne and is able to direct the police to her home address. When they knock on the door, the place is empty. They force an entry, on the grounds that it may be necessary to preserve evidence, but find no one inside. They're still searching the place at 4 a.m. when Sean gets home. At which point, they naturally break the news to him.'

'How did he respond?' asked Anna.

'Supposedly, he didn't. At least, that's the gossip I've been picking up. He just took it in and said nothing. It was almost like . . .'

'Like he knew already?' suggested Anna.

'Or a delayed response. As I'm sure you know, people

respond to grief in different ways. Some burst straight into tears. Some go into denial, or lash out. Others . . .' Pamela trailed off, giving a limp gesture with her hand. 'Though, supposedly, during a later interview, when they told him Leanne had been pregnant, he absolutely hit the roof. Took three officers to restrain him.'

Anna could tell Pamela didn't enjoy recounting that particular detail – and no wonder. She imagined they both had much the same image in their heads: large, powerful Sean being forced to the ground to prevent him from tearing the eyes out of whoever had been unfortunate enough to be tasked with breaking the news to him.

A fresh thought occurred to her.

'Was Sean wearing the grey hoodie when he showed up at 4 a.m.?'

'I'm not sure. I can try to find out.' Pamela made a jotting in her notebook.

Anna consulted her own notes again, running through the questions she'd wanted to ask. 'We're absolutely sure there's no possibility Leanne was killed inside the house?'

Pamela shook her head. 'The police seem pretty convinced she wasn't. Think about it: with a head wound like the one she had, you'd expect to find blood, or evidence that someone had done a clean-up job. But there was nothing. And it's not as if the forensics people didn't give the place a thorough going over. From what I understand, they took the place apart, top to bottom. Also, she was wearing her coat and shoes when she was found.'

'That's not necessarily conclusive. Maybe Sean killed her before she had a chance to take them off. And not everyone takes their shoes off inside the house.'

Right – not everyone's a clean freak like Zoe.

'Maybe,' said Pamela. 'Pretty sure most people don't wear their *coats* round the house, though.'

She sat there, frowning, clearly unconvinced. 'Oh!' she exclaimed suddenly, as a thought came to her. 'Handbag!'

'Come again?'

'What happened to her handbag? I mean, I'm assuming she must've *had* one, right?'

'Right.'

'Well,' said Pamela, clearly frustrated by Anna's inability to grasp what she was driving at, 'if it was found with the body, surely that would reinforce the case for her having never made it back to the house? I mean, if Sean *did* kill her at home and moved the body, I bet you anything it would never have crossed his mind to grab her handbag on his way out the door. That sort of detail just isn't how most men think – right?'

'Possibly not,' Anna admitted. 'I don't remember any mention of one in the press coverage – do you?'

They both spent some time consulting their respective jottings and scrolling through articles on their phones, before concluding that the elusive handbag hadn't been mentioned anywhere.

'I'll try to find something out,' said Pamela, again writing in her notebook. 'Also, there's the next-door neighbours.'

Anna gave her a quizzical look.

'Think about it. If Sean and Leanne got home in the wee hours, having this massive barney, and then Sean whacked Leanne over the head and killed her . . . don't you think the same neighbours who'd called the police out on three separate occasions over noise disturbances would've heard something?'

'You're on a roll today,' said Anna, not uncharitably.

Pamela grinned, seeming genuinely buoyed by Anna's rather backhanded compliment, and looked at her notes again. 'So what's next?'

Anna consulted her own notepad. 'I think we've covered pretty much everything. I'm planning to spend a bit more time going through Sean and Leanne's social media; see if I can persuade anyone in their friend circles to talk to me.'

Pamela nodded. 'What about Leanne's family?'

'What sort of family does she have?'

'Her parents are both still alive. And there are a couple of brothers. Both older, if memory serves.'

Anna considered this, then shook her head. 'I don't think I'd be doing anyone any favours asking them to revisit their daughter-stroke-sister's bloody murder. Plus, if they got even the slightest inkling that I was trying to get Sean off, I imagine I'd be lucky if the worst they did was run me out of town.' She shook her head again. 'No, I reckon I'm better off limiting my advances to people of the "friends and acquaintances" variety. Perhaps work colleagues. You know, people who knew them but still had that crucial bit of distance.'

Pamela shrugged philosophically. 'I suppose. You'll probably get a more objective picture from them too.'

They began to gather up their belongings. As Anna stood up to refold the map, she experienced another sudden, unanticipated rush of dizziness. She felt her feet buckling beneath her and stumbled, grabbing the back of her chair to steady herself. Noticing, Pamela dropped her bag and rushed to Anna's side, catching her arm and stopping her from falling.

'Whoa there! Are you all right?'

'I'm fine,' muttered Anna, both unnerved by the severity of what she'd just experienced and embarrassed by the spectacle she'd provided. 'Just stood up too quickly. I'm OK now.'

She shook Pamela off, one hand continuing to rest on the chair just in case.

'You sure?' Pamela eyed her uncertainly. 'You don't *look* OK.'

'It's nothing. I just skipped breakfast, that's all.'

Provided you don't count the two slices of toast . . .

'In that case,' said Pamela, 'I want you to promise you'll go straight and get something to eat as soon as we're out of here.'

'I promise,' said Anna, not meeting her eye.

.   .   .

'Listen,' said Pamela, as they made their way down the stairs, 'how d'you fancy grabbing a bite together, then heading out to Springburn for a little look-see? I'm not sure when I'll next be able to get through to Glasgow, so we might as well make the most of it.'

But Anna was only half-listening. She'd slowed to check her phone, which she'd set to silent while they were in conference. She saw now that she had a new voice message.

Holding up a hand to forestall Pamela, she tapped the Play button and put the phone to her ear. As she listened, she felt her jaw muscles tightening.

'Anna?' Pamela's voice radiated fresh concern. 'What's wrong? Has something happened?'

'Nothing.' Anna lowered her phone and stuffed it back into her shoulder bag. 'Everything's fine.'

She knew exactly how she sounded, her voice oddly high and overly brusque – both surefire signs that she was rattled. Taking a deep breath, she forced herself to turn and face Pamela, looking her directly in the eye.

'Actually, I'm afraid I'm not going to be able to do Springburn today. I've just remembered, there's something I need to take care of.'

'Oh.' Pamela was trying – and failing badly – not to sound put out. 'Well, if you're sure.'

'I'm sure. We'll sort something out another time.'

They continued down the stairs together, Pamela saying nothing but continuing to radiate disappointment. Anna saw her on her way back up to Great Western Road, then set off in the opposite direction, hurrying towards the staff car park. She swore under her breath as she rooted through her bag for her car keys, aware of each precious second that ticked by.

The call had been from the school secretary's office, asking her to come in straight away.

Jack had had another meltdown.

10

Anna strode in through the visitor's entrance to Thornwood Primary School and hurried along the corridor towards reception. The person at the desk, a prim-looking older woman who fit just about every school secretary cliché going, informed her that Mrs Johnson and Miss Smart were waiting for her in the former's office, along with Jack. Anna followed the by now familiar route along the linoleum-floored corridor to the door with its little gold plaque engraved with 'MRS A. JOHNSON – HEADTEACHER' and marched straight in without knocking.

Amelia Johnson, a tall and solidly built woman in her late forties, was standing behind her desk, arms folded behind her back. A younger woman in a floral dress – Jack's teacher, Miss Smart – stood a little off to the side, looking vaguely like a servant waiting at her mistress's beck and call. Jack sat on a plastic chair in the corner, arms crossed and with a face like thunder. He didn't look up.

'Ah, Professor Scavolini,' said Mrs Johnson, beckoning her closer. 'Thank you for coming in at such short notice.'

'What's happened?' demanded Anna. She was in no mood for beating about the bush.

'Would you like to take a seat?' Mrs Johnson gestured to the empty chair facing her desk.

Anna didn't particularly want to sit, but she recognised that a refusal would only drag things out further, and no doubt invite the spread of a whole lot of 'like mother, like son' gossip among the staff. So she obediently plonked herself down on the hard, foldaway chair, laid her hands in her lap and did her best to meet Mrs Johnson's gaze with a calm, neutral expression.

'Thank you.' Mrs Johnson resumed her own seat. 'Now, I'm sorry to have to tell you that there was a rather troubling incident in class this afternoon. Miss Smart?'

Miss Smart took a couple of halting steps forward. She really did look far too young to be in charge of a classroom full of rowdy five and six-year-olds, Anna thought.

'Jack became upset during a discussion about the solar system,' she said in a high, slightly tremulous voice, obviously reciting a pre-prepared statement. 'He challenged something I said – quite forcefully, I must add – and when I attempted to move on, he refused to let the matter drop. Things escalated and . . . well, he shouted and called me a liar in front of the whole class. And then he, um, used the F-word.'

'Do you mean "fuck"?'

It probably wasn't the most advisable comment to have made, but Anna didn't believe in mincing words, especially when it came to hiding behind euphemisms whose meaning everybody concerned understood perfectly well.

Miss Smart stared at her in horror. 'No!' she all but hissed, then added, with a curious mixture of sheepishness and defensiveness, 'He said "fart".'

'Oh,' said Anna quietly.

She winced inwardly. Brilliant. If the staff had been on the fence about her fitness as a mother, she'd just put any scope for uncertainty firmly to bed.

'Professor Scavolini,' said Mrs Johnson – trying her best, it seemed, to get the meeting back on track, 'the issue is less about the specific word Jack used and more about the sentiment behind it, not to mention the impact on the rest of the class.'

Partly in a bid to shift some of the scrutiny from her own questionable judgement, Anna turned to face her son, whose glare remained fixed on the floor.

'Jack?'

'It's true,' Jack said venomously. 'She *is* a liar.'

'*Jack!*' Anna hissed, appalled.

Jack just folded his arms tighter about himself and refused to look at her.

Mrs Johnson let the silence lie for a moment, then turned to Jack's teacher.

'Miss Smart, perhaps it would be best if Jack went outside while we discuss matters further.'

Miss Smart gave a brief nod and crossed the floor to Jack.

'Come on, Jack,' she said gently. 'Let's give your mum and Mrs Johnson some space.'

Reluctantly, Jack slid down off his chair and wordlessly accepted her hand. Together, they stepped out of the room, Miss Smart closing the door behind them.

Anna, who'd been craning her neck to watch these proceedings, turned to Mrs Johnson expectantly.

'Well?'

Mrs Johnson folded her hands on the desk. 'Professor Scavolini, I appreciate how difficult it must be to—'

'I'm not disputing what happened,' said Anna stiffly. 'I just want to understand *why*.'

'I suspect that's a question you're better off asking Jack – at any rate, to understand what it was about Miss Smart's lesson that caused him such obvious distress. The point is, this isn't the first time something like this has happened. Since Jack started school at the beginning of the year, there have been five separate incidents that have resulted in class being disrupted.'

'I know,' said Anna.

Just like today, each previous summons had left her feeling as though her fitness as a mother was being quietly called into question – whether that was the intention or not.

'It all adds up to a pattern of behaviour,' Mrs Johnson went on. 'There's his refusal to follow instructions, his persistent daydreaming, his tendency to get up and wander around during lessons – and now arguing with his teacher, undermining her in front of the other children. Not only is it unfair on them to have their learning disrupted, it also sets a precedent we very much want to avoid. Children are extremely impressionable at this age. If they think this sort of behaviour is appropriate, they'll start to imitate it. That's why it's important we nip it in the bud, before—'

'Before the contagion spreads?' Anna suggested.

The comment was a little more barbed than she'd intended, but she couldn't help herself. It had always been this way, with her instinctively responding to any perceived criticism of Jack as if it was aimed squarely at *her*.

Mrs Johnson ignored the remark. 'Of course, we must take into account that Jack was late in starting school . . .'

'Due to circumstances beyond my control,' said Anna, once again on the defensive.

Mrs Johnson gave a patient smile. 'It wasn't intended as a rebuke. I'm aware of your personal circumstances. But it does mean the other children had a five-month head start on him. More time to gain an understanding of what's expected of them behaviour-wise in the classroom.'

She fixed Anna with a not unsympathetic smile. 'Look, taken individually, I know all these incidents might seem like minor, trifling things. But, as I indicated, it's the pattern that concerns us. Jack's clearly very bright, and when he applies himself, the results are first-rate. But his responses to what he perceives as slights or injustices are disproportionate, and he has difficulty letting things go.'

'So what are you suggesting?' Anna felt a strange sort of resignation as she spoke.

Mrs Johnson gave another smile, this one studiously neutral.

'For now, I think we should continue to monitor his behaviour. I'm not proposing any sort of intervention at this stage – but if things don't start to improve, we *will* need to consider what our next steps will be, and whether that includes the provision of additional support needs.'

Jack said nothing throughout the car ride home, and Anna, sensing that it was likely to do more harm than good, didn't attempt to break the silence. Back at the house, his mood continued, and she gave him the space she suspected he needed and focused instead on preparing dinner.

It wasn't until they were sitting down at the kitchen table, Jack sullenly stirring his spaghetti carbonara with his fork, that she finally felt she had no choice but to address the source of his ire. The last thing she wanted to do now was to make him feel like he was being backed into a corner, but at the same time, she knew they needed to have a conversation about the incident – preferably while it was still fresh in his memory.

'Do you want to talk about what happened?' she asked him gently.

No response. He continued to stir.

'Jack.'

He set down his fork with a clang and jerked his head up, scowling across the table at her.

'What's the point? No one listens.'

She bit back a retort. '*I'm* listening, Jack. So come on – tell me what today was all about.'

'She's an idiot.'

'Who? Miss Smart?'

'Yeah. Miss *Stupid*, more like.'

Anna folded her arms on the tabletop. 'Why's she stupid?'

Jack sighed noisily. 'She said there are nine planets in the solar system. There's not. There's only eight. Pluto's a dwarf planet, not a real one.'

'Yes, but—'

But Jack wasn't listening. 'August 24, 2006,' he chanted, his voice getting louder as he became more and more worked up. 'Pluto was downgraded from a planet to a dwarf planet by the International Astronomical Union. She's teaching outdated information. She's spreading lies.'

'Jack—'

'She's teaching it wrong!' Jack virtually shouted. 'It's not science if it's wrong!'

Anna took a deep breath and counted to ten in her head. Gave Jack a strained smile.

'So you told her.'

His ire spent, Jack lowered his head, staring down at his uneaten plate of spaghetti. A moment later, he raised it again slightly, looking up at her meekly.

'Was that wrong?'

His voice was small, uncertain.

Anna thought about how to respond to this. Whatever she said was likely to only increase either his anger or his confusion – or, worse still, both.

'No,' she said at length. 'I mean, no, you're not wrong to say that there are only eight planets. But . . .'

She trailed off, struggling to find the words to express what she wanted to say in a way someone of Jack's age would understand.

'Jack,' she began again, 'sometimes you need to pick your battles.'

Jack looked at her, baffled. '*Whit?*' he said, uttering one of the many Zoe-isms he'd picked up.

She sighed to herself. Why did explaining the world to a

six-year-old always have to feel like giving a lesson on quantum mechanics?

'Adults aren't always right, you know,' she said.

Jack rolled his eyes. '*That's* obvious.'

'And,' she went on, ignoring his impudence, 'it's not always appropriate to point it out to them. Sometimes, it's best to keep that information to yourself.'

Jack continued to stare at her. 'So I'm supposed to let someone be wrong? On *purpose?*'

Anna fought the urge to grab great clumps of her hair and pull them out. Why was she making such a complete pig's ear of this?

'Look,' she tried again, 'it's not about letting people be wrong. It's about . . . about knowing when being right matters, and when it doesn't.'

Jack frowned. 'It *always* matters. If people go around saying wrong things, then no one'll know what's true and what's not.'

'Maybe. But sometimes, correcting someone doesn't actually make things better. It just makes them angry or embarrassed, and then they stop listening to you altogether. Sometimes it's more important to be . . . kind. Compassionate.'

'Even if they're wrong?'

'Even then.'

Jack shook his head. 'That's stupid.'

Anna couldn't help but give a wry smile. 'Yeah. It is. But that's the way the world works.'

Jack glowered at his spaghetti, his mood once more darkening. Anna watched him for a moment, then reached across the table and laid her hand on his.

'I'm not saying don't speak up when you see something wrong or unjust. I'm just saying . . . not everything's a battle you have to win. Some things are more complicated than that. And sometimes, staying quiet isn't about giving up. It's about being the bigger person.'

Jack didn't say anything, but his frown had softened. He sat there for a minute, studying his spaghetti. Then he gave a brief, emphatic nod, picked up his fork and began to eat.

Anna sat back in her chair, letting out the breath she'd been holding in.

Well, Anna, she told herself, *all things considered, you handled that about as well as anyone could have.*

Or was that, too, a lie?

That evening, after putting Jack to bed, Anna sat in the living room, ruminating on the day's travails. She'd never been one for superstition, but she found herself wondering whether she'd inadvertently brought this on herself, or at the very least severely tempted fate, by her habit of referring to Jack, throughout much of her pregnancy and even after he was born, as 'Trouble'. No doubt about it, he was certainly living up to the nickname.

In an effort to banish these thoughts from her mind, she fetched her iPad and, nestled in the easy chair with a blanket wrapped round her and a glass of wine within reach, forced herself to knuckle down and make good on her promise to Pamela to conduct a thorough examination of Sean and Leanne's social media accounts. She'd already given them a cursory look earlier in the week – noting, among other things, that Sean was pictured wearing the same hoodie as the figure in the CCTV footage broadcast as part of the public appeal. Now, however, with Jack safely in bed and all her other commitments taken care of, she embarked on a far more systematic exploration.

Both Leanne and Sean had been active on Facebook, Leanne more so than Sean, and, much to Anna's gratification, she hadn't been particularly privacy-minded, with most of her activity set to public. Her timeline was a veritable catalogue of photos showing nights out and holidays to sunny climes, as well as a bunch taken at home. Anna spent the longest time studying the latter, trying to get a sense of what it had been like to inhabit the small semi-detached house on Millbrae Avenue, and, more pertinently, the dynamic between her and Sean.

Initially, Anna focused on the various photos in which the pair of them featured together, some with Sean's account tagged, some not. Most of these were the typical 'loved-up couple' snaps, posing with their arms around each other, one planting a kiss on the other's cheek – usually with one eye on the camera. It was strange to be confronted by the sight of Sean smiling and gazing at Leanne so adoringly – a stark contrast to his mug shot on the news and Anna's own in-person meeting with him. Based on these images, the average observer would have had no possible way of knowing about the cracks that, seemingly, had existed beneath the front the two of them had presented to the world. Approving – and occasionally borderline jealous – comments below the images sang their praises in positively gushing terms. 'Perfect couple!!!' said one, accompanied by a row of love hearts. 'We should all be so lucky,' said another, the lack of emojis implying a far more grudging tone.

The final photo of them together, posted on 5 January, was a selfie taken from their living room sofa, three days before Leanne's death. They sat side by side, each with an arm around the other, all smiles, Leanne's other arm extending out of shot as she angled her phone at them, while Sean clutched an open bottle of beer. A second bottle, also open, sat on an ornamental side table next to Leanne's side of the sofa. The table looked old and out of place among the modern, more utilitarian items of furniture that otherwise occupied the room – an heirloom passed down to one of them by a parent or grandparent, Anna guessed. A small, slightly crooked Christmas tree was barely visible in the background, and multi-coloured fairy lights adorned the back of the sofa. The text accompanying the picture read:

Last look at the 🎄 Xmas decorations #twelfthnight 😷 😷 😷
Here's to an absolute belter of a New Year #2022
#feelinghopeful 😷 😷 😷

Four days later, Leanne was dead.

Anna now went through Leanne's timeline for a second time, this time concentrating on the photos where Sean was absent. Most of these featured groups of women of around the same age as Leanne, dolled up on nights out – spray tans, cocktail dresses and bottles of WKD the recurring tropes. Leanne, though invariably the plainest looking of the bunch, with her mousy hair and pale, lightly freckled skin, had thrown herself into the festivities with just as much gusto as the others, never once fading into the background despite being outshone by her more glamorous friends.

Of the various other women featured in the photos, one appeared considerably more often than the rest. From the accounts tagged into the posts, Anna was able to identify her as Natalie Lennox – a dark-haired, perma-tanned woman of roughly the same age who, like Leanne, had attended All Saints Secondary School in Barmulloch, and was now, according to her profile, an assistant manager with the Radisson Blu hotel chain. Natalie was a recurring presence in the various group photos, but also appeared in several of just her and Leanne. 'Besties 4 ever!!!!' read one caption.

Until late last year, she was a regular fixture on Leanne's timeline. Then, around mid-November, her appearances abruptly ceased. Further inspection revealed that they were no longer Facebook friends. Scrolling up, Anna skimmed through the various messages of shock and grief posted on Leanne's timeline following her death – 'CAN'T BELIEVE IT 😷 ', 'Heaven gained an angel today' – and noted, with interest, that Natalie hadn't posted anything.

Anna leaned back in her chair, frowning. To go from inseparable besties to not even posting a message of condolence suggested a serious volte-face in an unusually short space of time. What could possibly lie behind this apparent reversal? And what, if any, significance did it hold?

Her finger hovered over the 'Message' button on Natalie's profile page. This all felt decidedly ghoulish – but, at the same time, she recognised she was flying blind here. Her social media trawl had given her few, if any, concrete insights into Leanne's life. Who better to correct that state of affairs than her one-time best friend?

She figured she had nothing to lose. Natalie was free to respond, or to ignore her, or to tell her to fuck off – whichever brought her the most comfort. She clicked the button, tapped out a quick message, hit Send, then shut off the iPad and tossed it onto the sofa on the opposite side of the room, safely out of reach, in the hope that it would dissuade her from checking for a response – at least until morning.

Then she gazed out of the window into the darkness, cradling her glass in her hand and willing herself not to think about whatever was going on inside that head of hers – or Jack's.

11

Saturday 5 March

The AnyTime Fitness Centre was a sprawling complex on the outskirts of Rutherglen, sharing a business park with a cinema, a bowling alley and a branch of Halfords. Anna had never been here before – it was on the other side of Glasgow, and she'd never been a fan of the concept of exercising in an enclosed space surrounded by people with the opportunity to sneak glances at you, eyeing you up and passing judgement on your technique. Not to mention having to breathe in the aroma of other people's sweaty arse cracks.

Still, she wasn't here today for exercise. This was where Leanne had worked, right up until her death.

She hadn't originally planned to come here today, but she'd found herself with an unexpected morning to herself thanks to a chance encounter at the school gate the previous afternoon. While she was waiting for Jack to come out, one of the other mums, Theresa Walker, had struck up a conversation with her, mentioning that she and her husband were hosting a football party in their back garden on Saturday for their son, Max, and a bunch of his classmates – and would

Jack like to come? Anna had been highly sceptical, Jack having never shown any interest in the sport before – or indeed *any* sport. But to her surprise, when she'd put it to him later that evening, he'd seemed genuinely intrigued by the idea – enthusiastic, even. It might even do him some good, she reasoned: spending some time with his classmates, doing something that required taking turns and working as a team. And so, earlier this morning, she'd dropped him off at the Walkers' house in Broomhill, promising to be back for him at two.

She stepped through the automatic doors and into the bright, airy foyer, with a turnstile and a reception desk, behind which a pale, scrawny youth sat, trying not to yawn as he stared off into space. He sat up a little straighter as Anna approached, doing his best not to look like he was operating on the strength of a couple of hours' sleep after a late-night bender.

'Hi,' she said. 'I'm looking for some information.'

'Have you looked at our website?' he responded. 'It's got everything you need to know about becoming a member.'

'Actually, I'm not looking to become a member. I was wondering if you could direct me to someone I could talk to about Leanne McColm.'

What little colour there was in the receptionist's face seemed to drain away instantly. He looked around, searching for someone to rescue him from this situation. His eyes alighted on a red-haired woman in her late twenties, passing with a water flask in hand, wearing a polo shirt emblazoned with the gym's logo.

'Oh, oh!' He waved frantically to her. 'Lynette! 'Mere a minute.'

Lynette stopped in her tracks, turned and made her way over.

'Sup?'

'This one's asking about Leanne,' said the boy, his voice a low, apprehensive hiss.

Lynette's face darkened, her expression instantly suspicious.

'That right?' She turned to Anna. 'And what is it you want with Leanne? You don't look like any friend of hers *I* ever saw.'

The receptionist, glad to no longer be expected to deal with this, sank lower behind the desk.

'I'm not,' said Anna, slightly ruffled. 'My name's Anna Scavolini. I'm a criminologist. I'm investigating . . . what happened to her.'

She'd learned from experience that, when she introduced herself as a criminologist in situations like these, there was a slightly greater than 50/50 chance that people would assume she worked for the police and was therefore there in an official capacity.

'Uh-huh.' Lynette still didn't sound too sure of her, though she'd at least dialled back some of the overt hostility. 'Got some ID on you?'

Anna fumbled in her bag and produced her university ID card. She held it up for Lynette, who leaned in, arms folded, squinting at it.

'Says there you work for Kelvingrove Uni.'

'That's right. But the police consult with me on a regular basis.'

'Regular' might have been stretching it a bit, but the police certainly *had* consulted her in the past. One officer in particular. More than once.

'And that's why you're here now?' said Lynette. And then, before Anna could formulate a response, 'All right, you can put your credentials away, officer. Just wanted to be sure you weren't press. We've had a shitload of hassle off of them.' She sneered. 'Public interest, my arse.'

Anna made what she hoped was an appropriately sympathetic expression.

'Truthfully,' Lynette went on, 'there's not a whole lot I can tell you. I never knew Leanne all that well. She was on reception; I'm a fitness instructor.'

'Oh,' said Anna, disappointed. 'Is there anyone here today who *did* know her?'

She glanced in the direction of the desk. The receptionist sank even lower behind the counter, a fearful look in his eyes.

Lynette scoffed. 'John-Paul? He hasnae got a clue. Only started here a couple of weeks back.' She pondered the matter. 'I suppose Jacqueline might be able to help you. She and Leanne were pretty tight.'

She made a gesture with her index and middle fingers, bringing them to her lips. It took Anna a moment to realise she was miming smoking.

'Is she about?'

'Somewhere. C'mon with me and we'll see if we can find her.'

Lynette buzzed Anna through the turnstile with her ID card and, together, they headed up to the first floor, where, after much to-ing and fro-ing, with Lynette speaking to various colleagues and receiving vague or contradictory responses, she eventually let out a triumphant 'Aha!' Up ahead, a man and a woman in AnyTime polo shirts were emerging from one of the exercise rooms, chatting together as they carried a large, rolled up gym mat between them.

'Jacs!' called Lynette, advancing towards them.

The woman glanced in their direction, a trace of laughter still on her face. She was in her mid-twenties, her dark hair in a long ponytail, face glowing with slathered on makeup, eyebrows drawn on in improbably thin lines. As Lynette and Anna approached, she let her end of the gym mat fall, leaving her colleague with no option but to do likewise.

'Hey-o!' she grinned. 'What's the craic?'

'Got a woman here who works for the police,' said Lynette. 'She's wanting to know about Leanne.'

Jacqueline frowned, more puzzled than suspicious. 'Thought the polis'd already spoke tae all of us.'

Anna decided now was the time to step in.

'Yes,' she agreed, 'but I'm new to the case and I'd like to clarify a few things my colleagues haven't shared with me. If you could spare me ten, fifteen minutes . . .'

None of this, strictly speaking, was a lie. Apart from the 'colleagues' part.

Jacqueline considered this, then shrugged amiably.

'Aye, all right. Stuart can manage on his own – can't ye, Stu?'

Stu glanced at Lynette with a not overly hopeful expression.

'Hey, don't look at me,' said Lynette. 'Herniated disc.'

Stu's shoulders slumped in defeat.

Anna glanced at Lynette, who continued to hover nearby, not making a particularly strong fist of concealing her nosiness.

'Is there somewhere we can talk?' she asked Jacqueline.

Now that she was closer, she saw that the excessive application of makeup was designed to conceal a serious case of acne scarring, which did nothing to mar the younger woman's open, friendly air.

'Café's usually pretty quiet this time of day,' said Jacqueline. 'C'mon – I'm about due a break anyway. You can buy me a hot choccy.' And then, before Anna could reply, Jacqueline laughed and batted her shoulder playfully. 'I'm just messing. It's on me. Perks of the job: free use of the facilities and drinks at the café.'

They set off, Jacqueline leading the way.

'Can I just say,' she said, 'your hair's proper *GOR-juss*? So long and thick. What conditioner's it ye use?'

'Just Tesco's own brand shampoo,' said Anna, surprised and slightly embarrassed by the adulation.

Jacqueline sighed fatalistically. 'Well, you must be blessed with good genes or something. Not me. Mine's is always dead thin and brittle. Dead unfair, that, don't ye think – how some folk win the genetic lottery and others just tap out?' She caught Anna's eye and grinned, indicating no hard feelings.

Anna smiled back. She'd decided she liked this woman, which was unusual for her on a first encounter. And it wasn't just the compliment about her hair. There was something inescapably likeable about her; something vaguely Zoe-like: outgoing, plain-spoken, and with a deep, throaty laugh as rough as a badger's arse. You could tell there were no airs and graces with her; that she took people as she found them and treated them all the same, with no hidden agenda.

All of which made it hard not to feel more than slightly guilty at lying to her, even if it was only by omission.

'I got to know her through a shared passion for sucking on the old space pipe,' said Jacqueline.

Anna gave her a questioning look.

'Vaping. Mr Macdonald doesn't like us doing it on the premises. Creates a negative impression, he says. Claims we're all about promoting a healthy lifestyle. But there's a fire escape out back where there's no security cameras. Me and Leanne used to head out there on our breaks and shoot the shit.' She shrugged. 'I liked her. She was a sweet wee thing. Bit clueless about the ways of the world, but that was part of the charm with her. She always saw the best in folk.'

They were seated in the bright, airy café on the first floor of the sports centre, at a table near a large window overlooking the swimming pool. Splashes and the periodic shouts of children wafted up from below, mingling with the inoffensive muzak playing on the speakers. Anna toyed with a cappuccino, Jacqueline with a hot chocolate.

'Not that she couldn't be right fierce when she needed to be,' Jacqueline went on. 'We get some proper heidbangers coming through these doors. See a nice-looking wee lassie and think they can chance their arm.'

'And how long had Leanne worked here?' Anna asked.

Jacqueline considered the question. 'Not sure. I've been here getting on for two years, and she was already here when I started.'

'And she'd always been a receptionist?'

'Yeah. It's a dead important job,' Jacqueline added, a touch protectively. 'You've gotta be on the ball.'

'I don't doubt it,' Anna reassured her.

'Cracking set of lungs on her too. End of each month, after payday, we have a staff karaoke night at Shanghai Shuffle in the town. Leanne was always game for it. Belted out Britney and Gloria Gaynor with the best of 'em.'

'Sounds like fun,' said Anna, suppressing the wave of horror that convulsed through her.

Jacqueline smiled fondly. 'It was, aye.'

A moment of silent, wistful recollection elapsed, which Anna almost felt guilty for breaking.

'And was she generally, would you say, a happy person?'

'She enjoyed her job, aye. And she was *amazing* with the customers. One of they people who could make an instant connection wae anyone.'

This wasn't precisely an answer to the question Anna had asked, but she let it slide for now.

Jacqueline's smile slowly faded. 'Ye know,' she went on, 'I couldnae believe it when they told us she was dead. Mr Macdonald called us all into the staff room on Monday morning and a couple of detectives broke the news to us. Something like this, it really puts things into perspexitive. Y'know, sorta "here today, gone tomorrow". A reminder to grab life by the bollocks 'stead of waiting for that perfect moment.'

'And when was the last time you saw her?' asked Anna, resisting the urge to tell her the word was 'perspective'.

Jacqueline frowned. 'Y'know, I did say this all already to the other detectives. D'yous no keep records?'

'We do,' said Anna, once again hating herself for lying. 'But sometimes it's helpful to hear things directly. It lets us get a clearer sense of what happened.'

Jacqueline looked briefly dubious, then shrugged. 'I get that. I'm always saying to my boss, "If ye want me to do something, tell it to my face. Don't go leaving me post-its I'm never gonnae read." ' She paused. 'What was it ye were asking?'

'When you last saw Leanne.'

'The Friday before,' said Jacqueline, without having to think about it. 'I was working on Saturday, but she was off. We do alternate Wednesday/Saturdays.'

'And how did she seem? I mean, was she anxious at all, or . . . ?'

'Nah, she seemed in good spirits. We were having a gab in the changing room as we got ready to leave. Talking about what we were getting up to for the weekend. She said she hadnae made plans but ye never knew what might come up.'

'Was that how she tended to be? Spontaneous?'

Jacqueline considered this. 'Not really, no. Like, she was always game for tagging along if you asked her if she fancied doing this or that after work. But she was never much of a . . . what's that word? An initiator. Like I said – sweet wee thing. Least till she'd got a few bevvies in her. Then she started coming out of her shell more.'

'And her boyfriend, Sean . . .' ventured Anna.

Jacqueline's expression instantly changed. The look on her face didn't resemble anger so much as regret.

'Aye. That was shocking. I mean, it's every lassie's worst nightmare, in't it? Take my Dougie, for instance. He's as sweet as anything. I'd trust him wae my life. But, deep down, there's always this part of me that wonders, "But *should* I?" I mean, how well d'ye really know *anyone?*'

Anna wasn't minded to disagree.

'Mind you,' Jacqueline continued, 'in Sean's case, I'd love tae say I was surprised . . . and, don't get me wrong, it was a proper shock an' aw. Just, I always had a feeling it was gonnae end badly. I just never thought it'd end *that* badly.'

'How so?'

Jacqueline looked away, clutching her cup so tightly her knuckles turned white.

'I mean, I already said all this before. Can you no just ask your colleagues?'

Recognising that Jacqueline was becoming genuinely distressed, Anna did something she wouldn't normally have done. She reached across the table and squeezed the younger woman's forearm.

'I'm sorry. I know this is hard. But it would be really helpful if you could go through it with me just once more. What caused you to have concerns about the relationship?'

Jacqueline sniffed loudly, composing herself. She sat up straighter. Drew her arms about herself protectively.

'Here's the thing. Leanne tended to . . . well, she could be quite *clumsy*. Or at least, that was *her* word for it.'

Anna felt something shift in her stomach.

'You'd call it something different?'

'Well, when a lassie shows up tae work time and again wae sore ribs or black and blue arms, there's only so many times you can hear her say "I bumped into the door handle" or "I'm just a total klutz" before you start looking at the boyfriend with fresh eyes.'

Anna gave no response. It was as if every suspicion she'd harboured about Sean, from the moment she'd first clapped eyes on his mug shot on the evening news, had been confirmed. Once again, she asked herself just what the hell she was doing getting involved in this. The man was so obviously guilty that any attempt on her part to probe the robustness of the charges against him was, at best, someone's idea of a sick joke.

'Know he used to come here?'

Jacqueline's voice shook Anna out of her thoughts. She looked at the younger woman questioningly.

'Sean? You mean as a customer?'

Jacqueline nodded. 'Before him and Leanne hooked up. That's how they met. Which I kinda thought was a bit funny in and of itself. I mean, far as I know, at the time he was staying over in Cranhill. Bit of a trek, coming all the way out to Rutherglen to lift some dumbbells, when there's any number of perfectly good gyms closer to home.'

'Are you saying he sought her out?'

'I mean, sorta looks that way, dun't it?'

Anna nodded pensively, tracing her finger round the rim of her coffee cup. She thought back to what Pamela had told her about Gerry; about the fact he and Leanne had once been an item. Her relationship with Gerry might have been well and truly over by the time she and Sean got together – but how soon before then had Sean started making plans?

'Did you ever meet him?' she asked, meaning Sean.

'Couple of times, aye, when he came tae pick her up from work. He'd stopped using the gym by that point. Found something closer to him. Like he'd already got what he was after fae here so no need tae continue paying the membership, am I right?'

Anna gave a noncommittal little 'mm'.

'What did you make of him?' she asked.

'I never liked him,' said Jacqueline, and, for a moment, her previously warm, pleasant face morphed into something decidedly off-putting. 'I can usually get the measure of a bloke pretty quick, and my gut was telling me this one was bad news. He was always dead possessive – like, putting his arm round her, keeping her close to him even when she clearly wanted space. And I could tell she was scared of him. We all could. Like, you'd see her flinch whenever he went to touch her. Also, there's something just . . . I dunno, *off* about a guy that size dating a girl of her stature, right?'

Anna, who, by virtue of being five foot two, had been with her fair share of men considerably taller than herself, said nothing.

'Look,' Jacqueline continued, 'I work in a sports centre. I'm surrounded by six foot four guys wae massive biceps all day. Plus, I'm not ashamed tae admit I like my men big and brawny. But when you're a six foot four guy and your girlfriend doesnae even come up tae your pecs in *heels* . . . well, it's like, if it ever came to a fight, you just *know* she'd have *nae* chance.'

Anna sipped her coffee in silence. She pictured the bruises on Leanne's arms; her poor, crumpled body at the foot of the steps and, later, lying naked on a mortuary slab . . . and the words 'PAIN' and 'GAIN' tattooed on Sean's scarred knuckles.

She cleared her throat. 'Did Leanne *ever* admit what was going on?'

Jacqueline shook her head. 'Don't think we didnae try tae get her to. We were all worried about her – seeing her wincing when she tried to bend or wearing long sleeves at the height of summer to hide her arms. I tried telling her he was no good for her; that she should leave him before something really bad happened. But she wouldnae listen. She'd just say, "Sean *loves* me," all earnest-like, and change the subject.'

'Did you mention all this to the police?'

It hadn't been in any of the press reporting from his petition hearing, and Martin Glazer hadn't mentioned it in her conversation with him, but, if the police had known at the time, Anna couldn't imagine it not having factored into the decision to charge Sean.

'*Aye,*' said Jacqueline, as if Anna was accusing her of a dereliction of duty. 'They hummed and hawed and wrote it all down. 'Course,' she went on, a distant look entering her eyes, 'now I can't help wondering, if I'd said something while she was still alive . . .' She shrugged helplessly. 'But I felt it would've been going behind her back – y'know, breaking her trust. And now, telling *you* – well, I know it can't make amends . . . but it can't do any harm either, can it?'

'I wasn't criticising,' said Anna gently.

Keen to move the conversation along, she cleared her throat. 'You said earlier Leanne could be a bit clueless. What did you mean by that?'

Jacqueline looked shamefaced. 'Och, I mibby shouldn't've said that. When you put it that way, it sounds pretty condescending, dun't it?'

'Still, there must've been something to make you say it.'

Jacqueline shrugged lightly, conceding this point. 'Again, I said all this tae the police at the time . . . and, like, in the grand scheme of things, I'm no sure how big a deal it is . . . but still.'

As patiently as possible, Anna waited for her to continue.

'About a year ago, Leanne had a bit of trouble wae one of the customers. This guy, Tony Duffy. A right smooth so-and-so – always came in looking like he'd spent an hour getting ready, even though he was only gonnae mess up his perfect hairdo getting all sweaty.

'Anyway, he used to banter with Leanne at the desk – y'know, ask her how her day was going, try out his jokes and chat-up lines on her. And she'd laugh along and ask after *his* day and that, totally unaware he was hitting on her. Which he *totally* was, by the way,' she added, quite vociferously. 'Any lassie who was even *slightly* street savvy could've told.'

'But not Leanne,' said Anna.

'She thought he was just being friendly. A bunch of us tried to warn her off – told her the guy had "sleaze" written all over him. But she wasn't for hearing it. Said not every guy wanted to get in your pants.' Jacqueline shrugged, as if to say, *What can you do?*

'He got more and more obsessive,' she went on. 'Started paying her all these compliments, saying how nice her hair was looking the day and such. Couple of times, he even brought her presents. Like, not big things – just wee trinkets. But it was so obvious he was desperate to get wae her. Everyone could see it, 'cept wee Leanne.

'After a while, it started getting proper creepy. He figured out her shift pattern and started timing his visits so he'd only show up when she was on. And he'd always time it so he'd just happen tae be leaving when she was going off shift. He'd do the whole "chivalrous male" routine, offering tae walk her tae her car, saying it wasnae safe, a lassie like her, out there on her own after dark.

'Eventually, Leanne got the message. She tried tae let him down gently, but he wouldnae back off. Started showing up more and more. At one point, he was in virtually every day. We tried tae get Mr Macdonald to bar him, or at least let Leanne change her hours, and when he wouldnae do either, a bunch of us stepped up tae the plate and swapped shifts with her. And we kept an eye out for her. Like, if we knew he was in the building, we'd make sure the coast was clear 'fore she left for the day.

'That got him off her back for a bit. But then, one evening, after Leanne had finished up for the night, me and Lynette were out front, hanging up a sign at the door, when we heard this scream coming fae the car park. We bombed it over and found Leanne at her car, practically in tears. Apparently, he'd come up behind her while she was looking for her keys – just appeared outta nowhere and tried to put his hands on her. He'd ran off as soon as she screamed. We tried looking for him, but it was dark, and he'd obviously known better than tae stick around after we came running.'

Jacqueline shook her head. Blew out a heavy breath. 'Mr Macdonald was in his element, I can tell ye. Started talking gleefully about logging it in the incident book. *And* he was all set to get on the blower to yous lot. But Leanne wouldnae have it. She just cried and cried and said she didnae want Sean finding out. No prizes for guessing why.'

'So what happened in the end?'

'Well, we could hardly go against her wishes, even though we all felt it'd do him a world of good tae get his collar felt by the filth . . .' She winced. 'Sorry, police.'

Anna dismissed her concern with a wave.

'So, instead, after doing nothing for months, Mr Macdonald *finally* declared he was persona non grata. Said he was barred from this and any other AnyTime facilities henceforth. That's the word he used – "henceforth". Not that he need've bothered. Guy never showed his face again. Guess he knew he'd been rumbled.'

'Guess so,' Anna agreed. 'You said his name was Tony Duffy?'

'That's right. Still got his photie behind the desk and everything. "Do not, under any circumstances, allow this man to enter the premises." '

'And is there anything more you can tell me about him?' Anna hesitated a moment, then decided to chance her arm. 'I suppose you've probably still got his details on file.'

Jacqueline met her eyes with a cold, hard stare. 'Aye, but ye'd need a warrant for me tae show you them. Data protection and that.'

'Of course.'

Dammit.

A thought occurred to Anna.

'But if there was anything else you happened to know about him . . . something, say, that was in the file but which you'd have known anyway, even without looking at it . . . that would be OK to tell me, wouldn't it?'

'S'pose,' said Jacqueline, slightly dubious.

'Something you might have picked up about whereabouts he stays, for example. Or what sort of line of work he's in.'

Jacqueline thought for a moment. 'That actually *does* ring a bell fae somewhere. Haud on.'

She turned to one of the café staff – an older woman,

collecting empty trays and plates and loading them onto an already stacked trolley.

'Here, Marydoll! Ye mind that guy, Tony Duffy? The one who was giving our Leanne grief?'

Marydoll confirmed that she did.

'Where was it Joanne said she ran into him?'

'Blue Ridge Motors,' said Marydoll, without having to think about it. 'Pollokshaws Road.'

'You're sure?' said Anna, leaning sideways past Jacqueline to make eye contact with the woman.

'Hundred percent. Her and her man were shopping for a new motor about six month back, and he was working there as a salesman. He pretended not tae recognise her, but she said it was definitely him.' She raised an eyebrow, as if to ask whether that was what they'd wanted to hear.

Jacqueline beamed. 'Cheers, m'dear.'

'Yes,' said Anna, 'thank you very much.'

Marydoll gave a grunt that was probably intended to signify *don't mention it* and moved off, the assorted crockery in her trolley clattering as she wheeled it away.

Jacqueline turned to Anna again. 'Is he in the frame, then? Only I thought they already charged Sean. They wouldnae've done that if they thought there was a chance he didnae do it, right?'

'The case against Sean is certainly strong,' said Anna, opting for as neutral a statement as she could muster.

'But there's a chance he might not have?' Jacqueline insisted. 'There's a chance it might've been someone else? Only the cops never seemed all that interested when I told them about that business wae Duffy.'

'There's always a chance,' said Anna, thinking that it wouldn't be the first time the police had ignored a potential lead because they already had a suspect who fit the narrative. 'But no, I don't think it's likely. There are already multiple independent lines of evidence that implicate Sean, and the fact

Leanne was getting grief off someone else doesn't invalidate them.'

Still, she knew this was something she was going to have to look into. It was just the kind of complication a defence lawyer would eagerly toss in to muddy the waters, creating reasonable doubt in the minds of a jury. Adding another semi-plausible suspect to the line-up might not prove Sean didn't do it, but, so often in cases like this, it was enough to merely suggest, however tenuously, that someone else *could* have.

Jacqueline's voice interrupted her thoughts. 'This is gonnae sound dead awful, but I sometimes wonder if there was something *about* her, y'know?'

Anna shook her head uncomprehendingly.

'I just mean . . .' Jacqueline grimaced. 'Look, I'm no saying certain women invite trouble or anything . . . but trouble's definitely got a way of finding certain women, dun't it?'

Anna managed a strained smile. Truthfully, she'd long harboured similar thoughts herself, as uncomfortably close to victim-blaming as it sometimes felt.

Jacqueline glanced at her watch. 'Listen, I'd best be getting back. My super loses her nut if you're so much as a minute over your break, and this one's already set a new world record.'

She got up to go.

'Jacqueline, wait,' said Anna. 'There's something I need to tell you.'

Jacqueline sat down again slowly.

Anna sighed. 'I don't actually work for the police. Your colleague just assumed I did . . . though I didn't make any effort to set her straight.'

Jacqueline gave a small, mischievous smile. 'I sorta figured that.'

Anna blinked in surprise. 'Really? Why?'

'Well, I thought it was a bit weird, you asking me all the same questions I'd already answered back then. Plus, you don't seem much like a cop.'

'Oh? How do I seem?'

Jacqueline thought about this. 'Nice,' she said eventually. Then, before Anna could think of anything to say in response, 'Listen – I just want ye tae know I approve of what ye're doing.'

'What I'm doing?'

'Aye – you're one of they . . . what is it they call them? Citizen investigators? Is that it?'

'I didn't realise there was an official name for it,' Anna admitted.

'Either way, I seen enough examples of the law cocking things up tae know it's never a bad idea having someone checking their homework.'

Jacqueline got to her feet again and paused, gazing down at Anna with a meaningful look.

'I'm just saying, you keep doing what you're doing.'

'How did you enjoy football?' Anna asked brightly as she drove Jack home later that day.

'It's stupid,' said Jack emphatically. 'They ran round after a ball and when they caught it all they did was kick it into a net.'

'That's the general idea of the game.'

'It's stupid,' said Jack again.

'Well, I don't disagree with you . . . but I hope you didn't say that to anyone.'

'Why?'

'Because, in my experience, people don't particularly appreciate being told their hobbies are stupid. They tend to take it personally.'

'You mean like when someone says Pluto's a planet and it isn't?'

'Yes, exactly like that.'

There was silence for a moment.

'And d'you know what else?' said Jack.

'What?'

'At lunch, they had only veggie burgers. I hate veggie burgers.'

'I know you do,' said Anna patiently.

'So I told Max's mum and do you know what she said I could have?'

'I can't imagine.'

'Cheese!' He sounded outraged and incredulous in equal measure. 'Cheese at *lunchtime?!*'

He stared at Anna in the rearview mirror, willing her to share in his indignation.

'Different people eat different things,' said Anna evenly. 'In some households, cheese is probably the most normal thing in the world to have for lunch.'

For a moment, Jack just looked at her in disbelief.

'I don't want to go there again,' he stated, with complete finality.

For a moment, Anna seethed with an almost unreasonable level of exasperation. *YOU were the one who wanted to go there in the first place,* she felt like saying. *I could have told you you wouldn't enjoy it.*

But then, what sort of a mother would she be if she didn't let her son figure out his likes and dislikes for himself? Experience was, after all, the best teacher. Her job wasn't to shield him from every disappointment – just to be there when it happened, and to validate his feelings. Within reason, at any rate.

'Then we won't,' she said firmly, and turned onto Southbrae Drive.

12

Monday 7 March

Anna awoke the following Monday with an intense headache, largely focused behind her right eye but also radiating outwards to encompass that entire side of her head. Clearly, her attempts to convince herself that her condition was getting better had amounted to wishful thinking of the most deluded kind.

At least she wasn't due to start work until the afternoon. And it was the beginning of the School of Social and Political Sciences' reading week, meaning that, while she was still technically beholden to her contracted working hours, she had no teaching commitments, and therefore had quite a bit more flexibility about how much time she spent at the university. Once she was back from driving Jack to school – there had been no possibility of her countenancing a run *today*, not in her present condition – she took some painkillers, ran herself a bath, tipped in enough bath foam to fill a swimming pool, stripped off her clothes and sank beneath the bubbles.

As she lay there, a cold compress pressed to her head and her 'soothing relaxation' playlist on the Bluetooth speaker, she thought about the Leanne McColm case. She hadn't been in touch with Pamela since Wednesday, so she hadn't had a chance to fill her in on her visit to the fitness centre. She knew Pamela wasn't going to take the news about Leanne's bruises at all well. Anna was going to have to enlighten her sooner or later, of course, but she'd decided she wanted to try to build a fuller picture first instead of feeding Pamela scraps of information piecemeal.

That, or she was simply delaying the inevitable.

She'd taken the liberty of looking up Blue Ridge Motors on Google Maps the previous night and had been toying with the idea of showing up there to confront Tony Duffy about his harassment of Leanne. The odds of him being keen to talk to her, she knew, were low in the extreme – but, on the other hand, she suspected a desire not to be exposed as a creep in front of all his colleagues was likely to prove a powerful incentive for him to cooperate with her.

In the end, the extent of her recovery made her decision for her. The headache, while still very much present, eventually subsided to the point of being just about bearable, but she found herself unable to focus on text, with *or* without her glasses, for any length of time before her vision blurred to the point of the words being indecipherable. Unable to get any meaningful work done and positively repelled by the prospect of mooching around the house accomplishing nothing till it was time to head into the university, she got dressed, collected her shoulder bag, put on a pair of sunglasses to shield herself from the overbearing light, and headed out.

Not trusting herself behind the wheel with her vision in such a parlous state, she caught a bus into town from the stop outside the old college campus, then another to the Southside, which deposited her a short walk from the Blue Ridge Motors showroom on Pollokshaws Road.

The place was trying a bit too hard to be swanky in what was an otherwise rather run-down area, the gentrification that had swept the Southside in recent years having yet to reach this particular stretch of the road. Nestled between a kebab shop and a tenement block that had seen considerably better days, the building was a squat, square structure, its large, tinted windows offering a tantalising glimpse at the various cars housed within. Several additional vehicles, looking almost unnaturally glossy in the pale morning sunshine, were packed into the forecourt, each sporting a large, laminate sign: 'JUST SERVICED', 'ULTRA LOW MILEAGE', 'DRIVES LIKE NEW'.

As Anna threaded her way between the cars, a woman dressed in a crisp blazer and pencil skirt emerged from the building and approached her.

'Welcome to Blue Ridge Motors. How might I assist you today?'

As she spoke, Anna glanced over the woman's shoulder towards the showroom, inside which a man in a similarly crisp suit, sporting short, wavy blonde hair and a compact but muscular physique, was engaged in earnest conversation with a middle-aged couple. There was no question about it: he was a perfect match for the photos on Tony Duffy's Facebook profile, which she'd scoped out earlier.

Anna turned to the woman. 'Actually, if it's all the same, I'd rather speak to *him*.' She pointed towards the showroom.

The woman appeared less than thrilled. 'I can assure you, madam, I'm more than qualified to help you with all your vehicular needs.'

Anna could guess what she was thinking. *Oh, so you'll only take advice on cars from a MAN . . .*

'I'm sure you are,' said Anna, reassuring yet firm, 'but I'd prefer to talk to your colleague.'

Visibly put out, the woman held her gaze for a moment, before finally relenting.

'Fine,' she huffed. 'Wait here.'

Spinning balletically on her heel, she marched back into the showroom, where Anna watched her drawing Duffy aside and speaking to him. Duffy gestured helplessly to his customers, but his colleague continued to insist. Eventually, he turned back to the couple and offered his apologies, complete with effusive shrugs and a wincing smile. Then, leaving them with his colleague, he emerged, beaming, into the forecourt.

'Good morning, madam,' he drawled, in a curious blend of Glaswegian and a rather grating Mid-Atlantic affectation. 'What can I do for you on this fine day?'

Now that they were standing a mere arm's length apart, Anna could both see the steely glint in his eyes that belied his effusive smile and smell the overpowering reek of his aftershave.

'I'm interested in buying a car,' she said.

Duffy's smile widened. 'Well, you've certainly come to the right place. Did you have anything particular in mind?'

'Well—' Anna began.

'Buying a vehicle is a lot like buying a pair of shoes,' Duffy declared grandly. 'You've got to be sure you're choosing something that matches your sensibility. Something that projects the right image to the world. And, if you don't mind my saying so, you look like a woman with discerning tastes.'

Shoes. Of course he'd gone straight to shoes for his comparison. No wonder his colleague had been so affronted when Anna had dismissed her. She was probably on the receiving end of enough overt misogyny from this guy without having to contend with what she perceived as the internalised variety from customers as well.

Anna smiled and shrugged sheepishly, leaning into the part. 'I'm not sure. There's so many to choose from. I was rather hoping you'd be able to help me.'

Duffy beamed, clearly convinced he'd found the ideal mark. 'I most certainly can. And let me assure you, you couldn't be in safer hands. Now, are you after a nippy wee thing for dotting round town, or more of your classic family-size motor?'

Suspecting that the question was intended to be purely rhetorical, Anna didn't even attempt a response.

'Let's see. I've got a lovely wee Corsa right over here – reliable, cost-effective, complete doddle to park. Or maybe you're after something with a bit more kick to it. Maybe a Focus ST-Line or this Astra Turbo – handles like a dream, plenty of torque. Or, if longer drives are more your thing, you'll be wanting something with adaptive cruise and lane assist – a Golf, maybe, or there's the Skoda Octavia VRS if you're after something compact yet stylish.'

He stepped sideways, gesturing with a flourish towards the row of cars to Anna's right. 'Now, if you're in the market for a hybrid, we've got a Yaris Cross just in – regenerative braking, full suite of sensors, whisper-silent on pull-away. But maybe you're after something higher off the ground? Depends whether you want the full tech package: blind-spot monitoring, autonomous emergency braking, reverse camera, all that jazz. 'Course, if all that's not enough to tickle your fancy, we can talk dual-clutch gearboxes, paddle shifters . . . We've got DSG, MMI, DAB – the whole alphabet soup. All depends how deep you want to go, love.' He flashed her a wink.

Anna met his gaze from behind her dark glasses, her expression studiously blank. She waited till just enough time had passed for the silence to become slightly uncomfortable.

'I'd like something red,' she said.

'Something red,' Duffy repeated.

He seemed both deflated and more than a little irked – all that effort expended on his pitch, and for nothing. He gave a strained smile.

'Well, we can certainly manage that.'

He set off, threading his way between the tightly packed cars. Anna followed just behind him, feeling more amused at having successfully burst his bubble than she supposed she had any right to be.

They came to a stop next to a red hatchback, as plain and unoriginal as the mind could conjure.

'Here she is,' said Duffy. 'Red Corsa, ultra-low mileage, 1.2-litre engine. Solid little runner. This the sort of thing you had in mind?'

'Something like that, yes.'

'Well, you can't go wrong with this one. Five-seater, air con, Bluetooth, full service history. Now, if you'd like me to show you—'

'Actually,' said Anna, 'if you don't mind, I'd like to get behind the wheel. See how it feels from the driver's seat.'

'Oh.' Duffy seemed thrown again. 'Er, right. Sure, knock yourself out.'

'Thanks. You can carry on your pitch from inside.'

She opened the driver's door and got in. Duffy opened the passenger door and folded himself in. The car was far too small for a man of his height, and his hunched-over posture only served to further emasculate him.

He cleared his throat, patting the dashboard. 'Nice soft-touch materials, good visibility. There's—'

'Just so you know,' said Anna, cutting him off mid-flow, 'this is a personal safety alarm.' She pointed to the device attached to her wrist, which resembled a budget watch. 'I only have to press this button and it'll set off a siren loud enough to blow out your eardrums.'

'Aye, good enough,' said Duffy, not sure what to make of this.

'Good. You're Tony Duffy, right?'

'I—'

'You used to work out at the AnyTime Fitness Centre in Rutherglen.'

'How did you—'

'Name Leanne McColm ring any bells?'

A look of fear momentarily flashed in Duffy's eyes, before his face hardened.

'What d'you want with me?'

'Just to ask you some questions.'

'Who the fuck *are* you?'

'I'm a citizen investigator.'

It was the first thing that came into her head. She was aware of how ridiculous she sounded as soon as she'd said it, but by then it was too late to take it back.

'A what? Like, you're some sort of conspiracy nut or something?' He scoffed derisively.

It was a feeble attempt to hide his unease, and one that only hardened Anna's resolve.

'Or something. I take it you're aware Leanne McColm is dead.'

'I had nothing to do with that,' Duffy snapped.

'That's an interesting leap. I never said you did.'

'But that's why you're here, in't it? Some cunt or other's said something to you, and you've got it into your head I had something to do with it. Who was it? I'll sue 'em for defamation.' He paused for a beat. 'They've already got her boyfriend locked up for it, you know.'

'Been following the case closely, have you?'

Duffy didn't dignify that with an answer. He just scowled, then shot a wary glance across the forecourt towards the showroom, where his colleague was still attending to the couple he'd abandoned to talk to Anna.

'Do your co-workers know you harassed her, out of interest?' said Anna, following his gaze.

Duffy turned to her, a wild and furious look in his eyes.

'*Fuck* you! What gives you the right?'

'I've got some questions to ask you,' Anna said levelly. 'You can either cooperate or not – it's up to you.'

'But the cost of my refusing is you telling my colleagues I'm some sort of mental stalker-slash-serial killer, is it? Oh aye, I'm pure spoiled for choice.'

'Actually, to be a serial killer, you need to have killed at least three people.'

Duffy's eyes flared in righteous fury. For a moment, he looked to be on the verge of saying something. He opened his mouth, then changed his mind and shut it. A few seconds passed.

'Look,' he finally said, in a low, insistent near-whisper, 'I dunno what you heard or who you heard it from, but you're far off the mark. *So* far off you're practically in another *continent*.' Another pause. 'If you actually want to know, she was the one who led *me* on.'

'That's how it was, was it?'

'That's right. Fluttered her eyelashes at me, kept telling me how buff I was getting, perfectly happy to accept all sorts of gratuities off of me. Then, when I happen to run into her in the car park one night and I make some passing remark about maybe going for coffee some time, she starts screaming the place down, like I'm some sort of *predator* or something. Thought she was a nice, easy-going lassie. Turns out she was a lying fucking snake.'

'Find that happens to you a lot with women, do you?' said Anna dryly.

Duffy snorted disgustedly. 'Of course, you'd have to be one of *those*.'

'One of what?'

'*You* know.'

Anna felt she was getting a pretty good sense of how Duffy viewed the world. In his reality, women were either potential conquests or duplicitous liars, leading him on, then stabbing him in the back the moment he let his guard down. She supposed, on balance, her actions here today were more likely to have reinforced that view than shown him the error of his ways.

Duffy glanced back towards the showroom again. Sucked in a breath through his nose, as if steeling himself.

'You know what? Go ahead and tell my workmates what you're accusing me of. Tell the whole world, for that matter. I don't care. I've got nothing to hide cos I've *done* nothing. Now, why don't you fuck off and let me get on with my job, seeing as how it's pretty obvious you're not actually here to buy a motor?'

Anna studied him intently. She wasn't sure she believed him, but he was certainly insistent, and the threat to tell his colleagues had been her main trump card. Without it, she didn't have anything meaningful to threaten him with.

'Look,' she said, aware she was playing a weak hand, 'it's possible we got off on the wrong foot. If I could just have a few more minutes of your time, I—'

'No, not just a few minutes,' snapped Duffy. 'Leave, *now*, or I'll be phoning the polis myself and making a complaint of harassment.'

Anna looked at him. He met her gaze defiantly.

'That's your final word on the subject?'

'It is.'

She considered one last push – appealing to his better nature rather than resorting to further threats – before concluding that she was on a hiding to nothing.

'Fine.'

She opened the door, preparing to leave.

'Thanks for showing me the car,' she called in an unnecessarily loud voice, 'but I don't think I'll be taking it. There's a bad smell lingering inside it.'

With that, she got abruptly to her feet, ignoring the momentary rush of dizziness as she stood up, then strode off, leaving the door lying open.

. . .

Anna sat near the back of the bus, mulling over her confrontation with Duffy. Now that the initial adrenaline rush had subsided, she was forced to admit she'd gone in a bit too gung-ho, and in the process had probably blown her one chance to get him to open up. On balance, she still found his denials convincing, though she supposed it was possible she was merely mistaking vehemence for candour.

As the bus wound its way up towards the city centre, it occurred to her that she wasn't far from the spot where the bar worker had seen Sean dragging Leanne towards High Street Station on the night of her murder. The one who'd given the interview to the *Post*. Kasia something, wasn't it? Anna wondered whether she was working today.

Well, nothing to be lost by trying. It wasn't yet noon, and with no concrete commitments at the university till later in the afternoon, it wasn't as if anyone was going to be wondering why she wasn't in her office, catching up on the admin she'd been planning to get through before three o'clock, when she had a supervision meeting with one of her PhD students.

Oh, what the hell . . .

Getting to her feet, she hit the stop button and made her way unsteadily down the gangway as the bus juddered to a halt.

13

Strangeways, a fifteen-minute walk from the bottom of Hope Street, where the bus had dropped her, was nestled between an estate agent and an Indian restaurant on Trongate, the busy thoroughfare connecting the city centre and the East End. Beyond the outdoor seating area, unoccupied in the early March chill, the tinted windows were almost opaque, giving away nothing of what lay inside.

Anna pushed through the heavy front door and stepped over the threshold. She removed her sunglasses, but it still took her eyes a moment to adjust to the gloom. The place was dimly lit, furnished with dark wood and battered leather booths. Mellow rock music hummed quietly in the background, and the smell of grease and stale beer hung in the air.

At this hour, the place was almost empty. A couple of men in high-vis vests – builders on their lunch break, she assumed – were perched at the bar, busy ignoring each other as they scrolled on their phones. At the far end of the room, a gaggle of what Anna took to be students occupied a booth, their animated conversation generating by far the most noise in the otherwise tranquil setting.

Anna approached the bar, where a young man with

bleached blonde hair gelled into a coif was restocking mixers with practised efficiency. He looked up as she drew level with the counter.

'What can I get ya?'

'Nothing for the moment,' she said. 'Actually, I was hoping to speak to Kasia. Is she in?'

'Aye, she's in.'

He strode to the end of the bar and leaned through the door at the back.

'KASH!' he hollered. 'Someone to see ya!' He turned to Anna. 'She'll be with ya in a mo,' he told her, then returned to restocking the mixers.

Not long after, a young woman emerged from the back. Kasia Wiśniewska was in her early twenties, with multiple facial piercings and jet-black hair styled in a French braid. She stepped out from behind the bar and approached Anna, frowning.

'Hi?' she said, her voice rising uncertainly.

'Hi. Kasia Vis . . . Vis-new-ska?' said Anna, enunciating the unfamiliar name as best she could and wishing she'd had the presence of mind to look up the pronunciation before coming here.

'Veesh-NYEV-ska,' said Kasia in a forbearing tone.

Anna smiled apologetically. 'Sorry. I'm guessing you get that a lot.'

Kasia dismisses her with a wave. 'It's fine,' she said, and, for the first time, Anna registered her strong Eastern European accent, confirming what she'd already suspected: that her surname wasn't merely an ancestral relic. 'You Scottish are hard for me to understand sometimes, so it's teat for tat. Not you, though. You speak very clearly.'

'Oh,' said Anna. 'Well, thank you.'

Kasia studied her closely. 'I think I don't know you,' she declared.

'You don't. I'm Anna Scavolini. I'm investigating the murder of Leanne McColm.'

Kasia's eyes narrowed. 'You are police? I don't wish to talk to them. They already give me lecture for speaking to the newspaper.'

'No,' said Anna quickly. 'I'm investigating in a . . . personal capacity.'

Kasia appeared more confused than ever. 'This is a thing?'

'Sort of. I'm a professor of criminology, but I should tell you, this visit wasn't authorised by anyone connected to the official police investigation.'

She wasn't sure why she was being so honest when her previous encounters with witnesses had been predicated on being less than forthcoming with the truth. Perhaps, in some strange, irrational way, she was making amends for these past deceptions.

'Look,' she went on, 'you don't have to talk to me, but I'm trying to build up a picture of Leanne's movements in the hours leading up to her death, and I was sort of hoping you'd be willing to take me through what you saw that night.'

Kasia sucked the inside of her mouth dubiously. 'You are aware this is very strange thing to be asking.'

It wasn't a question. Nonetheless, Anna responded, rather helplessly, 'Yes.'

Kasia considered this for another moment, then gave a slight shrug.

'OK. I talk to you. And then you go. Yes?'

'Yes,' said Anna.

Kasia turned to her colleague at the bar. 'Felix. It's OK if I go for smoke?'

Felix shrugged. 'Nae skin off my nose. We're hardly slammed.'

Kasia turned to Anna. 'That was yes, I think. Come on. I show you.'

They headed outside, where Kasia produced a pack of

cigarettes and offered it to Anna, who demurred. Kasia shrugged, then selected one for herself and pocketed the pack.

'So have you been in Glasgow long?' asked Anna, attempting to break the ice.

'Yes. I come here to study the interior design. End up working in Strangeways Bar. Not many jobs for graduates, no?'

'No,' Anna agreed. 'The market's really tough right now.'

Kasia nodded. She produced a Zippo and used it to light her cigarette.

'So,' said Anna, as Kasia inhaled, 'the night of the eighth of January, you came outside at about 11:15 . . . ?'

'Correct. I am asked to take out the trash for pickup next morning. I don't mind. Is change of scenery, plus . . .' She held up her cigarette between two fingers by way of explanation.

'So you dumped the bags there, I'm guessing.'

Anna nodded to the square black bin by the kerb.

Kasia gave a slight smirk. 'Yes. This is funny, I think. They make a sign saying "PEOPLE MAKE GLASGOW", I assume as celebration, but they put it on a trash container.'

Anna acknowledged the ubiquitous slogan fixed to the side of the bin with a smile.

'Quite. What happened next?'

'I stop for some moments to enjoy my Benson & Hedges. Then, as I'm about to go back inside, a man and woman pass me on pavement. I notice because the man almost knocks into me. He shouts swearword at me and keeps going. He's dragging woman by the arm.'

Anna nodded. 'Keep going.'

'The woman is trying to stop. You know, like putting on brakes? But the man, he is too strong. He pulls her along the pavement. I watch. They go a bit further, then stop. He turns to her.'

She shut her eyes momentarily, imagining the scene. Anna waited as patiently as she could.

After a moment, Kasia's eyes opened again. 'Man is

standing on right side. Woman on left. They face each other. She is very small. He is very large. He has fists clenched. He is shouting. She tries to back away. He moves more close.'

She stepped towards Anna, extending both arms towards her, cigarette still clenched between her fingers.

'This is OK?'

Anna nodded.

'He does like this.'

She grabbed Anna by the upper arms. Leaned in, their noses almost touching.

'And he shouts at her face – like "RAAAAAAH!" '

Not anticipating the ferocity or the volume of her roar, Anna recoiled involuntarily, wincing.

Kasia released her and took a couple of steps back.

'And you didn't happen to hear what he said?' Anna asked, once she'd recovered from her surprise.

Kasia took a drag on her cigarette. Shook her head. 'No. Is too far away. Plus there is noise from the bar. Also . . .' She gestured with her cigarette. 'Scottish.'

Anna nodded her understanding.

'How far away were they at this point?'

Kasia frowned, shut one eye and tilted her head sideways, as if gazing down the scope of a sniper rifle. She pointed with her whole arm, cigarette clenched between two fingers.

'See where traffic light is? Outside Maggie's Rock 'n' Rodeo?'

Anna nodded, following her gaze. 'So about forty to fifty metres. And you were able to see them clearly from where you were standing?'

'Mm-hm. I have strong eyes.'

'I don't doubt it. But you're certain the woman was Leanne McColm and the man was Sean Kerevan?'

Kasia nodded emphatically. 'One thousand percent. The police show me photos. CCTV. I say, "It's them." Same clothes.'

'Did the man have his hood up or down?'

'Up,' said Kasia immediately.

'So you never saw his face clearly?'

'Only for an instant when he swear at me. But I remember it well. A face full of hate.'

Sounds like Sean, thought Anna.

'It was definitely the same man who was in the photos the police showed you?' she said.

Kasia looked at her as if she was spectacularly dense. 'Yes. He wore same shirt.'

'And the woman was definitely Leanne McColm?'

This time, Kasia sighed and stopped just short of rolling her eyes. Clearly, this was starting to bore her.

'Short. Skinny. Brown hair. It's her.'

'And after he was done yelling at her . . . ?'

'He take her by the arm again and they walk on. I turn and go back inside.'

'Did you ever . . . consider intervening?'

Kasia wrinkled her nose. 'I think it is not my place. I see this exchange often.'

'Oh?'

Kasia shrugged. 'Couples. They fight. They make up. They fight again. It's normal behaviour.'

Anna passed no comment on this depressingly familiar refrain.

Half a minute or so elapsed, during which Kasia finished her cigarette in silence while Anna pondered her own thoughts.

'Just one more question,' she said eventually. 'Could you tell from the way they were interacting that the man and woman were a couple – or is that something the police told you when they questioned you?'

Kasia thought about this. 'I don't remember. Too much time since that night. But when you see man and woman together, usually couple, yes? Why?'

'I'm not sure,' said Anna distantly.

At the back of her mind, an idea had begun to take shape. It was intangible, impossible to grasp, but there was the seed of something there. Something she needed to interrogate more, once she could figure out what it was.

Kasia eyed her, visibly impatient now. 'We're finished? I can go now? You have no more questions?'

Anna was dimly aware that she probably *did* have more questions, but right now she couldn't think what they might be.

'Yes, of course,' she said. 'You've been very helpful. Thank you.'

Kasia gave a crooked grin. 'It's all good. Makes day more interesting.'

She ground out her cigarette on the ash plate on top of the bin, then turned and headed back into the bar without a backward glance.

Anna remained standing there for a few moments, still preoccupied by her thoughts, then turned and headed back the way she'd come.

As she waited at the bus stop on Hope Street, she continued to mull over what Kasia had told her. She wasn't sure she'd actually learned anything new, besides getting confirmation that there was no possibility of Sean's behaviour towards Leanne that night having been in any way open to interpretation. Different people, she reasoned, had their own standards when it came to what constituted aggression, but she doubted even the most generous assessment could explain away grabbing someone by the arms and screaming in their face as a civil exchange of viewpoints.

She became aware of the sound of her phone trilling. She fished it out of her bag and checked the screen. The caller ID read 'Maybe: NHS Greater Glasgow & Clyde.'

A pang of tightness gripped her chest. Her heart thudding, she accepted the call, gingerly raising the phone to her ear.

'Hello?'

'Anna, hello,' said a woman's voice – brisk, businesslike, but not unkind. 'It's Elizabeth Maitland.'

'Dr Maitland,' said Anna, rather unnecessarily. 'What can I . . . how are you?'

'I'm well, Anna. So listen, the radiologist completed his examination of your recent MRI and forwarded his report to me. I have it here in front of me.'

Anna couldn't bear the prevarication. 'What does it say?' she demanded.

'Anna, I'd like you to come in for another scan – this one with IV contrast.'

'Why?' said Anna faintly.

For a moment, Maitland hesitated. 'I'll be level with you, Anna. The scan showed a shadow in the region of your right posterior communicating artery. That's a vessel at the base of the brain, running close to the nerves behind your right eye.'

The sounds of the street around Anna faded away to nothing. Her heart, which until now had been beating nineteen to the dozen, seemed to stop completely.

'Anna? Are you still there?'

'This shadow,' Anna managed to say. 'What is it?'

'It would be unwise to speculate at this stage. At the moment, the most important thing is that we—'

'Is it a tumour?'

There. She'd said it. Made it real.

'It could be any number of things,' said Maitland carefully, 'not all of which are necessarily anything to be concerned about. Now, as I was saying, it's important we get you in for a contrast scan in order to gain a better understanding of what we're dealing with.'

She paused for a second. 'As you'll no doubt be aware, the current backlog means that waiting times are far in excess of what they were pre-COVID. Realistically, you could be looking at a three-to-four-week wait. If you'd prefer to have the procedure done privately, I can—'

'It's fine. I'll wait my turn like everyone else.'

'All right,' said Maitland, in a tone that suggested she didn't entirely approve of this choice. 'I'll make the necessary arrangements. You should get a letter within the next few days with the date and time of your appointment. And Anna?'

'Yes?' said Anna distantly.

'I do have to stress that, even if it turns out to be something sinister, there's an excellent chance we've caught it in time. It really is far too early to start worrying.'

Easy for you to say, Anna thought – but she managed to avoid saying this, or anything else equally cutting.

'Well, thank you for your call,' she said instead, and hung up before Maitland could say anything else.

She lowered her phone. Slowly, the sounds of the city returned. She sank onto the bench inside the bus shelter, clutching the phone in both hands between her knees. Next to her, a young man with dreads was speaking animatedly into his phone in a language she didn't recognise, his voice loud and filled with laughter, while, on her other side, two elderly women who seemed to have run into each other unexpectedly embraced with great enthusiasm.

All around her, the world went on, oblivious to the body blow she'd just been dealt.

PART III

HOUSE OF CARDS

14

Somehow, Anna managed to get through the rest of the day. She made her way to the university and threw herself into a variety of administrative tasks, staying late in order to avoid going home to an empty house. It was after 6 p.m. when she finally switched off her desk lamp and headed back to Jordanhill to collect Jack from Theo's house. She made a monumental effort to appear normal in front of him, asking him about his school day and refusing to accept his monosyllabic non-responses, then expressing appropriate interest as he sat hunched over his jumbo sketchpad at the table in the living room, drawing furiously with his brows pursed together and his tongue protruding between his teeth.

It was only after 7:30, when she'd eventually succeeded in cajoling him into the bath, that she finally slipped off the metaphorical suit of armour she'd been wearing all afternoon and sank into her chair by the window, allowing all the thoughts she'd refused to dwell on to rise up and engulf her.

Brain tumour.

Just two words. Two utterly terrifying words that, in the blink of an eye, had completely upended her entire existence. Of course, she'd had an inkling already – since long before her

GP had referred her to Dr Maitland. Indeed, her innate incli-
nation to expect the worst meant she'd already prepared
herself for the possibility that this was coming. Or so she'd
thought. But actually hearing those words – 'The scan showed
a shadow' – was another matter entirely. She realised now that,
no matter how prepared she'd thought she was, there were
some things you were never truly ready to hear.

She stirred at the sound of the front doorbell ringing.

'Doorbell, Mummy!' Jack called from the bathroom.

'I hear it, Jack!' Anna called back, already on her feet.

'Answer or they'll think you haven't heard!'

'Yes, Jack, I'm going now!'

She headed into the hallway, took the door off its chain
and opened it. Standing on the doorstep was a tall, heavily
tanned woman in her early forties, wearing a fawn overcoat
over a charcoal trouser suit, her blonde hair scraped back into
a severe bun.

'Professor Scavolini,' she said. 'Long time no see. Mind if I
step inside for a chat?'

Even as Anna registered the fact that she knew her from
somewhere, the woman was already stepping forward, leaving
Anna, utterly unprepared for this intrusion, with no choice but
to back up and let her in.

'Nice place you've got here,' the woman said as she stepped
past Anna into the hallway. 'I've always liked these four-in-a-
block arrangements. A very efficient use of space.' She turned
to Anna expectantly. 'Well? Shall we do this out here or can we
go somewhere more comfortable?'

Anna's shoulders slumped in resignation. 'This way.'

The last time Anna had seen Vanessa Tope, she'd been
standing in a police observation room, watching from behind
the safety of a two-way mirror as Tope grilled Sean Hanlon,
the estranged son and killer of the infamous family annihilator,

Sandra Morton. Suffice it to say that Tope had lost none of her poise, unflappability or the unmistakable whiff of self-satisfied superiority she'd always seemed to exhibit. Now, as they sat facing one another in the living room, Tope with her overcoat spread across her legs, hands folded on top of it, Anna found herself experiencing the same familiar sense of indignation and exasperation that always seemed to overcome her when she had to deal with law enforcement figures.

'Detective Chief Inspector——' she began.

'Actually, it's Detective Superintendent now.' Tope gave what Anna suspected was intended to be a friendly smile. 'Snagged myself a cushy promotion a year or so back.'

'Good for you,' said Anna, wholly uninterested in the woman's career advances. 'All right, then, Detective *Superintendent*, I hope you won't think me rude if I ask you what this is about.'

'That strikes me as only fair,' said Tope genially. 'As it happens, my visit tonight was spurred by a complaint lodged by a member of the public regarding an incident that took place earlier today. An incident involving *you*.'

'Oh?'

'A certain Anthony Duffy alleges that you appeared at his workplace this morning, inveigled yourself onto the premises under false pretences and proceeded to subject him to a variety of threats and accusations.'

Anna felt her eyes widening involuntarily, shocked that Duffy had actually gone to the police about this of his own accord.

Tope cocked her head slightly. 'Well? Anything to say?'

'That's . . . not exactly what happened,' said Anna carefully. A thought occurred to her. 'Also, I'm fairly certain I didn't tell him my name.'

'Perhaps not, but I recognised you from the description he gave.'

'Which was?'

'Sure you want to hear this?'

'Positive.'

A flicker of a smile crossed Tope's lips before she next spoke.

'He referred to you as "an angry hobbit".'

This time, Anna's eyes practically popped out of her skull.

'And that was enough for you to connect it to *me*?'

'That, and your general modus operandi. Apparently, you've been going around telling people you're a citizen investigator.'

Anna winced internally.

Tope paused for a moment, letting her words hang in the air. Then:

'You're investigating Leanne McColm's murder, aren't you?'

'Perhaps I am,' said Anna carefully. 'Either way, I'm not aware of having broken any laws.' She got to her feet. 'So, unless you've got specific charges to bring against me, I'd prefer if you—'

At that moment, there was a sound of pounding footsteps in the hallway. The door swung open and Jack came striding in, stark naked apart from a pair of swimming goggles, clutching a plastic submarine and dripping with water and soapsuds.

'*Jack!*' Anna exclaimed, mortified.

Jack glared at her indignantly. 'Why does it float if it's called a submarine?' he demanded. ' "Sub" means "under". It should go *under*! That's the whole point. If it doesn't go under, it's not a submarine – it's a *boat*.'

As Anna simply stared at him, lost for words, Jack noticed Tope for the first time – or, perhaps, finally decided she was worthy of his attention.

'Do *you* know why?' he demanded, advancing with the submarine outthrust towards her. 'Because it doesn't make any sense.'

If Tope was at all fazed by any of this, she didn't let it show.

'Well,' she said, in a tone of perfect reasonability, 'I suppose it's got air in it. Air makes things float.'

Jack examined the submarine with a frown.

'It's still false advertising,' he declared, after giving the matter due consideration.

They faced each other for a moment, Jack studying Tope intently, Tope accepting the scrutiny of this unclothed, overly inquisitive six-year-old without objection.

'I don't know you,' Jack eventually declared.

'No,' agreed Tope, 'but I know *you*. You're Jack.'

'That's right. Who are you?'

'She's a police officer, darling,' said Anna, finally spurred into action and hoping that these words, which she'd have regarded as more than a little ominous when she was his age, would persuade him to vacate the scene.

But Jack did no such thing. He continued to stare at Tope, more intrigued now than ever.

'Are you here to put my mother in prison?'

'I wasn't planning to, no,' said Tope. 'Not unless you think there's a reason I should.'

Jack thought about this for a moment, then shook his head.

'No,' he said, 'I don't think so.'

'Well,' Tope smiled, 'that's a relief, because I didn't bring my handcuffs.'

'If you're a police officer, does that mean you carry a gun?'

'*Oooo*-kay,' said Anna, firmly stepping between the two of them, 'I think that's enough questions for tonight. Time for you to run along, kiddo.'

She took Jack by the shoulders and turned him in the direction of the door.

'Get yourself dried off and put on your jammies and I'll come and read to you in a bit.'

She gave him a gentle push and he took off, ambling out of

the room without a backward glance, leaving a trail of suds on the carpet.

Anna shut the door behind him and turned to Tope, her cheeks burning.

'I am *so* sorry about that.'

'Don't be,' said Tope amiably. 'My nephews are the same. Don't give a stuff *who* sees their unmentionables. You've got to admire it, haven't you? I fancy we'd all have a lot fewer hangups about ourselves if we adopted their attitude towards public indecency. Now, where had we got to . . . ?'

'I was asking if you planned to charge me with something, or if you were going to leave me to get on with my evening.'

'Oh – yes. Well, it'll no doubt please you to hear that the answer is no, I'm not going to charge you with anything. Believe it or not, this *was* just a friendly visit to try – possibly futilely – to talk some sense into you . . . and to set the record straight about something.'

'Oh really? What's that?'

'Tony Duffy had nothing to do with Leanne McColm's death. Of that we can be completely certain.'

'Why?'

'Quite simply because Mr Duffy was holidaying in Tenerife at the time. He boarded both his outgoing and return flights as scheduled. And, if that's not enough for you, we also have CCTV footage of him in a bar in Puerto de la Cruz, drinking himself into a stupor on the night of the murder.'

'Oh,' said Anna quietly. 'How clear is the footage?'

'Crystal.'

'Oh,' said Anna again.

'You sound disappointed,' said Tope.

'I'm not.'

But she was. In fact, she was surprised by just *how* disappointed. She hadn't realised it until now, but a part of her had indeed been clinging to the possibility that Duffy might have been responsible for Leanne's death. Not because any part of

154

her hoped Sean was innocent. Far from it. Rather, she supposed, because the dyed-in-the-wool contrarian in her invariably ended up willing the official version of events to be proved wrong.

'Well, now you know,' said Tope. She got to her feet. 'And now I'd better be on my way. Wouldn't want to take up any more of your valuable time.'

Anna saw her to the door. As she stepped outside, Tope once more turned to face her.

'I'm going to say something, even though I know it'll probably fall on deaf ears.'

'Don't be so sure,' said Anna.

Tope gave her a look, as if to convey that they both knew that was unlikely.

'I know there's some intractable part of you that feels the need, for reasons best known to yourself, to insert yourself into matters such as these. But I can assure you, in this instance, there *is* no miscarriage of justice. No cover-up. Sean Kerevan killed Leanne McColm. Sometimes, a pipe is just a pipe.'

'Freud?'

'Magritte.'

Tope smiled briefly – a weary, companionable smile with no scorn or sarcasm that Anna could detect.

'I mean it. You'll do whatever you have a mind to – I know that much. But you'll be wasting your time. Believe me, the case is as cut and dried as they come. We don't need your help with this one.'

And, with that, she turned on her heel and strode off into the night.

15

Tuesday 8 March

The train pulled into Springburn Station just before a quarter to one. As Anna stepped off, she spotted Pamela Macklin waiting for her on the platform. Pamela grinned and waved animatedly. Anna returned the wave rather more discreetly and made her way over to her.

They'd caught up by phone the previous evening, with Anna filling Pamela in on everything she'd found out since they'd last spoken, including her conversations with Jacqueline and Kasia. Pamela had clearly been crushed to learn about Leanne's bruises – though, to give her her due, she hadn't attempted to come up with an 'innocent' explanation for them. Anna had also told her about her encounter with Tony Duffy and her subsequent visit from Vanessa Tope. Pamela, whose hopes had momentarily been raised by the prospect of another suspect, had struggled to hide her disappointment upon learning that Duffy could be categorically ruled out.

'Thanks for accommodating my schedule,' said Pamela, as they began to make their way up the platform. 'I know you're meant to be working.'

'It's fine,' said Anna, batting Pamela's concern away with a dismissive wave. 'There are no classes this week, so I've a bit more flexibility than normal.'

She didn't mention that she nonetheless had a PhD student's draft thesis chapter to read and half a dozen essays to mark – all of which she was going to have to somehow get through this evening instead.

'Oh, by the way,' said Pamela, as they climbed the steps out of the station, 'I managed to find out about Sean's hoodie. You know, the grey one with the Nike logo? Turns out he wasn't wearing it when he got back to the house at 4 a.m. He was just in joggers and a T-shirt. The SOCOs found it in the washing machine along with a bunch of other clothes.'

'He could easily have gone back to the house after he planted Leanne's body, chucked it in the washing machine along with a full load to muddy the waters, then gone out again,' Anna pointed out.

'Perhaps. Or perhaps it was in the wash all along and it *wasn't* him who was seen with Leanne that night.'

Anna, who didn't trust herself not to respond with something utterly caustic, said nothing.

'Also, Leanne's handbag,' said Pamela. 'There was no sign of it, either at the crime scene or inside the house. What d'you make of *that*?'

It sounded like she was laying down a challenge.

'Honestly, I'm not sure,' Anna admitted. 'Sean *could* have thrown it away after he planted the body . . . though I'd be at a loss to explain *why*.'

They reached the top of the steps and emerged onto Atlas Road. The long, curving stretch of road, with its hodgepodge of new-build flats and old tenements, felt sad and desolate beneath the overcast sky. A solitary Union Jack attached to a lamppost fluttered slightly in the breeze, making Anna feel decidedly uneasy, as overt displays of nationalism invariably did. She considered making some pithy remark, then remembered that Pamela's grandfather had been a grandee of the Orange Lodge and decided she might not appreciate it.

Less than forty metres from the station steps, they found the flight of steps leading down to the car park at the back of the old library, at the bottom of which Leanne's body had been found. It was undeniably a steep drop, and, even knowing that Leanne hadn't *actually* fallen, Anna nonetheless felt her extremities tingling at the thought of losing her footing on the way down. She took it slowly, holding onto the railing and willing herself not to suffer another sudden attack of dizziness.

Mercifully, they reached the bottom without incident. From there, referring to the map on Pamela's phone, they took the most direct route south towards Millbrae Avenue.

'I'll tell you something for nothing,' said Pamela, as they walked side by side down a residential street. 'If Leanne *was* killed at home, then whoever moved the body to those steps was really pushing his luck. This whole area's really densely populated, and I bet it's well-lit at night too. All it'd take was someone out for a late-night walk or happening to look out the window and he'd've been spotted. If *I* wanted to get rid of a body, I'd've gone in the exact opposite direction – towards the scrubland north of Sighthill Cemetery. *Way* less chance of being seen.'

Anna said nothing, but she suppressed a smile. Not because the situation was remotely funny, but because she'd suddenly been confronted by the absurd mental image of prim, strait-laced Pamela dragging a body into the undergrowth under the dead of night.

They soon reached Millbrae Avenue, a long, gently curving street lined with council and ex-council houses built in the postwar push to empty the old slum tenements of the city centre, banishing their former inhabitants to the various newly constructed satellite estates. The housing stock was all much the same: roughcast walls, slate roofs, small front gardens and cramped little windows, most of the buildings sporting at least one satellite dish. Still, the lawns were well-tended and the pavement largely clear of litter. And, while the houses were all the same shape and size, several of them nonetheless exhibited flashes of individuality: different coloured doors of varying styles, and a wide array of carefully chosen plants and shrubs. The residents might not be rolling in money, but they evidently took pride in their little patch of home.

'Which house is Leanne and Sean's?' Anna asked, as they made their way along the pavement.

'Number 113,' said Pamela.

They came to a halt outside the house in question, a light brown pebbledash affair with a low hedge separating the two halves of the building. The remnants of a strip of police tape hung from the door of the right-hand half, number 113, while the empty beer cans and other assorted detritus that had accumulated in the garden handily illustrated what the other properties might have looked like without a rigorous upkeep regime.

'So,' said Anna, 'which house d'you want to hit first?'

Their plan had been to knock on as many doors as possible in an effort to persuade some of the residents to share their experiences of Sean and Leanne. Which, now that Anna thought about it, wasn't much of a plan at all. More of a wild stab in the dark, really.

Pamela considered the question, eyes glancing over the various buildings within her field of vision, then gave Anna a stealthy nudge.

'Don't make a big deal out of it, but we appear to have an audience.'

'What?' said Anna, turning to follow her gaze. 'Where?'

'I said don't make a big deal out of it!' Pamela hissed.

Anna's eyes fell on the ground-floor window of the opposite half of the McColm/Kerevan house – number 115, where an elderly woman with large-framed glasses stood, peering out at them with what appeared to be a mixture of suspicion and undisguised curiosity.

Seeing that there was no hope now of them pretending not to have noticed her, Pamela raised her hand in a cheerful wave. The woman withdrew from the window. At first, Anna assumed Pamela's less than subtle acknowledgement had frightened her off, but a few moments later, the front door opened and the woman emerged. She was short and barrel-chested, wearing an ill-fitting sweater and corduroy trousers, and she descended the steps leading up to the door in a curious crab walk, clutching the rail with one hand, before making her way gingerly down the path towards them. Anna and Pamela stood on the pavement, Pamela shifting nervously from one foot to the other.

'Are yous Jehovah's Witnesses?' the woman asked in a fifty-a-day smoker's rasp. Now that she was seeing her up close, Anna guessed she was probably in her sixties but passing for older, the wear and tear of a hard life etched into her face.

'Oh *no!*' exclaimed Pamela immediately, sounding genuinely horrified by the very idea. 'Not at all! And we're not selling anything either. As it happens, I'm a solicitor. Pamela Macklin. I'm with Riddoch MacLetchie.'

Beaming, she extended her hand. The woman eyed it suspiciously.

'That meant tae impress me?'

Pamela's smile faded. She continued to hold her hand out towards the woman for a couple of seconds; then, when it became obvious it wasn't going to be accepted, she withdrew it sheepishly.

The woman turned her gaze on Anna. 'What about you? You an ambulance chaser an' aw?'

'What?' said Anna, taken aback. 'No, no. I'm a crimi-nologist.'

'Crim*o*logist?' repeated the woman, mangling the unfa-miliar word. 'You work for the polis, then?'

Gotcha.

'From time to time, yes.'

The woman's eyes lit up behind her massive glasses. 'Then you'll be here about that poor lassie who died.'

'That's right,' Anna began, 'we——'

'You know, I can't *tell* yous how pleased I was tae finally see that basturt get done.'

The woman spoke with undisguised relish – which, in fairness to her, she seemed almost immediately to realise was inappropriate under the circumstances.

'Terrible, *terrible* thing that happened tae yon lassie,' she added hastily, adopting an appropriately pious expression. 'But then,' she sighed fatalistically, 'I always say, lassies wae reckless tastes in men always end up living tae regret it.'

It took all Anna's willpower not to point out that that choice of words was profoundly inappropriate when referring to someone who'd been brutally murdered.

'What was reckless about Leane's taste in men?' she said instead.

The woman gave her a contemptuous look, as if merely asking this question was evidence of a severe mental deficit.

'Well, I mean, is it no *obvious*? Kilt her, didn't he?'

'That's what we're trying to establish,' said Pamela brightly.

''Course he done it,' the woman scoffed. All they screaming matches, the crashing and banging, yon Leanne slinking about like a beaten dug, bruises all up her arms, scared out her wits of that beast.'

Anna took a step towards her. 'Am I right in thinking . . . sorry, I don't think we caught your name.'

'Mrs Graham,' said the woman, and didn't elaborate any further.

'Mrs Graham,' Anna repeated. 'Would I be right in thinking it was you who complained to the authorities about the . . . about the disturbances?'

Mrs Graham snorted. 'For all the good it done! Sent a couple of plods round tae nod their heids and tut-tut about how terrible it was, and then – zip. My Billy works nights, you know! Couldnae get a moment's rest, what wae yon racket going on in there.'

'Billy's your . . .'

'My son. Works in security over at the technical college in Haghill.' She drew herself up a little taller, clearly proud on his behalf. 'Disnae pay near enough, *and* he has tae work every weekend, but it's a VERY IMPORTANT JOB. He can't be turning up for his shifts bleary-eyed and unslept!

'No that he'd ever complain *himself*,' she muttered, seemingly as an aside to herself. ' "Just leave it, Maw," he'd say. But I wasnae having it – no for him, and no for that poor lassie either.

'Would yous *believe*,' she huffed, seeming to suddenly remember Anna and Pamela were still there, 'she'd chap on the door the day after and actually *apologise* for that basturt? How he didnae mean it, how he just got carried away. Unbelievable! Mair than once, I told her, if she knew what was good for her, she'd up and leave the cunt. And d'yous know what *she* said?'

'What did she say?' asked Pamela, staring at her wide-eyed.

'Said she'd never do that. "He loves me really," she said. "He just gets these . . . moods . . . sometimes." ' Mrs Graham shook her head contemptuously. 'Well, 's like my auld mammy used tae say: if ye willnae help yersel, then there's fuck all anyone else can dae fer ye.'

It was hard to escape the impression that Mrs Graham believed Leanne's fate, while a terrible shame, was nonetheless at least partly self-inflicted. Anna had encountered this sort of thinking before: some men, being little better than animals, were unable to help themselves, and the responsibility therefore lay with women to avoid providing them with the opportunity to do what came naturally to them. Those who failed to heed the warning signs had only themselves to blame.

She forced herself to focus on the matter at hand.

'The night Leanne was . . . the night she died, did you hear anything at all? An argument, or maybe the sound of someone entering or leaving the house?'

'Not a peep,' said Mrs Graham. 'But then, how would I? He never kilt her in the hoose. I know. I seen it on the news.'

'Right enough,' Anna agreed. She racked her brains for any other questions to ask. 'Um . . . is your son about, by any chance?'

'He's oot.' Mrs Graham shook her head fatalistically. 'It's a sin, so it is – him working the hours he does. Makes it impossible tae have any sort of a social life. D'yous know, this is the first time in three months he's been able tae meet up wae his pals?'

'I'm sure neither of us can even *begin* to imagine what that's like,' said Pamela.

Mrs Graham stared at her for a long moment, no doubt trying to work out whether Pamela had just insulted her – or her son. Pamela, oblivious, merely smiled at Mrs Graham and then at Anna, as if to say, *What's next?*

'Are yous wanting a look round the hoose?' said Mrs Graham suddenly, eyeballing them both expectantly.

'I'm sorry?' said Anna, blindsided by the question.

'Only I've got a spare key, so I can let yous in. Previous tenant gave me it,' she went on, before Anna could even begin to formulate a response, ''case she ever needed me tae pop in while she was oot. Which I'd've done in a heartbeat,' she added quickly, evidently keen for Anna and Pamela to know what a good neighbour she was. 'I'd a much better relationship wae her. Would've done *anything* for that wumman. 'Cept, she moved out, and those two moved in, and . . . well they never changed the locks. So are yous wanting in or not?'

'That would be incredibly helpful,' said Anna, simultaneously unable to believe their good luck and wondering just how Mrs Graham happened to know the locks hadn't been changed. 'Have you got it on you?'

'Not *on* me,' Mrs Graham scoffed. 'I'll have tae go back in the hoose and get it. Two ticks.'

They watched as she made her way back up the path and performed the same ungainly crab walk up the steps. As the door swung shut behind her, Pamela turned to Anna, wide-eyed with delight.

'What a helpful old lady! Bit too free with the old sailor talk for my tastes, but "let he who is without sin" and all that.'

'It's the son I feel sorry for,' Anna admitted.

'Because he's got her as a mother? I don't see what's so—'

'Billy *Graham?*' Anna raised an eyebrow.

Pamela looked back at her blankly. 'I don't get it.'

Anna considered explaining, then decided it wasn't worth the effort.

'Never mind. She's coming out.'

Pamela turned and followed her gaze as Mrs Graham once more made her way awkwardly down the steps. She approached them, clutching a metal hoop jangling with an improbably large number of keys.

'Well?' the older woman said. 'Don't stand there gawping. This way.'

They followed her up the next-door driveway obediently, then waited as she began sorting through the keys, looking for the one that would open the door. As she watched, Anna wondered just how many of the neighbouring houses she had keys for, and how she'd come to get her hands on them.

Finally, Mrs Graham gave a grunt of triumph and produced a Yale key, which she detached from the ring and successfully inserted into the lock, then opened the door.

'That's wonderful, Mrs Graham,' said Anna, hurrying to intercept her before she could step inside the house herself. 'Really, you've been incredibly helpful. We can take it from here.'

'Oh.' Mrs Graham was unmistakably put out. 'You're sure?'

'Yes, absolutely. If we need anything, we'll come and find you.'

'Oh,' said Mrs Graham again. 'Right.' She nodded towards the key, still in the lock. 'Yous'll bring that back when yous're done?'

'Absolutely.'

For a moment, Mrs Graham looked to be on the verge of making a fresh attempt to inveigle her way inside. But as Anna stood there, deliberately blocking the entrance with her shoulder, she admitted defeat.

'Just . . . don't take too long,' she grunted, then turned and began to make her way back down the driveway.

Anna and Pamela waited till she reached the street. For a brief moment, she turned and looked back at them, the expression on her face seeming almost forlorn. Anna, who'd taken possession of the key, smiled awkwardly at her, then gave a little goodbye wave and swiftly ushered Pamela inside, shutting the door behind them and locking it for good measure.

16

Alone at last, they stood in the narrow, dimly lit hallway, taking in their surroundings. The house followed the typical 'two up, two down' layout: stairs directly ahead, a door to the left leading to the front room, and another beyond the stairs, behind which the kitchen presumably lay. Dust coated every surface, and the air felt heavy and still. At their feet lay a pile of unopened mail – a silent testament to how long the house had lain unoccupied. The faint sound of voices reached their ears – a man and a woman having a heated exchange. For a moment, Anna had the irrational thought that new tenants had already moved into the house and were about to come charging out to demand that they leave. Then she heard a burst of music and realised it was just the sound of the TV filtering through the wall from the Grahams' half of the building.

'What exactly are we looking for in here?' said Pamela, her voice sounding unnaturally loud in the stillness.

'I'm not sure,' said Anna. 'I reckon we should start by just having a general wander round and see if anything jumps out.'

They took the front room first. The noise from the TV next door grew louder as soon as they opened the door – a booming, bass-heavy din that practically reverberated in their bones. Anna couldn't imagine having to live with this level of disturbance day in, day out. Sean had a point – Mrs Graham had some nerve complaining to the council when she herself was pumping out this amount of noise.

Inside the room, they found ample evidence of the police operation that had come and gone. The place didn't exactly look like a tornado had hit it, but one could easily believe that a mild earthquake had occurred in the vicinity. The room bore a resemblance to the one glimpsed in photos on Leanne's Facebook page, but that resemblance was only fleeting. The same items of furniture were present, but everything had the look of having been shifted and dumped back haphazardly.

The three-piece sofa that was the room's centrepiece sat at an odd angle, partially blocking the doorway, the discolouration visible on the carpet indicating its original placement. The same went for the two reclining chairs that had once faced it at ninety-degree angles, while the TV lay face down on the floor, its wall brackets still clinging to the space above the fireplace. Books had been crammed back onto shelves with their edges facing out, and the trio of framed prints behind the sofa, each boasting a different positive affirmation – 'YOU CAN BE ANYTHING', 'SHE BELIEVED SHE COULD SO SHE DID' and the dreaded 'KEEP CALM AND CARRY ON' – were all askew to varying degrees.

Anna tried to suppress the shudder that coursed through her. She knew those responsible had just been doing their jobs, but the space felt violated in a way she couldn't quite shake – and she couldn't help imagining the same thing being done to *her* home.

The disruption was even more pronounced upstairs. In the main bedroom, the large double mattress lay propped against the wall, while the contents of the wardrobe and dresser had been dumped in an unceremonious heap on top of the empty bedframe. Tights and lace panties mingled with socks and men's boxers, while the empty drawers lay strewn on the floor. There were even a couple of luminescent pink dildos standing upright on the nightstand, looking for all the world like they'd been placed there to cause maximum embarrassment.

Pamela gave a nervous laugh. 'Gosh! *There's* something you don't see every day. I didn't realise they came in that colour . . . or, um, size.'

Anna gave a strained smile. She knew Pamela was as uneasy as her, her attempt to lighten the mood clumsy but well-meaning.

She moved across to the dresser, where a 5x7 picture frame lay face down. She lifted it up, revealing a photo of Leanne and Sean in each other's arms, smiling up at the camera, both showing their pearly whites. The sun was shining behind them, and Sean was in a T-shirt and shorts, Leanne a flimsy sleeveless smock. Slender and diminutive, she was completely dwarfed by Sean's muscular frame, his tree-trunk arms wrapped around her protectively – or perhaps possessively.

She felt Pamela's breath on her shoulder and stirred, wondering how long she'd been standing there, gazing down at the picture.

'It's funny,' said Pamela.

'What is?'

'To look at them, it's hard to believe there was any strife in that relationship. They look so happy. So loved up. Don't you think?'

Anna said nothing. What was there to say? *Looks can be deceptive? You never know what's going on behind closed doors?* Empty, meaningless platitudes which did nothing to change the fact that, despite multiple people having seemingly known – or at least suspected – that she was at risk, Leanne was dead, and the two of them were sneaking around her former home, ostensibly looking for evidence that might exonerate a man who could hardly have looked more guilty if he'd tried.

'He did it, didn't he?' said Pamela quietly.

Anna turned to her in surprise.

Pamela gave a small, sad shrug. 'It's what you've been trying to tell me all along. You and Ger and everyone else. I'm the only one who thinks he could be innocent . . . and I think, deep down, even I never truly believed it.'

Anna gazed at Pamela. She saw the hurt in her eyes; how utterly crushed she was by the realisation. Why she'd come to it now rather than at any number of earlier points in the investigation when presented with infinitely more compelling evidence than a seemingly innocuous holiday snap, Anna couldn't say. She supposed everyone had their own personal tipping point. Pamela, it seemed, had reached hers.

She laid a comforting hand on Pamela's shoulder.

'Well,' she said gruffly, 'no harm in making sure, right?'

She smiled at Pamela. Pamela returned the smile weakly, her eyes moist but the tears, for now, successfully held at bay.

'Come on,' said Anna. 'I think we're probably done here.'

They emerged from the house, locked up and trooped round to number 115. There was no response when Pamela rang the bell, but the continuing sound of the TV blaring from the front room suggested Mrs Graham was in there somewhere.

Anna crossed over to the window and peered in. Mrs Graham was nestled in an armchair, eyes fixed on the TV in front of her.

She turned to Pamela, motioning to her to ring the bell again. Pamela did so. Mrs Graham didn't so much as look up.

Anna rapped on the window. This time, Mrs Graham did glance up, though not in the direction of the window. She seemed to sense that something had made a noise, but was unclear as to what, or where. Anna banged again, and, for good measure, waved both arms above her head, hoping the older woman would notice the movement.

Finally, Mrs Graham turned. She locked eyes with Anna,

standing with her arms still in the air, no doubt looking every bit as ridiculous as she felt. Mrs Graham muttered something to herself. Anna didn't need to be an expert lipreader to know that the three syllables had been 'what', 'the' and 'fuck?'

With some effort, Mrs Graham levered herself out of her chair and made for the door. Anna headed back to join Pamela, who looked like she was trying extremely hard not to laugh. Half a minute later, the door swung inwards and Mrs Graham peered out at them, seeming not in the least bit embarrassed at having made them wait.

'That's us off now, Mrs Graham,' said Pamela cheerily. 'We just stopped by to say cheerio.'

'And to give you this,' said Anna, handing over the key.

'Thanks again for letting us look around,' Pamela added, as if Mrs Graham was the house's authorised custodian.

'Find what yous were looking for, then?' said Mrs Graham, trying to and failing spectacularly at sounding disinterested.

'Just clearing up a couple of loose ends,' said Anna evasively. 'Our, uh, colleagues already did a commendably thorough job.'

'Just so long as there's nae chance of that arsehole getting off.' Mrs Graham's eyes flared in warning, as if she intended to hold Anna and Pamela personally responsible if it happened. 'You hear about it all the time – folk getting let go on technicalities just cos someone forgot tae take the right DNA scraping or what have you.'

'I can assure you, nothing like that's going to happen here,' said Anna.

'That's right,' said Pamela eagerly. 'We took all the right scrapings.'

Mrs Graham didn't seem to hear either of them. She was in full flow now, her voice becoming louder, her gestures more animated.

'Y'know, if yous are needing a character witness tae stand up in court and tell them all what a basturt he was, I'd be mair than happy tae volunteer.' She smiled briefly, clearly warming to the idea of taking the stand. 'Take it fae someone who's been aroon the block a few times – I had that man's number the moment I clapped eyes on him. That poor lassie never stood a chance.'

She tapped her glasses' frame and shot a meaningful look at Anna and Pamela. 'Some folk, you can just *tell*. You see it in their *eyes*. And he mair than lived doon tae expectations, that's for sure. First it's the shouting matches, then it's him leathering his missus black 'n' blue, then he's out there brawling in the street on Christmas Day like it's Saturday night on Sauchiehall Street, then—'

'Hold on,' said Anna, interrupting. 'What's this about brawling in the street?'

Mrs Graham seemed to realise she'd said more than she'd intended. She gave a dismissive shrug, attempting to affect an air of nonchalance.

'Just, you know, fights and such.'

'You mentioned Christmas Day, though,' Anna insisted. 'Something specific must have happened then – significant enough for the date to stick in your mind. What was it?'

'Now you're just putting words in my mouth. I never said anything about Christmas.'

'Um, you did, actually,' said Pamela tentatively.

Mrs Graham scowled at Pamela, who shrank back like she'd just been spat on.

'Now the two of yous are ganging up on me,' said Mrs Graham, her voice warbling with unconvincing emotion. 'I'm just a confused auld wumman. Yous ought tae be ashamed of yersels!'

'I don't think that's true at all,' said Anna levelly. 'I think you're a very sharp and observant individual. Nothing that goes on in this street passes you by – am I right? So I'm asking you, what happened on Christmas Day?'

Flattery seemed to do the trick. After some further half-hearted bluster, Mrs Graham relented.

'Awright, but only cos ye asked nicely. It was the middle of the afternoon. Billy was in his bed, resting up for his shift that night. Miserly shites wouldnae even give him bloody *Christmas Day* off. I was down the stair watching the telly. The adverts came on and I got up tae make a cup of tea, and that's when something out the windae caught my eye. I went over for a closer look.

'Leanne was standing at the bottom of her driveway, talking tae these two blokes. Big, burly men in suits and ties. Looked a bit like bouncers if ye ask me. One of them pushed her, and then her man came running out, like he was looking tae gie them both a square go. Never managed tae land more than a single punch, though, 'fore they beat him tae the ground. Gave him a right proper doing, so they did. It was – what's that word? Therapeutic.' She smiled briefly at this obviously fond memory.

'Then, after a minute or so, they stopped. Got bored, or tired, or mibby they just figured they'd made their point. One of them said something tae Leanne – jabbed a finger at her, like he was warning her. Then they got back in their motor and drove off, Sean still laying on the ground with his hands over his heid. And that's what happened.'

She shrugged and looked at them expectantly, as if opening up the floor for questions.

'You didn't mention any of this to the police,' said Anna. 'How come?'

It was just a guess, but an educated one. She knew, from the nature of Mrs Graham's initial slip and her evasiveness when questioned, that this was likely to be the first time she'd shared this story – with anyone she believed was connected to the investigation, at any rate.

The woman shrugged. 'I just never thought it was relevant.'

'I'm not sure that was for you to decide,' said Pamela.

Anna gave an involuntary wince. *Not helping, Pamela.*

Mrs Graham turned on Pamela, eyes flaring. 'I wanted tae make sure he got done, OK? I thought, if yous lot knew about this . . .'

'. . . it would muddy the waters too much,' finished Anna.

She understood all too well what Mrs Graham's thought process had been. From her description of the incident, it sounded like the men had been there for Leanne, with Sean only getting hurt because he'd got in their way. That Leanne had been threatened by a pair of violent thugs just a fortnight before her death was obviously pertinent information, and something that could well have taken some of the heat off Sean if it had been known about at the time.

Which, inevitably, begged the question: why hadn't *Sean* mentioned it either?

'I just didnae want yous getting sidetracked,' said Mrs Graham, her tone now verging on petulant. 'I know what yous lot can be like. Cannae see the wood for the trees half the time. One minute, it's all "pursuing multiple lines of enquiry". Then, next thing ye know, some basturt who everyone knows done it walks free cos there's too much "reasonable doubt".' Her expression hardened, and she shot a defiant glare in Anna's direction. 'Oh aye. I've watched enough murder dramas tae know how it goes.'

Anna met her gaze levelly. 'And that's your view of Sean, is it? He must have done it, because everyone just "knows"?'

She wasn't sure why she felt compelled to challenge that particular statement so vociferously, but it had stirred something deep within her. Perhaps it was the latent idealist in her – the bleeding-heart part of her that abhorred the thought of anyone, however unsavoury, being condemned by mob mentality; the notion that 'common sense', whatever *that* meant, somehow trumped the combined weight of knowledge, expertise and cold, hard evidence.

Or perhaps she was starting to accept the idea that Sean could be innocent after all.

Mrs Graham held Anna's gaze for a moment, staring at her belligerently. Anna could tell she was rattled; that she didn't know how to respond to her challenge.

'Well,' she said eventually, 'even if he didnae kill her, he still deserves tae rot after how he treated yon wee lassic. I'll no be shedding any tears if he never sees the light of day again – will *you?*'

Now she was throwing down a gauntlet of her own – one Anna had little desire to pick up, not least because a part of her very much agreed with the sentiment.

'Let's go,' she said to Pamela instead. 'I reckon we've heard everything we need to. Thanks again for talking to us, Mrs Graham.'

She set off down the path, Pamela trailing somewhat reluctantly behind her. As she reached the street, Anna halted and turned to face Mrs Graham, who hadn't moved from the doorway.

'Just one more question. Those men who beat Sean up – is there anything else you can tell us about them?'

Mrs Graham shrugged. She too was clearly done with this conversation.

'Nothing much. Just that they were professionals.'

'You mean because they wore suits?'

Mrs Graham gave a thin sneer. 'Naw, cos any eejit could tell they'd been sent tae do a job. And that job wasnae giving that basturt a kicking. Mark my words: they two left wae UNFINISHED BUSINESS.'

She gave a single, emphatic nod, then slammed the door and disappeared from view.

17

They remained in the neighbourhood for the next half-hour or so, knocking on several more doors and managing to persuade a handful of the street's residents to speak to them. However, none of them had anything of any real substance to impart. The consensus was consistent: Leanne had been friendly and good-natured, always finding the time for a how-d'you-do, while Sean was remembered as surly and standoffish – someone who, in the two years he and Leanne had lived there, had made no effort to ingratiate himself with his neighbours.

They headed back to the station and caught a train into town together. At Queen Street, they went their separate ways, Pamela remaining on the upper level to wait for a train back to Edinburgh while Anna headed downstairs for one bound for Partick. They parted company with a brisk hug and a promise from Anna to keep Pamela in the loop about any further developments.

The journey into town had passed mostly in silence, and what little they *had* said to one another had been about trivial matters with no connection to the case. Their conversation with Mrs Graham had clearly left them both with plenty to think about. Indeed, Anna was already formulating her next steps. Top of her to do list was trying to secure another meeting with Sean. She now felt she had enough new questions to justify a fresh visit – not least regarding the Christmas Day altercation and why he'd never mentioned it. Suspecting that she'd have an easier time getting Sean to talk if she went on her own, she made no mention of her plans to Pamela.

In the end, she didn't go back to work, barring a pitstop to her office to collect some paperwork. She'd decided enough of the afternoon had already disappeared for there to be no point. Instead, she resolved to work into the night if necessary to get herself caught up, then rang Zoe to tell her she was picking Jack up from school herself and that she and Sal could there-fore stand down. Zoe was clearly disappointed – she looked forward to the days when she had Jack almost as much as Jack did – but Anna was secretly rather relieved to be avoiding another potential encounter with Sal. Anything to delay having that conversation about getting her act together, which Anna *still* hadn't worked out how she was going to tackle.

It was after 10 p.m. by the time she finally finished her essay-marking, having delayed getting underway till Jack was safely in bed. Still wired from the day's events, and knowing she'd only toss and turn for hours if she went to bed now, she reached for her iPad and once more turned her attention to her ongoing quest to persuade Sean and Leanne's friends to talk to her.

She'd had little success with anyone from Sean's circle. With a single exception, all the Facebook friends she'd reached out to had either ignored her messages or sent short, sharp responses of the four-letter variety. The sole conversation she'd managed was a brief Messenger chat with Craig Leckie, a drinking buddy and occasional co-worker in his capacity as a fellow sparky-for-hire.

On the matter of the crime itself, Craig had little to say

besides recapitulating his shock. 'I can't believe he'd do something like that,' he wrote. 'Sean WORSHIPPED Leanne.'

If didn't feel much like a defence of Sean so much as a grim acknowledgement that you could never truly know what another person was truly capable of – even someone you counted as a friend. Either way, Anna doubted Sean would be calling Craig as a character witness at the trial – at least, not if he didn't want the whole thing to end in disaster.

She'd had marginally more success in her overtures to Leanne's friends and acquaintances. Of the few who'd actually responded, most had given her similarly short shrift to those in Sean's circle. One message, however, had borne fruit. After a lengthy silence, Natalie Lennox, the apparent best friend who'd mysteriously disappeared from Leanne's friends list a couple of months before her death, had finally responded to the DM Anna had sent her nearly a week ago. Over a couple of evenings of back-and-forth messaging, Anna had managed to get her to agree, in principle, to an in-person meeting. And, that night, just as Anna was finally preparing to wind down, her iPad pinged a message update from Natalie:

> Early lunch break tomorrow. Be at the hotel for 12 and I can give you 20 minutes.

18

Wednesday 9 March

Next morning, shortly before the appointed hour, Anna arrived outside the imposing, glass-fronted hotel, which stood on the corner of Argyle Street and Oswald Street, just across the road from Central Station. A couple of minutes after twelve, the woman who'd appeared in umpteen photos on Leanne's Facebook page came striding out of the front entrance in a navy-blue trouser suit, looking simultaneously harried and officious. She clocked Anna and gave a slight frown, no doubt making a mental comparison between her and the photo Anna had sent her to prove she was genuine. Anna greeted her with a small wave.

'Thanks for agreeing to see me,' said Anna, as Natalie drew alongside her. 'I know this is a bit weird, meeting up like this to talk about your friend.'

'Can we go somewhere else?' said Natalie, in a tone that perfectly matched her appearance. 'I don't fancy having my colleagues rubbernecking while I'm stood out here talking to . . . what was it you said you were?'

'A criminologist,' said Anna. 'And yes, of course. You lead the way.'

They set off down Oswald Street, making for the Broomielaw, the stretch of road that ran parallel to the Clyde between Jamaica Street and the Kingston Bridge.

'It was a bit surprising,' said Natalie as they walked, 'you getting in touch with me about Leanne after all this time. I kept waiting for that knock on the door from the police, but it never came. Is it normal policy, then – reaching out to folk on Facebook?'

'Not as such, no,' said Anna, who'd employed her usual technique of letting Natalie surmise that she worked for the police without explicitly stating it. 'Strictly speaking, this is something I'm following up on my own steam. But I'll be sure to pass anything pertinent on to the main inquiry.'

'Right enough, then,' said Natalie, clearly still somewhat bemused by the whole affair.

It wasn't so surprising, Anna reasoned, that the police hadn't been in touch with her. If Natalie and Leanne had cut one another out of their lives some months before Leanne's death, there was a good chance she simply wouldn't have been on their radar. The direction of a criminal investigation often depended heavily on what witnesses and family members chose to disclose. If no one had offered up Natalie's name, then she would naturally have fallen through the cracks. Anna wondered again what had come between the two women, but resolved to keep her powder dry for now.

They fell into silence until they arrived at the Broomielaw. Crossing at the traffic lights, Anna followed Natalie as she ducked under the old sign for the long-defunct Clyde Water Bus Service and came to halt at the railings overlooking the river.

'Aye,' said Natalie, once they'd dealt with the preliminaries, 'Leanne and me went back a ways. Same reggie class at All Saints

Secondary. We weren't pally right from the get-go, but over time we just sort of gravitated towards one another. You know how it is – find yourselves in the same place at the same time often enough and you start to become mutual co-dependents, I guess.'

'I know what you mean,' agreed Anna.

What Natalie had described reminded her a lot of herself and Zoe – only, with them, the mutual affection had been far more immediate and unapologetic than the sort of 'marriage of convenience' Natalie seemed to be alluding to.

'And you kept in touch after you left school?'

'That's right. I went to Clyde College to do my hospitality HNC while Lee found work right off the bat in a call centre. We were never top of the class, so it was obvious neither of us was destined for a life in the fast lane.'

'But you've done pretty well for yourself.' Anna gestured to Natalie's sharp suit.

'All hard graft,' Natalie retorted, as if to suggest Anna had merely fallen into her own lofty position. 'No one ever gave me a leg up. Some of us have no choice but to make our own luck in this world.'

Anna decided it would be wise to change the subject.

'I saw the photos of you and Leanne on her Facebook page. You obviously remained close for a good many years.'

'Aye, we were,' said Natalie, giving a brief smile of fond remembrance, which she hastily suppressed. 'She was always game for anything, that one. Dead impulsive. Seemed to have a limitless supply of energy. It'd be Friday night and I'd be knackered after spending all week on my feet but, five o'clock, come rain or shine, she'd be on the blower to me, saying, "Right, slag, where're we going dancing the night?"'

That didn't sound a whole lot like the Leanne that Jacqueline had described to her at the sports centre. What was it she'd said?

She was never much of a . . . what's that word? An initiator. Least till she'd got a few bevvies in her.

Then again, Anna supposed it wasn't that uncommon for different people to form radically different impressions of the same individual. We all, to some extent, tailored our behaviour depending on who we were with. She knew for a fact that she herself was a radically different person around Zoe than, say, her work colleagues. It didn't necessarily point to someone leading a double life.

'So you stayed in touch all through your twenties,' she said. 'You'll have known Sean, then?'

Natalie's expression clouded. 'Not well. I only met him a handful of times. Lee liked to keep her social life separate from her love life. She was funny that way.'

'What did you make of him?'

'Doesn't really matter what I made of him, does it? He killed her and he's banged up for it – for life, if there's any justice in this sorry world.'

'Probably not,' said Anna, trying to sound as reasonable as possible. 'But just humour me, if it's all the same. I'd like to know what you thought of him. How did they seem together? Did they seem like they were in love, or . . . ?'

Natalie sucked her teeth, considering the question – or, perhaps, whether or not to answer it.

'He seemed dead protective of her,' she said eventually. 'I can tell you *that* much. Like, any time I'd see them together, he'd always have his arm round her, like he was keeping her safe . . . or stopping her from getting away.'

Anna nodded. This much, at least, tallied with Jacqueline's account.

'And putting aside everything that's come to light since her death, at the time, did you ever feel you had any reason to fear for her safety? Did Sean ever seem like he could be a threat to her?'

Again, Natalie hesitated. When she next spoke, she chose her words carefully.

'I thought he wasn't a good fit for her. He was this big,

181

hard, alpha male type, and Lee . . . Lee was this delicate wee thing. She needed someone sensitive; someone who'd treat her like a princess. I figured he was always gonnae bring her a world of hurt, one way or another. I just never thought it'd be quite like this.'

They both fell silent, Natalie's words weighing heavily in the space between them.

'I met the guy she went with before Sean a couple of times,' said Natalie, breaking the silence. 'Thought he was way better suited to her. Big softie.' She gave a somewhat condescending smirk.

'Gerry, you mean?' said Anna. 'Big guy, red hair?'

'Aye. You know him?'

'He's Sean's brother.'

Natalie started to scoff, then saw Anna's expression. Her eyes widened in disbelief.

'Seriously? Jeez-*o*. I'd no idea. I mean, you wouldnae think it, would you? Two of them were like polar opposites. Hard to believe they share the same DNA.' She shook her head, letting out a nervous chortle. 'Christ almighty, *that's* gotta've been awkward. Y'know, the two of them, brothers, both knowing they'd had the same woman, knowing she'd be . . . y'know, comparing them.'

She hesitated, as if unsure whether to say what was on the tip of her tongue.

'Lee told me once Sean had a really small penis.'

'Oh,' said Anna, not sure how to respond to this information.

'She wasn't making fun of him or anything,' Natalie added quickly, clearly determined to preserve her dead friend's honour. 'Can't help the way God made you, right? Just, we'd had a few and had got down to comparing notches on our bedposts and it sort of slipped out. She was dead mortified basically as soon as she said it. Made me promise not to tell anyone. But everything made a bit more sense after that.'

'In what sense?'

'Well, I figured that's what was behind the tough guy act. Y'know – overcompensating.'

'People've accused me of being pushy cos I'm such a short-arse,' said Anna. 'I suppose it's not that different, really.'

'S'pose not.'

There was a further lull in their conversation. A pair of seagulls repeatedly divebombed the surface of the Clyde, shrieking at each other as they wheeled and swooped above the murky water, their cries echoing off the underside of the bridge above them.

'One of Leanne's colleagues told me she often turned up to work with bruises on her arms,' said Anna after a moment. 'Did . . . did you ever notice anything like that?'

Natalie hesitated before responding.

'Lee always used to bruise dead easily,' she said reluctantly, as if loath to cut Sean any slack. 'I remember it from when we were in school. Many's the time her legs'd be black and blue after PE. 'Course,' she went on quickly, 'just cos someone bruises easy doesnae mean they got those bruises by being clumsy.'

'No,' Anna agreed.

But it *was* another mitigating factor, she thought, and one which Sean's defence team really should be told about.

She hesitated again, bracing herself from the inevitable fallout from the question she'd been edging towards asking for a while now.

'Natalie . . . I noticed you and Leanne were no longer friends on Facebook.'

'Aren't we?' said Natalie, unconvincingly.

'No.'

'Oh.' A beat. 'Well, mibby it's automatic when someone dies.'

'It's not. Plus, her account's still friends with a bunch of other people.'

Natalie scoffed – a transparent attempt to appear uncon-
cerned. 'Prob'ly a glitch, then. Or one of us clicked the wrong
button by mistake. What difference does it make? The lassie's
dead, and I bet she'd want to think folk had better things to do
than go through her socials, seeing who she was friends with
and who she wasn't.'

'Natalie,' said Anna levelly, 'if something happened
between the two of you, you'll get no judgement about it from
me. I don't care who said what to who. I just want to know
what happened. Why'd she cut ties with you?'

A long, heavy silence elapsed, during which Natalie turned
her back on Anna and leant heavily on the railing, fists
clenched, gazing down into the depths of the water below. At
length, she inhaled heavily, the breath racking her entire body.
She held it in for a few seconds, then slowly released it.

'Actually,' she said, without turning to face Anna, 'I was the
one who cut ties with *her*.'

Anna waited for her to continue.

'I said Lee could be impulsive. She had . . . I guess you
might call it an addictive personality. About . . . let's see, when
did things start to open up again last year after lockdown?'

Anna thought about it. 'End of May?'

'Sounds about right. Around early June, then, the two of us
got invited to a get-together at a casino. It was a "friend of a
friend" sort of thing – celebrating the end of all the restrictions
in style. A bunch of us ended up going. I wasn't fussed, but Lee
couldn't get enough of it. The fruit machines, the poker tables
. . . it was like she'd discovered sex for the first time.

'She lost a ton of money that night, but she didn't care.
And, in the weeks after, all she'd talk about was when were we
going back? And I humoured her a couple of times. Tagged
along. Watched her fritter away great wads of cash on bets
only a complete mug would've made. Occasionally, she'd get
lucky and actually make back some of what she'd put in. But
that'd just spur her on to place bigger and bigger bets, and it

always ended the same way: her getting cleaned out and being asked by the bouncers to leave.'

She pushed herself upright and swung round to face Anna, her face drawn and grey.

'After a bit, I stopped going with her. Said I wasnae interested in watching her bankrupt herself. She yelled at me. Called me a fair-weather friend and a lot of other things I'll not repeat. She rang me up a couple of days later. Said she was sorry for the things she'd said. Told me she'd quit. That she wouldn't be going back there again.

'And it lasted . . . oh, I'd say about two weeks? Then I heard on the grapevine she'd been back. And I kept my mouth shut, cos I knew how she'd react if I said anything, and at that time I valued our friendship too much to put it at risk.'

'What ultimately changed?' Anna asked.

'Towards the end of last year, she came to me in a flap. Said she'd got herself into serious trouble. Owed a bunch of money in overdraft fees and credit card debt.' Natalie gave a curt, humourless laugh. 'And, like a big mook, I agreed to bail her out. Transferred her over a thousand quid. Now, I don't know about you, Professor, but in my line of work, a thousand quid's not just something you lose down the back of the sofa and don't miss. It took a serious chunk out of my savings. So when I heard she'd gone to the bank that very night, withdrawn the lot, then headed straight to the casino and blown it all on the roulette wheel, I'd reached my limit. I told her we were done. Said I wanted her out of my life. From now on, she'd have to find another sucker to pay for her addiction.

'That was the last time I ever saw her. I unfriended her on Facebook, deleted her number off my contacts, cut all ties with her so I couldnae be tempted to have a change of heart. Not that she couldnae've found a way to get in touch with me if she wanted to. But she never did. I never seen or heard from her again, till one of our mutuals rang to say she was dead.'

She fell silent, her arms slumping by her sides. Anna sensed that Natalie had reached the end of what she was prepared to say, and she couldn't think of anything else to ask her.

'Thanks for telling me this,' she said, rather uselessly. 'I know it can't have been easy to talk about.'

'It's not that,' said Natalie gruffly. 'It's not like it's any big secret – not really. Everyone knows we fell out. It's just . . . the way we left things. She went to her grave thinking I couldnae stand her. All those years we were pals, and we let it come apart over *money*.'

She spat the word out disgustedly, as if it came with a foul taste.

She shook her head. 'I should've tried harder,' she said – seemingly more to herself than to Anna. 'Should've made her get help.'

'From what you've told me,' said Anna gently, 'it sounds to me like she wouldn't have thanked you for it. If you'd pushed her, she'd only have resented you for it more. Sometimes . . .'

She stopped. Waited till she'd formulated the proper words before continuing.

'Sometimes, the kindest thing you can do, for the sake of both parties, is to walk away.'

Natalie's lips curled in a slight smile of gratitude, but Anna could tell she wasn't convinced. A moment passed, then she composed herself, straightening her back, throwing back her shoulders officiously.

'Well, I'd best be heading back. Dunno if you were keeping score, but I reckon that was way more than twenty minutes.'

She turned to go.

'Natalie, wait,' said Anna. 'One last question.'

Natalie stopped. She turned to Anna with an air of impatience.

'The casino you and Leanne went to – where was it?'

Natalie laughed. Shook her head humourlessly.

'You're looking at it.'

'Sorry?'

Turning to face the railing again, Natalie pointed across the water to the opposite shore.

'There.'

It took Anna a moment to realise what she was pointing at, but, eventually, her eyes settled on the squat, low-rise building just off to their right, its grey, utilitarian panelling contrasting with the large, cursive lettering fashioned in garish colours above the entrance:

The Palisades Casino.

19

Thursday 10 March

The following day, Anna received a letter from the hospital with the date and time of her repeat scan: Monday 28 March at 11:05 a.m. All things considered, it wasn't too long a wait. In fact, at bang on three weeks since her call from Maitland, it was about as swift a turnaround as she could have hoped for.

She noted the date in her diary, then tried her level best to put it out of her mind – something which proved to be considerably easier said than done. The headache which had started on Monday might have lessened somewhat in the intervening days, but it had never really gone away, meaning it served as an ever-present reminder of her situation, dogging her every step like her own personal black cloud.

At one o'clock, she finally had her long-overdue lunch date with Farah Hadid. Farah blethered away enthusiastically about some subject or other that had got her greatly exercised, and Anna gave what she hoped were the correct responses, but her mind was very much elsewhere, and afterwards she couldn't remember a single word of their conversation or even what it had been about.

In the afternoon, when she was between meetings, she contacted the Scottish Prison Service and started the ball rolling on arranging a fresh visit to Sean. She wasn't overly optimistic about Sean cooperating, not after how things had panned out last time – something for which, she was forced to admit, she bore more than her fair share of responsibility. But there was nothing to be lost by trying, and at least she'd now set the process in motion.

She also rang Pamela to update her about her conversation with Natalie. Perhaps predictably, Pamela was only too keen to latch onto Natalie's alternative explanation for Leanne's bruises. She was, it seemed, firmly back in the 'Sean didn't do it' camp. She was also intrigued to hear about Leanne's apparent gambling problem. Certainly, she said, it wasn't something Gerry had ever mentioned to her. But then, it wasn't as if it was the sort of thing Sean would have been likely to confide in him about – assuming he'd even been aware of Leanne's problem, and even if he and Gerry *had* still been on speaking terms at the time.

'Please, Anna,' she said, 'not one word to him about this. He's got enough on his plate at the moment.'

Anna, who'd had no intention of speaking to Gerry about this or indeed any other subject, nonetheless promised that the information wouldn't reach his ears from her, and ended the call, hoping her words had done enough to put Pamela's mind at ease.

After work, she headed through to Cowcaddens to pick up Jack from Zoe and Sal's. She tramped up the stairs towards the third floor, the question of Leanne's bruises continuing to absorb her. *Could* she have got them through innocent means after all? Many couples argued, she supposed, some more vociferously than others. It didn't necessarily mean Sean had been hitting her. But then she thought about Leanne's responses when she'd been questioned about them, all of which came straight out of the 'battered women's excuses' handbook: making excuses for him, insisting that he loved her really. And as Natalie had pointed out herself, the fact someone bruised easily didn't mean that *every* bruise they got came about by innocent means.

She rang the bell, which set off the now-familiar cacophony of furious barking inside the flat. A moment later, the door swung open to reveal Zoe, her eyes lighting up as she clocked Anna standing on the mat.

'Oh, *hey*, doll!' she gushed, clearly fired up about something. 'I've been *waiting* for ye tae get here. Listen, gonnae tell me—'

But the rest of what she said was drowned out as Captain Pugwash came barrelling out of the kitchen and down the corridor towards them. He came to a halt at Zoe's feet, bouncing up and down as he subjected Anna to his demented tirade of barks, not letting up until Zoe scooped him up and kissed his forehead, cradling him in her arms as she cooed at him.

'*What's* the matter, wee man? Oh, dear, oh deary *me* . . .'

At least she hasn't got him wearing one of those God-awful doggy outfits, Anna thought.

She followed Zoe into the flat.

'Where's Jack?'

Zoe pointed to the living room door, from beyond which cheerful, plinky-plonky music was playing.

'Through there on the Nintendo. Sal's letting him tan her arse at *Mario Kart*. Listen, d'ye fancy a coffee or something before ye drag him away? Feels like we've no had a proper catch-up in forever.'

Anna sensed that this offer was a pretext for something, presumably relating to whatever Zoe had been about to ask her on the doorstep before they were so rudely interrupted.

'Sure,' she said.

''Mon through, then. Just as long as ye don't mind bearing with me while I get his nibs something tae occupy him.'

They headed through to the kitchen, Zoe still cradling Captain Pugwash in her arms. She produced a rawhide bone chew from one of the cupboards, placed it in his mouth and set him down on the floor. He scampered over to his bed in the corner and settled down, then proceeded to attack the treat with gusto, emitting a litany of contented grunts and snorts.

'I thought he was supposed to be on a diet,' said Anna.

Zoe winced. 'Och, I know. And I try – I honestly do. But then he gets this look in his eyes, like . . .' She stuck out her bottom lip and wobbled it, making puppy-dog eyes at Anna. 'And I just have tae give in.'

She began to make coffee for them both, telling Anna this and that about her day as she worked. Anna, seated at the kitchen table, nodded, making appropriate noises at the correct intervals, but her mind was once again elsewhere and she knew she wasn't taking in a word Zoe was saying.

Zoe finished making their drinks and settled into the seat opposite from Anna, sliding a steaming mug across the table to her.

'There ye go – thick enough tae eat affy a spoon. So listen, doll – whit's this about you getting a visit fae the polis?'

'Come again?'

'Jacko tells me ye had a lady cop over the other night. Wouldnae stop banging on about it. Apparently the two o' yese were in conference for pure *ages*.'

'Oh really? Did he also tell you he came charging out to greet her with no clothes on?'

Zoe cackled. 'Naw, he left that detail out.' She leant across the table intently. 'So c'mon – what's the skinny? Don't tell me ye're working wae them again. I thought ye'd swore off that after last time.'

'Not in so many words.'

'Well, what, then?'

Reluctantly, Anna explained to Zoe about the Leanne McColm case and Pamela's strong-arming of her into looking into it, then proceeded to give her a brief rundown of her activities to date. Zoe listened intently, her expression shifting between disapproval and fascination multiple times throughout the account. Anna was just getting into her conversation with Natalie Lennox when the door opened and Sal wandered in.

'Hey, babe,' she called to Zoe.

'Hey, sausage,' Zoe responded.

'Hi, Sal,' said Anna, feeling a pang of unease as she remembered her promise to Zoe and her continued failure to act on it.

'Game over?' said Zoe, craning her neck to look up at her girlfriend.

'Finito.'

'Take it Jacko won?'

Sal grinned. 'Whooped me big time, as per. He's getting in another round himself before he leaves.' She glanced at Anna uncertainly. 'Hope that's OK . . . ?'

'Yeah, it's fine,' said Anna, suspecting she probably didn't have much choice in the matter – not if she wanted to get Jack out the door tonight without a tantrum.

Sal ran a hand through her hair, which, lately, she'd been cultivating into a mullet – currently olive-green with purple highlights.

'Listen, don't mind me. I'm just gonna make myself something to eat before I pass out from malnutrition. Yous carry on with whatever you were talking about before I came barging in.'

As she crossed to the fridge, Zoe reached across and gave her backside a playful squeeze. Sal gave a shriek and darted out of range with a grin. Anna, who'd had a ringside seat to the whole display, sipped her coffee and pretended not to have noticed. Some people had no shame when it came to PDA, meaning all the discomfort fell on the observer – a most unfair state of affairs, she thought.

'Ye were saying . . . ?' Zoe prompted her, as Sal deftly stepped over Captain Pugwash, briefly stooping to rub his ears as he continued to gnaw on his chew.

'Was I?' said Anna, shaken from her thoughts. She tried to remember where she'd got to in her account. 'Right – so it turns out Leanne had what might be described as a serious compulsion for frittering away her own and other people's money. Natalie said she used to drag her along to the Palisades Casino down by the quay.'

'What's this about the Palisades?' Sal mumbled, turning from the fridge with a thick hunk of Hovis Soft White clenched between her teeth.

'Just a place that came up in relation to someone whose death I'm looking into,' said Anna – aware, as she spoke, just what an utterly absurd sentence that actually was.

Sal, however, seemed to take it in her stride. She nodded philosophically, as if private citizens investigating suspicious deaths was something that went on all the time.

'And you reckon . . .'

She paused to extract the slice of bread from her mouth before beginning again.

'And you reckon her death's got something to do with the casino?'

Anna considered the question. 'On balance, probably not. But it's an angle the police don't seem to have considered. Not yet, at any rate.'

'Been to check it out?'

'Not yet, no.'

'Only my old mucker Snudge used to work there. Might still do.'

Zoe cackled in disbelief. 'Snudge? Is that his name?'

Sal grinned. 'I know – mental, right? But he's a sound guy. Him and me go way back.' She looked at Anna. Shrugged.

'Could be an in's all I'm saying. Don't mind hitting him up for you, if you want me to.'

Anna could feel herself becoming flustered. She hadn't expected to be put on the spot like this.

'Um . . . I mean, sure if you—'

'It's cool,' said Sal.

She'd already plonked the bread on the countertop and had her phone in her hands, thumbs dancing as she composed a message at blistering speed. Less than twenty seconds after she'd sent it, it pinged with a response. Sal read the message on the screen and grinned.

'It's on. Snudge says he'll meet us on his break tonight at half eight.'

Zoe turned to Anna with a grin of her own. '*That* was dead easy, wun't it? Is this one no worth her weight in gold?'

Sal beamed at the compliment, before grabbing a jar of peanut butter from the fridge and beginning to spread massive quantities of it on her bread.

Anna, dazed at the speed with which things had moved, could only nod distantly. She hated it when plans involving her were made on the fly, especially when she hadn't been adequately consulted about them beforehand – and doubly so on nights like this, when she was tired and worried about whatever was going on inside her head and wanted nothing more than to curl up under a blanket in her own home and listen to something soothing on the radio.

'It's just,' she began weakly, 'I haven't got anything arranged for Jack . . .'

'Ach, away 'n' shite,' said Zoe. 'Me and Jacko'll hold the fort while yous are away.'

Anna racked her brains for another reason to object, but she couldn't think of any. With a weary smile, she admitted defeat.

'Thanks, Zo. And thank *you*, Sal. What would I do without the two of you, huh?'

'I'll go let Jack know you'll not be prising him away from Mario for a few hours yet,' said Sal.

She ducked out, the slice of bread, now thickly buttered, once more clenched between her teeth.

Anna sat there at the table, slowly reconciling herself to the fact that her evening would not be going as originally planned. And it wasn't that she was ungrateful. On the contrary, she knew she couldn't very well pass up this golden opportunity. People who worked at an establishment designed to part people with their money by any means necessary might not be too inclined to talk to a stranger about the goings-on within their walls, but someone with a personal connection to one of those employees could prove to be an unexpected boon.

She realised Zoe was looking at her, smiling at her in a manner that might best be described as persistent.

'What?'

'That'll be nice, won't it – the two of yese, off on a mission the gether?'

'Um . . . yeah, I guess.'

'Give yese a chance tae have a blether . . . talk some things over . . .'

Still smiling, Zoe gave an encouraging nod, clearly trying to nudge Anna towards some unspoken goal.

It took Anna longer than it probably should have to understand what Zoe was driving at, but when she did, she felt like kicking herself. Of course – her promise to talk some sense into Sal about her lack of direction in life. Partly by design and partly because it was simply how things had panned out, she'd managed, so far, to steer clear of any circumstances that would have lent themselves to such a conversation, only to have blundered into the perfect opportunity – and one partly of her own making at that.

She managed a strained smile. 'Yeah. Lots to talk about.'

20

They set off just after eight, Anna behind the wheel of her Skoda, Sal beside her in the passenger seat, beaming at what she evidently regarded as an unexpected treat. To avoid the slow crawl through the city centre, Anna took a more round-about route, cutting along West Graham Street before joining the M8 as it curved south towards the river.

The first half of the journey took place in almost total silence, apart from Sal humming a merry little ditty and slapping out a rhythm on her thighs. This awkwardness between them was nothing new. Anna had never been quite sure what to make of Sal. She was never less than effusively pleasant to Anna, but they always seemed to dance around one another, regarding each other if not with outright suspicion, then definitely with a degree of uncertainty. It didn't have to be this way, Anna told herself. She and Zoe were, after all, the living embodiment of that, well-worn adage, 'opposites attract'. With Sal, though, no such spark seemed to exist, and she'd been unable to force one into being for love nor money. They both loved Zoe, but that was where any similarity between them ended.

As they passed the Mitchell Library, Sal broke the silence.

'So listen, how come I never see you round my sister's place anymore?'

'What d'you mean?'

Sal shrugged. 'Just, you and her used to be dead tight for a while, but now, all of a sudden, it's like you're total strangers. Did you guys have a falling out or something? I tried talking to Jen about it, but she just changes the subject.'

'No, nothing like that,' said Anna. 'We've both just . . . you know, been really busy with work and whatnot.'

She thought back to the last conversation she'd had with Jen Brinkley, sitting in Jen's car on a warm summer's night just over six months ago, minutes after their shared investigation into Hugh MacLeish's suicide had reached its bloody conclusion. At the time, they'd both agreed that it was for the best if they didn't have any further contact for a while. Anna wasn't sure how long Jen's idea of 'a while' was and had more or less been waiting for her to declare this period of enforced separation over.

She glanced across at Sal, who, having seemingly accepted this explanation at face value, was gazing idly out of the window, once again humming to herself.

Come on, Anna. Time for you to make good on your promise.

She cleared her throat.

'You're, uh, still working at Costa, aren't you?' she said, cringing inwardly at the clunkiness of this attempted segue.

'Uh-huh.' Sal halted her ditty long enough to respond, then resumed it immediately.

'How long is it you've been there again?'

Smooth, Anna, real smooth. You should do this interrogation thing for a living.

'Since, oh, spring of 2018, I think?'

'That's quite a shift to have put in at the same place. And you've always been part-time?'

'Uh-huh,' said Sal cheerfully. 'Longest I've stuck with any

job. They're a cracking bunch there. We have a right old laugh, and the hours suit me great.'

'You've never been tempted to put yourself forward for a supervisor's role? I mean, you've obviously got the experience by now . . .'

Sal screwed up her face in disgust. 'A promotion? Not on your nelly! All that added responsibility? And the extra hours, cutting into my free time?' She laughed good-naturedly, as if Anna had just cracked a particularly funny joke. 'No *thanks*!'

Recognising that this approach had been comprehensively shut down, Anna made no further attempt to raise the subject, and they settled into silence again. A minute or so later, Sal began to hum and tap her thighs once more.

They parked at the end of the busy car park opposite the casino and made their way across the concrete towards the front entrance. As they walked side by side, Anna realised she and Sal must look like quite a pair: her still in her smart work clothes, Sal in dungarees and a long-sleeved T-shirt with holes in it. Anna had never understood the appeal of dungarees. They must be an absolute faff when you needed to take a piss, or have a shit.

A thickset security guard in a heavy fleece stood at the door, the coil of an earpiece running up the side of his trunk-like neck. Anna found herself instinctively lowering her eyes to the ground, feeling he would somehow sense that she wasn't here for recreational purposes. Sal, however, strode boldly on ahead, nodding cheerily to the man as she passed him.

'Ladies,' he nodded back.

Inside, the air was warm and thick, filled with the low murmur of conversation and the mechanical trill of slot machines. They passed the reception desk, staffed by a man and a woman in matching white shirt and black tie outfits, and headed onto the main floor. There, pools of light in the otherwise dimly lit space highlighted the various gaming tables and the ubiquitous rows of slot machines. Despite the luxurious furnishings and obvious efforts to mark this out as a high-class establishment, the place had a curiously stagnant feel to it, the handful of patrons only serving to underscore how cavernous and devoid of life the place was.

As they stood there, eyeing up the sight before them, a young man of about Sal's age emerged from the shadows and came loping towards them. He was tall and gangly, with a shock of dark, curly hair and a pronounced Adam's apple, and wore a similar outfit to the pair at reception.

'Well, well!' he boomed, in a voice far deeper than his skinny frame ought to have been able to accommodate. 'The Sallie Army has arrived! How's it goin', ya absolute mental rocket?'

'It's going great, ya big vagina!' Sal yelled back, grinning.

The young man, who Anna concluded could only be Snudge, bounded over and joined Sal in a boisterous hug. After a moment, they released each other. Snudge looked Sal up and down.

'You're looking good, Salvation. Take it you're still a great big massive lesbo, then?'

'Last time I checked,' said Sal cheerfully.

Snudge nodded approvingly. 'Good stuff. Good stuff.'

Sal thumbed over her shoulder towards Anna. 'Snudge, this is the woman I told you about.'

Anna, who until now had been standing a little back, feeling a bit like a spare part amid this joyful reunion, gave Snudge a nod of acknowledgement, not really sure how to introduce herself.

'Awright?' Snudge nodded back at her, then turned to Sal again, lowering his voice.

'And you're saying she just wants to ask some questions? That's all?' He sounded somewhat incredulous.

'That's all,' confirmed Sal. 'She's not with the rozzers –
promise.'

'Pinkie promise?' He held up the finger in question.

Sal sighed. 'What are you *like?*'

She nonetheless extended her own pinkie, and they 'shook'
on it. As they released each other's fingers, Sal turned to Anna
with a theatrical eyeroll.

'Seriously, this guy.'

'Ach, she wouldnae have me any other way,' said Snudge.
He clapped his hands together. 'Right, then, that's me all yours
for the foreseeable.' He glanced at Sal. 'You sticking around,
or . . . ?'

'Actually,' said Sal, 'think I'm gonna leave you guys to it.'

'You sure?' said Anna, not altogether certain how she felt
about being left alone with this unfamiliar and, to her mind,
intimidatingly gregarious young man.

'Yeah, plenty round here to amuse myself. Thought I might
check out the fruit machines; see if they're all they're cracked
up to be. Come and find me when you're done, yeah?'

Before Anna could object, Sal clicked her tongue and shot
them finger guns, then turned and slouched off towards the
glowing displays.

'Catch ya later, Salvation!' Snudge called.

Sal responded by raising her middle finger behind her as
she kept walking.

Anna watched her go, then turned to face Snudge, who
suddenly seemed a good deal more taciturn now that it was
just the two of them.

He shrugged at her. 'So, what do I call you?'

'Anna,' she said, deciding that would do for now.

'And what is it you're wanting to know?'

Anna opened her mouth to respond, then changed her
mind. The sounds from the slot machines were doing her
head in.

'Actually, is there somewhere we can go? Somewhere . . .'

'Somewhere a bit less sensory overloady, ya mean? Yeah, follow me.'

They set off, Snudge leading the way.

'The place seems quiet tonight,' Anna observed.

'Give it time. 'S only half-eight on a weeknight. Won't get properly jumping till getting on for midnight, when the zombies rise to walk the earth.'

He led the way over to the bar area, located in a secluded alcove far enough away from the machines to limit their noise to a barely audible thrum. Having demurred when Sean asked her if she wanted anything, Anna waited at a banquette table in the corner as he headed over to the bar to procure a refreshment for himself. He soon returned, can of Coke in hand.

'So,' he said, 'you were saying . . . ?'

'I'm trying to find out about someone who used to come here as a customer. It's possible you might remember her.'

She took out her phone and showed him a picture of Leanne from her Facebook page. Snudge examined it.

'Yeah, yeah, I recognise her. The lassie who died, right?'

'That's right. Her name was Leanne McColm. So she was in here a lot?'

'All the time, aye. Served her drinks a couple of times. Nice lady. Always tipped well.'

He popped the tab on his Coke and took a large swig.

'And she generally came here with a friend, or . . .'

'Sometimes she had a gal pal or two with her, yeah. Not always the same ones. But a lot of the time, she was on her own – 'specially the last couple of months before she . . .'

He trailed off, contemplating the Coke can as he spun it in his hands. After a moment, he continued.

'I always thought she looked dead lonely – this wee slip of a woman, wandering about on her lonesome ownsome. Couldn't help thinking she looked like easy prey. And if *I* was thinking it, you can bet your bottom dollar others were as well. Others a whole lot less upstanding than yer old pal Snudge.'

Anna frowned. 'How do you mean?'

'Place like this, someone on their own, someone who doesn't look like they know what they're doing – they're vulnerable to getting took advantage of. And I don't mean the staff. I know places like this get a bad rap, but we've got dead strict rules about influencing the punters; about not encouraging them to spend more than they can afford. I'm talking about external forces.'

Anna felt herself growing impatient. 'And just who *are* these external forces?'

'She was kind of notorious,' said Snudge, ignoring her. 'Folk knew what an easy mark she was. Someone who'd never turn down a chance to make back her losses, even if any eejit could see the odds against her were, like, a gazillion to one. After a while, a bunch of us started feeling dead sorry for her. I mean, you know the saying – the house always wins – but after a while, you start to think, is this even ethical, letting her lose everything, over and over and over?' He glanced up at Anna. 'D'you think some folk are just born unlucky?'

'I'm not sure luck's something I believe in,' said Anna carefully. 'But no,' she conceded, 'I don't think misfortune is something that's equitably distributed. Some people invariably end up getting more than their fair share.'

'Well, I *do* believe in luck,' said Snudge, 'and some folk seem to have it all, while others get the complete opposite. Working in this place, I seen too much evidence of both not to. You mind the cat in that cartoon, *Bad Luck Blackie*? Poor wee soul couldnae catch a break. That's what I always thought of each time I saw her getting cleaned out like clockwork.'

'You said something about "external forces" earlier,' Anna pressed him once again. 'Could you be a bit more specific?'

Snudge didn't answer immediately. He sucked in his cheeks, looking this way and that. Anna was aware of his left leg jiggling under the table.

Eventually, he seemed to come to a decision.

'All right, look. There's folk who stand to make big money out of the ones who can't catch a break but can't tear themselves away from this place. One night, I seen your woman get completely rinsed at the roulette table. Bet the house and lost everything. Left looking like . . . I dunno, like this emptied-out shell with nothing left inside her. Then, later, after my shift ended and I was leaving, I saw her round the back of the building, talking to one of Jonny Lawlor's men.'

'Who's he?' asked Anna.

Snudge stared at her incredulously, as if he couldn't believe she was even asking this. When Anna continued to stare back at him expectantly, he shook his head in disbelief before speaking.

'He's a loan shark, and a majorly nasty one at that. Small-time – otherwise he wouldn't need to have his lackeys hang round places like this, hustling for business. But that doesn't make him any less bad news. They've been told heaven alone knows how many times to stay away from here. To stop giving the clients hassle. But they just take the piss. They bugger off for a week or two, then they're back, like nothing ever happened. And what's the likes of me supposed to do? Hardly gonna confront them myself, am I? Like, I'm quite attached to my kneecaps. I don't need the aggro.

'Anyway,' he went on, 'next week, your woman's back, flush with cash and acting like she just won the EuroMillions. And straight away, I knew what happened. I thought, "Poor cow. He's got her by the short and curlies." Cos when Jonny Lawlor gives you a loan, he's not doing you a favour. He's *buying* you.'

A sudden image flashed into Anna's mind of the two burly men in suits and ties squaring up to Leanne outside her house on Christmas Day. Of Sean intervening and being beaten to the ground. She remembered, too, Mrs Graham's final words on the subject.

Mark my words: they two left wae UNFINISHED BUSINESS.

She cleared her throat. 'Let's say, theoretically, this Lawlor had lent someone money and they couldn't – or *wouldn't* – pay it back . . . how would he respond?'

Snudge gave a grim smile. 'Well, let's just say I wouldn't put it past him to – y'know.'

He dragged a finger across his throat, making a *krkk* sound.

Anna gave him a sceptical look. It wasn't so much that she didn't *want* to believe him. Illegal money lenders, she knew, preyed upon the poor and the desperate, and certainly weren't above making life seriously uncomfortable for their victims. But the notion that any loan shark, especially a small-time one, routinely went around deep-sixing those who'd fallen behind on their repayments was so utterly far-fetched as to be almost laughable.

She tried to rearrange her face in a way that hid her incredulity.

'And have you ever *met* anyone Lawlor – y'know . . . ?' She mimicked his throat-slashing gesture.

She wasn't expecting a serious response, but Snudge simply stared back at her, his expression deadly serious.

'Met that Leanne, didn't I? And *she's* dead, right?'

She supposed she'd walked right into that one.

'Did you ever consider telling any of this to the police?' she asked.

Snudge sucked his teeth. 'I mean, I *considered* it, then I decided it wouldn't be conducive to my wellbeing.'

'What do you mean?'

'Just . . .'

Snudge hesitated, then leant in, beckoning Anna closer.

'Look, a few years back, I got done for possession, all right? It was a piddly wee amount, barely enough to dust the end of a key. Still enough to land me with a criminal record, but. Since then, let's just say myself and the authorities don't exactly see eye to eye. All's I want's to keep my head down and my nose clean – literally *and* figuratively. That can't be too much to ask, surely?'

Anna decided not to press the matter. She leaned back in her seat, mulling over this latest development. It seemed somehow significant that, in the last forty-eight hours, all her enquiries had seemingly brought her to this juncture. It was, she supposed, possible that the idea merely appealed to her because it represented a fresh development in an investigation in which, for so long, all roads had seemed to lead in one direction: Sean. However, she couldn't deny that a supposedly ruthless loan shark from whom Leanne had apparently borrowed money and who might well have sent his enforcers to her door to threaten her mere days before her death deserved, at the very least, to be treated as a person of interest.

At length, she broke the silence that had settled around their table.

'Supposing I wanted to find Lawlor . . .'

Snudge looked up sharply, practically choking on the dregs of his Coke. He stared at her, aghast.

'Have you got a death wish or something?'

'I only said "supposing",' said Anna, a tad defensively.

'Seriously, have you listened to a word I said? The man's bad fucking news. He'd chop you into pieces and feed you to the fishies like *that*.' He snapped his fingers. 'Believe me, you don't *want* to find this guy.'

'But supposing I did.'

Snudge stared at her, exasperated and unable to believe what he was hearing. Anna met his gaze, unblinking.

Finally, his shoulders slumped.

'Fine. It's pretty well-known round these parts that he drinks at O'Leary's on Saltmarket. But if I was you . . .'

'But you're not,' said Anna simply.

'No,' said Snudge, and it seemed to her that he felt profoundly grateful for this state of affairs.

. . .

Anna and Snudge headed back the way they'd come. As they reached the outer fringe of the gaming floor, Sal materialised from over by the slot machines and came bounding over to them, in obvious high spirits.

'That you done, then?' she asked, practically bouncing up and down with pent-up energy.

'That's us done,' Anna confirmed. 'Did you, uh, have a nice time, then?'

Sal grinned. 'Yeah, smashing. I can see why folk bankrupt themselves in a place like this. It's dead moreish.'

'End up getting lucky?' said Snudge, markedly more subdued now than he had been during their previous interaction.

Sal laughed. 'Nah, blew the equivalent of a week's wages. But hey – ya win some, ya lose some. Sure what you're really paying for is the experience.'

Anna's heart sank. So much for encouraging her to adopt a more responsible outlook towards life!

'Well,' said Snudge, addressing them both, 'much as I'd love to stay and shoot the breeze, duty calls. Was nice running into ya again, Salvation. Try not to be a stranger, now.'

'Right back atcha, ya big minge.'

Snudge flashed a grin, which died on his lips as his eyes met Anna's, and he shot her a silent, warning look. Anna, pretending not to understand the meaning behind it, nodded a farewell to him, then took Sal by the arm and steered her towards the exit.

'So,' she said, as they headed back through the reception area, 'I have to ask – him calling you "Salvation", is that some sort of in-joke or something?'

Sal sighed heavily. 'No, that's just my name.'

Anna waited for her to say she was joking.

'No, seriously, it *is*. My dad had this whole New Age spiritual awakening phase while I was still in utero. Didn't last, but it meant I got landed with Salvation while at least Jenelle's kind of an exotic twist on an old classic. But Snudge found out and made it his mission to make sure I'd never hear the end of it.'

'You couldn't just use your middle name?'

'My middle name's Guinevere,' said Sal flatly. 'So no, I couldn't. Still,' she declared philosophically, as they emerged into the night air, 'could be worse. His real name's Nigel.' She screwed up her face in disgust. 'Can you imagine? Wouldn't wish that shite on my worst enemy.'

As they drove back to Cowcaddens, Anna furnished Sal with a condensed version of her conversation with Snudge. Sal was positively buzzing from the whole experience, expounding with great enthusiasm on the many and varied delights of Rainbow Riches, and Anna wondered if it was possible to catch the gambling bug from a single encounter. If so, she'd potentially just made things a whole lot worse from the perspective of imbuing Sal with a sense of responsibility.

'Out of interest,' she said, 'you and Snudge – how is it you know each other?'

'We were at college together,' said Sal. 'Used to spend hours goofing off in the back row together while some poor schmuck was trying to teach us proper life skills.' She considered this. 'Hmm. Prob'ly got something to do with why our grades were both so shocking.'

For a moment, Anna said nothing. Then, reluctantly concluding that she couldn't let the evening pass by without trying once more to engage Sal about her future, she spoke again.

'And have you ever thought about going back?'

'Into education, y'mean?' Sal didn't even try to hide her incredulity.

'Yeah – finish what you started. Get some qualifications to buff up the old CV.'

Sal snorted, as if repelled by the very idea. 'Pfff! *Fuck* no!

Go back to school in my thirties? Can't think of anything sadder.' She seemed to remember who she was talking to. 'Um . . . no offence.'

'None taken,' said Anna, and resolved to leave it at that.

Back at the flat, Anna couldn't find it in herself to tell Zoe about her failure. She studiously avoided ending up alone with her, responding to her questions about the trip to the Palisades in the most cursory fashion, telling her Sal could fill her in on the details. She insisted on leaving more or less immediately, ignoring Jack's protestations and Zoe's efforts to point out that, if he wanted to stay, his bed in the spare room was all made up and ready for him.

As they headed for the door, Jack dragging his feet and wearing a mutinous expression, Anna pretended not to notice Zoe's questioning looks and repeated attempts to catch her eye.

At least I tried, she told herself, as she slunk off into the night.

21

Friday 11 March

O'Leary's Traditional Pub sat at the bottom end of Saltmarket, on the corner of Greendyke Street and within spitting distance of the High Court – which was either bitingly ironic or a blatant provocation.

Anna gazed up at the façade – the name in chipped gold lettering against peeling black paint; the windows clouded with grime and nicotine residue. The place looked like a throwback to the 1980s, before all the decades of accumulated soot and other assorted grot were sandblasted off the buildings and the place was dragged kicking and screaming into the tail end of the twentieth century.

She'd thought long and hard about whether to come here today. On the face of it, it seemed foolhardy, to put it mildly – walking alone into a hard man's pub looking for a loan shark famed for his take-no-prisoners approach to recouping his debts. And, she supposed, there were other, less reckless approaches to information-gathering than marching alone into the belly of the beast to demand answers. But patience had never been her strong suit, and she had no desire to waste hours or perhaps even days being given the runaround by people who knew as much as – or potentially even less than – Snudge. She remained convinced that Snudge had been exaggerating Lawlor's bogeyman status; that it was unlikely he'd killed Leanne, or *had* her killed, simply because she owed him money. But if there was even the faintest chance Lawlor knew something, then she was duty-bound not to leave this particular stone unturned.

And so, this morning, she'd woken from a fitful night's sleep determined to fit in a visit between finishing work at one and collecting Jack from school at 3:15.

She'd considered asking someone to come with her – strength in numbers and all that – before reluctantly concluding that everyone she could realistically have called on was either at work or, for one reason or another, someone she didn't want to involve. It would be useful, she supposed, in situations like this, if she had more male friends – particularly those of the burly, brick shithouse variety. Farah's boyfriend, Émile, who worked as a private personal trainer and was over six feet tall, might just about fit the bill, but she didn't feel she knew him well enough to rope him into something like this.

Ultimately, she'd decided she had little to fear in broad daylight. At least, that's what she kept telling herself. The odds of her finding Lawlor just sitting there waiting for her were, she knew, slim. And even if he *was* there, it seemed unlikely he'd go full gangster mode on her in a public place, in front of multiple witnesses, for merely asking questions. Plus, she had her personal alarm with her. One press of the button and the whole street would be suffering from tinnitus for a week. If it was enough to repel a would-be mugger or rapist, it was enough to repel a loan shark.

She steeled herself and headed inside.

The smell hit her first – thick, dizzying, a mixture of stale beer and even staler sweat. The carpet was worn and sticky underfoot, what little light there was coming courtesy of a couple of dim overhead bulbs and the paltry amount that managed to filter through the grubby front windows. A wall-mounted TV was screening horse-racing on mute, the handful of punters – exclusively male and down-at-heel – paying it scant attention. Near the back, a crowd of regulars sat huddled round a table, muttering in a fashion that was presumably friendly but definitely didn't sound it. A few others propped up the bar, while a solitary figure in an RAF-style flying jacket sat at a table towards the back, poring over a newspaper and peri-odically nourishing himself from a plate of chips drowned in mayonnaise. He was small, bald-headed and beady-eyed – one of those classic Glasgow scrappers who could be anywhere between thirty-five and sixty-five.

Acting far more boldly than she felt, Anna strode over to the bar, where the bartender – a squarish woman of similarly indeterminate age, sporting a face like a clenched fist – looked up.

'Sure ye're in the right place, darlin'?' she growled, in a voice deeper than that of several of the men Anna knew.

'Oh yes, I think so,' said Anna pleasantly, dialling up the 'just popping into Waitrose' energy and pretending not to have noticed the woman's undisguised hostility. 'This is O'Leary's Pub, isn't it?'

''S what it says above the door,' the bartender grunted.

'Well, in that case, I think I'll have something to drink.'

The bartender stared at her for several seconds, as if she was convinced this was a wind-up and that, any moment now, Anna would drop the act. When she didn't, the woman scoffed to herself and shook her head.

'What'll it be, then?'

'I'll take a lemonade.'

'A *lemonade*?'

The woman's tone couldn't have been more contemptuous if she'd tried.

'Yes,' said Anna.

The woman held her gaze for a moment longer, then abruptly turned towards the small portable fridge behind the bar, stocked with a variety of 250ml bottles. Anna watched as she selected a bottle of off-brand lemonade and poured it into a glass that looked almost as cloudy as the windows. No ice. She turned back to Anna, slamming the glass down on the counter.

'Three fifty.'

It was an outrageous amount for such a small serving, but Anna wasn't going to argue. She fished a fiver out of her wallet and handed it over, neither expecting change nor receiving it.

'Thanks.'

She slid the glass towards her and began to idly trace the rim with her index finger.

'So listen,' she said, as casually as possible, 'I was wondering if you could help me. I heard on the grapevine that there's a man who drinks here who, in these parts, is the person to see about money issues. Jonny somebody. Jonny . . . Lawlor?'

The barmaid gazed back at her, deadpan.

'Never heard of him.'

Anna affected a look of surprise. 'You're sure about that? Only I had it on good authority he was a regular fixture here.'

The woman met her gaze stonily, giving no reaction whatsoever to this statement.

Anna glanced towards the various punters. 'What about this lot?' she said, raising her voice just enough for those nearest to her to hear. 'D'you reckon any of *them* know where I can find Jonny Lawlor?'

The bald man in the corner gave what sounded like a chuckle and popped another chip in his mouth. The other patrons didn't so much as look up.

'Look, lady,' snarled the bartender, 'someone's been filling yer heid wae a load of shite. There's no Jonny Lawlor here. Never has been.'

Anna held her gaze. The woman stared back at her stonily,

her desire for Anna to leave unmistakable. Anna had no intention of giving her – or any of the other decidedly unhelpful people in this place – the satisfaction.

'I'll just sit anywhere, shall I?'

Not waiting for an answer, she took her drink and made her way over to a vacant table, feeling the eyes of every person in the building on her. The silence that she belatedly realised had fallen on the pub continued for upwards of a minute, and, though she steadfastly avoided looking, she was sure everyone was still glowering at her with naked hostility. Then, as if by unspoken agreement, the low murmur of conversation resumed and the mood grew marginally less oppressive.

As Anna sat there, sipping from her glass and trying not to think about where it had been, she ruminated on the challenges facing her. Top of the list was the fact that she had absolutely no idea what Lawlor looked like. She'd searched for him online the previous night but had been unable to find a single scrap of information about him, let alone a picture of him. He certainly appeared to be a man with a determination to avoid the limelight. She idly wondered whether he even existed. It was always possible, she supposed, that Snudge had made him up, or had simply been passing on Chinese whispers. For all she knew, he could be one of those fictional bogeymen people warned each other about, or an amalgamation of multiple real figures – like Sawney Bean and his cannibal brood, dreamt up by the English press to spread Scotophobic sentiment in the fifteenth century.

Time passed. The small man finished his chips, tucked his paper under his arm and left without a word. Otherwise, the lineup remained unchanged. The crowd at the table near the back continued their low, borderline snarling conversation. The bartender polished glasses with a cloth that looked as filthy as the receptacles she was supposed to be cleaning.

When Anna had been there for over an hour and a quarter, she reluctantly concluded that Lawlor wasn't planning on making an appearance anytime soon. Not that she'd have recognised him if she did, but the fact that no one new had come in since she'd arrived meant she at least knew he hadn't materialised in all the time she'd been sitting here. Besides, it would soon be time to pick Jack up from school.

She got to her feet and left without a word.

She emerged onto the street. The sky, which had exhibited the odd sliver of blue amongst the white, puffy clouds when she went in, had turned grey and overcast, the atmosphere almost as leaden as it had been inside the pub. It was so dark, in fact, that she could almost have believed time worked differently in there and that several hours had passed outside while she was sitting there, trying to make a miserly glass of lemonade last.

She made her way up Saltmarket and along Bridgegate towards the subway station at St Enoch Centre. As she tramped along the pavement, past the grotty-looking shops with their graffiti-strewn grilles, she was dimly aware of a car pulling up behind her. Of footsteps approaching her. Of a sense of impending threat that she couldn't quite place. And, in the split second she spent trying to decide whether to listen to her instincts, her fate was sealed.

Rough hands grabbed her, one on each bicep, another on the scruff of her neck. A sack came down over her head. A drawstring was pulled tight around her neck. She had neither the time nor the presence of mind to scream, far less to acti-vate her personal alarm. She felt her heels scraping the ground as she was dragged backwards and bundled into the back seat of a car. Someone got in next to her. The door slammed shut.

'Go!' shouted a voice.

The car took off like a rocket. As Anna frantically sucked in air through her nostrils, the man sitting next to her grabbed her wrists and fastened them in front of her with a zip-tie, the plastic biting deep into her skin. A blade snicked her flesh as it sliced through the strap of her alarm. It bounced off her foot as it fell to the floor, out of reach and useless.

The car continued at speed. Instinctively, she turned her head, trying to work out where they were going, even though she knew she wouldn't be able to see anything. This earned her a sharp cuff to the side of her head.

'Sit still,' her captor growled into her stinging ear. 'Don't make this any worse for yerself.'

She didn't need to be told twice. She remained perfectly still, trying to breathe and to fight the overwhelming sense of panic threatening to engulf her. The string around her neck was tight – not enough to choke her or restrict her airway, but enough to seal the sack over her head completely, preventing even a sliver of light from getting in.

With her vision out of commission entirely, she found her other senses greatly heightened. She was aware of every twist and turn the car took. Every pothole it hit. The smoothness of the leather upholstery under her thighs. Her captor's knee pressing against hers. The smell of his aftershave, thick in her nostrils, even through the bag. The roar of the engine and the discordantly cheerful chatter of Clyde 1 on the radio, and the total silence of her two abductors.

22

Time is a funny thing when you're sensorially deprived and scared out of your wits. Every moment seems to both last an age and be over in the blink of an eye. As such, it didn't take long for Anna to lose all conception of time. They could have driven for an hour, or only ten minutes. All she knew was that, eventually, she felt the car slowing. The crunch of gravel underneath the tyres. Finally, it came to a standstill. The man seated next to her nudged her in the ribs.

'Look sharp. We're here.'

She was hauled out of the car and onto her feet, then frog-marched between her two captors across the gravel and into a building – somewhere cramped and made of stone, judging by the chill and the boomy acoustics. She was led down a long corridor, then through a door and into a room.

She was shoved into a hard chair. The zip-tie round her wrists was slashed with a flick of a blade. The drawstring around her neck was loosened; the bag whipped off her head. Gasping and blinking, she struggled to adjust to the harsh over-head lighting after so long in pitch darkness. When her eyes finally came into focus, she found herself in a small, stone-walled room, lit by a single searingly bright overhead bulb.

Facing her, perched on a table with one leg folded over the other, was the small, bald man from the pub. He looked at her with a smile that seemed part-curious, part-amused.

'Welcome. I trust a pleasant journey was had by all.'

His voice was soft, almost melodic, and unexpectedly well-spoken.

'W-who are you?' she managed to stammer.

'W-who am I?' He grinned, spreading his hands wide in an exaggerated shrug. 'I'm the one you've been looking for!'

'You're . . . *you're* Jonny Lawlor?' Anna stammered in disbelief.

He grinned past her. 'No flies on this one, are there?'

Gruff, dutiful laughs behind her on either side as her two abductors humoured their boss.

Lawlor turned back to Anna. 'So, we've successfully established who I am. Question is, who are *you?*'

He gave a quick, almost imperceptible nod of his head. Immediately, one of Anna's captors stepped into view from behind her. Tall, heavily built, with dark, closely cropped hair, for a fleeting moment Anna was struck by how much of a resemblance he bore to Sean Kerevan. She noticed he was carrying her shoulder bag, which she'd forgotten about until now and realised she must have dropped in the fracas of being grabbed. He handed it to Lawlor, who rooted around inside it with an almost childlike eagerness while his lackey stood dutifully by his side, hands folded in front of him.

Lawlor took out her wallet. 'Let's see . . .'

He opened it. Fished around inside it till he found something. He held it up to the light. Her university pass.

'Well, well – Professor Anna Scavolini of Kelvingrove University.'

He returned the card to her wallet. Rifled through its contents until something else caught his eye. With an expression on his face not unlike that of a doting uncle, he took out and held up the picture of Jack that Anna kept in the photo slot. Anna felt a fresh lurch of terror.

'And who's this strapping young lad?'

'He's none of your business,' said Anna immediately.

Lawlor pursed his lips as if disappointed.

'Ah, now, that's not strictly true, is it? You see, by coming into *my* watering hole, asking questions about me, you've chosen to make yourself my business. And, since I'm willing to take a punt and say he's your son, then I'm sorry to have to tell you that makes *him* very much my business too.'

Anna said nothing. Fear gripped her like a vice: a deeper, more nerve-shredding fear than she'd felt at any point up until now – not even in that frozen instant of her own abduction.

'But all right,' said Lawlor, as if sensing what she was thinking. 'If it allows us to make some progress, we can put Junior to one side for now.'

He returned the picture to the wallet, shutting it with a snap, then faced her with a smile that felt somehow both disarming and deeply sinister.

'So, what would you be wanting with old Jonny Lawlor, then?'

Anna, her fear and disorientation leaving her at a loss for words, said nothing.

'Cos you see, Professor, thing is, you've been asking a lot of questions.' He tutted and shook his head disapprovingly. 'That's an awfy bad habit.'

His expression suddenly turned deadly serious, his small eyes like tiny black coals.

'So I'll ask you again,' he said, an edge in his voice now, 'what do you want with me?'

Anna licked her dry lips and swallowed heavily. Somehow, she found her voice.

'I've been investigating the death of Leanne McColm,' she began falteringly. 'I was led to believe you'd lent her some money.'

'I see. And, presumably, it must therefore follow that I'm the one who killed her. Am I right?'

Anna said nothing. The idea no longer seemed half as ridiculous to her as it once had – not now that she'd been grabbed off the street in broad daylight and spirited away to this . . . whatever this place was.

''Fraid you're going to have to walk me through your thought process here,' Lawlor said. 'See, I'm having a hard time following.'

'You're a loan shark, aren't you?'

Lawlor made a show of being offended. 'I prefer the term "private financier" myself – but yes, in a manner of speaking, that's what I am.'

'And when people don't pay up, you . . . apply pressure.'

'Me personally? No. Why would I, when I have my associates to do it for me?'

The 'associates' laughed again. The one behind Anna ran a hand through her hair, making her flinch.

Lawlor grinned, appreciating his own joke, before his expression grew serious again.

'But yes, I can confirm that Ms McColm and I had a business agreement. I was awfy cut up to read about what happened to her in the papers. That's a crying shame, so it is. And her boyfriend facing trial for the heinous deed.' He shook his head, tutting once again. 'Some might call it ironic – that the very man who ought, by rights, to have protected her with his life was responsible for ending hers.'

'From where I'm sitting,' said Anna, 'he's not the only one in the frame.'

Lawlor feigned an expression of surprise. 'And the polis are of the same opinion, are they? I'm to expect a knock on my door any day now?'

Anna said nothing. Her words had been bold – impudent, even – but beneath the bluster, she was still terrified out of her wits. Somehow, though, she sensed that Lawlor was unlikely to be moved by tears or pleading – in which case, it seemed better to brazen it out and at least try to get some information out of him. Besides, his whimsical attitude was starting to seriously grate on her.

'Thought not,' said Lawlor, when she didn't respond. 'Professor Scavolini, while I'd love nothing more than to entertain your delightful fantasies, I'm afraid the simple truth is this: neither myself nor my men had anything to do with this poor woman's death. Why would we? Why would *I*? She can hardly pay me what she owes now she's no longer in the land of the living.'

It was a fair point, and one Anna was forced to admit she hadn't previously considered.

'And, naturally, her boyfriend's in no position to inherit her debt – not while he continues to be held at Her Madge's pleasure. I could, of course, use my not insignificant connections to make life seriously unpleasant for him in there . . . but what would that accomplish? It won't get me my money, and I fancy the poor sod's suffering enough already.'

He sighed philosophically. 'So, I'm afraid I'm just going to have to chalk this one up as a loss.' He smiled. 'See? I'm solicitous that way. Aren't I, boys?'

'That's right, boss,' said the man behind Anna.

The other one – the one who reminded her of Sean – merely nodded.

'All right,' said Anna, 'but tell me this – did you send your men to Leanne and Sean's house on Christmas Day?'

'As it happens, yes, I did,' said Lawlor.

He seemed almost impressed that she knew this.

'I reckoned there was a fair old chance she'd be home,' he continued, 'celebrating the birth of our Saviour, and I must admit I also held out a sliver of hope that, in the spirit of the season of goodwill, she'd prove complaisant and meet her financial obligations. Regrettably, that was not the case, and her boyfriend even saw fit to get involved, assaulting my men unprovoked. Mr McGovern still has the bruises to prove it — isn't that right, Mr McGovern?'

'That's right, boss,' said the one standing next to him.

'But they never laid a finger on Leanne?' said Anna.

Lawlor looked her in the eyes.

'Not then, not ever,' he said firmly.

She believed him. She recognised that he was an unscrupulous gangster who hid his cruelty and malice behind a false veneer of amiability, but she also couldn't see what he had to gain by lying about this. He held all the cards here.

'Now,' said Lawlor, a twinkle in his eye, 'was that all the questions you had . . . or would you like to ask me if I also had something to do with the downing of Pan Am Flight 103 and the death of Princess Di?'

The heavies laughed again.

'No,' said Anna stiffly. 'That's all.'

'In that case, said Lawlor, 'I'll bid you good-day and leave the task of helping you on your merry way to my colleagues here.'

He returned her wallet to her shoulder bag, then got to his feet and made his way over to her, laying it in her lap. He gazed down at her, his dark eyes twinkling with amusement.

'You're a spirited woman, Professor Scavolini of Kelvingrove University. Ballsy. Headstrong. I admire that. But my tolerance when it comes to nosiness about myself and my business practices only extends so far. Ask about me again and you may not find it conducive to your long-term health. Yours and that of your son.'

He held her gaze for a moment, his pleasant smile all the more chilling for its incongruity. Then he glanced at the man behind her, gave another almost indiscernible nod, and the bag went over Anna's head again, consigning her to darkness once more.

· · ·

The car journey seemed shorter this time, but that might just have been how Anna perceived it. In what seemed like no time at all, she felt them coming to a standstill. Then, a gust of cold air as the door was thrust open. A hand grabbed her by the elbow and she was hauled outside. The bag was whipped off her head and, before she had time to even process what was happening, she heard a screech of tyres as the car took off without her. By the time she'd recovered sufficiently to turn in its direction, it was too late to identify it among the multitude of other vehicles thundering up and down the busy road on which she found herself.

She was at the edge of the pavement overlooking a dual carriageway, flats on one side, a stark industrial park on the other. The clouds overhead were virtually black, offering little indication as to the time of day, and heavy rain lashed down, plastering her hair to her face, getting into her eyes. She clutched her shoulder bag, which she'd held onto throughout the car ride as if her life depended on it, and tried desperately to get her bearings. Beyond a vague sense that she might be somewhere in the East End, she hadn't a clue where she was.

It had just occurred to her to get out her phone and check her location on there when a car pulled up behind her. She turned, thinking for an irrational moment that Lawlor's heavies had changed their minds and come back to cart her off again. But the two men getting out of the silver Ford Mondeo at the kerb weren't the ones who'd snatched her from the city centre. They were both in their mid-thirties, solid-looking, professionally dressed. They made their way towards her, fanning out to hem her in from either side.

'Miss? Is everything OK?' one of them said to her.

At least, that's what she *thought* he said. She could hardly make him out over the noise of the traffic, the wind and rain, not to mention her own ongoing state of disorientation. One of the two men – it might have been the one who spoke, or it might have been the other one – flashed something in front of her. ID of some sort, she thought. She was still too shaken up to process anything. One of them said something, and she found herself nodding, though she had no idea what she was agreeing to. Then she found herself being taken by the arm and led over to the Mondeo.

As she slid into the back seat and the door shut behind her, she noted to herself that this felt remarkably like a second kidnapping, only this time with her going along with it willingly.

23

'You're *detectives*?'

She wasn't sure why she was so surprised, or why it had taken her so long to actually ask them. It all made sense: the polished but anonymous car, the utilitarian suits, the flash of ID, their officious, presumptuous manner. Not to mention the building to which they'd taken her – a drab, anonymous-looking grey-brick affair in Tradeston, in one of whose cramped, multi-desk offices she was currently seated.

'That's right,' said the one nearest to her. 'I'm DS Anderson. This is DS Mackie.'

His companion, perched on the edge of an adjacent table, gave a cheery wave.

'We're with the Scottish Illegal Money Lending Unit,' said Anderson.

'As you've probably managed to work out,' said Mackie, 'we were watching when you were nabbed off the street after you left O'Leary's.'

'See, we've had our eye on Jonny Lawlor for a while now.'

'That's . . . reassuring,' Anna managed, not feeling reassured in the slightest. What if something had happened to her? Would these men have intervened, or would they just have stood back and watched it play out, all in the name of not breaking their cover?

'Aye,' said Mackie. 'Little does he know it, but the man can't so much as break wind without us knowing about it.'

'I'm glad to hear it,' said Anna impatiently. 'Now, look, I hope you don't think I'm speaking out of turn here, but I really need to pick up my son. He gets out from school at three-fifteen, and it's . . .'

She looked up at the wall clock – her personal alarm, which doubled up as a basic watch, now presumably lying on the floor of Lawlor's lackeys' car.

'Jesus. Quarter past *five*!'

'All in good time,' said Anderson smoothly. 'First, we'd like you to help us by answering some questions. First, what exactly is your connection to Lawlor? I can't imagine he had you snatched off the street for a jape, or that your visit to O'Leary's had nothing to do with it being his regular boozer.'

'Plus,' Mackie added with a smirk, 'there's the small matter of you being Anna Scavolini, mystery magnet *extraordinaire*.'

Anna wondered if *every* police officer in Glasgow had been warned about her behaviour.

'Ask your colleague Detective Superintendent Tope,' she said. 'She'll be able to fill you in. Now, if you don't mind . . .' She began to rise to her feet.

'*Just* a minute, Ms Scavolini.' Anderson held up a hand, halting her in her tracks. 'Your private comings and goings are your own affair, but not when they infringe on an active police operation.'

Anna was so unprepared for this response that she didn't even object to his failure to address her using her proper title. Instead, she lowered herself back into her seat.

'What do you mean?' she asked.

'As we indicated earlier, we've been aware of Mr Lawlor's "enterprise" for some time,' said Anderson.

'You could say we're intimately familiar with the man,' said Mackie.

'In fact, we know things about him even his own mother doesn't know.'

'Nice lady, actually. Volunteers at her local food bank twice a week. Shame about the way her son turned out.'

'If you're so familiar with his comings and goings,' said Anna, 'why don't you just arrest him?'

Anderson sighed philosophically. 'Would that it were that simple. The reality is, for all his bluff and bluster, Jonny Lawlor is but a small fish in an expansive pond . . .'

'. . . which means we aren't ready to move on him,' said Mackie. 'Not yet.'

Anna was beginning to understand. 'Why take out the bagman when he can lead you to the one signing the cheques?'

Anderson grinned. 'Precisely.'

'So we'll ask you again,' said Mackie, 'what's your connection to Lawlor?'

And so, on the assumption that the quicker she answered their questions, the quicker she'd be out of there, Anna told them. She was somewhat circumspect with her answers, giving them what she hoped was just enough detail to make them think they were getting everything – though she got the sense, from their periodic knowing looks at one another, that they knew far more about what she was up to than they were letting on.

'Look,' she said when she'd finished, 'I've answered your questions. Now can I *please* phone about my little boy?'

Anderson considered the request, then shrugged magnanimously.

'If you like, though it's not strictly necessary.'

'What?'

'We already contacted the school on your behalf. Your son's

with your emergency contact . . .' He checked his notebook. 'Zoe Callahan.'

'The school called her when you didn't show and she came straight out to collect him,' Mackie explained.

Anderson scoffed incredulously at Anna's stupefied expression. 'What – you didn't think we'd leave a literal *child* standing at the school gates, did you?'

Anna gawped at the two of them. She couldn't believe they'd left her hanging, imagining Jack waiting for her, and for no good reason. But then, did that not just sum up a certain type of men and the power games they played? There was no greater point to what they did than the knowledge that they *could* do it, and the powerlessness of their victims to do anything about it.

She got to her feet stiffly.

'In that case, can I go?'

'Certainly,' said Anderson, also getting to his feet, 'but there's no rush – not now that we've established your wee laddie's in no immediate danger. You hang tight. We'll give you a ride. Save you the taxi fare.'

He gave her a cheerful wink.

Anna would have loved nothing more than to tell them where to stick their ride, but she sensed that anything other than total, servile obedience was liable to result in them finding a reason to delay her further. So instead, she thanked them for their generosity and consented to being driven to Cowcaddens in the back of the silver Mondeo.

As they cruised through the now darkened streets, the two men conversed in low voices. Anna, seated behind them like a child – something she was sure had been deliberate – couldn't make out what they were saying. As they passed the dark expanse of Blythswood Square, however, and continued along towards Hope Street, Anderson, who was driving, suddenly raised his voice to address her.

'I've just realised – you're Paul Vasilico's ex, aren't you?'

Anna, who couldn't imagine many things worse than her erstwhile relationship – if you could call it that – being the subject of office gossip, managed a sullen, noncommittal, 'Right.'

'Shame things didn't work out for the pair of yous. Mind you, his new wife's a lovely lass.'

'Aye,' Mackie agreed, 'proper made for each other, so they are.'

'And as for that wee babby o' theirs . . . What was it again?'

'A boy,' said Mackie promptly.

'That's it! A boy. Gabriel. After the angel himself. Apple of his father's eye.'

'The spit of him, I'm told.'

Anderson glanced at Anna in the rearview mirror. 'Don't suppose you've been to pay your respects to the happy couple?'

'Somehow I haven't got round to it,' said Anna tightly.

'Ah. Pity. Sure they'd only be delighted to see you.'

Anna concluded, at this point, that the only way to shut down the conversation and avoid any further humiliation was to pretend to take a call, so she made a big play of fishing her phone out of her bag, putting it to her ear, and proceeded, for the remainder of the journey, to hold a one-way conversation with a fictitious colleague about a non-existent research proposal that was due tomorrow.

'D'you think I'm in any danger?' she asked, in as civil a tone as she could muster, once the car had come to a stop in the shadow of the flats on Dundasvale Road.

What she really meant, of course, was, *Is my* son *in any danger?* But she couldn't bring herself to give voice to that possibility.

'From old Lawlor?' said Mackie cheerfully. 'Nah, nae chance. He's a businessman, or thinks of himself as one. Doesnae need the hassle. You'll be fine . . . just so long as you don't go poking the nest again.'

'Aye,' said Anderson, as she got out of the car, 'don't you worry, miss. We've got our eye on you.'

A statement which somehow managed to sound far more unsettling than reassuring.

24

Tuesday 15 March

'Have you got everything?' said Anna. 'Pencil case?'

'Yes,' said Jack.

'Gym shoes?'

'Yes.'

'Packed lunch?'

Jack held up his plastic lunchbox in lieu of an answer.

Anna nodded slowly to herself, running through a mental checklist of other items that could potentially have been forgotten. Ultimately, though, she was forced to conclude that everything had been accounted for.

No excuses left for delaying the inevitable.

She straightened up. Pasted on a bright, enthusiastic smile.

'Right, then. Time to go.'

She opened the front door and peered outside. Apart from the continual churn of traffic, all was peaceful on Southbrae Drive. Still, she made a point of looking both left and right before allowing Jack to exit the house. She hurried him down the footpath to her Skoda, parked in the driveway, safely installed him in the back seat, then looked around again before getting in herself.

As she eased the car out into the street, she caught sight of movement at the edge of her vision – a figure striding along the pavement towards them, arms pumping with an aggressive rhythm. Her heart lurched. Every muscle in her body tensed. Her foot hovered over the brake.

Then, the details resolved themselves. It was just the man from number 140, getting in his daily power-walk before disappearing into his home office for another day doing whatever it was that earned him his keep. He strode on by without giving her a second look, and the icy grip on her chest loosened. She really had to stop jumping at shadows.

She told herself she'd feel better once she had her new personal alarm. She'd ordered one online, but had been told delivery could take up to twenty-eight days. Not that the previous one had done her much good when push came to shove. She was starting to wonder whether these things weren't, in fact, a complete con, selling people the false impression of safety and encouraging them to take greater risks as a result.

For her, the lesson had been well and truly learned. Alarm or no alarm, she was determined to play things as safe as possible. She'd spent the weekend holed up at home with Jack, refusing to let him out of her sight and working overtime to distract him from his various demands to take him to the swing park or the swimming baths or the Lego shop – each more insistent and single-minded than the last. She'd only grudgingly allowed him to go to school on Monday, and only then after rearranging her schedule so she could leave work early to pick him up at the gates herself, rather than letting him go home with Theo.

Throughout it all, she'd been dodging Pamela Macklin's various texts, asking for an update on the case, and, latterly, the solicitor's attempts to call her. She hadn't yet worked out the diplomatic way of telling Pamela that her experience on Friday had left her giving serious thought to throwing in the towel. As things stood, Lawlor had turned out to be another red herring. She believed him when he'd said he had nothing to do with Leanne's death. But even if she never crossed paths with him again, the encounter had nonetheless served as a timely reminder that asking awkward questions was a dangerous pastime. The next time she poked the wrong hornet's nest, she might not find herself dealing with someone quite so pragmatic.

Instead, she threw herself into her work, determined to distract herself at all costs – and devote herself to the job that, lest she forget, she was actually being *paid* for. It proved to be easier said than done: the headaches continued to worsen, the pressure behind her right eye increasing to the point that sometimes she thought her entire eyeball was going to be pushed out of its socket. Even worse, she now found herself periodically struggling with her vocabulary, words she used multiple times a day proving inexplicably elusive at the most inopportune times. The most extreme manifestation to date had come the previous afternoon during her first-year lecture on victimology, when she'd lost her train of thought altogether and spent a deeply uncomfortable spell standing in front of a crowd of gawping students, not a single coherent thought in her head as she desperately tried to remember what came next in a lecture she'd delivered on more than a dozen separate occasions over the years.

Shortly after two o'clock, she emerged from a lecture in the Gladstone Building to find yet another missed call from Pamela waiting for her. She knew she couldn't put off talking to her indefinitely, but it wasn't a conversation she was looking forward to having – or had the headspace to deal with right now.

As she made her way along the corridor, she noticed a man standing with his back to her at the far end. He was tall and muscular, wearing a tracksuit with the hood up. For reasons she couldn't pinpoint, she felt a jolt of anxiety running up her spine. As she drew nearer, he turned in her direction and, seeing her, lowered his hood. For the second time in the last few days, she briefly thought she was looking at Sean Kerevan. Then she realised where she'd seen this man before, and why the sight of him had felt so much like déjà vu, and panic took over.

'I'll scream,' she jabbered, as the man Lawlor had addressed as 'McGovern' moved towards her, his thick arms swinging menacingly. 'There are at least a dozen people within shouting distance of this corridor. You won't have time to—'

'Fuck's *sake*!' McGovern groaned in frustration. 'I'm not here tae do ye in. I just wanna talk.'

Anna stared at him for several seconds, blinking stupidly.

'You want to *what*?' she eventually managed to say.

25

_____

'The other day,' said Anna, 'in the back of the car – that wasn't you with me, was it?'

'No,' said McGovern, 'that was Rat—' He stopped himself. 'That was my associate. I was driving.'

'I see.'

They were making their way up through the cluster of buildings at the southwestern end of the university campus. It had turned into an unexpectedly sunny day after a run of damp, overcast ones, and the place was teeming with students whiling away the interval between lectures. McGovern, however, had his hood up again – something which, to Anna's eyes, only succeeded in drawing further attention to him than if he'd left it down.

He glanced at Anna briefly. Something was clearly on his mind, but he seemed reluctant to articulate it.

'He didn't . . . ill-treat ye, did he?' he eventually asked.

'Apart from manhandling me off the street, zip-tying my hands, putting a sack over my head, slapping me and hauling me around by the scruff of the neck . . . no, he treated me just grand.'

McGovern looked pained, but he neither apologised on

behalf of his accomplice nor attempted to explain why such treatment would have been justified.

They reached the open-air plaza outside the medical school with its curved glass façade. Anna led the way over to a vacant bench and took a seat. McGovern followed her lead and sat, hunched over, looking decidedly uneasy. Anna had made it clear she'd only talk to him if they did it somewhere public. McGovern, clearly, would far rather not be seen by anyone.

'I never wanted it tae go down like that,' he said after a moment. 'We're not normally in the business of . . .'

'What? Abduction? Assault? Grabbing defenceless women off the street and scaring the shit out of them?'

'Hey!' McGovern snapped. 'It wasn't my idea.'

'And yet you went along with it.'

McGovern sighed, shoving a hand under his hood and running it over the bristles of his skull.

'Ye don't get it. Jonny Lawlor's not someone ye say no tae. When he tells ye tae do something, it's no up for debate.'

'Then why work for him?'

McGovern didn't respond. He sat in silence with his head low, hands squeezed between his knees.

Anna watched him for a moment before speaking.

'So what was it you wanted to talk about?'

McGovern raised his head and looked across at her.

'You wanted tae know about Leanne McColm, right? Well, there's some stuff I can tell ye that might shed a bit of light. Or it might not. I dunno.'

'I already know she'd racked up some pretty serious gambling debts. I know Lawlor had given her a loan and was putting increasing pressure on her to pay it back.'

'Aye, but did ye know she came tae see him the night she died?'

Anna opened her mouth, then stopped. She looked at McGovern.

'No, I didn't know that.'

'The showdown outside her house on Christmas Day must've spooked her good and proper. You could tell she'd no been expecting us tae turn up like that. Far less for it to turn violent. Like the boss said, that was down tae her man getting too big for his boots – but still. My guess is that was the point it became real for her, if ye know what I mean.'

Anna nodded. She thought she did.

''Bout a week later, she gets in touch. Says she wants tae agree a realistic payment plan. I mean, that's no how it normally works. Normally the client doesnae get tae set the terms. But the boss was full of the Christmas spirit or something and he said OK, come and see me at The Stag on the night of the eighth.'

'The Stag? Where's that?'

'It's a restaurant, just off Ingram Street. The boss likes it. Nice wee place. Good, straightforward food; nothing foreign. Dead discreet too. Staff know not tae ask questions. Sometimes he conducts his business there. Rents out their private room and makes a night of it.'

Anna waited for him to continue.

'So she shows up about quarter to ten, and by that point the boss has already ate and drank his fill. He's in a generous sort of mood. And so, when she explains she's worked out how she's gonnae pay him back in instalments, and even gives him a complete, itemised breakdown of the timescale, he's honestly kinda touched – or leastways he's amused by all the effort she's gone tae, working it all out down tae the last penny, taking account of the interest rate and everything. And he tells her he's gonnae go along with her little scheme. He warns her, though, this is positively the last time she's gonnae find him so accommodating.'

Anna nodded, with him so far.

'So she left The Stag at about when?'

'Not till nearly quarter to eleven. He makes her stay for a

drink with him. Says it's only polite tae raise a toast together after concluding a successful business deal. 'Course, any fool can see he's ripping the piss out of her, but she's too gormless to realise it. I can still see her sitting there with her glass of bubbly, grinning away like a ninny, thinking she and him are on equal footing now just cos she caught him in an indulgent mood that night.' He shook his head and scoffed derisively.

'And presumably that was the last time you saw her.'

McGovern lifted his head and turned to look at her.

'No. See, that's the whole point of this story. Ten minutes later, the boss is preparing tae make tracks. Tells me and Rattray he's finished wae us for the night.'

Anna noticed he'd just inadvertently named his 'associate', but said nothing.

'We all go our separate ways,' McGovern continued. 'I head down towards Parnie Street. There's an all-night chippy there, and I'm feeling a bit peckish after watching the boss stuff his face all evening. But, as I turn onto Trongate, who do I see standing outside of Ladbroke's?'

'Leanne,' said Anna quietly.

At the back of her mind, something slotted into place with a satisfying click. She was too focused on listening to McGovern's account to properly process what it was, but she nonetheless recognised that a fatal error in the police's reconstruction of what happened that night had just been – or was just about to be – revealed.

McGovern nodded. 'Right. So you can imagine what's going through my head. Daft wee cow has no idea how lucky she is. She's just been gien a second chance by a man who *never* gies folk second chances . . . and what's she do? Heads straight tae the bookie's.'

He ran a rough hand over his face, his seething frustration still palpable, even now.

'Folk like her, they cannae help theirsels. Shouldnae be let within a hunner feet of a betting shop. And I'm sorry tae say I wasnae exactly gentle wae her. I went straight up tae her and said, "Are you completely stupit? What part of 'last warning' did ye no get?" And she kept on insisting, "I was only looking, I wasnae actually gonna make a bet," all sulky-like, like I'm the unreasonable one here.

'Well, obviously, after that, I'm hardly gonnae just let her go on her merry way, am I? So I ask her how she got intae town. She says the train. What station? High Street, she says. So I grab her by the arm and I haul her up there, wait wae her till the train comes, then get on wae her and make sure she gets off at her stop.

'And she pleads, PLEADS wae me no tae walk her home. Says if her man sees her showing up tae the door with another bloke, he'll kill her. 'Course, knowing what I know now, I wish I had. Walked her tae her door, I mean. But "beggars would ride" an' aw that. So I trust her tae go straight home, and then I head off myself – walk back tae my own place through in Barmulloch. Figure the night air'll do me good.'

He shrugged, indicating that his account was at an end, and fell silent. Anna, too, sat in silence for several seconds, quietly digesting everything she'd heard.

'You know the police are under the impression it was Sean Kerevan who was seen dragging Leanne up the street?' she said eventually. 'And they think it was him who was caught on CCTV with her at the station.'

McGovern looked up sharply. 'Aye, and I'm no going tae set them straight, so don't even ask. I can't talk to them. No with my . . . associations. Plus,' he added petulantly, 'they'll just take it as proof *I* killed her and pin the whole thing on me.'

'I'm not sure that's true,' said Anna.

But how sure *was* she, really? If she was being honest with herself, she was far from convinced she'd put it past them. And it still didn't resolve the question of what had happened to Leanne between McGovern leaving her at Springburn station and her turning up dead at the foot of the steps just a hundred metres or so away. None of what she'd heard proved Sean's innocence. In fact, there was, she now realised, a plausible scenario in which he'd found out about where Leanne had been that night and why, flown into a blind rage and killed her.

'Why tell me all this?' she asked at length.

McGovern shrugged. 'Cos,' he said gruffly.

She waited for him to elaborate.

He sighed. 'Cos I wasnae keen on how we treated you the other day. And I wanted tae help.'

Anna nodded slowly, saying nothing. She was thinking about what he'd told her. She wasn't convinced there was anything she could meaningfully do with any of it – not if he wasn't prepared to go on the record.

At length, something occurred to her. Something she'd like to put to the test. It was unlikely to change anything in and of itself – but still, she'd like to try it all the same. To satisfy her own idle curiosity, if nothing else.

She turned to McGovern again.

'Have you got any plans for the rest of the day?'

Three quarters of an hour later, Anna stepped into the Strangeways Bar for the second time in less than a week. In terms of overall activity, the place was every bit as quiet as it had been the last time she was here. The main difference, this time, was that Kasia Wiśniewska was on duty at the bar. She frowned as Anna approached.

'You again. You have more questions?'

Anna came to a stop at the counter. 'Just one or two things I'd like to run through again, if you don't mind.'

From the expression on her face, Kasia very much *did* mind, but she nonetheless dropped the cloth she'd been polishing glasses with and faced Anna, arms folded across her chest.

'OK. You ask.'

'Thanks. So I'd just like to check, the time you came out of the bar on the night of the eighth – you said quarter past eleven?'

'This is correct,' said Kasia, patently irritated to be going through all this again.

'And you came outside, dumped the rubbish bags by the bin, stopped to have a smoke, and then . . .'

But Kasia was no longer listening. She was staring past Anna, towards the figure who'd just come in through the door.

'But . . .' she stammered, 'but this is him. The man I see making argument with the dead girl.'

With a sense of satisfaction more deeply pleasurable than she would ever have admitted, Anna turned to face McGovern, who stood in the doorway, looking uncomfortable and vaguely sheepish.

'I should phone for police?' Kasia suggested tentatively.

26

Thursday 17 March

Casa Bellini bore a certain resemblance to a giant glass cube that had been plonked at random in the middle of Jordanhill. Stepping across the threshold, Anna was hit by a blast of warm, temperature-controlled air, along with the rich smells of garlic and wine. The floor underfoot was polished concrete, while overhead lights picked out individual tables from the otherwise shadowy expanse of the main floor.

As Anna's eyes swept the room, past the serving staff who flitted by with the grace of ballet dancers, Vanessa Tope rose from her seat at a table for two towards the back and lifted a hand in greeting. She was wearing a sleeveless sparkly top and svelte black trousers, her blonde hair cascading over her shoulders.

Anna headed over with a self-deprecating laugh.

'Sorry. Didn't recognise you without the overcoat and your hair in a bun. You look amazing.'

She slid into her seat.

'Flatterer.' Tope flashed a grin. 'So do you.'

'Thanks,' said Anna, knowing she didn't. She looked tired

and harangued, her hair unbrushed, bags under her eyes as deep as canyons. For the past week, a combination of the headaches and gnawing anxiety about her health had pushed the prospect of a full night's sleep firmly out of reach.

Tope looked around approvingly. 'This was an excellent choice. I've never been here before. You?'

Anna shook her head. 'No, but I've heard good things about it.'

She didn't want to admit she'd only chosen it because it was convenient for her to get to. With the visual disturbances becoming increasingly severe, she'd given up driving after dark altogether, and wrangling with the city's patchy public transport if it turned into a late one was most assuredly *not* top of her list of ideal ways to spend a Wednesday night.

'Know what you're having?' said Tope. 'I wasn't sure whether to order red or white.'

Anna shook her head. 'You choose. I'll go with the flow.'

She made a play of studying her menu, trying to disguise the fact that the words were blurring together into an unintelligible mush. Eventually, she gave up and set it down, facing Tope across the table.

'Detective Superintendent—'

'Vanessa – please.'

'Vanessa, then. As lovely as all this is, I'm still not entirely clear what I'm doing here.'

'Well,' said Tope, casually examining her own menu as she spoke, 'I wanted to arrange this wee get-together because I heard on the grapevine about your encounter with Jonny Lawlor and his band of merry men.'

'Brought me here to give me a finger-wagging, did you?' said Anna, immediately defensive.

'Actually, it was to make sure you were OK, and to commend you for your tenacity. You didn't hear me saying this, but not many go toe to toe with Jonny Lawlor and come out in more or less the same shape as when they went in.'

Anna looked up in surprise. Tope smiled and gave a slight shrug.

'I see,' said Anna, still on her guard. 'Did you also hear on the grapevine about how I was treated by your colleagues from the Illegal Money Lending Unit?'

'Surprisingly, that part got missed out. Of whose company did you have the pleasure?'

'Detective Sergeants Anderson and Mackie.'

Tope's expression soured. 'Och, they're a pair of arseholes. Tweedledumb and Tweedledumber. What happened?'

Anna told her.

'Cunts,' said Tope, once she'd finished her account. 'I can help you make a complaint if you like.'

Anna considered it, then shook her head.

'It's fine.'

She'd long since come to the conclusion that such endeavours were more trouble than they were worth, knowing from experience that any disciplinary proceedings brought against them would most likely only result in a typical 'cops look after cops' stitch-up, the likes of which she was acutely familiar with.

Tope shrugged. 'Your choice, but I want to make it clear you'd be entirely within your rights, and that you'd have my full support.'

'Thanks,' said Anna, noting how much more cordial things seemed between them than the last time they met. She wondered if it was simply because they were no longer in what might loosely be termed a work setting, or if Tope recognised how heavy-handed she'd been before, when she turned up at the house.

A waiter arrived, gliding over to them as if he was levitating off the ground.

'Good evening, ladies,' he purred. 'Have we decided?'

Tope finished consulting the menu.

'We'll have the Montepulciano.'

'A *fine* choice,' said the waiter approvingly, which Anna

suspected he'd also have said if they'd ordered a carafe of Diet Coke.

'Can you bring us a bottle of sparkling water for the table?' she asked.

She thought she'd better try to limit her alcohol intake, suspecting it was unlikely to mix well with her condition.

The waiter departed with a flourish, leaving Anna and Tope to resume their conversation.

And, for a time, Anna managed to forget about her symptoms and her impending brain scan, or came as close to it as she'd been able to in as long as she could remember. To start with, they discussed matters which had nothing to do with Leanne's murder and Anna's investigation. Tope asked Anna about her work, about recent developments in the field of criminology, and about Jack and how he was getting on at school, and Anna found herself almost unreasonably grateful for the distraction.

It wasn't until their main courses had been cleared away and they'd entered into that interminable period of waiting to catch someone's eye to summon the bill that Tope, as casual as anything, once again steered the conversation back to the reason she'd arranged this get-together in the first place.

'So, Jonny Lawlor. You believe he had something to do with Leanne's death?'

Anna pursed her lips. 'No. At least, I don't think so.'

Tope gave her a questioning look.

'I did consider it for a while,' Anna explained, 'but no – I no longer think he's anything more than a red herring.'

She hesitated, uncertain as to whether to divulge what was on her mind. After weighing up the pros and cons, she decided to go for it.

'Having said that, my encounter with him did lead to a conversation that I believe has a significant bearing on the case.'

'Oh yes? What sort of bearing?'

Tope's tone was casual, almost disinterested, but Anna wasn't fooled for an instant. She hesitated again, aware that sharing this would, technically, constitute a betrayal of McGovern's confidence. She'd tried once more, before they parted ways the other day, to persuade him to tell the police what he'd told her, but he'd again refused. She reminded herself that, strictly speaking, she'd never promised not to tell them herself. Most people, she knew, would take his willingness to talk to her in the first place as an unspoken condition of confidentiality – but she decided she was going to lean into the overly literal mindset she was so often accused of having.

Without naming McGovern, she told Tope about his appearance at the university and their subsequent conversation outside the medical building, concluding with their visit to Strangeways.

'Kasia Wiśniewska is ready to go on the record that the man she saw with Leanne that night wasn't Sean after all,' she said.

'And this mystery man of yours – the man you claim everyone, including Kasia Wiśniewska and several of Police Scotland's most eagle-eyed pixel peepers, mistook for Sean Kerevan – would he happen to have a name?'

Anna, not responding, focused on her glass to avoid meeting Tope's eye. This, she felt, would be one betrayal too far.

'No matter,' said Tope. 'I'd lay odds on him being known to us already.'

Anna smiled weakly. Somehow, she didn't think McGovern would regard her failure to explicitly name him as a mitigating factor if he received a knock on his door as a result of this conversation.

'Are you going to look into it?' she asked, half-apprehensive and half-hopeful.

'I'll certainly pass it on to my colleague who's leading the case,' said Tope. 'Though I feel compelled to point out that it doesn't prove Sean's innocence.'

Anna didn't respond. She'd been expecting Tope to say this.

'The other possibility, of course,' said Tope, 'is that this admittedly upstanding-sounding criminal, whose identity you've admirably gone out of your way to protect, is the one who killed Leanne.'

Anna had also been prepared for this.

'It's certainly possible,' she conceded, 'but I don't think it's likely. I don't see what he'd have to gain from putting himself in the frame by telling me. In any event, he says he didn't do it, and the vibe I get from him is that he's telling the truth.'

Tope gave a dry smile that Anna, had her mood not been mellowed by a tenderloin steak of rare good quality and an unexpectedly pleasant evening overall, would have regarded as deeply patronising.

'I'm afraid we police officers need more to go on than "vibes" when it comes to ascertaining a man's guilt or innocence.'

'Perhaps, but I'm in danger of losing track of the number of planks that have collapsed in what you yourself must admit is an almost entirely circumstantial case since I started looking into it.'

Tope's tight smile suggested she was conceding nothing.

'And then there are the leads you've missed altogether,' Anna went on. 'Take Natalie Lennox, for one. She was Leanne's best friend since school, and yet the police never even saw fit to question her. It's only thanks to her that the gambling angle came to light at all – and, by virtue of that, the fact that the man seen with Leanne on the night of her murder wasn't Sean.'

'Yes, that was a nice bit of detective work,' Tope acknowledged. 'We knew all about the state of Leanne's bank balance, of course, but I'll concede we didn't probe too deeply. Sometimes, you can have all the information in front of you but don't possess the necessary context to assemble it into a coherent picture. Unfortunately, in the real world, we have to make difficult decisions about how to prioritise our resources.' She gave an impish smile. 'We can't all afford to spend hours scrolling on Facebook.'

Anna laughed dryly. 'Now *there's* a backhanded compliment if I ever heard one. Can I ask you a serious question? Did you lot ever consider, even for a moment, the possibility that Sean didn't do it?'

She realised, as she spoke, that her stance had shifted dramatically since McGovern's intervention. Maybe it was just the dynamic at play – speaking to a police officer who, by nature and duty, felt compelled to defend the investigation over which she'd presided, and, in the process, pushing Anna into the opposite side of the good cop/bad cop dynamic she'd had with Pamela Macklin.

But then, she supposed, it was just possible that she was in danger of becoming a true believer.

Tope gave a forbearing smile. 'Yes, believe it or not, the possibility did occur to us. In the early days of the investigation, we cast the net wide. We scrutinised everyone we knew of who had a connection to Leanne, from her immediate family to her work colleagues to her past lovers. I take it you know she used to go out with Sean's brother?'

'Of course.'

'Well, in the beginning, we gave very real consideration to the possibility that *he* could have killed her out of jealousy. The whole "spurned lover" trope, you know. When he came in to talk to us with his legal representative . . . Richard somebody? The guy he went into business with.'

Anna nodded.

'Well, when he came in, he was obviously in a state of some distress. He told us he'd found out about Leanne's death in the paper. Needless to say, not an ideal situation – for him *or* for us.'

'No, definitely not.'

'It was literally the morning after her death, and the team was just getting up to speed on everything. At the time, we weren't aware of Gerry's past connection to Leanne, so he wasn't yet on our radar – otherwise we'd have reached out to him ourselves and hopefully avoided all that . . . unpleasantness. But it was painfully clear he didn't know anything – unlike Sean, who didn't even seem surprised when he was informed of her death.'

'Were you there when they broke the news to him?'

Tope shook her head. 'No, but the whole thing was corroborated by multiple officers. At first, he was pissed off to get home to find a bunch of coppers swarming all over his house. Then, when they took him aside and explained why they were there, he just sort of shrugged and said, "Oh. Right." '

'Delayed reaction?' Anna suggested. 'You know as well as I do that people respond to grief in different ways.'

'Right. But, equally, I'm willing to bet *you* know as well as I do that over sixty percent of femicides are committed by the husband or boyfriend.'

'And over seventy percent are murdered in their home – but you're confident that wasn't the case here.'

'For reasons with which I have no doubt you're already intimately familiar, so I won't bother rehashing them now – save to assure you that the SOCOs did as thorough a job as anyone could ask for and didn't find a single *scintilla* of evidence there.'

'I know,' said Anna absentmindedly, recalling her own visit to the house. 'I saw the state they left it in.'

Tope glanced up sharply. 'What do you mean, you *saw* it?'

Anna immediately realised her mistake.

'I . . . I just mean,' she stammered, backtracking furiously, 'I know what people's homes tend to look like after the police have gone to town on them. Furniture moved, drawers tipped out onto the floor, ornaments shoved onto whatever surface happens to be nearby.'

Sex toys left on the dresser . . .

Tope's expression remained utterly deadpan. She made no attempt to fill the awkward silence now unfolding between them.

'I mean,' Anna continued, growing increasingly animated in her attempt to distract from her earlier slip, 'you go looking for the kettle and find it in the airing cupboard, or . . . or your hairbrush wedged behind the sofa cushions. Honestly, I don't know how anyone finds anything again after you lot have been and gone.'

Tope sat there for a long moment, her piercing eyes boring into Anna. Anna knew she was far too sharp to have bought such a feckless cover-up.

'Sadly,' Tope said, after a long, uncomfortable moment, 'we don't have the time or resources for the full *60 Minute Makeover* treatment. But I can assure you, not a single item was removed from that house – not even a clothes peg. So, in the event that Mr Kerevan is acquitted, everything will still be there – and he can celebrate his newfound freedom by putting it all back just the way he likes it.'

Her dry, derisory tone ably conveyed just how remote she considered that particular outcome to be.

They emerged into the chilly night, fastening their coats as they left the warmth and light of Casa Bellini behind them. As they made their way down the steps, Tope spoke for the first time since they'd settled up.

'I suppose, for the record, I should reiterate that I'm duty bound to implore you, in the strongest possible terms, to give up this investigation and leave matters to the professionals.'

'Supposing you did,' said Anna, 'do you think I'd listen?'

'I think I'd have a slightly greater chance of persuading my dog to stop licking his own balls.' Tope glanced at Anna with a smile. 'I'd better let you go. Away home to your wee boy before he starts flashing the babysitter. Night, Anna.'

'Night, um . . . Vanessa,' Anna murmured, as she watched the detective superintendent go striding off into the night – a tall, upright figure in a long fawn coat, cutting a determined swathe through the darkness.

27

Monday 21 March

'Well, well,' said Sean, 'look what the cat dragged in.'

He gazed up at Anna from his table in the visitation room with a weak, lopsided grin, showing off both a fresh black eye and a gap between two of his front teeth that Anna was pretty sure hadn't been there the last time she saw him.

'Don't tell me,' she said. 'They started it.'

'In this case, it's true.'

She took a seat opposite him.

'What, no chocs this time?'

'That was Pamela's idea,' said Anna shortly. 'She's not here today.'

'No,' agreed Sean, making a show of looking for her. 'It's just you. Why *is* that?'

'I thought we could have a chat, just the two of us.'

Sean gave a slow, amused smile, clocking her refusal to answer the question.

'Well,' he said, 'whatever she's paying you, I guarantee you it's not enough.'

'She's not paying me anything,' said Anna.

Sean stared at her. 'You're doing all this for free? What's *wrong* with you?'

'I've been wondering that myself,' said Anna, more to herself than to Sean.

'Huh?'

'Nothing,' she said quickly, realising she'd momentarily allowed her mind to drift to her own ongoing issues. 'Look, I wanted to thank you for agreeing to this. I thought, after the way I came in all guns blazing last time, you'd probably never want to hear from me again.'

Sean shrugged. 'S'pose you could say I was sort of impressed, really.'

'Impressed?'

'Aye. The way you came at me, like a bat straight outta hell – I figured, if I've got someone *that* fierce on my side, I might just stand a chance after all.' He paused. ''Sides, no one else's asked to visit.'

'Still nothing from Gerry?'

He shook his head. 'Hee fuckin' haw.'

Sitting there all alone with a black eye and a missing tooth, abandoned by everyone he ever knew, Anna couldn't help but feel just a sliver of sympathy for him. Then she thought of Leanne, and the bruises on her arms and her frail little body, and her resolve hardened.

With brusque efficiency, she brought Sean up to speed on everything she'd found out since she'd agreed to take on the case, including having established that the man seen with Leanne on the night of her murder hadn't been him after all.

'See?' said Sean, when she'd finished detailing her conversation with McGovern. 'I *told* you.'

To her ears, he honestly sounded more aggrieved that she hadn't believed him in the first place than pleased that she now knew the truth. She was tempted to suggest to him that he was in danger of not seeing the forest for the trees, but she bit her tongue.

'It's good, though, from your point of view,' she said instead, opting for what she hoped was an encouraging note. 'Don't you think? It means the prosecution has one less round of ammo in its arsenal against you.'

'Aye,' said Sean, once more retreating into morose self-pity, 'but they've still got plenty more to throw at me.'

Of course, thought Anna, *no need to thank me.*

She decided it was best if she moved on.

'I'm curious about one thing,' she said. 'How much did you know about Leanne's gambling problem?'

Sean shifted uneasily in his chair, reluctant to make eye contact.

'You knew she *had* one, I take it.'

'Aye,' said Sean quietly, 'I knew. Not at first, but. She managed to keep it from me for a good long while. We had separate bank accounts, so I never . . .' He trailed off.

'You knew *something* was up, though,' said Anna.

Sean nodded. 'Right. She started going to that casino last summer – her and her pals. But whenever I asked about it, she'd always blow me off. Tell me she just went for the vibes, not the actual gambling. I never found out how bad it'd gotten till those cunts shown up to the house at Christmas.'

'I hear you got into an altercation with them.'

Sean gave a crooked half-smile. 'S'pose that's one way of putting it. Bit of a one-sided altercation, but.'

'Tell me what happened.'

'Do I have to? Wasnae exactly my finest hour.'

In response, Anna simply folded her arms and gave him the silent treatment.

At length, he sighed heavily. 'All right. Since you asked so nicely. I'd just got done having a shower when I heard voices out front. I went to the window and looked out and I could see her standing at the gate wae these two blokes, both of them giving off proper "hard bastard" vibes. I couldnae hear what was being said, but I could tell she was dead agitated. One of 'em jabbed his finger at her, like poked her right in the tits, and I obviously couldnae just stand there and watch after that. I went charging outside. Asked 'em what the fuck they wanted. One of 'em gave this sort of smirk and said, "Ask yer missus." I looked at her and I could see she was scared out of her nut. So I . . .'

He trailed off. Looked down at the table, riven by shame. Anna waited. After a moment, he continued.

'S'pose I done what I always do. I went for 'em. Only, turns out, they weren't all just swagger. I got mibby one punch in before the other one decked me. He was a right big bastard. I went down like a sack o' spuds. And they're laying into me wae their feet and Leanne's screaming and crying and the neighbour's dug starts barking the place down and then I hear one saying tae the other, "We better beat it. The boss said no tae cause a scene."

'They stopped kicking me, and when I managed tae look up, they were backing off towards their car. One jabbed his finger at Leanne and said, "End of next week. Then we do to you what we done to him," or something like that. And they got in the car and drove off.'

He fell silent, eyes downcast, massaging his knuckles as if he'd been the one dishing out the beating. The words 'PAIN' and 'GAIN' were stark against his pallid, sun-deprived flesh.

'What then?' said Anna.

He stirred again. 'I was pretty bashed up. Leanne got me inside and cleaned me up, and I asked her what the fuck that'd all been about. At first, she tried to brush it off. Said it was nothing – just a couple of guys she'd borrowed some money off of. But I kept pushing, and she eventually caved. It all came out: the money she'd lost, the debts she'd racked up wae her pal Natalie and then this Lawlor bloke. How she owed thousands and he was jacking up the interest every week.

'I offered to talk to Lawlor for her. Try and smooth things over wae him. Make her see she was just a daft wee girl who'd got in over her head. And she looked at me and said, "Yeah, cos that worked out real swell just now, didn't it? Face it, Sean, unless you've got a few thou in your back pocket, you're pretty much useless to me." '

He gazed glumly down at the tabletop, his huge, muscular arms folded on top of it. Watching him, Anna sensed that this was, for him, the worst part of the whole affair. Not being beaten up, not learning that Leanne had got herself into debt with a loan shark – being told she had no use for him.

'Why didn't you mention any of this before?' she said.

Once again, his seeming unwillingness to do even the smallest thing to help himself was beyond comprehension.

Sean shrugged tetchily. 'What would've been the point?'

Anna fought the urge to scream.

'Well, I don't know,' she deadpanned. 'Maybe the fact that the same thugs who beat the shit out of you threatened to do the same to Leanne just a fortnight before she was found dead *might* have given the police some other avenues to explore!'

'So everyone would remember her as a gambling junkie, you mean?' Sean snapped back. 'Yeah, no fucking thanks.'

He folded his arms about himself and sat back, glowering. Anna, gazing across the table at him, couldn't help thinking that, on balance, this reflected well on him. Once again, he'd turned down the opportunity to attempt to sow doubt about his guilt – and all to defend the honour of a woman who wasn't around to thank him for it. Maybe he really *didn't* do it, she thought.

Then, as invariably happened whenever she entertained such thoughts, she remembered the bruises.

'Out of curiosity, did you know she was pregnant?'

Sean glowered at her. 'You know I know. The police told me.'

'But before that. You had no idea?'

She wondered why this felt so important to her. Perhaps it had something to do with Pamela's suggestion that it was harder to imagine Sean killing Leanne if he knew she was carrying his child – something she'd dismissed at the time but, she was forced to admit, no longer found completely impossible to discount.

Sean shook his head. 'No. I never knew. Not till . . .'

'Not till the police told you. And when you found out, how did you feel?'

'Angry.'

Sean's answer was immediate and unequivocal.

'Why?' said Anna. 'Because she hadn't told you?'

'No. I'm not even sure *she* knew. If she did, surely she'd've . . .'

He trailed off, the words catching in his throat. A moment later, he composed himself and once more fixed Anna with a surly glare.

'I was angry cos *they* kept it from me so they could spring it on me right when I was at my lowest. It's like they wanted me to lose my rag.'

'And you happily obliged them by doing so.'

'Right, cos you'd be perfectly calm if you'd just been told *your* kid was dead.'

'Or maybe,' said Anna, ignoring Sean's provocation, 'maybe the truth is you were angry with yourself because, when you killed Leanne, you hadn't realised you were also killing your unborn child.'

''Cept I never killed her.'

'And the bruises? The sore ribs and the black and blue arms? I've heard about them from multiple people, so don't bother trying to deny it.'

'I never touched her,' said Sean immediately.

'Walk into a lot of doors, did she?'

'*Fuck* you. I never laid a finger on her, EVER.'

'OI!' one of the prison officers snapped, taking a couple of steps towards the table.

Sean held up a hand in acknowledgement of his faux pas,

bowing his head in a gesture of supplication. The officer hovered for a few more seconds, then gave a curt nod.

'Just watch it,' he growled, and moved off.

Sean waited till he was out of earshot, then leant towards Anna, his tone as plaintive as his expression.

'I mean it,' he insisted. 'I was brought up not tae hit lassies.'

But hitting men is fine? Anna thought. She'd never been remotely swayed by the idea that committing violence against one half of the population was unacceptable but the other half was somehow fair game. She considered raising the matter of his conviction from 2018 again, but decided there was no point. He'd only reiterate his claim that it had been an accident – and, for all she knew, perhaps it would be the truth.

'Well,' she said instead, in a tone she hoped conveyed an openness to being convinced, 'if you didn't give her those bruises, can you suggest who *did*?'

Sean said nothing. He just shook his head and looked dejected.

'There must be *some* explanation for them,' said Anna.

'I can't explain it,' Sean muttered.

'Just like your alibi.'

Sean shot her an angry glower and lowered his eyes once more.

'Come on.' Anna leant across the table towards him, trying desperately to catch his eye. 'I want to believe you when you say you didn't do this. I'm ready to be persuaded. But you're not doing yourself any favours.'

Sean said nothing. He didn't even look at her.

'Is there *anyone* you can think of who might have had a reason to harm Leanne?'

It was a last throw of the dice on her part – a vague, non-specific plea to persuade him to come up with something, *anything*, that might make his guilt appear marginally less cut-and-dried.

And, to his credit, Sean did appear to give the question genuine consideration, before shaking his head unhappily.

'There's no one. Leanne was the life and soul of the party. She lit up every room she walked intae. Everyone loved her.'

Anna felt herself physically deflating, slumping in her seat, as if the effort of holding herself upright had become too much.

'It's not like she went looking for trouble,' Sean continued, frowning to himself, as if this was a logic problem he was slowly working through in his mind. 'She didnae mix wae a rough crowd or anything. *I* was probably the roughest person she knew. She was a classic girly girl. Liked her spa treatments and spending time with her girlies. Her favourite colour was pink, for Christ's sake. And she never had any guy friends in all the time I knew her . . . and that's gotta count for something, right? Cos whoever done that to her *has* to have been a bloke.'

Anna said nothing, but Sean didn't seem to have been expecting a response. He gave a sad, wistful smile before continuing.

'I used to joke about it wae her. Said she'd make the perfect girlfriend for a paranoid schizophrenic, cos he'd never have to worry about where she was or who she was seeing.' He smiled weakly. 'Funny, right?'

Anna smiled out of obligation.

'Thing is,' Sean went on, his tone quiet and almost dreamy, as if he was talking to himself, 'those last few weeks, she wasnae really herself. Always off somewhere. Nipping out at weird times, saying she was going to the shops, then coming back hours later with nothing.'

Anna felt herself sitting up a little straighter.

'And you never asked her where she'd been?'

'Sure I did,' said Sean. 'She'd just laugh it off. "Out and about," she'd say. "Nowhere special." '

'And you didn't push?'

'What was I meant to say?' Sean retorted sharply. 'Every

time I brought it up, she'd just go on about how I was on her case the whole time. How I didnae trust her. How she never kept tabs on *me*.

'She started leaving her phone at home too,' he went on, reverting to the same soft, reflective tone as before. 'Said it was for her "mental health". But I know what that means. Meant she didnae want me seeing where she was going. I tried guessing the pin, but I never got it right. Then, about a week before—'

The words caught in his throat. He took a moment to compose himself, then carried on.

'I was putting on a wash, and I remembered tae go through her coat pockets, cos she was always leaving stuff in them. Sweet wrappers and that. And I found a receipt. Café in Shotts called Dawn and somebody's. Rose I think. Aye, Dawn & Rose's. Timestamp said it was midday on the twenty-eighth of December.'

'Shotts?' said Anna.

'I know. Right old distance to go for a cup of tea. Doesnae take a genius to work out she went there to meet someone.'

'And you think it was a man,' said Anna quietly.

Sean shook his head. 'I dunno. Not for sure, anyway.'

He fell silent. Anna thought he was finished. But, as she opened her mouth to speak, he stirred once more.

'But she was hiding something,' he said, with conviction. 'That much I *do* know.'

28

Wednesday 23 March

Shotts is a small North Lanarkshire town with a population of less than 9,000. Its chief attribute of note is that it is situated roughly halfway between Glasgow and Edinburgh – two stops away on the train from Glasgow Queen Street, three from Edinburgh Haymarket.

Dawn & Rose's Café was located half a mile up the hill from the station, past several rows of pebble-dash semis and squat bungalows with tiny gardens and wrought iron fences. Normally a brisk walker despite – or perhaps to compensate for – her short legs, it took Anna a good five minutes longer to reach the café than the twelve her phone had estimated. Over the last few days, a growing lethargy seemed to have crept up on her that went beyond mere tiredness from lack of sleep. At times, it felt like she was wading through wet cement, and the headaches – or more accurately *headache*, since it was an ever-present feature of her life now – were making even getting out of bed increasingly feel like an ordeal.

Upon entering the café, Anna was struck by how tiny the place was, crammed with more tables than she imagined was

allowed by any of the various pieces of health and safety legis-
lation. A pair of elderly women sat at one table, conversing
over coffee and scones. A middle-aged man sat alone at
another, reading a paperback book. The counter, meanwhile,
was occupied by a woman in her late thirties – Dawn or Rose,
Anna assumed, though she wouldn't have liked to guess which.

'Hi,' said the woman cheerily, as Anna approached the
counter. 'What can I get you?'

Normally, to avoid it seeming like she was *completely* taking
the piss, Anna would have ordered something before launching
into her spiel. Right now, though, she hadn't the headspace for
anything but the barest of essentials.

'I don't want anything to eat or drink, thanks,' she said. 'I
just have some questions.'

'Right,' said Dawn-or-Rose, obviously nonplussed. 'What
sort of questions?'

'It's about someone who came in here between Christmas
and New Year. A woman. I was wondering if you happened to
remember her. Here.'

She handed over her phone, showing a photo of Leanne
from her Facebook profile. The woman – Anna had decided
just to assume she was Rose, because otherwise she'd only
continue to wonder and be unable to concentrate on anything
else – studied the picture carefully.

'I know her,' she breathed, a note of awed surprise in her
voice. 'I mean,' she clarified, 'I don't *know* her know her. What
I mean is I recognise her face. That's that poor girl who
was . . .' – she dropped her voice to a hushed whisper –
'. . . *murdered*, isn't it?'

Anna confirmed that it was.

'And you're saying she came in *here*?'

Anna couldn't tell whether Rose was alarmed or excited by
this possibility.

'That's right. Around midday on Thursday the twenty-
eighth of December.'

'Ah, see, I don't work Tuesdays. Hang on a minute, but.'

She turned and poked her head through the doorway behind the counter.

'STRUAN! Out ye come a sec!'

A moment later, a young man emerged. He was more of an overgrown boy, really; tall, rake-thin, with a large, protruding bottom lip and what looked to be a permanent stoop – possibly on account of the café's unusually low ceiling.

'Struan was on that Tuesday,' Rose explained to Anna. 'Weren't ye, Struan?'

'December the twenty-eighth,' added Anna.

'Tell him what you told me,' said Rose.

Anna explained briefly what she wanted to know, showing Struan the picture of Leanne. Struan took the phone in his hands and examined it carefully, bringing it close to his face and squinting with one eye, as if he was nearsighted.

'Not sure,' he said, after a moment. ''S not a great picture.'

Well, here at least was someone who wasn't intimately familiar with the various twists and turns of the Leanne McColm case. Given his age, Anna surmised, his media consumption was probably limited to fifteen-second TikTok videos which had a tangential at best relationship to current affairs.

'She was probably with someone,' she said. 'Possibly a man?'

Struan suddenly seemed to come alive. 'Aye. *Aye!* I remember now. I *did* see her. Her and her boyfriend.'

'Boyfriend? Why do you say that?'

Struan shrugged, as if it was self-evident. 'Cos of how they were with each other.'

'How they were?'

'Aye. Dead close, like. They were sat at that table over there, leaning across to each other, heads practically touching. Whispering, like, in dead low voices.'

Anna followed his gaze. 'Is that right?' she murmured.

'My sister's that way with her boyfriend all the time,' said Struan, who didn't seem to have heard her. 'Intimate, like. Pure gives me the boak.' He pulled a face.

'And this man,' said Anna, 'can you describe him at all?'

Struan thought about it. 'He was a big guy. Way bigger than her.'

'You mean taller?'

'Aye, but not *just* taller. Bigger in the other direction too.'

'He means "fat",' said Rose bluntly.

Struan looked mortified, but Anna was past the point of sparing anyone's blushes.

'Is there anything else you can remember about him?' she pressed him. 'Any distinguishing features? Apart from his size, that is.'

'Aye. He was, y'know, ginger. A redhead. Had it tied back in, like, a man-bun or something.'

Something cold and icy ran down Anna's spine. She snatched her phone back and tapped furtively at the screen till she found what she was looking for, then angled it towards Struan again.

'Was this the man?'

Again, Struan squinted at the screen for a moment, then nodded emphatically.

'Aye, that's him. Defo.'

A feeling of deep dread settled in the pit of Anna's stomach.

'You're sure?'

'Hundred percent.'

Anna fought the urge to shut her eyes in despair. Instead, she took her phone back and gazed at the screen herself, as if to convince herself she'd somehow got the wrong end of the stick. But there was no hope of explaining it away. Her worst fears had just been confirmed.

'That wasn't the only time they were in,' Struan went on, oblivious to Anna's mounting horror. 'I seen them again, just after we opened up again after New Year. Wednesday, mibby, or Thursday. Same deal as before – leaning in, heads close together, like they were gonna kiss any second.'

'Uh-huh?' said Anna distantly.

She continued to stare at her phone. The browser was open on the website for Viventis Software Ltd. Under the section labelled 'Our Team', a professional black and white portrait of Gerry Kerevan smiled back at her.

Gerry, who'd sworn blind he hadn't seen Leanne since she and Sean got together more than three years ago.

PART IV

UNRAVELLING

29

Monday 28 March

Another day, another round in the MRI scanner, this time with an intermission partway through to allow a nurse to inject IV contrast via the cannula in Anna's inner elbow. Lying there on the hard, rigid surface, the machine clanging and banging overhead, she found her mind working overtime, bouncing from one idea to the next and refusing to listen to her repeated attempts to empty it of all conscious thought. So many different thoughts, but they all led to the same conclusion.

I have a brain tumour and I'm going to die.

Anna had never given her own mortality all that much thought, in spite of all the hair-raising situations she'd got into over the years – many of which, she was forced to acknowledge, had brought her perilously close to the edge. But now, the thing she'd always regarded as a distant, far-off concern felt terrifyingly immediate and real.

Her thoughts, as they had on so many occasions in the recent weeks, turned to Jack. Who was going to take care of him if she was no longer around? Zoe would obviously be her first choice, and Anna knew she would do it gladly. But she also knew that such an outcome wouldn't be automatic. Zoe might be the closest thing Jack had had to an unofficial co-parent for the first four years of his life, and, in a sane and just world, that would count for something, but she wasn't his next of kin. Anna wasn't sure how that particular aspect of the law worked, but she supposed that, officially, it would be either her mother – and raising a child at her grand age wasn't something Anna wanted to inflict on her, *or*, for that matter, on Jack – or his father, which was a can of worms she had no desire to open up. Should she be talking to a lawyer? Making a will?

Her mind was still churning over these matters when the table slid back out of the scanner and the nurse came in to remove the cannula. As he helped her sit up, Anna caught sight of the radiographer through the observation window, removing her headset and jotting something down.

Before the nurse could stop her, Anna slid off the table and made a beeline for the control room.

'Excuse me.'

The radiographer looked slightly panicked, as she supposed most people probably would be when confronted by the sight of a patient in a hospital gown invading her private space. A patient who should, by all sensible measures, be taking it easy.

'The scan,' said Anna. 'Could you . . . did you see anything?'

The radiographer's expression softened into one of compassion.

'I just take the pictures, love. 'S not my job to pass comment on them.'

'But you've seen enough of them in your time, right?' said Anna, trying to keep her voice steady. 'You must have some idea.'

The radiographer was doing everything she could to avoid Anna's eye. 'Like I say, I really can't comment. You need to wait for the consultant to write to you. Your scan's flagged for priority review. I'm sure it'll not be long.'

Anna felt the nurse's hand on her arm. She resisted the urge to shake him off and instead, after spending a few more seconds staring at the radiographer with helpless insistence, allowed herself to be led out of the room.

Woodcroft Nursery was located in the Broomhill area, west of Hyndland, on a quiet side street just off Crow Road. Anna stepped off the bus and made her way up the pavement, one arm trailing the wall beside her just in case she suffered another sudden onset of dizziness. She knew Zoe normally took her lunch break around now and was banking on catching her. And, as she drew level with the nursery's wrought iron gates, she was rewarded by the sight of her friend sitting in her colourful staff tabard on a bench under a tree in the otherwise empty grounds, her phone in one hand and a half-eaten sandwich in the other.

As Anna approached, Zoe looked up with a grin that was as delighted as it was surprised.

'Ahoy, sailor! Whit's the occasion?'

Somehow, Anna managed an easy shrug. 'Just passing by,' she lied. 'Thought I'd look in and see if you were about.'

Truth be told, she wasn't sure precisely what *had* brought her here, beyond a sudden, overpowering desire to see her friend. It wasn't as if it was on the way to the university – which, officially, was where she was meant to be heading after the hospital.

'Well,' said Zoe, moving her juice can so Anna could join her on the bench, 'it's aye a joy tae see ye, come rain or shine. Park yersel here, doll, an' you tell me what's what.'

Anna did as she was told, seating herself next to Zoe and immediately lapsing into silence. Now that she was here, she realised she had no idea what she wanted to say. A part of her wished dearly that she could tell Zoe all about her problems – completely unburden herself of all her worries to her oldest and closest friend, submitting to her judgement and wisdom. The only trouble was, after keeping it all to herself for so long, she had no idea how to even begin to broach the subject.

'Listen, don't be taking this the wrang way – but should you no be at work?' Zoe's puzzled question broke the silence.

'My one o'clock class was cancelled,' Anna explained. 'I've not got any teaching commitments till three now, so there's no rush.'

The unspoken truth was that *she* was the one who'd taken the precaution of cancelling the class pre-emptively, fearing that there could be any number of unexpected delays at the hospital.

Zoe grinned. 'Aw, well that's nice. I always did appreciate an unexpected free period.'

Anna returned the smile. 'Don't I know it! What was it you used to call them?'

'Accidental parole!' they both chanted in unison.

'Well, anyhoo,' said Zoe, when it became clear that Anna was waiting for her to carry the conversation forward, 'it's actually dead fortuitous, you dropping by. See, I got a wee favour tae ask. More of a massive one, really.'

'What is it?' said Anna, already bracing herself.

'You don't work Wednesdays, right?'

'Right.'

'Well, thing is, me 'n' Sal are both gonnae be tied up the whole day. Sal said she'd cover her pal Griff's shift at Costa, and I've got this course over in Toryglen. "Integrative Strategies for Multimodal Soft Play." ' She rolled her eyes, grinning at the absurdity of it. Then her expression turned serious.

'Thing is, it means Captain Pugwash is gonnae be on his own in the flat all day, and the wee soul doesnae cope well wae being left alone. The vet says he's got separation anxiety, on account of how his last owners used tae abandon him for hours on end. Ye couldn't swing by early afternoonish, could ye? Take him out tae do his business; keep him company for an hour or two?'

Seeing the faintly desperate gleam in Zoe's eyes, Anna hadn't the heart to say no, no matter how sorely tempted she might be.

''Course I will,' she said, fixing the brightest smile she could muster on her face.

Zoe beamed. 'Ach, ya absolute dancer!' She wrenched Anna into a brief but vigorous hug. 'See, this is how I never bother asking anyone else about things like this – cos I always know you'll say yes.'

Anna gave a strained smile. 'Old reliable, me.'

'Mind and get the spare key fae me or Sal when ye swing by for Jack the morra night.'

She grinned again, slurping noisily and contentedly from her juice can.

Silence settled, and, after the brief distraction of Zoe's dog-sitting dilemma, Anna once more found her thoughts taking a turn for the doom-laden. She sat, leaning forward with her elbows resting on her knees, gazing off into the distance. She felt like she was being crushed beneath an all-encompassing sense of hopelessness, powerless to alter the trajectory on which she found herself. Even the knowledge that the diagnosis she feared and expected wasn't necessarily a death sentence did little to assuage her. To her horror, she felt an ache developing at the back of her throat and her eyes growing moist.

'Hey,' said Zoe, oblivious to Anna's growing distress, 'speaking of favours, been meaning tae ask – d'ye get a chance tae talk tae Sal yet?'

'Not as such, no,' Anna muttered, trying to wind her unspooling emotions back in. 'I've not really had the time.'

'God's sake, hen,' Zoe scoffed good-naturedly, 'I only asked ye tae *talk* tae her, not tae mentor her through a five-year life plan wae PowerPoint slides!'

'I know. It's just . . . things've just been really busy lately,' Anna managed to choke through the tears that, to her immense shame, had begun to flow.

Zoe stared at Anna – first in disbelief, then in concern.

'Oh babydoll, what's the matter?'

By now, Anna had lost control completely, covering her face with her hands as if to try to force the tears back into her eyes.

'It's just stress,' she sobbed. 'I've got a lot on my plate right now.'

Zoe enfolded her in her arms, drawing Anna's head to her chest and stroking her hair, murmuring reassuring nothings to her until her sobs finally subsided.

'It's this case, in't it?' she said, releasing her. 'If I've said it once, I've said it a hunner times: it's no good at all, you getting involved in they things.'

'It's not the case,' said Anna, wiping her nose on her sleeve. 'It's just . . . y'know, life stuff.'

Zoe gave her a pointed look. 'Anna, I hope ye'll take this question in the spirit it's intended . . . but when's the last time you had a really good wank?'

The response Anna choked out was somewhere between a fresh sob and a laugh.

'I'm serious,' said Zoe. 'Since you an' yer Italian stallion broke up, you've no been getting any – 'least no as far as *I'm* aware. Ye gotta have *some* way of relieving all that stress.' She shrugged. 'Just sayin' – a good, vigorous hand shandy's a tried and tested method.'

Anna gazed back at Zoe – at her friend who'd always been there for her, through thick and thin, no matter how insurmountable the challenge.

TELL her, said the voice at the back of her head.

'Zoe . . .' Anna began.

'Aye?'

Anna opened her mouth to continue, but at that moment,

272

there came a sound of approaching footsteps. They looked up as a girl of about twenty, wearing a tabard similar to Zoe's, made her way over, slowing as she reached the tree and edging tentatively towards them.

'Zoe, sorry,' she said, clasping her hands in front of herself awkwardly. 'It's just, Lesley's wet herself again and she'll only let *you* change her. Can you come?'

'Go,' said Anna immediately.

Zoe looked at her. 'Ye sure?'

Anna nodded tightly. 'Yeah. You've got work to get back to, and I . . . I should be doing the same.'

Zoe looked up at her colleague, picking nervously at her fingernails, then at Anna, concern and reluctance writ large on her face.

'It's *fine*,' said Anna firmly. 'I'll see you later.'

Reluctantly, Zoe got to her feet.

'We're putting a pin in this conversation. This isnae over.'

It sounded dangerously close to a threat.

Anna gave no response, and, after a moment, Zoe, unable to keep her colleague or the unfortunate Lesley waiting any longer, turned and headed back towards the nursery.

For several minutes after she'd gone, Anna remained seated under the tree. Rarely in her life had she ever felt so utterly alone – or, at least, rarely had it ever bothered her to the extent that it did now. She sensed that the moment had passed – that this had been her one opportunity to come clean, and it had been snatched from her by circumstances beyond her control.

Slowly, she got to her feet and made her way across the empty grounds, sloping off down the street with nothing but her all-consuming fear for company.

30

Tuesday 29 March

'Vanessa Tope.'

'Detec— Vanessa, hi. it's Anna Scavolini.'

'Anna, hey,' said Tope, her tone instantly more personable than the brisk, officious one with which she'd taken the call. 'Half a second.'

At the other end of the line, the chatter in the background faded as Tope presumably moved to somewhere quieter.

'Now, what can I do for you?'

'Just a small favour. I was wondering if I could ask you about something?'

'Does it concern the Leanne McColm case?' said Tope, a note of wariness entering her voice.

'Well . . .'

Tope sighed. 'Anna, I feel obligated to point out that I can't possibly discuss a live investigation with a member of the public.'

'Even if that member of the public has already provided information indicating that the investigation in question has been found wanting?'

Anna could practically *hear* the steam rising from Tope's ears.

A beat, then:

'This is all off the record.'

It was a statement, not a question.

'Of course.'

Tope sighed again. 'Ask away, then.'

'The other night, you mentioned that, when you interviewed Gerry Kerevan—'

'Well, technically, it wasn't *me* who interviewed him. It's pretty rare for a DSU to be that hands-on. DI Drysdale, the senior investigating officer, did the honours.'

'Granted, but presumably you know, broadly speaking, what was discussed during the interview.'

'Presumably.'

'Was he asked to account for his whereabouts on the night of Leanne's death?'

'That would be the normal procedure when interviewing a person of interest in a murder inquiry.'

'And?' Anna was beginning to tire of these half-answers.

'And what?'

'What did he give by way of an alibi?'

'Strictly speaking, he didn't. At least, not one that could be corroborated.'

Anna waited for her to elaborate, hoping silence would succeed where badgering had so far failed.

'Gerry told us he was at home alone on the night of the murder,' said Vanessa, after a moment. 'His better half − your sidekick, Ms Macklin − was off visiting her rellies in some far-flung locale. Stromness?'

'Stornoway,' said Anna.

'Close enough. And, not that I'm under any obligation to share this information with you, but the GPS data taken from his phone backs up his account.'

Just like the GPS data that showed both Sean and Leanne at home

when her body was being dumped at the bottom of the library steps?
Anna resisted the urge to say.

'He never mentioned attending a technology conference in
Dundee?' she asked instead.

'Not that I'm aware of. Why?'

'Never mind. Just checking.'

'Can I ask *you* a question?' said Tope.

'Of course.'

'Is this your current modus operandi? You can't prove
Sean's innocence, so you've moved on to bending the evidence
to try to make it fit Gerry?'

'Of course not!' Anna snapped, then immediately regretted
it. 'Sorry. But no, that's not what I'm doing. I'm just trying to
clarify a few things in my own head. Call it laying some ghosts
to rest if you like.'

Stony silence from Tope.

Anna hesitated for a moment, then decided to chance
her arm.

'I just had one more question.'

'Go on, then,' said Tope, in the tone of a weary parent
indulging a particularly demanding child.

'I appreciate it. Now, you mentioned that, when Gerry was
questioned, his business partner, Richard Duncan, came along
as his legal representative.'

'If you say so.'

Tope, it seemed, was determined to admit to nothing.

'And whose idea was that?' Anna asked. 'Did you – or
rather, did DI Drysdale suggest he should have a lawyer
present?'

'No, that was Gerry's idea. The two of them turned up at
the station together.'

'And did that strike you as suspicious at all? Presumably he
wasn't being interviewed under caution.'

Tope laughed dryly. 'If we arrested everyone who walked
into an interview with legal counsel, the cells would be full to

bursting. No, Anna, there's nothing remotely suspicious about it. It's a right that's extended to every citizen, not a honking great "guilty" sign.'

That stung, and Anna couldn't help feeling like she'd probably deserved it. She should never have suggested it – certainly not to someone who was only ever going to respond one way.

'Now then,' said Tope, when Anna had remained silent for several seconds, 'is there anything else I can assist you with today, or would you like me to set you up with your own personal login to the SID database?'

This was one sardonic jibe too far, and Anna had no intention of entertaining it.

'That's awfully generous of you,' she said, as blithely as possible, 'but no thanks. Sorry to have taken up your time.'

She ended the call before Tope could say another word and gazed down at the iPad lying in her lap, still showing the events page on the Dundee City Council website. Trade fairs, antique shows, even a stamp collectors' convention – all neatly catalogued as part of the council's 'What's On in 2022' calendar.

Her conversation with Tope had merely confirmed what she knew already. Gerry couldn't have been attending a technology conference in Dundee on the weekend of Leanne's murder, because there had *been* no such conference that weekend.

She made herself a coffee and wandered over to the window with the steaming mug, gazing out into the darkened street. Ever since her trip to Shotts the previous week, she'd been doing everything she possibly could to avoid thinking about the implications of what Struan had told her. But now, with Jack tucked up in bed and only her newfound fixation on her own mortality to occupy her, she'd concluded that reopening this particular can of worms was a far more palatable option than the alternative.

The case against Gerry, as she saw it, while hardly cast-iron, was only marginally less convincing than the one the police had assembled against his brother.

First, there was the fact that he and Leanne, with whom he'd had a prior romantic relationship, had met in secret on at least two occasions in the week leading up to Leanne's death, their manner towards one another so clearly intimate that the eyewitness who'd seen them had assumed they were boyfriend and girlfriend.

Then, there was his decision to bring his lawyer friend to his police interview. Whatever Vanessa Tope might think – or, perhaps more accurately, feel obliged to say – Anna doubted she'd be able to find a single person who wouldn't consider it at least somewhat suspicious. She supposed it was a bit like the 'not proven' verdict: in the eyes of the law, it was every bit as much of an acquittal as a 'not guilty', but ask any rando on the street and they'd tell you, without a second thought, that it *really* meant the jury was saying, 'We're pretty certain you did it. We just can't *prove* it.'

Finally, there was the simple, incontrovertible fact that *Gerry had LIED*. He'd lied to Pamela about not having seen Leanne since she and Sean got together three years ago. He'd lied to her about his whereabouts on the weekend of Leanne's death. And, most damning of all, he'd *continued* to lie, even when his own brother was charged with her murder. One thing was certain: people didn't behave like that unless they had something seriously incriminating to hide.

Anna was under no illusions about the crossroads at which she found herself. Whatever Gerry was hiding, even if it was nothing more ignoble than an affair with his ex-girlfriend, the ructions were going to be positively cataclysmic for him – and for Pamela. For all Pamela's many irritations, Anna was genuinely fond of her, and the thought of her getting hurt was almost too much to even contemplate.

But there was no getting around it: Pamela deserved to

know the truth. And, if Gerry *had* murdered Leanne in cold blood, then it was incumbent upon Anna to warn her as soon as possible – if for no other reason than to save her from the possibility of meeting a similar fate.

Setting down her now lukewarm coffee, she dragged a hand roughly over her face, forcing herself to get a grip. She'd procrastinated for long enough. With a heavy heart, she picked up her phone and rang Pamela's number.

Pamela was both surprised and pleased to hear from Anna, though it was obvious, from the note of consternation in her voice, that she was more than a little miffed about not having received word from her sooner.

'I've been trying to get hold of you for *yonks*,' she exclaimed, her booming voice causing Anna's already pounding headache to spike. 'What's happened? Have you not been getting my messages?'

'It's been a really busy time,' said Anna, hating herself for her dishonesty. 'I've been following up a few leads and wanted to be absolutely certain of them before I shared them with you.'

'And *are* you? Absolutely certain, I mean.'

Anna hesitated. 'I think, perhaps, it would be best if we met up so I can tell you what I've found out face to face.'

'Why not tell me now?' A note of irritation entered Pamela's normally affable voice. 'If it's important—'

'I'd *really* rather we spoke face to face,' said Anna firmly. 'How's your calendar looking for the rest of the week?'

There was a pause at the other end of the line as, Anna suspected, Pamela suppressed the urge to argue the toss.

'I'm working from home tomorrow,' she said eventually. 'I haven't any client meetings, so I'm treating it as an admin day.'

'In that case, I can come to yours. Is mid-morning OK?'

'It's fine. But Anna—'

'I have to go now. I'll tell you everything when I see you.'

She hung up before Pamela had a chance to protest any further, then slowly sank into the easy chair facing the window, filled with foreboding about the bomb she was about to detonate at her friend's feet.

31

Wednesday 30 March

Anna woke the following morning – if 'woke' was the right word after having spent most of the night dozing fitfully – to the worst headache she'd experienced so far. The pressure behind her right eye was immense, her entire skull felt like it was being squeezed in a vice, and her vision was a blurry mess unless she shut her bad eye completely and squinted through her remaining good one.

With a great effort, she got out of bed, roused Jack, got him fed, watered and safely off to school, then proceeded to potter about the house with a cold compress and the curtains left drawn to keep out the harsh sunlight until it was time to leave for Edinburgh.

As the train sliced its way through the vast expanse of countryside beyond Falkirk, her phone rang. It was the same NHS number that had called her the day she learned about the shadow.

'Hello?' she said, her mouth suddenly dry.

'Anna, it's Dr Maitland,' said the consultant, without preamble. 'I have the results of your repeat scan in front of me.'

'And? What do they say?'

Maitland hesitated. 'I think it would be better if you came in at your earliest convenience and discussed them with me in person.'

Time seemed to stop. A sick heat rushed to Anna's face. Her body tingled with an impulse to get to her feet and run, even though there was nowhere to go. Everything around her – the murmured conversation of the other passengers, the click-ety-clack of the train's wheels – seemed absurdly distant, as though she was watching the world from behind a pane of thick, soundproofed glass.

'I'm in my office now,' Maitland continued. 'I can see you this morning if that suits.'

'I can't,' Anna blurted. 'I'm otherwise engaged. Just tell me now.'

'Anna, I *really* think it would be better if—'

Anna ended the call.

She sat there, heart hammering like a fist against her ribcage, skin hot and clammy beneath her clothes, her thoughts spinning out in every direction, yet landing nowhere. Why the hell did she just *do* that?

The phone rang again, startling her so much she almost dropped it. NHS Greater Glasgow & Clyde again.

She rejected the call.

I can't I can't I can't I—

She set her phone to silent and shoved it into her shoulder bag, burying it deep beneath all the accumulated detritus inside it, then sat up straight and faced forward, hands folded in her lap, one leg crossed over the other.

I have a mission. Nothing can get in the way of that.

Nothing.

. . .

'It can't be.' Pamela shook her head vehemently. 'It's not *possible*.'

'I wouldn't be telling you it if it wasn't true,' said Anna gently.

'But . . . but you didn't see him yourself, did you?' said Pamela, her voice high and desperate. 'You weren't *there!*'

'No, but the boy at the café was sure it was him. I'm not trying to be cruel, but Gerry's quite . . .' Anna searched for the appropriate word. 'Distinctive.'

Pamela sat on the sofa, hands behind her ears, each clutching a great clump of hair, slowly shaking her head over and over. Anna, perched on the chair facing her, bit the inside of her mouth and tried her best to give her friend the space she needed to come to terms with the news she'd just received.

At length, Pamela appeared to come to a decision. She let go of her hair and composed herself, sitting up straight and smoothing down her skirt.

'No,' she said, with finality. 'You must be mistaken. Gerry would never do something like that.'

'Pamela . . .' Anna began wearily.

'No! Don't "Pamela" me. You don't get to come into my house and start casting aspersions like this.'

Anna shrugged helplessly. Where to even *begin* to respond to any of this?

Pamela jabbed a finger in Anna's direction, a look of unhinged triumph burning in her eyes.

'I know what this is about. You've got nowhere with the investigation so you're clutching at straws, latching onto every hare-brained rumour you come across just so it doesn't look like you've got nothing to show for it.'

Anna opened her mouth to speak, then decided against it. She pinched the bridge of her nose, fighting the blistering headache that was only being exacerbated by Pamela's high-pitched exclamations and refusal to see reason.

Pamela was on her feet now, pacing the room in small,

frantic circles, her words tumbling out in a rush, sharp and laced with high-handed opprobrium.

'The boy was mistaken. It was someone else with Leanne. Or . . . or it wasn't Leanne either. People are always rubbish at recognising faces, especially after the fact. Eyewitness testimony's completely overrated. You know people think it's the second most reliable form of evidence after forensic science but it's actually the least? Folk watch too many courtroom dramas on the telly. Think everything's decided by the one star witness who saw everything. And-and-and maybe the council forgot to list the conference on their website, or maybe I misremembered and it wasn't Dundee but Dunfermline or . . . or Dalkeith or—'

'Pamela, *please* . . .' Anna began, raising her voice wearily.

'NO!'

Pamela stopped pacing and whirled around to face Anna, her face flushed, trembling so hard she was practically convulsing.

'Why would you come here and lay this at my door? How could you possibly think it would do a lick of good? He's my bloody *fiancé*!'

'Hey!' said Anna, rising to her feet and responding to Pamela's tirade with equal ferocity.

She'd promised herself she wasn't going to respond emotionally, no matter *what* Pamela threw at her, but that was easier said than done. Even when she was at her best, there was only so much abuse she could take before she felt compelled to strike back – and right now, she was a very long way indeed from her best.

'I didn't *choose* to do any of this,' she reminded Pamela, doing her best to make sure her words were firm but measured. '*You* were the one who asked me to go digging.'

'Well, I wish I hadn't,' said Pamela, her voice a brittle whisper.

A silence settled on the living room, both of them seeming

to recognise that they'd hit an impasse. Slowly, Pamela sank back onto the sofa, her face expressionless and drained of colour. Anna remained standing.

The lull was broken by the sound of the front door opening and shutting, followed by heavy, lumbering footsteps in the corridor and a booming voice in a playful, singsong tone.

'I come bearing sustenance! Where's my little Night Elf queen?'

Gerry stepped into the room, carrying a bag laden with groceries. His eyes alighted first on Anna, then on Pamela.

'Paz?' he said, a note of worry creeping into his voice. 'What's going on?'

For a moment, Pamela just stared at Gerry, her expression unreadable. Then, with a howl of rage, she went charging across the room towards him and began to pound his chest with her fists.

'Bastard!' she wailed. 'Evil, shitting bastard! How? How could you *do* this to me?'

Gerry dropped the bag. Oranges spilled out and rolled across the polished hardwood floor in multiple directions. He didn't fight back or even try to restrain Pamela. He just stood there, allowing her to pummel him, gazing across at Anna with a sad, broken expression.

And, in that instant, Anna knew that he understood precisely what this was all about, and that the game was up.

32

'It's true,' said Gerry. 'I did go to Shotts to meet Leanne. But it wasn't what you think. We weren't having an affair.'

He sat at one end of the sofa. Pamela sat at the other, looking, to Anna's eyes, like she was determined to stay as far away from him as possible. She'd calmed down considerably since her initial, frenzied outburst, and now sat there in silence as Gerry spoke, periodically sniffing or dabbing at her reddened eyes with a paper tissue.

'She rang me up out of the blue just after Christmas,' Gerry went on. 'It was the first time we'd spoken in years. She told me about the debts she'd gotten into and the business with the loan sharks.' He hesitated. 'She also told me she was pregnant.'

Anna heard Pamela inhaling in shock. *But you already knew,* she wanted to say. Then she realised that what Pamela was actually responding to was the fact that Leanne had chosen to confide in Gerry.

'She said Sean didn't know,' said Gerry. 'She was scared for her safety, and for the baby's, 'specially after the beating they gave Sean and the threat to do the same to her. She didn't know who else to turn to . . . so she came to me.'

He shrugged helplessly, as if he still couldn't quite make sense of it himself.

'I'm not sure why. I'd have thought I was the *last* person she'd want to involve. The whole situation with her and Sean and me was . . . messy, to put it mildly. But then, maybe it *does* make a certain amount of sense – like she knew the odds of me getting on the blower to Sean to tell him what she'd just told me were pretty much nil. And she was absolutely crystal clear about that. He couldn't know – about the baby or the . . . other stuff.'

'But Sean already knew,' Anna pointed out. 'About the debts, I mean. Leanne told him after the incident on Christmas Day.'

Gerry turned to look at her, a brief flicker of what might have been resentment in his eyes.

'I know,' he said, 'but it was much, much worse than she let on to him. He thought she owed a few thousand. In reality, it was *tens* of thousands.'

He fell silent for a moment. He rubbed his hands together between his knees, as if trying to warm them.

'She reached out to me cos she knew I'd made a mint off that app I developed. She figured I could get my hands on a lot of money without too much hassle. I said to her, "Leanne, if you think I'm just going to hand over a cheque to write off your debts, you've got another thing coming."

'I thought she'd curse me out. Call me every name under the sun. Tell me that whatever happened to her and the baby as a result would be on me. But she never. She just looked defeated.

'So I told her, "Here's how it's going to be." I said I'd work out a payment plan for her to take to these creeps to get them off her back for good. And then, I'd give her the money in scheduled instalments, on the understanding that she got professional help for her condition.' He gave a small, humourless laugh. ' "Condition." Until I said the word, I don't think she'd ever really acknowledged to herself that that's what it *was*.

'She said Sean could never know,' he went on. 'If he found out we'd met up . . . that I'd helped her like this . . .' He shrugged helplessly. 'I dunno. He always had a chip on his shoulder about my . . . my success. Made out like I done better than him just to spite him. That I lorded it over him every chance I got. If he found out I was paying off Leanne's debts for her – for the *both* of them, really – it'd be like I was rubbing it in his face. 'Least, that's how Leanne saw it. And I'm not sure she was wrong.'

He looked at Pamela. 'And I couldn't tell you, because . . .' He hesitated. 'Well, cos I didn't think you'd approve,' he finished weakly.

'You could have talked to me,' said Pamela. 'That's what couples are *supposed* to do.'

She spoke quietly, but every word was loaded with a raw, understated fury.

Gerry winced, but he made no further attempt to justify himself. He just sat there, gazing miserably at his scuffed trainers, so incongruous against the polished floor.

'Why continue to keep this to yourself, though?' Anna asked him. 'After Leane was killed, surely . . .' She trailed off.

'Because I didn't want anyone asking where the money'd come from,' said Gerry.

Anna stared at him uncomprehendingly and waited for him to continue.

He sighed. 'I'm nowhere near as loaded as folk assume. We made a load of money off of the app, Richard and me, but most of it went straight back into the business. Licencing fees, operating costs, and . . .' He gestured to their surroundings. 'Things like this place. So I shuffled some funds, bounced a few invoices between companies, invented some non-existent consultancy expenses. I didn't want HMRC getting involved . . . so I said nothing.'

Pamela stared at Gerry, appalled. 'In the name of *God*!' she moaned softly.

Gerry drew his arms about himself, unable to look her in the eye.

Anna, meanwhile, realised she felt strangely let down by the explanation. It was grubby and, in most people's eyes, undoubtedly immoral, but it was so mundane, so utterly banal, that it couldn't help but feel like an anticlimax.

She forced herself to move on from her own misplaced sense of disappointment.

'When the police interviewed you, you took Richard in with you, even though you hadn't been charged with anything. What was that about?'

'*I* made him do that,' said Pamela quietly.

Anna turned to her in surprise.

'You?'

'When he rang me up in Stornoway, I told him straight away, "If the police want to talk to you, make sure you take legal representation. You never know what they might try and pin on you." ' She shrugged limply. 'I'd have advised anyone in his shoes to do the same.'

'Oh,' said Anna.

She felt a bit foolish. This was more or less exactly what Tope had said to her, and she'd dismissed it at the time, convinced it was a sign of guilt. Now, knowing it had been Pamela's idea all along, the whole thing suddenly seemed infinitely more innocuous, not to mention commonsensical.

Something else occurred to her.

'What about the conference? I already checked the council website. There *was* no tech conference in Dundee that weekend, and you never mentioned one to the police. Your alibi was false.'

For the first time since she'd confronted him, Gerry appeared genuinely furious. His eyes flared and he glared across at Anna with a look akin to disgust.

'You're trying to make out *I* killed her? *Me?* What the hell possible reason could I have had? What would I have had to gain?'

Anna didn't answer. Truthfully, she couldn't think of a solid reason, beyond a general sense that Gerry's actions still felt, in some indefinable way, like those of a guilty man.

'Seriously,' said Gerry. 'What could she possibly have done to me that was so terrible it'd justify me going all the way through to Glasgow in the middle of the night to bash her skull in?'

'Why did you lie, then?'

Anna and Gerry both turned to face Pamela, caught off guard by her softly spoken intervention.

Gerry gazed desperately at her. 'Baby . . .'

'Don't "baby" me,' said Pamela, her voice almost unnaturally quiet after Gerry's outburst. 'I want you to answer me. You told me you couldn't come with me to Mum and Dad's cos you were tied up all weekend with the conference. "It's something I can't get out of," you said. Why would you say that if it wasn't true?'

Gerry continued to gaze miserably at her. To Anna's eyes, it seemed as if he was pleading with her not to force him to go there. But Pamela remained resolute, sitting up straight with her hands folded in her lap, meeting his gaze. Gerry's eyes briefly flashed to Anna, silently cursing her for putting him in this position.

Eventually, he angled himself towards Pamela once again, his entire body hunched forward, head bowed low, unable to face her directly.

'I made it up cos I didn't wanna go with you,' he muttered.

'What?' Pamela's voice cracked in disbelief.

'Your folks,' said Gerry unhappily, lifting his head slightly to meet her gaze. 'They've never liked me. I've never been good enough for you in their eyes: big fat working class scruff, getting his grubby great hands on their precious little daughter.

Sure, he's made some money for himself, but at the end of the day he's still just a glorified schemie. You can take the boy out of the council estate but you can't take the council estate out of the boy, right?' He flashed a humourless smile.

Pamela shook her head in slow disbelief. 'I don't understand,' she said, in the same small, plaintive voice as before.

'I'm never able to relax around them. I can always feel them, looking down on me, waiting for me to say or do the wrong thing. And I couldn't face an entire week trapped in that house of theirs, feeling like a failure. So I lied.'

Pamela continued to stare at him. 'You never said.'

'I didn't want to upset you.'

'We're getting *married*.' Pamela's voice cracked with emotion. 'We're supposed to *tell* each other these things.'

Gerry stared unhappily at his trainers and said nothing.

As the silence between him and Pamela continued to grow, Anna risked another question.

'You told the police you were at home alone on the night of Leanne's murder. What did you spend the night doing? And please don't say you don't remember.'

Gerry swung around to face Anna again, fresh anger flaring in his eyes – perhaps because she'd interrupted his moment of quiet reflection with Pamela or perhaps, more likely, because he'd simply had enough of being interrogated by her.

'You want to know what I was doing that night, while my ex was being bludgeoned to death?' he snapped. 'I was sat here in the flat, looking at porn. That's what I was doing.'

On the periphery of her vision, Anna was aware of Pamela clasping an involuntary hand over her mouth. Anna guessed she didn't approve, and that she probably regarded this as yet another betrayal on top of all the others.

'I was lonely,' continued Gerry, more softly now, but no less bitterly. 'And I was missing Paz, and so I . . .'

He trailed off, leaving them to complete the picture themselves.

'I can show you the browser history if that's what you want,' he said after a moment, directing his words at Anna in the same tone of bitter resentment. 'It's all there.'

Anna shook her head. 'No,' she said, not without some degree of sympathy. 'That won't be necessary.'

She felt genuinely awful about this. She'd known, either way, that it would be bad, but this was somehow worse than she imagined it would have felt if it had turned out Gerry had murdered Leanne – something she no longer even remotely suspected. At least then, she told herself, she'd have been saving Pamela from a killer. This, though, just felt . . . sordid. The lies, the omissions, the creative accounting – even the admission that he'd spent the evening of Leanne's murder in front of the computer with his hand down his trousers – it all just added to the grim sense that, rather than unearthing some grand conspiracy, all she'd really done was force Pamela to confront a series of squalid truths she'd have been happier not knowing about.

Slowly, Anna got to her feet. Gerry followed her with his eyes.

'What happens now?' he said. 'Will you go to the police?'

She knew what he was referring to: his cooking of the books.

'I don't know,' she said truthfully. 'I don't suppose it really changes anything in a material sense. It's not like anything you've told me has any bearing on Sean's guilt or innocence, does it?'

'No,' said Gerry quietly, 'I suppose not.'

Anna gazed down at the pair of them; at the wreck of their relationship. Or rather, she gazed at Gerry. She made sure Pamela remained lost in the indistinct blur of her right eye, convinced that, if she saw her face clearly, all it would reflect back at her was unbridled hatred for bringing this into their home.

'I'll see myself out,' she muttered.

Then, without another word, she turned and walked out, as quickly and in as dignified a manner as she could muster.

33

The journey back to Glasgow was as grim and morose as any Anna could remember. The pain in her head was excruciating, the pressure behind her eye close to unbearable, and the thought of her brain scan, the results of which she was certain she already knew, was enough to make her want to vomit. Checking her phone, she saw she had half a dozen missed calls from Dr Maitland. She ignored them all and tossed her phone back into her bag. She couldn't face them. Not now. Not yet. Besides, they'd all say the same thing.

Anna, please come and see me in my office to discuss the devastating, life-altering news that, for some reason, I categorically refuse to tell you over the phone.

And then there was the case. The case, where her latest grand wheeze had taken her right back to square one, with nothing but a ruined relationship to show for it. She doubted Pamela would ever forgive her. And perhaps she didn't deserve to be forgiven. After all, if she'd wanted to avoid a showdown like the one this morning, surely she could have made some more covert enquiries of her own before marching into Pamela's living room and presenting her with the worst possible interpretation of Gerry's activities.

The reality, she concluded, was that her current condition, and the gut-gnawing worries that came with it, had prevented her from approaching this case as diligently and systematically as she should have done. She'd been cutting corners, latching onto easy answers, going with whichever theory seemed the most expedient at any given moment.

And now? Leanne was still dead, Sean continued to languish in prison, and, in her heart of hearts, Anna knew she would still be lying if she claimed she believed, with any great conviction, that he was innocent.

Things would have been better if she'd held firm and met Pamela's plea to look into the case that night in February with a polite but firm 'no'.

An hour later, she found herself back at Queen Street Station. She was making her way down to the lower level to catch a train home when she belatedly remembered she'd promised Zoe she'd look in on Captain Pugwash for her. Exhausted, in pain and sick with worry, she turned round and trudged back up the steps, silently cursing herself for agreeing to yet *another* favour for a friend.

She and Zoe never had got round to the heart-to-heart they'd been on the verge of having in the nursery grounds. The previous night, when Anna had stopped at the flat to pick up Jack, she'd been back into full-blown deflection mode, taking full advantage of the fact that Zoe was on the phone to the factor about some issue with the central heating to make as speedy a getaway as she could. It was as if her moment of vulnerability on Monday had never happened.

It was getting on for two when she finally reached Cowcaddens, the tramp up the hill through the city centre having taken nearly twice as long as it would have done back when she was still fighting fit. Before she'd even unlocked the door, she was treated to the now-customary tirade of barking, hacking and spluttering from her would-be charge, who proceeded to follow her around the flat, yapping at her non-stop as she went in search of his collar and lead.

Five minutes later, the two of them were standing together in the communal garden area, a cold wind eddying around them, slicing through Anna's coat as she waited for the dog to do its business. It had quickly become apparent that the conventional act of walking to heel was something that was beyond Captain Pugwash, who'd turned on the brakes the moment they alighted on the grass and continued to refuse all overtures by Anna to coax him to move. He simply stood there, looking as miserable as she felt, gazing down at the ground as if he was waiting for it to open up and swallow him.

'You,' she informed him, 'are a sorry excuse for a dog. You know your ancestors were once wolves?'

Captain Pugwash licked his chops, then let out an almighty sneeze, the force of which sent him flying backwards onto his rump.

A drop landed on Anna's cheek, then another. She stood there, neck tucked into her collar, hands jammed into her coat pockets, as it proceeded to piss with rain.

After ten minutes of exposure to the elements, she called it quits. She trudged back up the steps, soaked and exhausted, Captain Pugwash – who'd discovered that he *could*, in fact, move the moment Anna decided to turn for home – trotting behind her. Inside the flat, she let her sodden coat fall in the hallway and staggered through to the living room, where she promptly collapsed on the sofa.

Just a few minutes, she told herself. *I just need to recharge my batteries.*

The clack of paws on the floor heralded the arrival of

Captain Pugwash, who came to a halt at the foot of the sofa and once more proceeded to assault her eardrums with his tirade of barking.

Anna groaned and massaged her aching head.

'Dog, you are *not* helping me here.'

Captain Pugwash stopped barking for all of three seconds, then resumed with even greater ferocity.

Anna shut her eyes, trying to will both the pounding behind them and the dog's barks to silence. The right side of her head felt like it was being crushed in a vice. She pressed the back of her hand against her temple, but the pressure only intensified – hot and sharp, like her brain was trying to force its way out through her skull.

Suddenly, it hit.

If what she'd felt until now had been pain, a new word would have to be added to the dictionary to describe what she now found herself experiencing. It was like nothing she'd ever felt before – fast, cataclysmic, exploding from somewhere deep behind her right eye and radiating outward like a thunderclap. Her vision whited out. Her whole body turned rigid.

Dimly, she registered the dog's yelp as she tripped over him in her senseless rush to get to her feet. She dropped to the floor, hard, landing shoulder-first on the unyielding surface.

She lay there on her side, one arm pinned beneath her, the other sprawled limply beside her. Her eyes darted helplessly this way and that as she tried to move. Tried to speak. But nothing happened. Her breath came out in short, panicked gasps. She felt the hot surge of vomit rising in her throat, then dribbling from her slack mouth onto the carpet.

She heard the pad of paws. Captain Pugwash approached, his wrinkled face gazing down at her with a look so akin to concern that she almost wanted to laugh.

'Hmmmphwww,' she told him. 'Gwwwwhwmphhlllphhhh.'

Captain Pugwash stood there for a moment, his head cocked slightly to one side. Then he turned and trotted off, disappearing from view. For a brief, euphoric moment, Anna convinced herself that the dog had understood her plea and had gone to summon help.

The moment soon passed. A few agonisingly long seconds later, she heard the sound of approaching paws again as he re-entered the room. He trotted up to her, carrying a large pink squeaky bone, which he dropped in front of her, then sat down, gazing at her with a look Anna now realised was not concern but expectation.

'Fffffuuuucckkksake,' she managed to groan, before everything turned black.

34

The world came back together in fragments.

At first, there was only light – blurry, diffuse light, seeping through her eyelids. Then came sound – a soft, rhythmic beeping, almost comforting in its predictability. And a voice – or perhaps multiple voices – hushed, murmuring, too quiet and muffled to understand.

Anna stirred. Her limbs felt leaden, her head woolly, like it had been stuffed with cotton wool.

She opened her eyes a crack, cautiously letting in the light.

The ceiling above her was unfamiliar, tiled white and grey. Cold, clinical colours, to match the sound of the beeping.

She attempted to open her mouth, but her lips were stuck together. Tried to speak, but only managed a low moan.

'I think she's awake,' said a voice.

A voice she knew, but her head was too woozy to connect it to a face.

And then she opened her eyes fully and saw the faces staring at her. They seemed to come into focus one by one.

Zoe, leaning over her, her long red locks cascading over her shoulders, her freckled face even paler than usual, worry and elation vying for dominance in her wide, grey-green eyes.

A stocky woman with dark hair in a bun, wearing blue hospital scrubs. A nurse, she thought. Filipino, perhaps. Or perhaps not. She didn't want to make assumptions. Assumptions were bad, especially when it came to race and ethnicity.

And then, standing at the foot of the bed, beyond the twin hillocks that Anna assumed must be her feet beneath the pale blue blanket, tall and erudite, ash-blonde curls framing her long, serious face – Dr Elizabeth Maitland, consultant neurologist.

'Hey.'

Zoe's voice, a gentle, quavering whisper, caused Anna's focus to rack back to her friend's face.

'Ye're back. Ye know ye scared the ever-loving *shite* out of us?'

'What . . . happened?' Anna managed, her voice raspy and unfamiliar in her ears.

'You collapsed,' said Maitland matter-of-factly. 'The paramedics brought you in. You've been in and out of consciousness for the past few hours. You don't remember any of it?'

Anna shook her head.

'It looks like you experienced a sentinel haemorrhage – a small leak from the aneurysm. That's what caused the sudden pain and collapse. Not a full rupture, but they're often a warning sign that one is imminent.'

Anna shook her head again, struggling to process this. Most of it had sounded to her like gobbledygook. She forced herself back to the beginning of Maitland's explanation – to the first thing she'd said after 'You collapsed.'

'Paramedics . . . what . . . how?'

Zoe grinned. 'Captain Pugwash. His barking cheesed off the neighbours so much they called the cops. They figured he'd been abandoned, so they broke the door down; found *you* lying on the flair. Wee soul prob'ly saved yer life.'

Anna let out a shuddering breath. 'I take back . . . every bad thing . . . I ever said . . . about him.'

'Y'know, I think he actually *knew* ye were poorly? I read somewhere, dogs've got a sixth sense about they things.'

But Anna's thoughts had already moved on – or rather back, to something Maitland said.

'You mentioned . . . something about an aneurysm?'

'That's what I was trying to reach you about all day!' exclaimed Maitland, with all the enthusiasm of a literary detective announcing the solution to a particularly knotty locked room mystery. 'The results of your MRI. The shadow we saw on the original scan? It's a berry aneurysm – a bulge in one of the arteries at the base of your brain. It hasn't ruptured, but the symptoms you've been experiencing – the headaches, the visual disturbances, the nausea – those were all warning signs.'

Anna blinked hard, trying to force herself to make sense of what she was hearing.

'But . . . but I looked everything up online. The symptoms . . . all of them . . . tumour.'

'It's true,' Maitland agreed, 'your symptoms aren't consistent with the typical presentation of an aneurysm. In fact, most of the time, they're completely symptomless. But yours is atypically large, and because of where it is – on the right posterior communicating artery – it's been pressing on nearby nerves and tissue. That explains the headaches, the pressure behind your eye, the blurred vision, even the trouble finding words.' She paused. 'Are you aware your blood pressure's sky high?'

Anna shook her head dumbly.

'That would explain why the aneurysm's grown so quickly. And I suspect this isn't the first leak you've had. It would fit with the way your symptoms have been building over time.'

Anna stared up at Maitland in silence for several seconds – confusion, hope and a strange, irrational feeling of anticlimax vying for dominance inside her head.

'I don't . . . I don't have a brain tumour?' she managed to say.

Maitland smiled. 'You don't have a brain tumour.'

She let the news settle for a moment, then her expression became solemn once again.

'That's not to say your condition isn't serious. A ruptured berry aneurysm is a major medical emergency – potentially fatal. You're extremely lucky yours hasn't reached that stage.'

She paused again, letting her words sink in. Then her face softened once more.

'We've started you on medication to manage the intracra-nial pressure and lower your blood pressure. The aneurysm's size and the tricky location preclude the possibility of more conservative treatments, meaning our only option is to perform an intercranial procedure known as surgical clipping. We'll monitor your condition overnight; make sure your blood pres-sure remains stable. Then, assuming all's well, Mr Bhakti, the consultant neurosurgeon, will operate on you first thing tomorrow morning.'

Anna blinked again. Her heart was racing, her brain still not quite managing to compute what it was hearing.

'Have you got any questions?' Maitland asked.

Anna licked her dry lips. Gazed up at Maitland, like a small child looking to an adult for reassurance.

'I'm not . . . going to die?'

Maitland smiled. 'As things stand, you're stable and in good hands. I fully expect you to make a complete recovery. But it's important we act promptly – which is precisely what we're doing. I'll let you get some rest now.'

She turned to the nurse, then nodded surreptitiously in Zoe's direction.

'Don't let her stay too long,' she said in a low voice.

She slipped silently out of the room. As the nurse continued to monitor the various machines, Zoe perched on the end of the bed and slid a hand under the covers, finding Anna's and squeezing it. For several moments, they remained like that, Zoe gazing down at Anna affectionately, Anna gazing back up at Zoe, overwhelmed by gratitude towards her for simply being there.

'Where's Jack?' she asked eventually.

'I brought him in wae me,' said Zoe. 'Didnae have time tae organise anything else. One of the nurses is looking efter him.'

'Good.'

That was one less thing for her to worry about.

'Well,' Zoe went on briskly, 'I've gottae say, this is a bit of a turn-up for the books. Mind you, I always *did* figure, if one us was ever gonnae have a brain aneurysm, odds are it'd be you.'

Anna managed a weak smile.

Zoe's expression turned serious. She fixed Anna with a look of consternation.

'Anna, how the hell did ye no *tell* me?'

'You heard the doctor,' said Anna weakly. 'I didn't even know I had this . . . this berry aneurysm till now.'

Zoe shook her head reproachfully. 'Ye know what I mean. You, carrying all this around inside that big auld heid o' yours, no saying a word tae me.'

'I didn't want to worry you,' Anna said helplessly.

Zoe stared at her with derision, as if she couldn't believe she'd stoop to that excuse.

'That's such fucking bullshit, Anna. Newsflash: I'm yer *pal*. It's my *job* tae worry about ye. How is it ye've got all they fancy diplomas framed on yer wall and ye still havnae got *that* intae yer thick skull?'

Anna winced apologetically. 'I'm sorry.'

'Don't be sorry. Just don't dae it again.'

'I won't,' said Anna, chastened.

Zoe got to her feet and circled the bed, hands clasped behind her back.

'It's aye been a bad idea,' she declared philosophically, 'this sitting on yer problems. All that happens is they get bigger and bigger and then – BOOM!'

'Hopefully not "boom" in my case,' Anna pointed out.

'Well, you heard the doc. Ye're gonnae be right as rain.'

Anna wasn't sure for whose benefit Zoe was asserting this with such certainty, but she opted not to argue. For one thing, she was too tired to.

'Right,' said the nurse briskly, 'enough talk now. Your friend needs rest. Big day tomorrow. Out, out.'

Zoe raised an eyebrow at Anna. 'That'll be me getting my marching orders, then. I'm no going far, but,' she added, with a pointed look at the nurse. 'You have yersel a nice wee snooze an' I'll be back in a bit.'

Anna did have a snooze – or rather several short ones, drifting fitfully in and out of consciousness multiple times over the course of what was left of the afternoon and into the evening. When she finally came round properly, Zoe was once again there, slouched in a chair by the bed, scrolling on her phone. Anna, observing her from the corner of her eye, noted how drawn her face looked – how, behind all the light-hearted banter and confident assertions that everything would be fine, Zoe was every bit as freaked out as she was.

She made a show of coming round and Zoe, pocketing her phone, instantly slapped on her happy face. They chatted for a while, about nothing of any great significance. Then, Anna asked Zoe to bring Jack in.

As Jack sat on the end of the bed, his drawing book and pens spread out before him, Anna explained to him that she wasn't feeling well and had to have an operation, but that she was going to be OK. Jack, who seemed rather disinterested by the whole affair, nodded and continued to scribble furiously in his book.

After some time had passed, Anna asked to speak to Zoe alone. One of the nurses – the one who'd looked after Jack earlier, she assumed – took him by the hand and led him out.

As the door closed, Anna turned to Zoe and began to speak in a low, urgent voice.

'Zoe, if anything goes wrong tomorrow—'

'It *won't*,' Zoe insisted. 'I looked up the op online. It's a bit gruesome,' she went on, with a certain amount of relish. 'They drill right intae yer skull just over yer ear. But it's dead straightforward. Folk have 'em done all the time.'

Somehow, she succeeded in making it sound as if it was a procedure people chose to undergo for cosmetic reasons.

'I know,' said Anna, 'but if something *does* go wrong . . .'

'Aye,' said Zoe quietly.

'. . . I want you to promise you'll take care of Jack.'

Zoe perched on the end of the bed. She took Anna's hand and gazed into her eyes with an intensity that was almost frightening.

'I will. Anna, ye *know* I will. But it willnae come tae that.'

Anna hoped that would be enough. She'd procrastinated endlessly about consulting a lawyer or making a proper will – and now? Now, she supposed, it was too late – a situation entirely of her own making. She resolved to write out a statement tonight once Zoe had left, setting out her wishes in clear, unambiguous language, along with the letter she planned to write for Jack, to be given to him if, somehow, she didn't make it.

It would do, she told herself. It would have to.

'There's something else I need to say,' she said after a moment.

'Aye?'

'I'm really sorry I haven't made a better fist of talking to Sal about . . . you know. I said I'd do it, but all I've done is bottle it at every opportunity.'

Zoe's face crumpled in tenderness.

'Aw, Anna, it doesnae matter. None of it fuckin' matters.'

'It does.'

'Naw, it *doesnae*.'

She scooted closer towards Anna, gripping her hand with a fresh intensity.

'Listen – I never got wae Sal cos I expected her to bring home a six-figure salary or buy us a mansion in Newton Mearns tae live in. I got wae her cos she's a mad fuckin' rocket who makes me laugh every day and treats me like a total queen. I don't care if she's happy spending the rest of her days working sixteen hours a week in a coffee shop – or if she decides, "Ye know what? Screw it. I'm gonnae pack it all in and live a life of sloth and indolence." I bring in enough moolah tae see us through. We're no living in the lap of luxury, but we do OK.'

She shrugged, like she was surrendering to something bigger than logic.

'Life's just too fuckin' short, y'know?'

Anna did know. Now, perhaps more than at any other point in her existence, she knew exactly what Zoe meant.

''Sides,' Zoe added with a grin, 'gotta admit there's a certain . . . I dunno, novelty 'bout being the responsible one for a change.'

Zoe left shortly afterwards, taking Jack with her. As Anna sat there in bed with a pen and notepad in her lap, fretting over how to begin her letter to him, one of the nurses – a solid, matronly figure of about her own age – came in to check her vitals. Anna realised she recognised her from before.

'You were the nurse who took care of my son earlier, weren't you?' she said. 'I just wanted to say thanks.'

'Och, it's no bother,' said the nurse, taking Anna's temperature with a digital ear thermometer. 'I'm the one folk turn to whenever there's wee ones needing looked after. In-house nanny, that's what they call me.'

'Well, I'm grateful. I know Jack's not always the easiest to deal with.'

'Honestly, it's fine. One of my nephews is autistic too, so I pretty much know the score.'

Anna blinked in surprise. 'But Jack isn't autistic.'

The nurse took a step back.

'Oh. Right. Well, my mistake.'

She finished doing her observations and cleared out quickly, obviously embarrassed by her faux pas. Anna found herself irritated by the exchange, though she couldn't put her finger on why. Perhaps it was the presumptive nature of it – the careless armchair diagnosis of another person's child. But then, she wondered, could it not also be because it had struck a nerve? She'd always resisted labels, especially ones that were forced on her by other people without her consent. She wouldn't accept someone defining *her* in that way, and she sure as hell wasn't going to let them define her son.

She forced herself to knuckle down and eventually succeeded in finishing both the letter to Jack and the statement setting out her wishes regarding his future care. But afterwards, she continued to lie awake long into the night – less preoccupied, now, by her surgery tomorrow and more by Jack. She'd always taken his various idiosyncrasies as mere quirks and oddities that made him unique. Lovely, maddening, irreducibly *him*. Yet now, try as she might not to dwell on one passing comment from a stranger who didn't know him, she couldn't stop herself from mentally rearranging every past moment with him, seeing them in an altogether different light.

Was it really possible, she wondered, that she'd been missing the blindingly obvious all this time?

The following morning, as soon as the ward rounds were over and the place was open to visitors, Zoe and Sal arrived with Jack in tow. The fact Zoe had brought Jack there to see her off was, in Anna's eyes, proof that, beneath all her bluster, Zoe had accepted there was a chance, however slim, that she might not come out of this in one piece. As such, she passed no comment about the fact that Jack ought be in school, treating him instead to an extended and decidedly possessive hug. Jack squirmed in her arms and moaned irritably – out of either embarrassment at the public display or discomfort at being held so tightly – or perhaps both.

The porters arrived to take her to the pre-op room, and suddenly, she was consumed by all the things she wanted to say and do, only now there wasn't enough time. She felt panic rising in her throat and found herself wanting to jump out of the bed and make a bolt for it – to go somewhere, *anywhere*, as long as it was far aware from here.

Seeming to sense her panic, Zoe moved towards her and gave her shoulder a reassuring squeeze.

'I'll take good care of him,' she whispered, correctly distilling the million and one thoughts bouncing around Anna's head down to their core.

'Time to go,' said the nurse briskly.

Zoe flashed Anna a wink. 'See ye on the other side.'

And then, Anna became aware that her bed was in motion, and she was being wheeled down the long corridor with its luminescent overhead lighting. She levered herself up into a sitting position and, craning her neck, gazed back the way she'd come. At the end of the corridor, Jack stood in the doorway, framed on either side by Zoe and Sal. Zoe held his hand in hers; Sal's arm was draped protectively over his shoulder.

And, for a fleeting moment, before she rounded the corner and the little group disappeared from sight, she thought they looked more like a normal, well-adjusted family than she'd ever been able to provide for him.

PART V

RESTRAINT

35

Thursday 7 April

Detective Superintendent Vanessa Tope checked her email inbox for the umpteenth time, once again reassuring herself that everything pressing had been either dealt with or delegated to one of her more capable underlings.

Low, late afternoon sunlight streamed through the large window of her office on the fourth floor of the sprawling, grass-fronted complex in Govan that served as the Major Investigation Team's base of operations. She checked her watch. 4:55 p.m. It was going to be something of a novelty to actually clock off on time for once. She couldn't remember the last time she'd done that. She kept thinking there must be something wrong. Something she'd overlooked. But no – she'd checked her list multiple times and there really was nothing she'd forgotten to do. An actual, honest-to-God blank slate.

For the first time since arriving at her desk at 7 a.m. that morning, she allowed herself to clear all thoughts of work from her head and look with anticipation towards the long weekend that lay before her. Four days of just herself and her

Weimaraner, Steve, on a self-led walking holiday in the Cairngorms. Plus her phone, obviously, already pre-loaded with
podcasts in anticipation of the lack of signal up there.

Right now, French lessons were her listening material *du
jour*. Not for any particular reason – neither of her current
lovers was French, and she wasn't planning a trip there anytime
soon. But she'd had her fill of Conversational Catalan, Begin-
ner's Czech and Advanced German, and she could do with a
palate cleanser.

She got to her feet and began to clear her desk. Nothing
worse than coming back to an untidy desk after time off. Not
that there was ever much clutter for her to clear away. She
wasn't born in a bloody barn! As she worked, she conjugated
verbs in a low murmur.

*Je pars, tu pars, il part, elle part, on part, nous partons, vous partez,
ils—*'

Her desk phone rang, shattering the serenity of the
moment. Cursing the device for its poor timing, she quickly
finished her arranging and snatched it up.

'Vanessa Tope.'

'Ma'am, it's DI Drysdale.'

'Scott, hi,' said Tope, recognising the gruff voice of her
underling even before he said his name. 'What can I do for
you?'

'Well, Ma'am, I'm sorry to bother you, only I've just taken
a call from DS Huxley in the incident room. *She* just took a call
from the duty sergeant at Yorkhill station. Apparently, someone
walked in off the street an hour or so ago, spinning a fair old
yarn about the Leanne McColm murder. And I figured, since
you'd asked to be kept in the loop about anything pertaining to
the case . . .'

Tope lowered herself back into her seat. Something told
her she wasn't going to be walking out the door on time today
after all. Or, in all likelihood, making it to the Cairngorms
tomorrow.

'You did the right thing, Scott. Now then, what's the skinny?'

'Urm, you'd probably better get down there right away. I reckon this one could be a game-changer . . .'

36

Wednesday 20 April

Anna lay in her easy chair in the living room, gazing out at the street, improbably far-off beyond the double-glazed window. The cherry blossom season was in full bloom. She'd always liked this time of year, and all the more so because of how fleeting it was. The trees barely seemed to have sprouted their pink cotton-candy foliage before, as quickly as it had come, it was gone.

It was a bit like life itself, she supposed: brief, brilliant, and gone in the blink of an eye.

Muffled by the glass, she heard the sound of an approaching vehicle. A moment later, a Tesco delivery van came into view. It pulled up to the kerb outside the house, and she watched the harangued-looking driver jumping down and jogging round to the side hatch. She waited till he'd loaded the two crates containing her supplies for the next week onto his barrow and was making his way up the path before awkwardly levering herself to her feet.

Slowly, she made her way from the living room to the hall-way, the umbrella she'd been using as a cane tapping on the ground with each shuffling step. Leaning one hand against the wall in case she lost her balance, she wrenched open the door before the man could ring the bell.

He inspected the printed manifest.

'Delivery for Scav . . . Scavo . . .'

'That's me.' She gestured to the crates. 'Can you lift them into the . . . into the . . .' She waved a hand vaguely behind her. '. . . thingummy?'

'Sure,' the man nodded. He looked at her uneasily. 'You want a hand getting them unloaded?'

She knew what he was thinking: how long was this going to take her?

She shook her head. 'Just leave them. I'll give them back next time.'

The driver looked uncertain – though whether because it wasn't protocol or because he wasn't convinced she'd manage on her own, she couldn't tell.

At length, he nodded and left her to it. As he departed, he shot her a look that, these days, was all too familiar to her.

Pity.

She'd come round after the operation on 31 March to find herself in, if anything, an even worse state than before. The surgical consultant assured her the procedure had been a complete success: the aneurysm had been clipped without complication. And yet the nausea, the intense pain in her skull, the pressure behind her eye – all seemed to be, at the very least, as bad as ever. To these familiar symptoms could be added memory lapses, aphasia and a crushing, bone-deep exhaustion. All of this, the surgeon insisted, was temporary, and in time she would make a full recovery – but for now, the feelings of shame and helplessness were so overpowering that, if there *was* any light at the end of the tunnel, it was impossible to even conceive of, let alone see.

They'd kept her in hospital for just over a week. During that time, she found herself with no shortage of visitors and was just sorry her condition made it impossible for her to appreciate them properly. Zoe was there at least once every day, sometimes on her own, other times with Jack in tow. She kept these visits short and sweet, partly to avoid tiring Anna out, and partly to shield Jack from some of the less agreeable manifestations of her present condition: the short-temperedness, the tendency towards random bouts of weepiness, the frequent forgetting of words.

Farah Hadid was another frequent flyer, as was Marion Angus, Anna's former student from the early 2010s. They mostly talked shop with her, filling her in on the goings-on at Kelvingrove University and in the academic world more broadly. Anna might not have been much of a conversationalist at the moment, partly out of fear of coming out with the wrong word and embarrassing herself, but she was content to sit and listen until her head started to hurt too much – something which invariably happened fairly quickly where Marion, who never could use one word when a dozen more were available, was concerned.

On one occasion, the pair of them even came up together with a selection of picnic items procured from the M&S downstairs. For a time, Anna actually managed to forget she was an invalid confined to a hospital bed. Listening to her younger friends chattering away happily, she almost felt normal – until she realised she couldn't latch onto the flow of their conversation at all and was knocked swiftly back to the stark reality of her current state.

Afterwards, Farah stuck around once Marion had left, hurrying back to work before her absence was noted.

'I have some news,' she said, as she perched on the end of Anna's bed. 'I've decided, I *will* go for the course director position.'

'Farah, that's wonderful,' said Anna, delighted for her friend. 'They'd be fools to entertain anyone else.'

Farah considered this. 'I think,' she said prudently, 'if I get the position, it's because no one else is crazy enough to want it.'

Anna considered telling Farah she needed to stop doing herself down all the time, but concluded that any such entreaty was likely to fall on deaf ears. In any event, she was just glad to know that the programme would be in safe hands and that she was off the hook. The prospect of her being in a position to take up the post again herself seemed even more remote now than it had before the op.

She'd been signed off work, of course, and Gina Fox – the new Head of School and a significant improvement on her predecessor – had told her she wasn't to even *think* about coming back till she was completely ready. In a previous life, Anna would have been filled with horror at the insinuation, however unintentional, that she was surplus to requirements. Now, however, she found herself overwhelmed with relief that there was no question of her resuming her duties while still in such a deeply diminished state.

'There's something else,' said Farah, her words interrupting Anna's thoughts.

'What?'

'Émile. He . . . well, he proposed to me.'

Anna looked at her blankly, waiting for her to finish the seemingly incomprehensible sentence.

'Proposed what to you?'

Farah laughed. 'That we should get married!'

It took Anna a moment to cotton on. When she did, she tried to dredge up the appropriate thing to say under the circumstances, only to find herself, as she so often did these days, at a loss.

'That'll be nice for you,' she said, for want of something more appropriate.

Farah laughed again, and Anna found herself laughing at her own absurdity, and then Farah flung her arms round her and drew her into a fierce embrace, and the pair of them hugged each other and laughed together until the ward sister came in to ask them to keep the noise down.

The feelings of elation soon faded after Farah left, however, giving way to a vague – and, to Anna's mind, rather unreasonable – undercurrent of disappointment. Even though Farah going for the course director's position was what she'd wanted – indeed, what she'd pushed for – it left her with the uncomfortable feeling of being left behind. Of having outlived her usefulness. This was how all mentors must feel, she supposed, when the day came that their former protégés overtook them.

Furthermore, loath though she was to admit it, she also felt the stirrings of envy in response to Farah's other bit of good news. Yet another of her younger friends was now tying the knot, while she, at forty, remained resolutely single. She reminded herself that this was the life she'd chosen. She knew, deep down, that marriage and all the trappings that came with it wouldn't make her happy – but, on a certain level, she envied the happiness it brought *them*.

She told herself to stop being so foolish. After all, she was perfectly content with it just being her and Jack.

Except, right now, there *was* no her and Jack. It was just her at home, alone. She'd been back now for just under a fortnight, during which the days and weeks had blurred together to the point that only the slow drift of cherry blossoms on the pavement gave her the vaguest sense of the passage of time. She often found herself caught unprepared when friends showed up out of the blue, only for them to gently remind her that they had, in fact, confirmed it with her earlier in the week.

Jack was still staying with Zoe and Sal. She'd had a number of what amounted to supervised visits from him over the last two weeks, with Zoe bringing him to the house for just long enough to avoid Anna becoming too worn out by it all. A handful of times now, Zoe had broached the question of when Anna would be ready to have him back, but on each occasion, Anna had succeeded in steering the conversation away from the topic.

What was she so afraid of? Truthfully, she wasn't really sure, beyond a vague sense that, if she had him back, something would go badly wrong. She wasn't herself. She wasn't ready.

She couldn't look after him.

Not that she wasn't thinking about him nearly every minute of the day. He was rarely far from her thoughts, and, inevitably, those thoughts ended up turning to the words of that nurse on the neurosurgery ward.

One of my nephews is autistic too, so I pretty much know the score.

She told herself over and over that it was hardly some sort of death sentence if he *was* autistic. It wasn't an illness or a disability – it just meant he was wired slightly differently. And really, when you thought about it, wasn't *everybody* wired differently from everybody else, whether or not they qualified as being on the autistic spectrum?

Try to stop thinking of it as a negative. Try to see the positives instead.

And she could see how it could be viewed through that lens. Yes, being neurodivergent in a world built for people who weren't brought challenges, but it could also have its advantages.

She reminded herself of Jack's many strengths. There was his impressive vocabulary for a start, which she often took for granted but which far outstripped that of most children his age. Then there was his fearsome intelligence, his problem-solving abilities, his aptitude for building things, to the point that he was already rapidly outstripping the Age 16+ Lego sets he seemed to burn through as quickly as she could buy them for him. He could more than hold his own in a conversation with grown-ups, and adapted far better to change than she suspected she would have at his age. Indeed, from what she'd been able to gather, he appeared remarkably unfazed by the fact he was now living with Zoe and Sal on a full-time basis. As far as he seemed to be concerned, that was now his life, and he seemed to neither expect nor want it to change anytime soon.

Really, when you thought about it, it was just his problems at school – the lack of concentration and the sporadic tantrums, which, based on the occasional hints dropped by Zoe, Anna was aware remained an ongoing issue. And it wasn't as if other children didn't struggle to adjust to the rigours of formal education, especially those who'd grown up during the upheaval of lockdown. All things considered, he was doing pretty well. Surely there was an argument for letting sleeping dogs lie?

But, on the other hand, if he wasn't getting the support he needed . . .

She finally finished unpacking the shopping. Really, she should have had the foresight to schedule the delivery for a time when someone would be around to help her. But it was done. It had taken the better part of half an hour, with frequent rest breaks, but she'd managed it. One to file under 'Successes'. God knows, she needed all of those she could get.

She checked her phone. Saw that an email had come in while she was lugging bags of frozen peas to the kitchen.

Anna,

This is your mother. I was sorry to hear about your recent difficulties. I hope you're continuing to take life at a more sedate pace and are drinking plenty of fluids.

Life here in Saint-Tropez continues in much the same vein as always, down to the local épicerie's refusal, despite repeated entreaties from myself and others in the expat community, to stock Ovaltine.

I hope to visit you and Jack (my grandson) at some point in the not-too-distant future, though it's difficult to organise anything just now with Les Bravades approaching. Once the festivities are over, I shall try to arrange a trip.

PS. If you need a little digestive encouragement, I've discovered a recipe for a very good prune and beetroot tonic that I'm forwarding to you.

Anna allowed herself a small smile. Truthfully, this was about the most positive response she could have hoped for. She'd only reluctantly allowed Zoe to inform her mother about her situation, fearing she'd jump on the next flight over – something that would have been good for neither party's blood pressure. She noted well the pointed reference to 'my grandson', though she knew, from her mother's eagerness to get her excuses lined up, that the threatened visit was unlikely to materialise any time soon. Not if she knew Leah.

As she made her way gingerly back towards the living room, the doorbell rang again. Biting back a curse, she corrected her course and shuffled to the front door.

She opened it to Vanessa Tope.

'Vanessa,' she said, surprised.

Tope smiled. 'Hi, Anna. Would you mind if I came in?'

Anna gazed out at the impossibly well-groomed Detective Superintendent, and suddenly pictured herself as Tope must see her: a pale, tired-looking woman in a shapeless pullover and baggy cords, her hair strategically combed across the right side of her head to mask the long, curving scar that arced from just above her temple up to the crown. Before the op, she'd been considering lopping off her long hair, on account of its weight and the hassle of washing it, but now, she'd never been more grateful for it.

'Sure,' she said, belatedly remembering that Tope was waiting for a response. 'Right this way.'

They headed through to the living room, Anna conscious of Tope deliberately slowing her own pace to match hers. She invited Tope to take a seat, then sank heavily into her own chair, hooking the umbrella over the armrest.

'I gather you've been in the wars,' said Tope. 'All well now, I trust?'

'Oh yeah, good as new, me,' said Anna, her own words sounding bitingly acerbic in her own ears.

'That's great to hear.'

An awkward silence settled on the room, punctuated only by the muffled sounds of traffic beyond the window.

Anna looked at Tope expectantly. Tope seemed to suddenly remember herself.

'Oh yes, sorry. I thought I'd drop by to let you know there've been a couple of interesting developments in the Leanne McColm case.'

'Oh,' said Anna, not sure how to feel about this. Of late, she'd made a conscious effort not to think about the case if she could possibly help it. In her mind, she'd come to associate it far too strongly with her recent brush with death, and continued to wonder whether the pressure she'd put herself under might have contributed to her nearly catastrophic collapse.

'A certain Andy McGovern recently turned himself in to the police,' said Tope. She paused. 'Friend of yours, I believe.'

It took Anna a moment to realise why the name sounded dimly familiar. Then it hit her: Lawlor's man. The one who'd been mistaken for Sean.

'He turned himself in?' she repeated, her mind too sluggish to do anything other than parrot Tope's words back at her.

'I don't know what you said to him, but it clearly did the trick. Sang like a canary to my colleagues at the Money Lending Unit – gave them chapter and verse about each and every one of Jonny Lawlor's dirty dealings, all the way back to the year dot. Thanks to him, they've been able to shut down Lawlor's outfit *and* the wider network he was part of.'

Anna wasn't sure what to say.

'That's . . . amazing,' she eventually managed.

'But I fancy that's not the part that'll *really* interest you,' Tope went on. 'We also got an on-the-record admission from him that he was the man seen with Leanne on the night of her death. And the cherry on top: Kasia Wiśniewska successfully picked him out of a fresh lineup.'

'Amazing,' Anna said again. A beat. 'And what happens to McGovern now?'

'Well,' said Tope, 'he's up to his oxters in some pretty shady practices himself. "Just following orders" doesn't carry much more weight with us than it did at Nuremberg.' She gave a philosophical shrug. 'But, if you scratch our back, we'll scratch yours, and he's done a fair amount of scratching. Besides, judges love a reformed sinner.'

Anna nodded. 'Good.'

Now that it came down to it, she realised she rather liked McGovern. Well, perhaps 'liked' would be putting it too strongly, but she recognised the favour he'd done for her, coming to her that day at the university – no doubt at considerable risk to himself.

'And how's this likely to affect the case against Sean?' she asked.

Tope pursed her lips, arms folded.

'It's early doors. There's still a long way to go till he gets to trial, and the prosecution's case against him could look very different by the time he's sitting in the dock.'

'Right,' said Anna, irritated by the noncommittal nature of

Tope's response but lacking either the energy or the mental clarity to challenge it.

A moment passed. Then:

'What was the other one?'

'The other what?'

'The other development. You said there'd been a couple.'

'Ah. Yes. That. Well, perhaps "development" was the wrong word. More an ongoing line of enquiry. On reflection, I think, perhaps, it would be unwise for me to comment on a situation that's still unfolding. It could turn out to be a total nothingburger. All will no doubt become clear in due course.'

Anna again tried to get Tope to elaborate, but she refused to bite. Had Anna been in a more robust frame of mind, she'd no doubt have persisted. As it was, the mere act of sitting here and talking had all but completely drained her, and she decided that, on balance, she'd rather not delay Tope's departure any longer than necessary, lest her thinly maintained façade of stoicism in the face of adversity crumble and Tope see her for the poor, diminished creature she actually was.

She saw Tope to the door, despite the detective's protestations not to put herself out. Tope entreated her to look after herself, then strode off down the path towards her Carrera sports car, every bit as sleek and polished as she was. Anna watched her go, remembering a time when *she'd* walked with that sense of purpose and confidence.

37

Monday 25 April

The following week, Anna had her follow-up scan at the Queen Elizabeth. Both Farah and Zoe had offered to come with her, but she'd refused their advances, instead booking a taxi and making her way gingerly down the path to the street, trusty umbrella in hand.

An hour and a half later, another taxi deposited her back on Southbrae Drive. As she manoeuvred herself out of the cab, she spotted a smallish figure sitting on the front step outside the house. It wasn't until she drew nearer that the figure stood up and she realised it was Pamela Macklin.

'Pamela,' she said, surprised and somehow apprehensive.

Pamela smiled sheepishly. 'Sorry. You weren't in and I couldn't get you on the blower.'

Anna hadn't checked her phone for messages since being reunited with it following her scan. The call must have come through while she was still inside the machine.

'. . . so I thought I'd better wait,' Pamela finished with a slight shrug. 'And here you are.'

'Yes,' Anna agreed. 'Here I am.' She remembered her manners. 'Would you like to come inside?'

Pamela beamed, as if she hadn't realised such an offer was on the cards.

'I'd be delighted to.'

The two of them trooped in together. As they stepped into the hallway, Pamela gave Anna a curious look.

'Have you had a fall?'

For a moment, Anna was confused. Then she realised Pamela was referring to her umbrella and slow, shuffling gait. It occurred to her that Pamela had no reason to know anything about the aneurysm, the surgery or her stay in hospital. Perhaps unsurprisingly, given how they'd left things, there had been no contact between them since the morning before she collapsed. On reflection, Anna realised she was quite happy with this state of affairs. There was something refreshing about coming across someone who didn't know every last detail about her recent brush with death.

'Something like that,' she said.

They made their way into the living room. Anna made a point of offering Pamela something to drink (she declined) and remaining on her feet till Pamela had taken a seat instead of collapsing straight into her easy chair, as had become her habit of late.

'First of all,' said Pamela, once they were both seated, 'I want to apologise for how I behaved the other week. I was upset and in denial and I took that out on you, which I shouldn't have done. Frankly, I disgraced myself.'

'That's all right,' said Anna. 'It wouldn't have been easy for anyone, hearing . . . that. Are you and Gerry . . . ?' She trailed off.

'We're taking some time off at the moment,' said Pamela flatly.

'Oh. I'm sorry.'

She didn't know what else to say.

'The flat's still in both our names,' Pamela went on, 'and I . . .' She hesitated. 'I like to believe we're still going to get married at some point. But we've . . . well, let's just say we've a few things to iron out before we can even *contemplate* moving forward with that.'

'Sorry,' said Anna again, feeling worse than useless in her inability to muster up anything more profound.

A silence settled on the room, both of them looking in vain for something on which to fix their gaze besides each other. At length, Pamela stirred again.

'I want to make it absolutely crystal clear I don't hold any of it against you,' she said. 'You did everything I asked you to. I'm not exactly in a position to complain just because I didn't like hearing what you uncovered.'

'Didn't do much good, though, did it?' said Anna. 'Gerry was just another red herring at the end of the day, and Sean's still in prison.'

Pamela's expression shifted, as though Anna's words had jogged something in her mind.

'Actually, that's what I came here to talk to you about.' She paused. 'You haven't heard, then?'

Anna stared back at her blankly. 'Heard what?'

'Sean's no longer in prison. He's been released.'

'WHAT?' Anna almost fell out of her chair.

'This Friday past. We got word just before they let him out.'

Anna stared at Pamela in disbelief, completely lost for words.

'But . . . what *happened*?' she eventually managed to say.

'His alibi? The friend he originally said he was with the night of the murder? Well, they came forward.'

'The one he changed his mind about and decided he'd been out for a run instead?'

'The very same.'

She might not be saying it, but, from her tone and the

dubious look on her face, it was clear Pamela found this development as surreal as Anna.

'And who is he – this friend?' Anna asked.

'Not "he". *She.* Her name's Melanie Phelan. It would appear she's a . . .' She trailed off.

'A what? She's a what? Just say it, Pamela.'

'Prostitute.'

She spoke the word in a hushed whisper, dropping her gaze to her lap to avoid eye contact with Anna.

'I suppose that might explain his reluctance to identify her,' said Anna, after a moment. 'Though surely, given that he was charged with *murder* . . .'

She cleared her throat, forcing herself to focus on what was important right now.

'And she came forward of her own volition?' she said.

'So it seems,' said Pamela. 'She turned up at Yorkhill Police Station, saying she'd remembered Sean was . . . you know, *with* her . . . that night.'

'And that was enough to get him released?'

'That, plus the sighting and the CCTV turning out not to be him. The Procurator Fiscal reassessed the case; concluded there was no longer a realistic prospect of conviction. So the charges against him were dropped and he was released.'

Pamela ended with a little shrug, as if presenting the whole thing as a fait accompli.

'The investigation remains ongoing, I take it?' said Anna.

'Oh, yes. Needless to say, if Sean didn't kill Leanne, then it means the police and – let's face it – the entire justice system spent months hounding the wrong man when the *real* killer's still at large somewhere.'

'Any suggestion of the police having someone in the frame?'

Pamela raised an eyebrow mischievously. 'I think you'd be better off asking your friend Detective Superintendent Tope that. Rumour has it you two are quite close these days.'

Anna gave a strained smile. 'I reckon the powers of my persuasion have been grossly exaggerated if you think that.'

Pamela smiled softly. 'Perhaps.'

She was silent for a moment. Then:

'Seriously, though, Anna, well done. And thank you. There's no way we'd be where we are today if it hadn't been for you.'

Anna gave a small nod of acknowledgement but said nothing. Truthfully, she doubted that very much. It sounded as if, in the end, she'd been almost entirely surplus to requirements.

'Have you had any contact with Sean since he was released?' she asked, attempting to shift her mind from her own navel-gazing.

Pamela shook her head. 'No. At least, not as far as I know. Gerry might have, but I . . . *we* aren't really doing a whole lot of speaking these days. To each other, I mean. I had thought about ringing Sean myself, seeing how he's getting on, but I decided against it. I figured he needs his own space. To process, and . . .' She trailed off.

'Where is he now?' asked Anna.

'Back at the house in Springburn, I gather. I'm not sure how he can stand it. I don't think *I* could. Not after . . .'

Pamela trailed off again. A moment passed, then she inhaled a deep breath and pasted on a bright smile that, under the circumstances, felt decidedly forced.

'It's the right outcome,' she said. 'He didn't do it.'

Anna nodded but remained silent. She knew she should be pleased – that this was exactly the outcome the two of them had been working towards all along. And yet, some part of her recoiled from the very idea of calling this justice. Perhaps it was the unsettling sense that her own illness and Sean's release had become strangely entangled in her mind – two narratives knotted together, both spiralling to conclusions that didn't feel earned. Or maybe it was the lingering distaste she'd never quite managed to shake; the fact that, guilty or not, Sean

Kerevan was still the kind of man she instinctively believed should not be walking free.

But there was something else. The whole affair, now that it had apparently been resolved, felt like a story she'd been written out of, her efforts rendered peripheral. Pamela's apparent gratitude only reinforced that feeling of dissonance. The truth was, Anna didn't feel remotely triumphant. It was as if she'd been chasing shadows while, beyond the fringes of her vision, the outcome was being shaped by forces beyond her control.

So she said nothing. She simply nodded again, trusting that Pamela would infer whatever she wanted from this silent gesture.

38

Friday 6 May

Two more weeks rolled by. Towards the end of the second, Anna received a call from Elizabeth Maitland, informing her that her follow-up scan showed that the aneurysm was completely sealed. The crisis, she was assured, was over.

So why did she still feel so off-kilter? So on edge? Gradually, she realised that it wasn't her health that was making her uneasy, but rather the outcome of the case – or, to be more accurate, the lack thereof. Something about it still troubled her – something she couldn't put her finger on.

She kept returning to the question she'd asked Pamela but to which she'd received no satisfying answer: if Sean hadn't killed Leanne, then who *had*? She'd already ruled out all the other potential suspects – at least, those she was aware of. There could be others in the frame. There *had* to be, if Sean didn't do it. She considered doing as Pamela had suggested and asking Vanessa Tope, but she resisted the temptation. Partly, it was because she knew Tope was unlikely to be drawn on the identity of any persons of interest in an ongoing inquiry.

But it wasn't just that. Reaching out to Tope would mean exposing herself and her vulnerability all over again – laying bare the fact that, despite her clean bill of health, she was still a long way from being herself. Tope, with her crisp suits and air of unshakeable authority, represented everything Anna currently was not: composed, sharp, fully in command. Their last encounter, when she'd dropped by to tell Anna about Andy McGovern's Damascene conversion, had been more than enough. She couldn't face that again. Not yet.

Still, she knew she couldn't just let things lie. Moving with a sense of purpose she hadn't experienced since before her collapse, she dug out her old notes and research on the case and began to go back through them from scratch.

It took her far longer than she'd anticipated. The fact she still had difficulty looking at screens and dense text for long meant she could only work in short bursts, taking frequent, lengthy breaks of the 'lying down in a darkened room' variety. But eventually, she got through it all. Then, having found nothing that leapt out at her, she began the process all over again.

The breakthrough didn't come in a single, sharp moment of clarity. It came when she least expected it, halfway between boredom and fatigue. One moment, she was scrolling through Leanne's Facebook profile for the umpteenth time, dragging her fingers on autopilot across the surface of her iPad. The next, she stopped dead, her heart thumping, the hairs prickling at the back of her neck. Slowly, she scrolled back up to the post she'd just passed: the photo of Sean and Leanne, seated together on their living room sofa, mere days before Leanne was killed.

Last look at the 🎄 Xmas decorations #twelfthnight 😭 😭 😭
Here's to an absolute belter of a New Year #2022
#feelinghopeful 😊 😊 🥳

She stared intently at the photo for almost a full minute, drinking in every detail of the room, comparing it against her memory from the day she and Pamela visited the house – a lifetime ago, or so it seemed. She took in the various props on display: the sofa, the framed prints on the wall behind it, the side table on which Leanne's beer bottle stood . . .

She'd been right about what she'd noticed. She was sure of it – and now that she'd seen it, she couldn't unsee it.

The doubt faded. The fog lifted. Something sharp and familiar began to stir in her chest.

And, just like that, the old drive was back.

39

Saturday 7 May

Once Anna actually got down to work, tracking down Sean's alibi didn't prove to be all that difficult. She surmised, from Pamela's account of her turning up at Yorkhill Police Station, that that was likely to be her local nick. A brief examination of the phone book revealed that a Melanie Phelan lived on a third-floor flat on Thornbank Street, close to the Ambulatory Care Hospital and within walking distance of the police station.

Anna stood in the street outside, gazing up at the thoroughly unlovely off-white building, framed against an overcast sky. The place had a depressing, anonymous feel, with small, uniform windows and mean little balconies – a poor venue for soaking up the non-existent sun. A single door on the ground floor served as the communal entrance.

Carrying her umbrella under her arm – she'd brought is more as a precaution than out of necessity – Anna made her way up the footpath and into the building. She was relieved to discover that there was a lift. It was small and rickety and smelled decidedly suspect, but it got her to the third floor in one piece and with considerably less effort than would have been required if she'd had to take the stairs. She made her way along the narrow, stone-floored corridor and knocked on the door to number 3/3.

The door was opened by a thin, ratty-looking woman of about thirty – give or take ten years in either direction. Her lank, curly hair was scraped back into a severe bun, and she wore a tired-looking dressing gown paired with incongruously fluffy-looking slippers.

'Aye?' she said, in a thirty-a-day smoker's rasp.

'Melanie Phelan?'

'Who's asking?'

'I wondered if I might ask you some questions.'

The woman glowered at her with unconcealed hostility. 'Oh aye? Questions, is it? And supposing, just supposing, I was tae tell ye tae take yer questions and stick 'em where the sun doesnae shine?'

The standoff might have continued indefinitely had one of the doors at the other end of the corridor not opened and an older woman with her hair in curlers peered out at them with a mixture of curiosity and suspicion. Anna could well imagine what assumptions she must be making, seeing a comparatively well turned out, professional-looking woman at the door of a known sex worker first thing on a Saturday morning.

Melanie glanced briefly in her neighbour's direction, then turned to Anna and gave a gruff, reluctant nod.

''Mon in off the landing, then,' she said ungraciously. ''Fore *everyone* decides they want a piece of the action.'

Knowing this invitation had nothing to do with hospitality and everything to do with discretion, Anna did as she was bidden.

Melanie directed her into a small, cramped sitting room that was in a severely dilapidated state. The carpet was thread-bare; the ceiling marked with condensation stains. A full

ashtray lay on a coffee table next to a sagging sofa, the upholstery worn thin at the arms.

As Anna gazed down at it, not sure she wanted to sit on it,
Melanie eyeballed her warily from near the doorway.

'You're not polis.'

It was a statement of fact rather than a question.

'No. I'm . . .'

Anna considered reaming off her credentials, but she
doubted this woman would be impressed by them. Not to
mention that it would seem somehow dishonest, given that she
was currently signed off sick. And the 'citizen investigator' line
seemed increasingly ridiculous the more she thought about it.

'I'm just a person,' she said simply.

'But you've got questions.'

'Yes.'

Melanie considered this.

'What's in it for me?'

It took Anna longer than it probably should have to cotton
on to the fact that she was being asked for payment. Opening
her wallet, she took out a couple of twenties, then added a
third when Melanie continued to meet her gaze, unimpressed.
Melanie snatched the notes, counted them like a pro and
slipped them into her dressing gown pocket.

She shrugged. 'So – what is it ye want tae know?'

'I wanted to ask some questions about . . .' Anna paused,
considering how best to word this. '. . . about an acquaintance
of mine.'

'Oh aye? "Acquaintance" is it?'

The 'lah-di-dah' was implied rather than spoken.

'And who is he, this acquaintance of yours?'

Anna noted the automatic assumption that the person
she'd referred to was a man. She wondered if Melanie thought
she was speaking to a scorned lover, and if she regularly
received visits from such people.

'Sean Kerevan,' she said.

Melanie Phelan had a good poker face – Anna would give her that much. But she couldn't quite hide the slight tremor at the corner of her left eye.

'That name s'posed tae mean something tae me?'

'It should do. You told the police he was with you on the night of the eighth to the ninth of January.'

Melanie drew her robe more tightly about herself.

'Mibby I did, aye. What's it tae you?'

'I told you. Sean's an acquaintance.'

'But ye're no his missus.'

'No, I'm not. I think you know as well as I do that his "missus" was killed on the night you told the police he was with you.'

Melanie looked uneasy. Her eyes glanced surreptitiously to one side, as if she was weighing up her chances of making a run for it.

'Well?' said Anna.

'Aye,' said Melanie curtly. 'I seen it on the telly.'

'Back in January, you mean?'

'Aye.'

'But you only came forward a month ago.'

'Didnae realise it was him till then, did I?'

Anna considered this. It was just possible, she supposed, that this was the truth.

'So you and he spent the night together. I take it it was a . . . business arrangement.'

Melanie sneered. 'Got some other kind of arrangement in mind?'

Anna smiled thinly.

'All right. So he came to you for your . . . services. Where did you meet?'

'Here.'

Anna stared at Melanie, incredulous. 'He came all the way here from Springburn just for sex?'

Melanie gave a sardonic smile, exposing two rows of

blackened teeth.

'Guess I'm just that good.'

'I'll take your word for it,' said Anna.

As she spoke, her gaze transferred briefly to the large TV facing the sofa. Its size and obviously high price tag were seriously at odds with its cramped, down-at-heel surroundings. It was clearly a recent purchase.

Anna returned her gaze to Melanie. 'Roughly how long was he here for?'

Melanie sighed, making clear her resentment at being made to go through again what she'd no doubt already told the police.

'Dunno. 'Bout three and a hauf, four hour? He left jist after three.'

'That seems like an awfully long time.'

'Whit kin ah say? I provide a very thorough service.'

She did a little flourish with her hands, like a magician finishing a trick.

'For which he paid handsomely, no doubt,' said Anna.

'Naw, I done it all for free.'

Anna gave another strained smile. 'How did he pay?'

'Contactless,' said Melanie, deadpan. 'I keep a card reader under the bed for punters who don't keep any money on 'em.' She snorted. 'He paid in cash. How the fuck d'ye *think*?'

Anna gestured to the TV. 'Paid for that, did he?'

'Aye. Look, are we done here?'

'Just about.'

Anna racked her brains, trying to think whether there was anything else she wanted to ask. Suddenly, she remembered something Natalie Lennox had said to her down at the waterfront, about a drunken confession Leanne had made to her one night when they were out on the lash.

'Sean's a pretty big guy, wouldn't you say?'

Melanie shrugged. 'Aye, s'pose.'

'Great big muscle-bound fella like that,' Anna continued, as casually as she could manage, 'I'm betting he was packing downstairs . . .'

'Oh aye. Big-time. Gave *me* plenty tae work wae, that's fer sure.'

Melanie cocked her head sideways, an amused smirk on her face as she studied Anna.

'You're getting off on this, aren't ye?'

'I don't know what you mean.'

'Aye ye do.'

Melanie nodded with smug satisfaction, convinced she'd well and truly got Anna's number.

'You're one o' they freaks that fall in love wae convicts – write 'em letters, send 'em yer used knickers, that sorta thing. That's what this is all about.' She shook her head mirthfully. 'Why's it always the posh wans?'

Anna said nothing.

Melanie chuckled to herself, as if this was a situation she often found herself in.

'Well, I hope ye got yer money's worth, but I reckon it's about time for ye tae bolt. Ye *do* know there's chat lines ye can call if ye're wanting someone tae talk dirty tae ye?'

'I'll bear that in mind,' said Anna.

She allowed herself to be escorted firmly to the door. As they passed down the narrow hallway, Anna clocked the wax Barbour jacket hanging from the coat stand – much like the TV, brand new and jarringly out of place amid its ramshackle surroundings.

She stepped out into the hallway, a gust of air ruffling her hair as Melanie slammed the door firmly behind her. She remained standing there for a moment, the conversation still echoing in her head – and with it, the creeping sense that she wasn't merely chasing ghosts.

She was on to something, and it was now firmly within her grasp.

40

It was approaching 9 p.m. when the taxi turned onto Millbrae Avenue. The last vestiges of twilight still clung to the darkened sky, but it was dimming fast, and the streetlights were already on. It wouldn't be long before it was fully dark.

As the driver pulled to a stop across the road from number 113, Anna, seated in the back, spotted the door to number 115 – the Grahams' half of the house – opening.

'Just keep the engine running for a minute, would you?' she said to the driver.

The driver did as he was instructed, and Anna watched as a heavily built man in a dark fleece emerged from the house, descended the steps and made his way down the path. Billy Graham stopped at the gate, paused to fit his headphones over his ears, then turned and set off, heading north towards Atlas Road and Springburn Station. Anna waited till he was out of sight, then paid the driver and got out. As the cab drove off, she crossed the road towards the house.

The lawn of number 113 was even more overgrown than it had been the last time she was here. Evidently, Sean hadn't been using his newfound freedom to catch up on the gardening. In addition to the drinks cans and other items of litter that had accumulated on the grass, some enterprising soul had taken the time to daub the word 'KILLER' in large red capitals across the front door and part of the wall.

She'd waited until now in order to maximise the odds of Sean being home. She wasn't sure how he'd been spending his days since his release, but she struggled to picture him just sitting all day in the house he'd shared with Leanne, with nothing but his own thoughts for company. Then again, perhaps that was *exactly* what he'd been doing. After all, had she not been doing much the same since she got out of hospital?

She gazed up at the house, clocking the light in the living room window. She took a couple of steps towards the driveway. Then, changing her mind, she corrected course, heading up the path towards the Grahams' front door instead. She stood on the step, listening. Beyond the drawn curtains of the front room, she could tell, from the frequent bursts of canned laughter, that someone was watching the TV at an obscenely high volume. She rang the bell a couple of times, and even pounded on the door with her fist for good measure, but the only response was a *ba dum tss!* drumbeat and a fresh gale of inane guffawing.

Her suspicions confirmed, she headed back down to the street and made her way up the driveway of the other half of the house with slow but determined steps. She hadn't bothered bringing the umbrella this time. It was more a hindrance than an aid now – and besides, she needed to project an aura of confidence and command. Tough to do that when you were reliant on a walking stick. She straightened her back, thrust back her shoulders and rang the bell.

Framed by the doorway of the tiny house, Sean seemed larger and more imposing than ever, and yet there was a weary, defeated air about him. Far from giving him a new lease of life, he seemed diminished since his release, as if a part of him had remained behind in his cell in Barlinnie.

'It's you,' he said.

'It's me,' Anna agreed.

She couldn't tell whether he was annoyed to see her or if his tone of flat detachment in fact signalled resignation – as if he'd been expecting this moment ever since he got out.

'Can I come in?' she said, when he made no move to invite her.

'Yeah, s'pose,' he muttered, then turned his back and headed down the hallway, giving no indication for her to follow.

She stepped inside, shutting but not locking the door behind her. Up ahead, Sean was already sloping through to the living room. She followed him to the doorway, where she stopped, taking in the view of the room beyond it. Sean had evidently made some attempt to tidy up the mess the crime scene investigators had left behind, but the furniture and overall layout matched her memory of her previous visit back in March. The sound of the TV next door leaked through the thin wall separating the two halves of the house, muffled but still loud enough to be intrusive.

Sean turned to face Anna, on the verge of saying something, but she cut him off before he'd even finished drawing breath.

'Before you say anything, I want to make you aware that I've texted this location to a dozen people. So, if anything happens to me, the police won't have to think hard about where to come looking. Are we clear?'

Sean looked at her for a moment, then gave a small nod. He didn't seem surprised by any of this. Again, it was as if he'd been waiting for this moment all along.

Satisfied, she advanced further into the room, till they were almost close enough to reach out and touch one another.

'It was a stroke of good luck, wasn't it?' she said. 'That woman coming forward to confirm your alibi.'

'Aye,' said Sean quietly, 'it was that.'

'Of course, if you'd just given her name and address to the police at the time, you'd have saved yourself a whole lot of bother.'

Sean glowered at her, saying nothing.

'Mind you, given her profession and the nature of your, uh, liaison with her, I suppose your reluctance could be seen as understandable.' She paused. 'Show me your penis.'

It seemed to take him a moment to process what she'd just said. 'Wh . . . what?'

'You heard. Show it to me.'

'What . . .' he began again; then, with a petulant stubbornness that put her in mind of a child refusing to eat its vegetables, '*No.*'

Calmly, Anna reached into her shoulder bag and produced a small plastic disc, not unlike a key fob in appearance and size. It had been delivered at the beginning of April, but she hadn't got round to taking it out of its packaging until today.

'This,' she said, 'is a personal safety alarm. The moment I press this button, it'll emit a one-hundred-and-forty-decibel alarm that won't stop till I press it again.'

One hundred and forty decibels. A full fifteen more than its predecessor, which was partly why she'd gone for this particular model, even though she knew, at that volume, it was merely splitting hairs.

'Do you want me to press it?' she enquired mildly.

For a moment, Sean continued to stare at her, disbelief mingling with something akin to fear. Then, with an angry, impatient sigh, he unbuttoned his jeans and yanked both them and his boxers down to just above his knees in a single movement. He stood there, gripping the waistband with his clenched fists, anger and humiliation coming off him in waves as Anna gazed dispassionately at his exposed genitals.

'That's fine,' she said, after a couple of seconds. 'You can pull your trousers up.'

Immediately, Sean hitched up his jeans, glaring daggers at her as he buttoned them.

'It's interesting,' Anna said.

'What is?' he snarled.

'You might claim to know Melanie Phelan, but I can tell you this for nothing: Melanie Phelan doesn't know *you*.'

Sean said nothing.

'So I guess my question is, who paid her to give you that alibi? Not you, obviously. You wouldn't have been in a position to do that from prison. But *someone* clearly did.'

Still no response – just the sound of the TV next door, the insufferably upbeat tone of the host utterly discordant with the tense atmosphere between Anna and Sean.

Anna took a step closer. 'It *was* you all along, wasn't it? You killed Leanne, right here in this room.'

That got a reaction from Sean. His eyes flared in momentary . . . what was it? Anger? Disbelief? Fear? All three? Then he caught himself and once more assumed his familiar expression of blank sullenness.

'Dunno what you're talking about,' he muttered.

'Oh, I think you do,' said Anna quietly. She paused for a moment. Then, 'Would you like to know how I know?'

Perhaps recognising that saying 'yes' would amount to an admission of guilt, Sean once again gave no response.

Taking his silence as permission to continue, Anna produced her phone. She unlocked the screen and angled it towards Sean, an image already loaded up.

'This picture.'

Sean gazed at the photo of himself and Leanne, seated together on the living room sofa. His expression remained blank.

'Taken in this very room,' Anna went on, 'just days before Leane died. Notice anything?'

Sean seemed to genuinely study the picture, examining it carefully in search of the telltale clue, then shook his head.

Anna pointed to an object visible at the corner of the image.

'The side table. Here in the picture, next to Leanne's half of the sofa. Gone just three days later when the police searched the house.'

'That doesnae prove anything,' Sean shot back. 'Mibby the cops took it away and forgot to bring it back. Or mibby they lost it. Should've seen the mess they made of this place.'

'I did,' said Anna calmly, 'and I know for a fact they didn't take it. The detective superintendent overseeing the case told me from her own mouth that absolutely nothing was removed from the house.'

She paused, letting her words sink in, before continuing.

'Someone got rid of that table between this picture being taken and the police arriving at the house on the night of Leanne's death. And that someone was you. You fought, and Leanne hit her head on the table, and that's what killed her.'

'That's absolute shite,' Sean retorted, shaking his head a little too vigorously for it not to be performative. 'If we'd had a fight, how come no one heard us?' A thought occurred to him. 'The neighbours next door.' He gestured towards the wall, through which the sound of the TV continued to leak. 'You can hear how thin they walls are. You know how it was. Two of us couldnae even raise our voices without them phoning the polis.'

'Billy Graham works nights,' said Anna. 'I called his employers earlier and checked: the night of Leanne's death, he was on security duty at the college in Haghill. And his mother's as deaf as a post. You could have been holding a rave in here that night and it wouldn't have roused her.'

She waited for Sean to attempt a fresh round of deflection, but he didn't respond. Slowly, he lowered himself onto the sofa and sat there with his head in his hands.

It was all the confirmation Anna needed.

'How did it happen?' she said quietly.

'It was an accident,' said Sean, his words muffled by his hands.

Anna scoffed. 'Right. Let me guess – a red mist descended on you, and you weren't responsible for your own actions, just like all the other times you beat the living hell out of her.'

'I TOLD YOU, I NEVER LAID A FINGER ON HER!!' yelled Sean, dropping his hands and raising his head to face her.

His sudden outburst caught Anna so off guard she instinctively took a step back. He glowered up at her, eyes seething with bitter resentment.

'I *loved* her,' he growled, more quietly but no less ardently. 'She was my everything. I'd DIE before I hurt a single hair on her head.'

Anna stared down at him, exasperated – but, at the same time, strangely intrigued – by his continued efforts to deny the undeniable.

'You say you didn't touch her,' she said, 'but she clearly died in this room, and you clearly moved the body – and then lied about it afterwards. How do you square that circle?'

'I can't,' said Sean unhappily.

'Then what happened?'

For almost a full minute, Sean sat there in silence, hunched over, squeezing his knuckles, one after the other – some sort of calming ritual, Anna supposed. She found her eyes instinctively drawn to the words inked on them.

'PAIN' and 'GAIN'.

Then, at last, Sean, began to speak.

41

'She went out that evening at the back of nine,' said Sean. 'Just did what she'd always do – suddenly announced she was going out, no explanation, no indication when she'd be back. "Just out," she said, when I tried asking where she was going. And out she went, slamming the door.'

He licked his lips and rubbed his palms together, still sitting hunched forward, staring straight ahead.

Anna, settled on one of the two reclining chairs that faced the sofa at a ninety-degree angle, continued to watch him intently. After his earlier outburst, an uneasy stillness had settled on the room. He spoke in a low, almost preternaturally calm voice, as if he too had recognised the almost hallowed quality of the air around him and didn't want to break the spell. The noise of the TV continued from next door, but it seemed less intrusive now – perhaps because the previous show had finished, the raucous laughter and strident tones of the presenter replaced by the comparatively more dulcet tones of what sounded like a nature documentary voice-over.

'She left her phone behind, as per,' Sean continued. 'I checked as soon as she was out the door. So I knew she was up to no good. I figured she'd gone back to the casino, or . . .

'I knew there was no telling when she'd be back. Sometimes, it'd be three or four in the morning when she came traipsing in, high as a kite off whatever buzz it is addicts get. Normally, I just let it lie cos I knew I'd get nothing out of her but dog's abuse. But this time, I decided I wasn't gonnae stand for it. I'd just found that receipt the other day, and my mind was churning like naebody's business with the thought she was having an affair. And so, I waited up for her. And the second I heard her coming in the door just after midnight, I was straight out to the hall to have it out with her.

'She never even looked at me at first. Just headed over to hang her handbag on the banister post like I wasnae even there, taking all the time in the world. I could tell she was in one of her moods. I asked her where she'd been. And she was like, "Don't fucking start with me, Sean. I've had my fill already the night of men telling me what the fuck to do."

'I was like, "What men?" And I wouldnae let it go. I said I'd had it up tae here with all the mysterious trips out, leaving her phone behind so's I couldnae see where she was. I said I knew she was seeing someone on the side.

'And she got this look in her eyes, like she'd been waiting for me to say it, *hoping* I'd say it. And she started goading me, saying it was true, she'd been shagging the entire town; that that was the only way she could get any satisfaction cos I sure as fuck wasnae giving it tae her.

'I said, "You're lying," and *she* said, "Mibby I am and mibby I urnae. You'll never know. Question is, which would you prefer? Cos see, thing about you, Sean, is I think, deep down, you actually *want* tae be cucked, cos then it'd justify all your mistrust and all your efforts to control me." '

He ran a hand down his face, as if trying to wipe away the memory.

'It went on like that for a bit. The two of us standing there in the hallway, her still in her coat, winding me up like there was no tomorrow. And she kept pushing and pushing, slagging me off harder and harder, trying to get me to break.'

'To get you to hit her, you mean?' said Anna. 'She knew you'd snap eventually if she kept goading you. She knew because it'd happened before.'

Sean's head jerked upright and, for the first time since he'd begun his story, he looked straight at Anna, eyes burning with bitterness and anger.

'For the tenth fucking time, I never fucking touched her! Not once in my whole life!'

'Then explain the bruises.'

Sean glowered. 'You wouldnae believe me if I told you.'

'Try me.'

Sean was silent for a moment, eyes fixed steadfastly on the fireplace in front of him. Then:

'She used tae do it to herself.'

'You're right,' said Anna. 'I don't believe you.'

But as she said it, an element of doubt crept into her mind. Right from the start, Sean had been utterly adamant that he'd never hit Leanne. It was the one truth he'd clung to throughout, even when he'd relented on virtually every other hole she'd poked in his narrative.

'She always bruised dead easily,' Sean went on. 'Delicate skin or . . .'

He gave a vague wave, the proper explanation beyond his grasp.

'From time to time – when we'd had a fight, when I done something tae annoy her, or just cos she felt like it – she'd grab her own wrists like this . . .'

He squeezed his left arm hard by way of demonstration, fingers digging deep into the skin.

'And she'd squeeze 'em and squeeze 'em till they were black and blue. And I'd watch her doing it and she'd say, sweet as anything, "See, Sean, if you insist on making things difficult, I might just have to tell someone you done this to me."'

'Far as I know, she never did. Not outright, away. Still dropped plenty of hints, but. Like, she'd never come out and say it, but I know she enjoyed letting her pals catch sight of her bruises, and she never set them straight when they assumed . . .' He gestured to Anna. 'Well, same as you.'

Anna dropped her gaze, twisting her hands in her lap. She hated to admit it, but she was finding it harder and harder to doubt him. If he was lying, he was doing a phenomenally good job of it. Contrast this with the utter flimsiness of his made-up alibis, and the difference was like night and day.

Sean inhaled a deep breath. When he next spoke, he was clearly making a concerted effort to moderate his tone.

'When I first got with Leanne, I was absolutely over the moon. I could hardly believe a lassie like her would ever so much as look twice at me. And, for the first year or so, things were really good. We were both completely besotted with each other. Couldnae stand to be apart. She was the last thing I thought about at night and the first thing I thought of the moment I woke up. The cracks never started to appear till after we started living the gether.

'And even after things begun to go south, ninety-nine point nine percent of the time, things were still really good between us. It was just that other point one percent. And I always said to myself, "You're not gonnae throw away the love of a lifetime on account of a measly point one percent, are you?" I could put up with the moods and the name-calling and the self-harming and—'

The suddenness with which he stopped suggested he realised he'd been on the verge of saying too much.

'And what?' Anna pressed him. 'What were you going to say?'

'It got worse, the last year or so,' he continued, with a forcefulness that suggested he hoped, if he just powered ahead, she'd let the matter drop. 'After the gambling problems started. At the time, I'd no idea that's what was causing it, but looking back, it's obvious that's where it all stemmed fae. She'd be stressed out her nut the entire time. She'd snap like *that*.' He clicked his fingers. 'The slightest thing set her off. I'd be treading on eggshells the entire time, feart that any minute she'd blow up, or start hurting herself, or . . .' He trailed off.

Anna stared at him, shaking her head. 'If that's what she was like, then why in God's name would you stay with her?'

'How many more times dae I have tae say it?' Sean exclaimed in exasperation. 'Because I *loved* her. D'you even know what that is? Have you ever experienced it?'

Anna didn't dignify that with a response.

'Plenty of folk've put up with worse, you know,' Sean continued. 'Ye wouldnae ask a battered woman why she keeps going back to her man, would you? Ye might try and persuade her not to, but you'd never act like it's some big mystery why she does it.'

Anna didn't trust herself to say anything. She ran a hand through her hair, inhaling heavily as she forced herself to concentrate on the crux of the matter.

'All right. Back to that night. You were standing in the hallway. She was winding you up, trying to get you to break. What then?'

'I decided I wasn't doing this anymore, so I just upped and walked away while she was still going on at me. I went back through here, but she came after me, like, "No, come on, big man. You wanted a fight, let's have a fight. Why don't you take a pop at me, huh? You're normally so good with your fists." But I wouldn't. And then . . .' He trailed off.

'And then?' Anna felt herself leaning forward.

'And then . . .'

She waited.

'And then she just fell and banged her head.'

It came out in a rush – a single expulsion of breath, the words running together in his hurry to get through them.

Anna stared at him in disbelief.

'That's *it*?'

It was his most feeble invention to date.

'What – you were just standing there, and then, spontaneously, she just dropped to the ground? You expect me to believe that?'

Sean glowered at the floor and shrugged, like an unrepentant schoolboy caught in a lie.

'Come on,' said Anna. 'You're going to have to do better than that.'

There was a long silence, broken only by the chatter from the TV next door and the loud, upbeat voices of a group of youths passing outside, their words muffled by the window. Sean neither moved nor spoke. He just sat there, hunched over, rubbing his knuckles obsessively.

Time passed. A fox yammered somewhere in the distance. And finally, in a low voice, Sean began to speak.

'The first time she hit me was just under a year ago.'

It took a second for Anna's brain to catch up with and process what he'd just said. Her eyes widened, lips parting in stunned confusion.

'The first time *she* hit *you*?'

Sean didn't respond to her. Instead, he continued in the same low, flat voice, as if she hadn't spoken.

'We'd been out for a drink with this couple we were pally with, and we'd had this argument about . . . honestly, I can't even *remember* what it was about. Something stupid and unimportant. We got in the door, still going at it hammer and tongs, and all of a sudden she just swung round and lamped me on the side of my head. I was so surprised, for a moment I just stood there, blinking. Then I felt the blood running down into my eye, and she was just staring at me, shocked at what she done.

'She got me cleaned up and was full of apologies, saying she didnae know what came over her; how she never done something like that before and she'd never do it again.'

He gave a small, mournful shake of his head. 'But it *did* happen again. And again and again and again. Face, ribs, balls – she was never picky about where she hit me. Usually, I could tell when it was coming. She'd get this . . . this light in her eyes. The air around her seemed to change, if ye can believe it. And by that point, I'd always know it was already too late. Once the cork was out of the bottle, nothing I said or done could put it back in. Not till she'd . . . got it out of her system.

'And afterwards, she'd be all over me, kissing me, telling me how much she loved me, how sorry she was. Sometimes, she'd make us have sex straight after, even though I was hurting and didnae want it. She'd just keep pushing me, grinding up against me, moaning, "Come *on*, Sean. I want to make you feel good." And so I'd just let it happen.

'She was dead big on keeping up appearances – y'know, the whole "document every minute of your life in pictures" arrangement. She was forever getting me tae pose for snaps so she could upload them onto Facebook and show everyone how happy we both were. She always seemed to want to do it right after we'd rowed.'

He gave a dry laugh. ' "Rowed". That's what she called it when she . . .' He trailed off. 'It was like . . . I dunno, like she thought, if she tried hard enough, getting the perfect shot and whatnot, she could somehow paper over the cracks and make the fantasy real.'

He fell silent. Watching him, Anna sensed that, deep down, there had been a part of him that had hoped in vain for that too.

'And you never hit back?' she said.

Her voice was soft, though still tinged with disbelief.

'Not once,' said Sean emphatically.

He lifted his head, looking straight at her with an earnestness that almost made her want to turn away.

'I don't expect you to understand, but it's like . . . like an honour thing, I guess. When I was a wee boy, a lot of my pals' mums were battered wives. Round where I grew up, it was practically expected. If their husbands gave them a split lip, it must've been cos they done something to deserve it. As a kid, I never knew that wasn't normal. But that didnae mean I didnae know it was wrong. And I knew, I just *knew* I never wanted to be like they men.' He shook his head emphatically. 'A man who does something like that – that's not a real man.'

Anna felt tempted to ask whether that made a woman who did something like that not a real woman, or if the inverse was true, but she resisted the urge to indulge in pedantry. Instead, she tried, once more, to move the story forward.

'So, that night, she started laying into you with her fists, like usual.'

'No.' Sean shook his head. 'At least, not right away. No, what happened first is I threatened to tell on her.'

'Oh,' said Anna.

She hadn't been expecting *that*.

'Aye – she kept on goading me to hit her, knowing I never would. And I said to her, "Leanne, this stops now. I'm done being your punching bag. And what's more, I'm done making up stories to cover for the bruises. I'm gonnae tell folk what you're really like."

'And she laughed at me. She stood there, head back, laughing her arse off. She asked me if I thought anyone was gonnae believe that – big brute like me against a wee slip like her. She said, if I told anyone, she'd just deny it, and not a person on this earth would take my side against hers. And supposing, just supposing they *did*, then I'd have to live with the shame of the whole world knowing I was the big strong man who let hisself get beat up by a girl.'

Another pause, another agonising silence.

'She was still right there in my face, goading me. "Come on – just one proper swing. Prove you're a man after all. Or've you no got the balls?" She gives this wee smirk; says, "Course, we both know you're deficient in *that* department."

354

'And I just seen red. The one time in my life, instead of standing there and taking it, I pushed her off of me. I never thought. I just wanted her out of my face. And she sorta staggered backwards wae this wide-eyed look. She kinda tottered on the backs of her heels for a moment, then she lost her balance and . . . and I heard the crack.'

He shut his eyes, clenching them tight, as if trying to will what had happened out of existence. Eventually, he opened them again, blinking heavily, and Anna saw that they were filled with tears. He gazed back at her desperately, almost as if he was pleading with her to make it go away.

'Why?' said Anna. It was all she could think to ask. 'Why did you never say?'

Sean's expression shifted into one of weary exasperation, tired of having to spell it out.

'Oh, c'mon. Use your imagination.'

'But even after you were accused of her murder, *still* you didn't say anything! Why wouldn't you even *try* to save yourself?'

Sean shook his head. 'You've got no *idea*. No idea of the shame that comes wae being a bloke who gets leathered by his own missus, 'specially where I'm fae. That sort of thing just doesnae *happen* to men. Plus,' he went on, gesturing to her with a meaty hand, 'I can see from your face, a part of you still doesnae believe me. A part of you's thinking it can't be possible. That I'm just telling you this tae save my own hide. Don't even bother trying to pretend otherwise.'

She didn't try, because she knew it would be pointless – and because he was right. However much she might not like it, a part of her, however small, *was* still struggling to accept what he was telling her. It clashed too starkly with everything she believed, everything experience had taught her, about a world in which men were the aggressors and women their victims. The notion that, in this case, the roles had been reversed felt like trying to force a square peg through a round hole. And yet, here it was, staring her in the face.

'All right,' she said heavily. 'Tell me what happened next.'

42

Sean took up the story again almost eagerly – relieved, it seemed, to be able to park his status as a victim of domestic violence. For now, at any rate.

'I dunno how long I just stood there. It might've been seconds, it might've been longer. But either way, I finally came out of it and looked down and there she was, just laying on the floor, not moving. The table was on its side next to her, blood on the corner of it where she'd whacked her heid aff it.

'I called to her. I shook her. I shouted her name over and over, but she didnae wake up. I'm not a doctor or anything. I don't know how to check for a pulse. But it didnae matter. I knew. Somehow I knew.'

He let the image conjured by his words rest for a moment, before continuing.

'And then, straight away, I panicked. I knew I had to get rid of the body. Make it look like she never made it home. That's when I thought of the steps behind the old library. Many's the night I'd thought anyone coming down they steps in the dark was taking their life in their haunds. So I lifted her over my shoulder and snuck out of the house.'

'That was a massive risk to take,' Anna couldn't help pointing out. 'Heading up through all that housing – you could so easily have been spotted.'

'I know,' said Sean. 'I figured I never had a choice. It needed to look like she'd fallen on her way home, and it stood to reason she'd've been coming that way. Plus . . .' He hesitated, then pulled a sheepish face that was almost a smile. 'I suppose I couldnae stand the thought of her lying for days, weeks somewhere, all alone. I wanted her to be found quickly. I figured, people use they steps all the time. Someone was bound to stumble across her.'

Anna nodded. This tracked.

'Go on,' she said.

'I got her to the steps and I laid her down. I meant to make a better fist of it, but I'd hardly set her down when I heard voices up at street level. I never even had time to think. I'd no choice but to take off. I bombed it all the way back here and never looked back. And when I got in the door, what's the first thing I saw?'

'Her handbag,' said Anna.

Sean nodded. 'Hanging on the banister where she left it. And I knew, if *it* was here, the polis'd know *she'd* been here too. So I grabbed it and the table she'd hit her head on and the throw rug she'd landed on and went and chucked 'em in a skip a couple of streets down, where this bloke and his missus were doing up their kitchen. Everyone in the street'd been using it for chucking stuff they didnae want. I figured no one'd ever spot a few extra bits of clutter. Then I came back here and took off all my clothes and stuffed 'em in the washing machine. I put on a full wash so it wouldnae look suspicious – just grabbed whatever I could find and jammed it in there.

'Then, I went for a long walk. I needed to clear my head and . . . and come to terms, I guess, with what'd happened. I dunno how long I walked for or where I went, but by the time I got back, the polis were already here, swarming all over the place like flies on shite. And then . . .' He made a limp gesture with his hand. 'Well, I reckon you know the rest.'

Anna nodded to herself as she digested everything she'd heard. Sean's account did seem to have covered everything. Everything, that was, except . . .

'I take it it was Gerry who paid Melanie Phelan to say you'd been with her?'

He was the only person with any connection to Sean who would have had the means and the potential motive for doing so, but she hadn't been able to work out the circumstances under which it had come about.

'Aye,' said Sean quietly. 'Came and visited me in the Bar-L at the start of last month.'

So not long after she'd confronted Gerry about the meeting in Shotts.

'It was the first time I'd seen him in ages,' Sean went on, 'and I was so overcome with – y'know, *feelings* – that I just sort of cracked. I poured it all out to him then and there. The beatings, the putdowns, and what really happened that night.

'He was horrified. I think a part of him blamed himself – y'know, for letting me . . .' He trailed off for a moment. 'Not that she was violent tae *him* . . . least, I don't *think* she was. I asked him straight out, and he said she never hurt him, but . . .'

He shrugged helplessly – *who can say?*

'He said to me, "Don't worry, Sean. I'm gonnae sort this." And I suppose, in a sense, he did. Next thing I know, I'm getting told it's my lucky day and Mr Hanley's shaking my hand, telling me, "Never doubted you for a second, sonny." And here I am.'

He shrugged again. This time, the gesture carried with it a sense of finality – like he'd emptied himself of everything he had to give. Now all that was left for him was to wait for judgement.

More than a minute passed in silence. Neither Anna nor Sean moved or spoke, both too preoccupied by their own thoughts. And though they were coming at this from opposite sides, Anna suspected their minds were both circling around much the same ground.

It was Sean who ultimately broke the silence.

'What now? What are you gonnae do?'

Anna stirred.

'I don't know,' she said at length. 'What do *you* think I should do?'

Sean just gazed back at her helplessly. Either he had no idea what he wanted, or he didn't dare voice what he hoped her decision would be.

Anna let out a long, slow breath, pressing her fingertips to her temples. She was overwhelmed by conflicting thoughts and emotions. A part of her wanted to walk straight out the door, right this minute, and keep walking without looking back. Pretend this whole conversation never took place.

But another part – the part that had spent hours talking to Leanne's friends and colleagues, listening to their stories, their concerns – the part that had spent weeks, *months*, constructing a picture of Sean as a violent bully who repeatedly assaulted his girlfriend and ultimately killed her – still wasn't ready to let go of that mental image. That part still wanted to get straight on the phone to Vanessa Tope. Urge her to rearrest Sean. Send him straight back to prison.

And it wasn't as if Sean hadn't committed a litany of offences. Concealing a death, moving the body, disposing of evidence, perverting the course of justice . . . He might not end up doing prison time for them – not if he ended up with a sympathetic prosecutor who deemed it not in the public interest to pursue a conviction. But there were no guarantees. None whatsoever.

She became aware of movement on the periphery of her

consciousness. Sean shifted on the sofa, head bowed, hands worrying each other so tightly that the knuckles, with their twin exaltations – 'PAIN', 'GAIN' – stood out white. When he finally spoke, it was with a flat, hollow calm that somehow hit harder than if he'd been shouting.

'You know what's worst? Even after all of it, there's a part of me still thinks it's my fault. If I'd been stronger, if I'd toughed it out, or . . . I dunno, if I'd just been a better *man* . . . mibby none of this would've happened. Mibby I'd still have her.'

A moment passed. The TV next door was silent now. Mrs Graham had presumably turned in for the night.

Sean sniffed hard, blinking as he fought back tears. For a second or two, it worked. Then, his shoulders began to heave and he made a small, strangled noise, which soon developed into a full-blown sob.

Anna stared at him, surprise mingling with discomfort that threatened to spill over into full-on horror. Every instinct in her body screamed at her to stay put. But then she saw the way he was clutching himself, rocking back and forth – a desperate, solitary figure hugging himself because no one else would – and something inside her gave way.

She got to her feet. Slowly, almost mechanically, she made her way over to the sofa. As she sank down beside him, he buried his face against her shoulder, the tears now flowing unchecked.

At first, Anna didn't respond. She sat there stiffly, consumed by her own discomfiture. Then slowly, tentatively, she reached out an arm and draped it across his broad shoulders. She shifted closer, no longer pushing his grief away but accepting it, soaking it up with her own body.

'I just . . . I miss her,' Sean managed to whisper between sobs. 'I miss her so much.'

It was an almost perverse statement – that, after everything

Leanne had done to him, he still yearned for her. Would give anything to have her back. But feelings, Anna knew, were messy things – rarely rational, far less conducive to our own wellbeing or survival. And, though she couldn't place herself in his shoes, she understood that much, at least.

'I know,' she said, and continued to hold him.

quiet, barring the sound of heavy snoring coming from the kitchen. Luckily, Captain Pugwash was a heavy sleeper.

She tiptoed along the corridor, pausing briefly to peer through the half-open door to the main bedroom. Zoe and Sal were fast asleep, a tangle of bedclothes and pale limbs, each of which could have belonged to either of them. Sal's head rested on Zoe's chest, a thin trickle of drool drying on the bare skin.

Anna slipped away, continuing till she came to the small spare room that, ever since they'd moved in, Zoe and Sal had kept made up in readiness for Jack, should he ever need it. Like the main bedroom, the door was half-open, framing Jack, lying face-down beneath a Lego Space Explorers duvet, as dead to the world as the rest of the flat's inhabitants.

She slipped in, picking her way past the various items of Lego and other toys strewn on the floor, before settling on the end of the bed. She watched him for a moment. Then, unable to help herself, she reached out and ran a hand gently through his hair.

Jack stirred. He rolled over and sat up, blinking at her in the semi-darkness, their faces partially illuminated by the glow of a nearby streetlight filtering through the thin curtains.

'Mummy,' he said, puzzled and, it struck her, a little put out. 'What are you doing here?'

Anna smiled. 'Jack,' she said simply, and drew him into a hug.

'Ow. Ow!' Jack squirmed agitatedly against her grip. 'Too tight, Mummy.'

'Sorry.'

She released him and shuffled up the bed slightly, giving him the space he needed.

He faced her, head tilted, studying her curiously, as if trying to figure out her agenda.

'Are you better now, Mummy?'

Anna considered the question, then nodded.

'Much better.'

'Am I coming home with you now?'

It was a simple, direct question, without emotion or judgement – as if suddenly, after several weeks, arriving to collect him in the middle of the night was the most natural thing in the world for her to do.

Anna smiled – weary, bone-tired and yet filled with warmth and something akin to relief. For reasons she couldn't quite articulate, she knew in her heart that now, at long last, the travails of the last few months were over. That normal life could begin again.

'Yes, my love,' she said emphatically, 'you are.'

ACKNOWLEDGEMENTS

First off, much thanks as ever to Suze Clarke-Morris for editing my scribblings with a deft hand. That this one turned out to be unusually smooth sailing was, I think, a pleasant surprise for us both.

Thanks to Gwen Hendren for answering my questions about school policy when a parent goes AWOL, and Dr Marion Simpson for allowing me to pick her brain about all matters neurological. Suffice it to say, any errors, deliberate or otherwise, are mine, not theirs.

Thanks to Tim Barber for once again designing a stunning cover, and to Neil Snowdon for allowing me to talk through various plot details with him while I was still struggling to come to grips with the story.

Thank you to my first wave of beta readers: Anne Simpson, Caroline Whitson, Catherine Mackenzie, Luiz Asp and Sarah Kelley. And to the second wave too, a.k.a. my trusty ARC team. You all have my well-deserved gratitude for all the feedback and typo-spotting.

And last but not least, thank you to YOU for reading this to the end.

Finally, continuing a tradition I started with *The Secrets We Keep*, now seems the most fitting time to apologise for impugning a variety of names throughout the course of this book. So, sorry to all the Billy Grahams out there, and all the Guineveres and Nigels too.

Most of them, anyway.

77437661R00218